Claudia, Susan
Mrs. Barthelme's madness

AUG 13 '76	DATE DUE	
AUG 13 '76	FEB 7 '77	OCT 15 '80
SEP 29 '76	FEB 16 '77	OCT 27 '80
OCT 6 '76	FEB 21 '77	FEB 16 '83
OCT 20 '76	MAR 4 '77	AUG 5 '85
NOV 3 '76	MAR 16 '77	AUG 31 '85
NOV 22 '76	MAR 25 '77	FEB 9 '87
NOV 26 '76	APR 13 '77	MAR 17 '87
DEC 6 '76	APR 22 '77	JUL 19 '88
DEC 17 '76	MAY 13 '77	AP 28 '89
DEC 27 '76	DEC 26 '79	NO 5 '90
JAN 10 '77	AUG 15 '80	JA 18 '94
	SEP 10 '80	JA 29 '94

GAYLORD 234   PRINTED IN U. S. A.

MRS. BARTHELME'S MADNESS

MRS. BARTHELME'S MADNESS

by Susan Claudia

FOUNDED 1838

GPPS

G. P. PUTNAM'S SONS
NEW YORK

SBN: 399-11761-X

Library of Congress Cataloging in Publication Data
Johnston, William, 1924-
  Mrs. Barthelme's madness.

  I. Title
PZ4.J724Mj   [PS3560.0395]   813'.5'4   76-3522

PRINTED IN THE UNITED STATES OF AMERICA

MRS. BARTHELME'S MADNESS

One

THE rain began to slacken as Rachel Barthelme reached her car in the O'Hare airport parking lot. Wet and reflecting the parking lot lighting, the black Eldorado glistened as if it had been sprayed with cellophane. Clutching her umbrella, Rachel fished in her shoulder bag for her keys. They eluded her. A gust of wind caught the umbrella, forcing Rachel to use both hands to keep it from blowing away, and for the moment she had to abandon the search for the keys. In her mind she heard her husband, Paul, reprimanding her.

If you'd used your head and got your keys out before you left the terminal, you wouldn't be in this predicament.

Chastened, Rachel closed the umbrella and stood bareheaded in the drizzle searching for the keys. They were nowhere in the bag. In a mild panic she dug into her raincoat pocket. The keys were there. Retrieving them, relieved, she heard Paul speaking to her once more.

You never know where you put things. Don't you know what you're doing? Doesn't anything register? Don't you think?

Inside the car, Rachel sat motionless for a few moments, shedding the tension brought on by the fear that she had lost the car keys. The Eldorado was conducive to relaxation. It was in some ways like a burial vault, strong, designed to hold the occupant in comfort. There was the illusion that it was airtight and impregnable, a weatherproof steel box in which to store the body after the spirit had ceased to twitch.

Rachel's spirit, however, was still stirring, still responding to the elbow nudges of duty. Stretching forward, she inspected her reflection in the rearview mirror to see how much damage the wind and rain had done to her hair. The image was easily repaired with a few deft pulls at the straggling strands. That done, she switched on the engine and left the parking lot. Approaching the airport exit, she looked at the clock on the instrument panel. A little after six. With any luck at all with the traffic she would be home in Cedar Point by seven.

When she had been on the west-bound highway awhile, she began to feel the bite of the October chill and turned on the heater. The Eldorado filled quickly with warmth. There was a lulling pleasantness about driving in the rain in the autumn dusk. The metronomic sweeping and clicking of the wipers . . . the buzzing of the tires on the wet pavement . . . the vaporish look of the drizzle in the fuzzy yellow light from the headlamps. . . . Rachel realized all of a sudden that her eyelids were closing. She sat up straight, blinking, exorcising the drowsiness. She shouldn't have let Loretta Cashman coax her into having that one more martini.

Now, in fact, Rachel wished that she hadn't gone to the airport to see Loretta off at all. She was feeling the pinch of envy. Loretta had what Rachel most wanted and would never have: a divorce, a generous settlement and enough good years left to make a new start. By now Loretta was on her way to St. Thomas. Something unknown was waiting for her. But the only thing in Rachel's future was the same old familiar harness, with its straps that rubbed unceasingly against the never-healing sores.

What really made it so sad was that Loretta didn't appreciate her good fortune. Crying in her drink. Wishing that her husband would come bounding into the airport bar like Super CPA and confess to being a fool and beg her to come back to him. Jesus God Almighty! Loretta, damned idiot, thought it was Rachel who was the lucky one.

Eighteen years, Rachel, and Paul still wants you. That's wonderful!

Oh, yes, he still wants me. Why not? I can still run and fetch. I can still snap to attention and salute when it's useful to him to play the part of the family man and he introduces me as his wife. And every six months or so, when an erection wakes him up in the middle of the night, I'm still convenient. But, tell me, Loretta, what's so goddamn wonderful about it?

Rachel, how have you held him? What's your secret?

Martyrdom, dear. I've sacrificed myself for the children. I've kept the home and family together. Children are entitled to that; they need it, a father, a mother, a place. So, when Paul belittles me, or ignores me, or uses me, I gulp back that faint memory I have of pride and carry on—for the sake of the children. It's not Geritol, it's not Chanel—it's pure and simple self-sacrifice. I begin each day by burning myself at the stake.

And now you have the new baby. It must be like having your marriage license renewed.

What it's like, Loretta, is having my pardon turned down. My son, B.J., is seventeen, my daughter, Holly, is sixteen. In two years they'll both be in college. With them gone, there wouldn't be any need to keep the home together. I had a plan for that day. I'd walk out the gates, free.

But now, as you say, I have the new baby. I've had seventeen more years tacked onto my sentence, until the baby too grows up and goes off to college. Seventeen more years of starting each day by tying myself to the stake and touching the flame to the faggots at my feet. That's what's really meant by keeping the home fire burning.

And what then, after the baby has grown up and gone? I'll be thirty-eight when Holly leaves for college. That's young. I could start again and do something with my life. But in seventeen more years when the baby goes, I'll be fifty-three. Too late. With all that burning at the stake, day in and day out, there will be nothing left of me but ashes. It's for more than seventeen years, it's for life.

Rachel turned the Eldorado onto Edens Highway, heading north toward Cedar Point. She wondered how the marriage had gone so wrong. She could still remember how idiotically happy she had been when she became pregnant with B.J. at eighteen. Maybe Paul married her because he thought he had to. No, he wanted to. Paul had not been so noble that he would have made getting through the university more difficult for himself if marrying her and taking on the responsibility of the child hadn't been what he wanted. And when she became pregnant again so soon after the first baby was born, that hadn't seemed to turn him against the marriage either. So it wasn't that he had been nursing a secret resentment over the years.

She and Paul were different kinds, that was the obvious reason. Paul was a hard driver. Ever onward, ever upward. From Dyne Plastics as a member of the accounting department, to assistant treasurer for American Tool & Die, to financial vice-president for the international division of Cumberland Steel, and now to United Machinery, Inc., as executive vice-president in charge of the company's expansion into overseas markets.

Rachel would have been satisfied to stop at the third plateau. They had the apartment on the east side of Manhattan, only a few blocks from Central Park and the museum, and she had it furnished exactly to her taste. B.J. and Holly were in the Barwick School. Rachel had friends in the neighborhood. From mid-July to mid-August there was the annual sojourn to East Hampton for her and Holly and B.J. Perfect.

She could have been content with less than that if she'd had a husband to go along with it. But Paul's sole interest, from the time he graduated from NYU and possibly even before then, had been the climb. He was aware of apartments and furnishings and schools and friends and summer places, but they were merely things to him, trappings that he acquired to advertise himself or help him along on the ascent. Rachel had once wondered what he would do when he got to the top. Jump off? She had decided that no, he would build the top higher so that he could continue the climb.

She wondered now if Paul had acquired her as a trapping. A young man who knew where he was going, up, would recognize the advantage of having the right kind of wife. He would want her to be attractive in an unostentatious way and comfortable with older and already-established people. That was

Rachel, even at eighteen. She had her mother's lithe slenderness and dark-haired, dark-eyed good looks. And her father having been a successful corporation lawyer who often entertained clients at home, she had grown up being at ease in the company of movers-and-shakers.

Not that, in those days, Paul would have made such a choice coldly. He hadn't yet become calculating. But he had an animal sense of what was best for him—a sense that over the years he had refined and given a name: logic. It was logical, for instance, that William Hoag, the chairman at United Machinery, nearing sixty-five, would soon step down and that Arthur Jahnke, the president, would step up, leaving the presidency open.

By then, according to the plot, Paul would have tight personal control over the overseas operation he was putting together. He would be a power in the organization, a man who had to be dealt with, a prime candidate for the vacated presidency. So, at the dictate of that logic, the Barthelme roots had been yanked up, painfully for Rachel, and Manhattan and the apartment and the friends and the Barwick School had been left behind.

Since she was asking herself why Paul had married her, it was only fair to ask herself why she had married him. Love, yes, but, hell, that didn't explain a thing. Why had she been in love with him? Mostly, she suspected, because he was something unknown to her, a rough diamond, son of a bartender father and alcoholic mother whose early home, playground and life school had been the back end of a West Side New York saloon. There was a satisfaction in polishing him. The idea may have been in the back of her mind that after she made him over, created him anew, she would own him. A heady notion, especially for a female, whose accustomed role was to be the possessed rather than the possessor.

What she now knew for sure was that the love was dead. What she wished was that she could hate him. Hate was strong. If she hated him, she could take the baby and leave. But unfortunately, because she realized that her reason for marrying Paul was probably as questionable as his for marrying her, the most she could manage was dislike. Dislike generated no power; it never boiled, it merely simmered. So she would stay, burning at the stake, becoming ashes.

A cloverleaf; then Rachel was on the road to Cedar Point, passing through the village of Melville. Most of the boxlike houses along the way had the porch lights on, giving the road the look of an airport landing strip. She saw a group of children in costumes and masks and carrying paper bags and understood why the stretch was so well lighted, remembering that it was Halloween. The lights were on for the trick-or-treaters.

The drizzle became a rain again. When the village of Melville fell behind, the road was no longer so well lighted. Rachel leaned forward at the wheel, squinting into the dimness, watching for the next turnoff. She was not yet familiar enough with the area to read the landmarks; she still needed the assistance of signs. Her own section of Cedar Point, in fact, a thickly wooded area of estates, was still a maze to her.

You're going home.

That was what Paul told her when he announced that he had taken the position with United Machinery in Chicago. Going home. There *was* a smidgen of truth to the statement. She had grown up in Winnetka, a few miles south of Cedar Point. But she hadn't been back there since she had gone east to college—because her parents, soon after her departure for New York, had moved to San Diego—and the only friend in Winnetka with whom she had kept any kind of contact over the years was Loretta Cashman—now free and on her way to the Virgin Islands. Home to Rachel was the apartment in Manhattan. Cedar Point was the unknown wilderness.

Paul, naturally, had a logical reason for choosing Cedar Point as the place to live.

This house is magnificent. Old Victorian. Rich stuff. Seventeen rooms. A guy in railroading built it. Trees all around. On the lake, too. The kids can learn about nature. It's all estates. The public

[6]

school, as you can guess, is as good as any private school, so that eliminates that expense.

The real reason, she learned later, was that Arthur Jahnke, the president at United Machinery, had a home in Cedar Point.

The sign at the entrance to the turnoff appeared. Rachel steered the Eldorado into the twisting two-lane road that was the estate area's main artery. The rain was letting up once more. Even so, because of her unfamiliarity with the road's contortions and the feeble lighting, she had trouble navigating, having to step on the brake quickly every now and then to avoid missing a sudden bend.

The headlamps picked up the sign that marked the private road to The Ridges, the first estate. Two more to go before she reached the Barthelme property, Catawba. That was the name, Indian, that the railroad man had given it. Paul would eventually change it, she assumed. No American Indians for him on his totem pole. He would give it a name that implied a long-standing link with some Caucasian aristocracy, possibly something British, like Blenheim or Buckingham. It would be a good joke on him if she could trick him into calling it Billingsgate.

Next came the road to Vallum. She wondered what kind of word that was and what kind of people had chosen it. Rachel had not yet met any of her neighbors. With the houses so far apart, closed in by woods, she doubted that she would ever meet any of them—or even see them, except when their Cadillacs happened to pass on Cedar Point Road. They weren't neighbors; they were a sect of strangers. To Rachel, used to apartment living, neighbors were people who lived within elevator distance.

The entrance to the road to Cooper's appeared and was left behind. Rachel leaned forward at the wheel again, anticipating the abrupt hill and sharp bend that she and the Eldorado would have to contend with before they reached the road to Catawba. Almost at once, sooner than expected, the slick-looking, rain-wet rise of the incline came into view; then the nose of the car began to lift. For a second, as the Eldorado topped the crest, Rachel felt weightless. Then down. Experiencing the sinking sensation, she pressed back against the seat.

Turning into the bend, Rachel saw a flash of white. A split instant later she felt a thud and heard a scream, telling her that she had hit someone. In that same minute fraction of time, Rachel saw a face, huge and plaster-of-paris white, with bright red, yellow and black markings. Horrified, she jammed her foot against the brake pedal. The Eldorado went skidding sideways. Instinctively, Rachel janked at the steering wheel. The car swung wildly into a half turn, then skidded along the road rear first. The end of the slide came quickly. The Eldorado left the road and came to rest in the ditch.

There was quiet. The engine was dead, the wipers had stopped, and the windshield was awash with drizzle. Rachel sat motionless, stunned. Apparently she was not hurt. She remembered the thud and the scream. Oh God! Grabbing frantically she found the door handle and shoved the door open. As she scrambled from the car, she lost a shoe. When her foot, without the shoe, touched the asphalt, she felt a sudden shock of cold and wet.

The car was completely off the road, with the lights focused back along the shoulder in the direction from which she had come. Through the mist and drizzle, Rachel saw children, youngsters, in masks. She stared, baffled. The scene was unreal. Then it began to make sense to her. Halloween. Children, trick-or-treating, wearing masks. Lord, God! She had hit a child!

Leaving the car, Rachel hobbled along the road toward the figures, hampered by the loss of the shoe. No, she kept saying to herself. No, no. no, the child isn't hurt. The figures looked too tall. If they were children, they were teenagers. She could see the masks more clearly now. Not ordinary Halloween masks. Face masks, made of papier-mâché, with brightly colored, painted-on features and markings.

[8]

One of the half dozen or so figures in the huddle turned outward, facing her straight on. Reflections, cold as frosted ice, peered at her through eye holes in the mask. She halted, jarred. The other figures in the huddle began shifting, staying in the circle but turning their masked faces directly at her. For a flick of a second the movement revealed the center of the circle. Rachel got an impression of a child's babyish face, pale, lifeless.

A girl's voice shrieked at her. "You killed my brother!"

The cry—confirmation of what she most feared—froze Rachel's mind and body in a state of excruciating shock. The moment became fixed, like a photograph. Raindrops stopped in midair; the clouds of mist became suddenly stationary. The masked figures were statuelike, the reflections behind the eye holes piercing, freezing, unblinking.

The girl's screams broke through.

"He's dead! You killed my brother!"

The figures moved toward her, staying in the circle, advancing on her like a nightmarish, many-headed monster. Terrified, she backed away, hobbling.

"It was an accident!" Rachel protested. "I didn't see you!"

"You killed him!" The cry was a rasp, choking.

"I didn't *mean* to!"

The figures were closing in on her. Their eyes, behind the holes in the masks, were icy glints, threatening. She saw young hands, long-fingered, talonlike, ready to claw and tear. In full panic, Rachel fled. Running into the glare of the headlamps, she was blinded. She ran awkwardly, one shoe on, one shoe off.

"Mur-derrrrrr!" the girl screamed.

Rachel reached the car. She looked about wildly for her other shoe. It was nowhere to be found. The figures, still in the tight circle, as if they were chained together in that configuration, came at her again out of the mist. In the car lights the masks were Satanic, the mock flesh a pebbled, ghostly white, the features exaggerated, luminous, contorted. Once more, Rachel fled, racing, limping, abandoning the other shoe.

The girl's shriek followed her. "Murder! You killed my brother!"

Running, hobbling, Rachel shouted her protest again. "I didn't *mean* to!"

Her ankle turned, and she stumbled and fell forward, sliding along the wet asphalt like a baseball player going into second base on a steal. Scrambling to her feet, she felt a sharp pain in the ankle. Her other shoe was gone. Running again, she looked back. There was a spot of white in the darkness. Facing foward, she ran as fast as the pain would allow, sensing that the masked figures were at her heels. She heard panting, dry, and for a moment thought that they had caught up with her, then realized that she was hearing her own frenzied gasping for breath.

The pain in her ankle was letting up. Now, though, there was an ache in her chest as her lungs sucked desperately for air, and her legs felt as if they weighed a ton apiece. At the same moment that she saw the entrance to the private road to Catawba, she stumbled again. This time she caught her balance before she went all the way down, only scraping her hands. Staggering, she plunged on into the darkness, running toward the house. From both sides the forest seemed to press in on her, tormenting her with a new threat. The children, the youngsters, might know a shortcut. They could spring out at her at any time from anywhere.

A light, faint. The house was in sight. Her legs were numb; she had no awareness of touching the ground; she was running on frozen stumps. Her lungs were now beyond pain; they were tissue-thin balloons, ready to pop. She could see the shape of the house now, black on black, high and broad and imperious, a forbidding dowager. Wetness glistened on the cone-shaped turrets. The faint light came from a bay at the main level, spilling out onto the wide porch and, by contrast, deepening the darkness at the entrance.

Rachel reached the drive that curved around the fountain with the stone swans and stumbled on, carried by momentum. Escape now was only yards away. As she began the climb up the steps to the porch, a foot slipped and she fell again. Rising was impossible. She crawled, step by step, listening to her own feverish wheezing, feeling the pressure against the walls of her lungs, anticipating the bursting that would leave them collapsed.

Arriving at the top of the steps, Rachel crawled on across the porch. At the door she found the latch and pulled herself up. The door gave way, swinging inward, and Rachel pitched forward. She had a glimpse of the foyer and the shadows beyond it; then she was down again. Sprawled in the entryway, unable to go an inch further, she began to sob.

Two

RACHEL heard her daughter Holly speaking to her, concerned. Raising her head, she found Holly kneeling beside her, looking puzzled and frightened.

"Mother, what's the matter?"

"I'm all right," Rachel told her, still short of breath. "I had—I had an accident. Help me. I've got to call the police."

"What *happened?*"

"The car . . . I hit a little boy . . ." Rachel said, rising to her hands and knees. "I didn't *see* him. They were trick-or-treating." With Holly's help, she got up, then moved toward the sitting room off the foyer. "They were just suddenly there. I heard a thump. Oh, God! I killed him." She wept.

"Oh, Mother!"

"They were after me."

"Who?"

"The others," Rachel told her as they entered the sitting room. "They didn't understand. It was an accident. I didn't *see* them!"

"The other children?" Holly asked.

"Yes. They were older. Except the little boy. I don't

know. . . ." She sat down limply in the black leather club chair beside the table that held the phone. "How do I call the police?"

"I'll do it," Holly said. She picked up the receiver and dialed. "Where did it happen?"

"On the road. The car is there. I ran all the way. Just before the turnoff. Tell them to send an ambulance. Maybe he isn't dead." She knew that hope was groundless. In her mind she could still see the child's pale, lifeless face.

Holly spoke into the phone, evidently to an operator, then, waiting, addressed Rachel once more. "The turnoff to the house, you mean?"

"Yes, yes."

Again, Holly spoke into the phone, in touch with a policeman now. Rachel listened closely. Holly had the details right and was transmitting them in the proper order, even though they had been out of sequence when she got them from her mother. Rachel was not surprised. Holly was like her father in that way, orderly-minded. She was also like him physically, large-boned, heavyset. Fortunately, she had Rachel's dark hair and dark eyes and other facial features. When she matured, she would be an attractive big woman. At present, however, her potential was not readily observable.

"They're sending someone," Holly said, hanging up.

"Here?"

"To the accident. They'll come here, too, I suppose," Holly said. "You're a mess," she told Rachel. "Look at your hands! How did that happen? Where are your shoes?"

"I lost them. I was running. That's what happened to my hands—I fell. I was so scared," she said, shuddering. "They were chasing me. They blamed me for what happened. But I didn't *see* them . . . until it was too late."

"Do you want to get cleaned up?" Holly said. "Do you want me to go upstairs with you?"

"I'd better wait for the police."

"They're not going to be here right away. You can wash your hands."

"I think I'm supposed to wait," Rachel said drearily.

B.J. came into the room. He was an emerging copy of his father, moderately tall and broad-shouldered and thick-chested. Like Paul, he was blond, with shaggy eyebrows over pale-blue eyes. The difference in their looks was that B.J.'s hair was a mop, while Paul wore his closely cropped and brushed down.

"What's going on?" B.J. asked.

Rachel began telling him about the accident, then interrupted herself. "Call your father," she said to Holly. "Tell him what happened, and tell him to come home. Tell him the police are coming. Tell him I don't know what to do."

Holly picked up the phone again. As she began dialing, Rachel turned back to B.J. and resumed the story. He frowned slightly as he listened. Otherwise, there was no reaction from him. Like Paul and Holly—and so unlike Rachel—he rarely let his feelings show.

"Maybe I'd better drive out there and see if I can do anything," he said when Rachel finished.

"We've called the police."

"I can find out what's going on," he said, departing.

"Tell them I didn't *see* them!" Rachel called after him.

"Okay."

Facing Holly again, Rachel found that she was no longer on the phone.

"He'd left," Holly reported. "He's on his way."

"Good. I just hope he gets here before the police do." She leaned back in the chair and closed her eyes. "Oh, God, that poor child. I just saw his face for a second—" She began sobbing again. "I killed him. . . ."

"Mom, you didn't mean to," Holly said sympathetically.

"But he's dead."

"You don't know that."

"No, I *know*. His sister was screaming at me. She said he was dead and I could see. . . ." She pressed her hands to her eyes, wiping away the tears. "I feel so tired. . . ."

"Why don't you lie down?" Holly said. "Try to rest or something."

"I don't want to be alone."

"I'll go up with you. I'll wash that dirt off your hands and put some spray on them."

"I don't know. . . ."

"Let's take off your raincoat, at least," Holly said.

"In a minute. . . ."

Rachel hung her head, totally exhausted. She had no more tears left in her. Dimly, she heard B.J.'s car start up, recognizing it by the throaty sound of its damaged muffler. She wondered what questions the police would ask her. They would want to know if she had been drinking and she would have to tell them about the martinis she'd had with Loretta Cashman. She couldn't lie about it because they would probably check with Loretta. After all, it was a serious accident; that poor child was dead.

They couldn't accuse her of being drunk, though. Not on a few martinis—no more than three, maybe four. They couldn't blame her for leaving the scene of the accident either. She had been *chased* away. Besides, she had to leave the scene of the accident to report it; she didn't have a phone in her car, and there were no phone booths on Cedar Point Road.

Rachel felt a warm wetness against the palm of her right hand. Opening her eyes, she found Holly kneeling beside the chair and daubing at her hand with a damp washcloth. The hand washing had a soothing effect. Rachel felt herself relaxing a bit. She looked idly about the room.

It was the only sitting room in the house that was fully furnished. Most of the rooms, in fact, were completely empty. This room held the furnishings from the main room of the Manhattan apartment, the couches and chairs and tables and lamps that Rachel had chosen so carefully and maintained so protectively over the years and felt so comfortable with. The dining room and master bedroom and Holly's and B.J.'s

[14]

rooms had the furnishings from the apartment too. The things in the nursery and in Mrs. Woolsey's room were new. That left almost a dozen rooms still to be stocked. In view of the fact that they probably would never be used, why bother? Well, she guessed, because, like the proverbial mountain, they were there.

"That's that, anyway," Holly said, rising. She held out the cloth. "Do you want to go over your face?"

To the police, Rachel realized, she would probably *look* like a drunk, with her face tear-streaked and her hair a mess and her shoes gone and her hose torn.

"I'll go upstairs and see if I can do something with myself," she told Holly. Getting up, she felt unsteady. Holly reached out to her. "No, I'm all right," Rachel said. The slight dizziness had passed quickly. "Watch for the police," she said, leaving the sitting room.

"I will."

Crossing the foyer and climbing the stairway, Rachel was conscious of the bareness of the walls along the way. She really had to do something about decorating the house. Paul was beginning to make remarks about it.

Less is more is okay, but this is getting ridiculous.

The reason for the procrastination, she knew, was that she just didn't give a damn. The apartment in New York had been the family place, and she had cared about it. But this house was Paul's alone, his monument of the moment to his progress. She had no more feeling for it than she had for a Holiday Inn.

Mrs. Woolsey was emerging from the nursery, closing the door quietly, when Rachel arrived at the second-floor landing. She was a dear woman—and looked the part, being plump and waddly and cherub-cheeked—and Rachel felt lucky to have her, but she did not want to become involved in a conversation with her. Not now. Every talk with Mrs. Woolsey, no matter how straight-lined and single-purposed it started out, got lost on a baffling detour of irrelevancies.

"I just put the baby down," Mrs. Woolsey whispered.

"Yes, fine," Rachel replied, edging on toward the master bedroom.

"B.J. told me you had some trouble with trick-or-treaters," Mrs. Woolsey said.

"Yes, an accident. I didn't see them."

"It's terrible," Mrs. Woolsey said. "They're putting razor blades in their candy bars and handing out dope pills. What's the world coming to?"

Nodding agreement, Rachel kept moving. "I've got to do something about myself," she said, indicating her general appearance. "The police are coming."

In the bedroom, Rachel got panty hose from a drawer and shoes from the rack in the closet, then went into the bathroom. As she was going over her face with a warm cloth, she heard B.J.'s car returning. She hurried back into the bedroom and looked out the bay window. Her son's car was not in the drive. Evidently he had gone on to the rear of the house, to the garage or the parking area.

As she started to leave the window, she saw lights on the private road, approaching the house. Two cars. The police, probably. She got a brush from her dressing table, then, tugging at the damp tangles in her hair, returned to the window. The first car reached the drive and passed it by, going on toward the rear of the house. It was Paul's Jag. The second car made the turn into the drive and stopped at the entrance. It was a police car.

Sitting on the edge of the bed, Rachel pulled on the fresh panty hose. Her hands were trembling. Would they take her to jail? Surely not. What would be the point of that? She wasn't a criminal; it had been an accident. But that poor little boy was dead; that might make a difference. What good would locking her up do, though? It wouldn't bring him back to life. Still, not everything made sense; maybe there was a rule that if someone were killed, someone had to be locked up. Stupid!

Rachel went back to the window. Paul had joined the policeman, and they were walking toward the porch together. She put on the shoes that she had taken from the closet, then took one more look at herself in the dressing-table mirror. At least her face was clean. Deciding that she looked as presentable as possible considering the circumstances, she left the bedroom and went downstairs.

Paul and the policeman were in the foyer. The policeman, a young man with sharp, set features, had his hat in one hand and Rachel's shoes in the other.

"This is Mrs. Barthelme," Paul said. "Rachel, this is Officer Morrisey."

"Is the little boy dead?" she asked the policeman. Her voice was thin and strained.

"We don't know," he answered. "We didn't find anybody. We're checking the hospital." He held up the shoes. "Are these yours?"

"Yes, thank you," she replied, taking them.

"Are you all right?" Paul asked her. "I didn't know what was going on. I was driving along, and there was your car in the ditch and the police all around. What did you run off without your shoes for?"

"They were chasing me."

"Who was chasing you?"

"Those children. The girl was screaming at me, and they chased me. I was afraid."

"Look, let's go in and sit down and get this straightened out," Paul said, motioning in the direction of the sitting room. "Morrisey, can I make you a drink?" he asked, leading the way.

"No, sir."

"Do you want some coffee or something? Jesus, what a night!"

"No, sir. Thank you."

Holly and B.J. were in the sitting room. The officer nodded to B.J. and smiled fleetingly at Holly, then, at Paul's invitation, sat down in one of the club chairs. Rachel joined Holly on a couch, and Paul settled in the chair that had the telephone table beside it. The officer opened a notebook and poised a pencil.

Rachel told her story as briefly as she could. To her own surprise, she spoke with relative calm. The officer continued to write in the notebook for a few moments after she finished.

"Kids don't look where they're going," Paul said.

The officer addressed Rachel. "But you didn't see the boy when you hit him?"

"No. I just saw his face for a second. It was so babyish." She had a lump in her throat. "They were holding him. That was when they started at me. I couldn't think." Tears came.

"Take it easy," Paul said.

"How old was he?" the officer asked.

"I don't know. How old would he be? They were walking along the road. Five or six, maybe. But he looked like such a baby."

The phone rang.

Paul picked up the receiver, identified himself, listened for a second, then turned to the officer. "I'm going to Rome tonight," he said, "and I've got a fellow on the line here with some figures I want to take with me—could you give me a minute?"

"Sure."

Paul got his wallet from his inside jacket pocket and flipped it open to the notebook section and began recording the information the caller was giving him. As promised, the interruption lasted only a minute. Hanging up, Paul nodded to the officer to proceed.

"Where were you coming from?" he asked Rachel.

"What do you mean? When?"

"When the accident occurred."

"Oh. From the airport. O'Hare. I was seeing a friend off. Loretta Cashman," she said to Paul. "She left today."

Paul grunted.

"Are you on any medication?" the officer asked.

"No."

"Had you been drinking?"

"No. I had a martini . . . two, three, maybe, with Loretta,

but I wasn't drinking. Not in *that* sense. I mean, I certainly—"

Paul broke in, speaking to the officer. "Listen, we really don't know what's happened yet, how the boy is," he said. "So I think it would be just as well if we held off on this till we have the facts."

"I only have a few more questions."

"Fine. But even so, I think we ought to hold off. Rachel is upset enough as it is. What you've got, in fact, I don't think is worth a damn thing. It's too soon after it happened. When she thinks about it and calms down, she'll be better able to get the facts straight."

"Are you saying she won't answer any more questions?" the officer asked. His expression had hardened.

"Not until she has the advice of counsel."

Officer Morrisey closed his notebook and rose and moved toward the doorway. Paul got up, too, and followed.

"How can I find out about the little boy?" Rachel called after the officer.

"Through counsel," he answered.

"Why did your father do *that?*" Rachel said crossly to B.J. and Holly when Paul and the officer had left the room.

"Because you said you were drinking," B.J. answered.

"I *didn't* say I was drinking. I said I *wasn't* drinking."

B.J. smiled faintly.

Rachel got up and went to the bay window. Officer Morrisey was on the porch, putting on his yellow slicker. She couldn't see Paul, but she assumed that he was in the doorway, talking to the officer, because the officer appeared to be carrying on half of a conversation. She could not hear the words or even the sounds of the voices, so solidly was the old house constructed. After another few minutes the police officer departed. As his car was pulling away, Paul came back into the sitting room.

"I knew this was going to happen someday," he said disgustedly, going to the telephone table. "Where was your mind this time?"

"What does *that* mean?" Rachel responded resentfully. She knew what it meant, of course. Paul was constantly accusing her of having a wandering mind.

"You know what it means," he said, getting the telephone book from the low shelf of the table. "Your head's always somewhere else."

She didn't argue. Not with the children present. She had to keep the home as pleasant as possible.

"I'm calling Jack Flanagan, in our legal department," Paul said, putting the phone book back on the shelf. "He lives in Glencoe; he can stop here in the morning before he goes in to the office." He began dialing.

"Are you really leaving tonight?" Rachel asked.

Paul dialed the final digit, then glanced at her curiously. "Yes. . . ." Obviously, he saw no reason for altering his schedule and was wondering why Rachel thought it should be changed.

The lawyer came on the line, and Paul began telling him why he had called. Rachel had hit a kid with her car, a trick-or-treater, apparently. Indications were that the boy was dead, but nothing was definite yet. A cop had been to the house, the usual questions, and Rachel had boo-booed, telling him that she'd had a few drinks. Could Jack handle it? Fine. In the morning? Good. Right—Paul would be in Rome.

Paul hung up. "He'll be here in the morning," he told Rachel. "In the meantime, he says, say nothing to nobody. Zero. If that cop comes back, or some other cop, tell him you can't talk without counsel." He began writing on the cover of a magazine that was lying on the table. "If, for some reason, you need Jack tonight, this is his number." He headed for the doorway. "Got to pack. Got to run. Oh, kids," he said, maintaining his pace, "I got those tickets to that Bears game." Then he was gone.

Rachel dropped into the chair by the phone table. There was silence. It was as if a hurricane had passed through the room and this was the quiet in the aftermath.

"What am I going to do about the car?" Rachel said, thinking aloud. "I left the keys in it."

"I think you'll have to leave it there until the cops get finished with it," B.J. said.

"What are they doing?"

"Looking around. They couldn't find anything."

"What were they looking for?"

"I don't know. They had flares up around the car when I got there. They were tramping around. They told me to go home. But then Dad came along. They told him about you calling them and telling them about hitting somebody."

"I called," Holly said.

"Whoever."

"What *happened* to those children?" Rachel said.

"Maybe they got a ride from somebody to the hospital," B.J. suggested.

"I've got to find out how that little boy is," Rachel said. "I'll call the hospital myself." She picked up the phone. But Paul was on the line, talking business. "Your father's on," she said, putting the receiver down. "I thought he was in such a hurry to get away."

"I'm hungry," B.J. said. He left the room.

"Do you want me to get you something, Mother?" Holly asked.

"No. Go on and eat."

"What are you going to do?"

"I've got to find out about that little boy," Rachel said. She picked up the phone again. As before, though, Paul was on the line. "He's still at it," she told Holly. "I think I'll go upstairs and wait for him to get off."

They left the sitting room together. In the foyer they parted, Holly going back toward the kitchen and Rachel heading up the stairs. Rachel wondered what Paul expected her to do about the slip, telling the policeman that she'd had the martinis with Loretta. If she was supposed to tell the lawyer something else, she wouldn't do it. Not just because it would

[21]

be lying, but because she had been over the effects of the drinks by the time she reached Cedar Point Road and she didn't want anyone thinking secretly—especially not B.J. and Holly—that she had been drunk when the accident occurred.

Paul was still talking on the phone when Rachel entered the bedroom. At the same time he was chucking clothing—shirts, socks, underwear and so forth—into a suitcase and watching the evening news on the small black-and-white television set that was positioned at the end of the bed on a mobile stand. She had always marveled at his ability to do several things at once and all of them fairly proficiently. Over the years that wonderment had grown, possibly because her own capabilities had lessened. These days she had trouble doing even one thing at a time and doing it right.

She took over the packing for Paul. Arranging his things neatly in the bag, she listened partly to his end of the telephone conversation and partly to the news. The rain was expected to end by morning. Paul's interpreter in Rome would be a Britisher named Pinero. Something catawampus about that: a British interpreter of Italian with a Spanish name. A witch, being interviewed on one of those inevitable Halloween features, claimed that she had cast a spell on the Wrigley Building. Paul was arguing against being hard-nosed with a man named Vanuti in Rome. Traffic was still backed up on the Dan Ryan Expressway owing to the weather.

Paul hung up.

"My shaver isn't in there, is it?" he said, going into the bathroom. He knew that his shaver wasn't in the bag.

"What do you want me to tell the lawyer?" she asked.

"Tell him what happened. Then listen to him and do what he says." He reappeared with the shaver.

"I don't see why you have to leave," she said.

"Because the deal is now."

"Paul, do you really understand what happened? That little boy is dead. Dead. A little boy. Don't you understand that?"

"I know how you feel," he said, closing the suitcase. "But

there's nothing I can do about it. I can't bring the boy back to life. What's done is done. What you need is a lawyer. I *got* you a lawyer."

"I don't see how you can go away."

"The deal is ripe," he told her, putting on his jacket. "What would be the sense of me staying here and losing it?"

"Can't somebody else go?"

"It's *my* baby." He picked up the bag. "Get some sleep," he said. Then he left.

Rachel sat down in the wing chair, feeling empty.

Paul reappeared in the doorway. "Look, I know what you're talking about," he said. The edge had gone from his tone. "You think I'm deserting you in your hour of need or some goddamn thing. But I'm not. Flanagan is the best I can do for you. I can't help you. I'm not the lawyer. Flanagan is the lawyer. Flanagan can help you." He was talking to her as if she were dull-witted. "See?"

"Yes."

"I've *got* to go to Rome," he told her. "I've got the momentum going for me. You can't stop when you've got the momentum going. If you stop, if you even slow up, you lose it."

Rachel nodded.

"Have Holly call a doctor for you if you think you need something. Got to run," he said, departing again.

He was right, it was better for him to go. Once his presence would have been important to her. Now she preferred the lawyer. The lawyer would be objective or, at least, would try to appear to be. Paul, on the other hand, had already made up his mind that the accident had been her fault, the result of drinking. She felt bad enough about what had happened; she didn't need Paul's condemnation to make it worse.

Sitting on the edge of the bed, Rachel picked up the phone and called Information and got the number of Cedar Point Memorial Hospital, then dialed it. The name evoked a bad memory. Cedar Point Memorial was where the baby had been delivered, by an obstetrician who was practically a stranger to her. Paul hadn't allowed her to stay in Manhattan to have the baby, to have the obstetrician who had brought her along over the months of pregnancy. It wouldn't "look right," he thought, to leave her in New York while he went on alone to Chicago. That was what was important to him, what looked right, as he saw it, not what she wanted or needed.

A woman answered:

RACHEL: I'd like to find out about a little boy who was brought in. He was . . . hit by a car. . . .
WOMAN: Yes, ma'am. What's the name, please?
RACHEL: I just want to find out if he's— How he is. . . .
WOMAN: The patient's name, I mean.
RACHEL: Oh. I don't know. He's a *little* boy, though. It happened on Cedar Point Road. About an hour ago. Two hours, I guess.
WOMAN: Hold on, please. I'll find out.

Waiting, Rachel half listened to the news. The word "coexistence" caught her attention. That was what she and Paul were doing, coexisting. He was providing her with the necessities—and, now that she was in trouble, with a lawyer—and in return she was playing the part of the devoted wife that he believed he needed to have on hand in case company dropped in. It was no wonder that coexistence between nations was so hard to maintain if it was as burdened with sham as the relationship between her and Paul.

The woman came back on:

WOMAN: Hello? I'm told that no little boy has been brought in. Are you sure you want Cedar Point Memorial?
RACHEL: Aren't you the only hospital?
WOMAN: In Cedar Point, yes.
RACHEL: Where would he be taken then?
WOMAN: Perhaps to a doctor's office.
RACHEL: No, he was dead.
(momentary silence)

[24]

WOMAN: We've had one accident case since noon, a woman. She wasn't hit by a car, she was driving a car.

RACHEL: Is there someone else you can ask?

WOMAN (crisply): I checked Admitting. Admitting would know.

RACHEL: All right. I'm sorry . . . thank you. . . .

She hung up, puzzled. If the boy had been taken to a doctor, wouldn't the police know by now? Why hadn't they contacted her? Maybe that officer was punishing her, making her suffer, because Paul had stopped her from answering his questions. No, surely not. The doctor simply hadn't yet reported to the police; that was the obvious explanation.

Rachel lay back on the bed. She could only wait. She couldn't eat; she was hungry, but she had no interest in food. She would wait another half hour, and if she hadn't heard from the police by then, she would call them. Even if they could only tell her that they were still looking for the boy, that would be better than nothing. Oh, God, that poor child!

Rachel recognized the street. She was back in the East Side Manhattan neighborhood. What she could not understand was why the street slanted so steeply downhill and why she was alone on it, feeling so frightened, running so desperately. Was she dreaming? No—the drizzle was real, the darkness was real. But how? Why?

As she raced on, gasping for breath, she realized all of a sudden that the street wasn't downhill. Her shoes, with the heels so high that she was almost on tiptoe, only made it seem that way. Why didn't she take the shoes off and run barefoot? Because she couldn't stop. She was pitched forward at such an acute angle that she had to keep running to stay on her feet. If she stopped, she would fall, and if she fell, they would catch her.

She saw the masks in the shopwindow. Plaster-of-paris white with red, black and yellow markings. They were alive! The jaws moved, making silent, rubbery mouthings. The eyes burned with a white, glistening fire, like liquid ice. Rachel ran faster, terror-stricken, but the window with the masks kept pace with her. She tried to turn away from it. It was everywhere. No matter where she looked the masks were there, staring at her with hot icy eyes, mouthing the soundless accusations.

Then the window was gone. In the yellowish light from a streetlamp, Rachel saw a child, a young boy. He, too, was running. But happily, as if he were chasing a falling leaf. Rachel cried out to him, warning him. He didn't hear. He ran into the street. She heard the screech of brakes. No car—only the sickening squeal of the tires. Then silence. She saw the boy lying in the street, his body twisted and broken, his tiny babyish face pale and lifeless.

The girl, only a shape to Rachel, was kneeling beside the boy's body, screaming. "You killed my brother!"

"I didn't see him!" Rachel sobbed. "I didn't see him!"

The girl screamed again. No words, only a shriek. She was on the television screen. Rachel could now see her clearly. She was an actress. The street was gone; the boy was gone. The actress was in a dark, shadowy room, screaming, screaming. For a second the screen went dark. Then a commercial came on, an advertisement for a toothpaste.

Staring at the screen, confused, Rachel began to understand what had happened. She had fallen asleep and had been dreaming. Why she had been back in Manhattan in the dream, she didn't know, but the other elements were easily explainable: They had been on her mind when she fell asleep—the problem with the shoes, the masks, the child, the screech of brakes, the screaming girl. The actual screaming, of course, had come from the television set, waking her.

Another commercial came on. Rachel looked at the clock on the bedside table. Almost ten! Perhaps the police had called. Quickly, she got up and left the room. When she reached the hall, she heard music, one of B.J.'s rock records, so she climbed the narrow stairway to the topmost floor and moved on to the door of his room and knocked.

"Yeah?"

Rachel opened the door. B.J. was lying across his bed on his stomach, with his head extending over the edge, reading *Rolling Stone,* which was on the floor. The music was coming not from his hi-fi but from his tape player.

"Hi," he said.

"Dear, did the police call? Or come back?"

"No."

"Are you *sure?*"

"There was just one call. It was for Dad."

"When am I going to hear from them? It's almost ten o'clock."

He shrugged.

"I called the hospital," Rachel said. "They told me no little boy had been brought in."

"I don't know. . . ."

"I just can't understand— Oh, well. You'd better get to sleep, dear. School tomorrow."

He nodded.

Rachel closed the door and returned to the stairway and descended. The rock music continued. Otherwise, the house was quiet. Mrs. Woolsey would be asleep, of course. Holly was probably reading, in her room or in the downstairs sitting room. B.J. and his music, Holly and her books. Rachel wished they were more active. They had been in New York. Here, though, they hadn't made any close friends yet.

Back in the bedroom, Rachel dialed Information again. This time she asked to be connected to police headquarters. After a second, an officer came on, identifying himself as Sergeant McDonald:

RACHEL: I'd like to speak to Officer Morrison, please.

McDONALD: We don't have a Morrison, ma'am. Morrisey, do you mean?

[27]

RACHEL: Yes, that's it, I think.

McDONALD: He's off duty, ma'am.

RACHEL: Who can I talk to then? I had an accident this evening. It was on Cedar Point Road. A little boy was hit, and I can't find out what's happened to him. I thought I'd hear from the officer.

McDONALD: Yes, ma'am, I've got that here. Lieutenant Lomax is handling that.

RACHEL: May I speak to him, please?

McDONALD: He's off duty, too, ma'am. He'll be in touch with you.

RACHEL: *When?*

McDONALD: He'll be on duty in the morning.

RACHEL: How can I find out about the little boy?

McDONALD: You'll have to talk to Lieutenant Lomax.

RACHEL: Where is he? How can I?

McDONALD: He'll be in in the morning, ma'am.

RACHEL: Sergeant, I am going out of my mind. I don't know what happened to that little boy, I don't know if he's dead or what. Can't you even tell me that?"

McDONALD: I'm sorry, ma'am. I don't have any information.

RACHEL: Does *anybody?*

McDONALD: You'll have to talk to Lieutenant Lomax, ma'am.

Rachel slammed down the receiver. Damn them! They were doing it on purpose.

She telephoned the hospital again, thinking that perhaps in the meantime the boy had been brought in. A different woman answered the phone. The result was the same, however. No child had been admitted. Maybe, the woman suggested, the boy had been taken to a hospital in Chicago. That was usually what was done, she told Rachel, when a patient required the services of a specialist who was not available in Cedar Point.

Rachel clutched the possibility and clung to it. The boy had been taken to a local doctor's office, then to a hospital in Chicago, and the police simply hadn't been able to track him down yet. The police wouldn't deliberately withhold information from her. The boy was alive, in Chicago, getting treatment from a specialist.

Rachel closed her eyes, exhausted, but then opened them after a second, afraid of falling asleep and having another terrible dream. She turned her attention to the television set, where the late news was on. A report about an infant girl being kidnapped from her carraige in a town in Indiana caused Rachel to feel suddenly apprehensive about her own baby girl. She realized that she hadn't looked in on her since arriving home. Alert again, she got up and left the bedroom and walked down the hall to the nursery.

The baby was asleep in her crib, covered. Rachel stood watching her for several minutes, then retreated, heading back to the bedroom. There had been no legitimate cause for anxiety, she knew. Mrs. Woolsey gave the baby the best of care. She was the perfect proxy mother, patient, gentle, genuinely loving. The baby would be better off if she had been born to Mrs. Woolsey. Everybody would be better off. It was a terrible thing to think, but it was true.

Back in the bedroom, she went to the bay window and looked out at the night. The rain had stopped; the sky was clearing. She thought she saw moving shapes at the edge of the woods. Immediately, she recalled the figures that had chased her along the road, and she felt the fear again. Now, though, the shapes were gone. She had imagined them, she supposed. But then they reappeared, casting shadows that reached out from the woods. The children! They had come for her!

The shadows receded, withdrawn. Again, Rachel told herself that she had been imagining. It made no sense for the children to be out there in the woods, scouting the house. Unless they were still after her. Unless they were waiting for her to come out so that they could do to her what they had intended to do to her when they chased her. But that was ridiculous. They were children, mere children, not fiends.

Rachel watched the edge of the woods awhile longer. She saw no more moving shadows. Set on staying awake, she got the uncompleted *Times* puzzle from the lower shelf of the bedside table, then sat down in the wing chair. She found it hard to concentrate on the puzzle, though. She kept glancing toward the bay window. Improbable as the notion was, she could not rid herself of the feeling that the children were out there in the woods, watching, waiting.

Three

RACHEL heard her name being spoken softly and felt her shoulder being shaken gently. Opening her eyes, she saw her daughter leaning over her. Rachel was still in the wing chair. The bedroom was bright with morning light. She couldn't remember falling asleep. But she was grateful for the respite from thinking about the accident and thankful that she had not dreamed.

"Mother, we're leaving for school," Holly said. "I thought I ought to wake you. That lawyer is coming this morning."

Rachel nodded. "Thank you, dear."

"Are you all right?"

"Yes. Go on. I'm fine."

"Mrs. Woolsey says do you want her to make you something for breakfast."

Rachel shook her head. "I've got to shower and change clothes. I'll be down soon, tell her."

"Did you find out anything?" Holly asked.

Rachel shook her head again.

"Well, that's probably good."

"I hope so. Go on, don't be late."

Holly left.

Rachel remained in the chair for several more minutes, kept there by the lingering feeling of exhaustion. When she heard B.J.'s car leaving, she forced herself to rise and went into the bathroom and got out of her clothes and into the shower. Standing under the warm spray, she wondered if it was too early to call the police. She should have found out exactly when that Lieutenant Lomax would be back on duty.

The shower revived her somewhat. In the bedroom Rachel dressed quickly, pulled a brush through her hair a few times, then went downstairs to the sitting room. There she telephoned police headquarters. Lieutenant Lomax was back on duty but not on hand at the moment, she was told. He would be informed that she had called, however. Having no other choice, Rachel settled for that.

Mrs. Woolsey was in the kitchen when Rachel entered, preparing a bottle for the baby and, while she waited for it to warm, putting the breakfast dishes into the dishwasher. She smiled sympathetically at Rachel. Apparently she had been told the details of the accident and was aware of the current uncertain status of the situation.

"Don't worry, dear," she said. "It's always dark before the dawn."

"So they say."

Rachel put water on to heat for instant coffee.

"The same thing happened to my sister," Mrs. Woolsey said. "A man backed out of his driveway and hit her smack-on. *That's* a story! He told her to go to a certain garage to get the repairs and she'd get a deal. She thought that was fishy right off."

"What happened?" Rachel asked, getting a mug from the cabinet.

"She didn't take it there. She took it to her own place," Mrs. Woolsey said. "Her insurance man told her she did the right thing." She sprinkled milk from the baby's bottle on the underside of her wrist to test the temperature. "Just right," she announced.

Rachel spooned instant coffee into the mug.

"The children had French toast," Mrs. Woolsey said. "I could make you some when I get finished upstairs."

"Thank you. I think I'll just have toast and coffee."

"You want to keep your strength up."

"I'll be all right."

Mrs. Woolsey departed with the bottle.

Rachel put a slice of bread into the toaster, then poured boiling water into the mug. As she was taking the kettle back to the stove, the doorbell chimed. Carrying the mug of coffee, she went to answer it. At the door she found a short, plump, conservatively dressed middle-aged man. He introduced himself as Jack Flanagan.

"Would you like some coffee?" Rachel asked, leading him into the sitting room.

"Had some, thanks. I'd rather get right at this, if that's okay with you."

He was like Paul in manner, crisp in his speech and in the way he moved. He had Paul's freshly barbered look, too.

"I can't tell you anything that Paul didn't tell you," she said as he sat down in the club chair beside the phone table. "Nothing new has happened. I can't even find out how the boy is. Or *where* he is. I called the local hospital and they say he's not there, and I called the police and they won't tell me *any*thing."

"Police don't tell, they ask," Flanagan said. "Give it to me again, though. Paul just sketched it in. Start at the beginning; give me the whole ball of wax."

Once more, Rachel told her story, beginning at the point when she heard the thud and saw the masks and ending with her collapse in the entranceway of the house after the chase.

"The boy ran in front of the car then," Flanagan said when she finished.

[32]

"I didn't *see* him in front of the car. I didn't see him at all. Except for just that glimpse of him afterward."

"But you were on the road," Flanagan said. "What I'm getting at is, you didn't swerve *off* the road and hit him, he was *on* the road, where he shouldn't have been."

"I didn't swerve. Not until after I put on the brake."

He nodded. "That's what we want. I saw your car down there on the road and stopped and looked around. I couldn't find any marks on the shoulder, except where you went off the road *after* the skid. So, obviously, the boy ran into your car; your car didn't run into the boy." He looked at her closely. "Are we in agreement on that?"

"That must have been what happened."

"Right. Now. According to Paul, you'd had a couple drinks. How many is a couple?"

"Three at the most," Rachel replied. "I was seeing a friend off at the airport. You know how things like that go. I didn't sit there counting my drinks."

"It could have been less than three then?"

Rachel sipped her coffee.

"Your friend—a she?" Flanagan said.

"Yes."

"How would she remember it, do you think?"

"I don't know."

"Give it some thought. We want to be right about it. And we want your friend to back us up—if it ever gets to that. Paul also said—"

Rachel, having heard a car approaching, had withdrawn her attention. "That might be that officer," she said, rising and going to the bay window. "Maybe now we can find out about that little boy."

It was an ordinary, unmarked car, though, not a police car, and not familiar to Rachel. It did not turn into the drive, where the lawyer's car was parked, but drove on toward the rear parking area.

"No, it's not him," Rachel said, leaving the window. "It must be somebody delivering something."

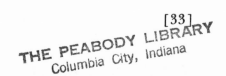

Flanagan resumed. "Paul said you told the cop that you'd been drinking. Did you—"

"Not that I'd been drinking, that I'd had some drinks."

"That's drinking," Flanagan said. "Did you mention any number of drinks to him?"

Rachel thought for a moment. "I can't remember."

"Did he give you any kind of sobriety test?"

"No."

"Any conclusion he reached about your condition, then, he reached purely by observation?"

"I guess so."

The doorbell chimed.

Rachel excused herself and went to the door. When she opened it, she found a big, smiling man of about forty standing on the porch. He was bareheaded, with shaggy, curly dark hair, and an open, pleasant face, and was wearing a loose, baggy dark-brown raincoat.

"Mrs. Barthelme?" he said amiably.

"Yes?"

"I'm Sam Lomax."

"What, uh?"

"Lieutenant Lomax," he said.

"Oh! Come in!" Rachel said, backing away from the doorway. "I saw your car, but it wasn't a police car, so I didn't realize."

"I put it back in your parking lot," he said, entering. "I try to stay out of driveways. I don't want to get blocked in."

"What about the little boy?" Rachel asked anxiously.

"We haven't found him."

"Not *yet?*" she said incredulously.

Sam Lomax shook his head. "I'd like to talk to you about it."

"Where can he be?"

He shrugged.

Rachel sighed discouragedly. "May I take your coat?"

"No, thank you, I'll keep it on. I won't be here long."

Rachel took him into the sitting room and introduced him to Jack Flanagan.

[34]

"They still haven't found the little boy," she told the lawyer.

Flanagan looked skeptically at Sam Lomax.

"That's right," the lieutenant said.

"That's a crazy one. . . ."

"A little bit," Lomax agreed. "So, I thought I'd better stop in and talk to Mrs. Barthelme about it."

"Of course," Flanagan said. "I'd like to sit in . . . no objection?"

"It's all right with me," Lomax responded genially, sitting down on a couch. He faced Rachel. "Your statement to Officer Morrisey was that you'd had two or three martinis. I wonder—"

Jack Flanagan broke in immediately. "We want to reserve any further statement on that aspect of it, Lieutenant."

Lomax shrugged. His manner was still genial.

"I was just thinking," Flanagan said to him. "If you haven't found the boy. . . . What charge did you have in mind?"

"We don't have anything to make a charge on," Lomax replied. "It's a funny thing. Mrs. Barthelme says she hit a child, and she says this girl was screaming at her that she killed her little brother— But where's the boy? He wasn't taken to the hospital. He wasn't taken to a doctor. We've checked every doctor in the area. So where is he?"

"You've talked to *all* the doctors?" Rachel said.

"I had men on the phones all night," Lomax told her. "And there are a couple other things," he said, addressing both Rachel and Jack Flanagan again. "When Officer Morrisey and his partner got to the car last night, there wasn't any sign that anybody but Mrs. Barthelme had been there. They found her shoes, one in the car and one on the road. And finally, there's no damage to the car. No dent, no scratch, nothing to show contact." He smiled amiably. "It almost looks as if it didn't happen," he said.

"It *did* happen!" Rachel snapped.

"Oh, I didn't say it didn't. We didn't find any tracks, but, it was raining, maybe the tracks got washed out, or maybe the kids stayed on the road—it's hard to leave prints on asphalt.

[35]

And that's a good solid car; it would take a good bump to dent it. How hard was the hit, would you say?"

"I heard a thump. Not a loud thump."

"Uh-huh."

"Lieutenant, it *did* happen," Rachel insisted.

"Suppose this," Sam Lomax said. "Suppose you came around that turn and these kids were walking along the road and you surprised them and one of them—scared—took a whack at the car and hit it. There's the thump. And then suppose they decided to give you the same kind of scare that you'd just given them. They *did* scare you, you say."

"Yes. . . ."

"That seems to be what it was, a bad joke, a prank. Or," he added, gesturing vaguely, "something else."

"What?" Rachel asked sharply. He seemed to be implying that the something else was something that he would rather not identify.

"Nothing in particular."

"How do you explain the child?" she asked. "I saw him. He looked—he looked dead."

"He could have been putting on."

"Pretending to be pale?"

"Maybe he's naturally pale."

Jack Flanagan got up. "Rachel, I don't see any further need for me here," he said tightly. "I'd better by on my way." He turned to Sam Lomax. "Nice meeting you, Lieutenant."

"Same here."

"Paul will be calling in from Rome," Flanagan said to Rachel, moving toward the doorway. "I'll fill him in."

She rose and followed him out.

"This isn't over," she said to him, keeping her voice low, when they reached the entranceway. "That little boy has to be somewhere."

"Just don't say anything more to that cop about your drinking," Flanagan counseled.

"Is that what you think?" she said indignantly. "That I was drunk and dreamed this all up?"

[36]

"Rachel, that's between you and Paul," he replied. "It's not in my line. I can't help you with it." He opened the door. "We'll get together sometime soon, you and Paul and my wife and me," he said. Then the door closed behind him.

Furious, Rachel stood glaring at the door and cursing Jack Flanagan in her mind. He *did* think that she had been drunk and had either imagined the accident or, for some reason, made up the story about it. Evidently that was what the lieutenant was thinking too. That was the something else that he had preferred not to put into words.

She strode angrily back to the sitting room.

"You think I was drunk, don't you?" she said fiercely to Sam Lomax.

That smile again. "It crossed my mind," he admitted.

"I wasn't!"

"Good," he said. "That backs me up. Because I lean toward the prank theory."

"You didn't see that little boy's face. He *wasn't* pretending!"

"Mrs. Barthelme," he said patiently, "let's suppose again. Suppose you *did* hit that kid and you killed him. He had to be taken somewhere, to a hospital or a doctor. He was with his sister, you say. What did she do with him? Throw him away, like an old pop bottle? What did she tell her parents? If the boy is missing, dead, the way you think, why haven't his parents reported it? We haven't had any report on any boy being missing. Not in the whole area, not one missing boy. So you tell me, where is he?"

He was right. It was almost impossible for her to believe that the children had been playing a joke on her, that the girl's rage and the hostility that Rachel had felt coming from the others hadn't been real. But Sam Lomax's logic was unassailable. He was right.

"I thought you'd be happy about it," he said.

"I am—of course. It's just so unexpected. It was so real and I went through so much, worrying about the little boy. And worrying about me, too. And now, all of a sudden, it's over. I guess I'm having a little trouble adjusting."

Sam Lomax stood up and reached into his raincoat pocket. "I've got your car keys here," he said. "You can take the car anytime you want. There's no damage and it's still running—I tried it."

She rose and took the keys from him. "Thank you."

"You can ride along with me if you want to get it now," he said. "I see you don't have any other cars in your garage."

"Yes . . . my husband drove his to the airport and my son drives his to school. Thank you again. I will go with you."

In the entranceway Rachel got a car coat from the closet, then they left the house and walked toward the rear.

"Paul, the one in Rome, that's your husband?" Sam Lomax said.

"Yes."

"On Officer Morrisey's report he said he talked to him last night. How did he do that? On the phone? He didn't mention that."

"No, Paul was still here last night."

"Mmmm."

"He *had* to go," Rachel said. "It's a business deal and . . . well, you know. . . ."

"Sure."

They reached the parking area. Beyond was the four-car garage, three doors open, then the forest.

"You must be right on the water here," Lomax said, opening the car door for Rachel.

"Pretty close, I guess," she said, getting in. "The children have been down there. There's a path through the woods, they tell me. I haven't explored it myself, though."

He closed the door, then circled the rear of the car and got in on the other side. Rachel watched him surreptitiously as he started the engine, then turned the car around. She was aware of being comfortable with him and was surprised. She had a leeriness of policemen. So far, though, he had not conformed to her concept of how a policeman acted: no brusqueness, no institutional politeness, no indication that he thought of himself as Supermale. He was more like his raincoat, loose and rumpled.

"How old are your kids?" he asked as the car moved along the private road.

"Seventeen, sixteen . . . and the new baby."

He glanced at her questioningly.

"Things happen," she said.

He laughed. "Seventeen and sixteen . . . you must have got married young."

"I was eighteen."

"I almost did that, too," he said. "But she changed her mind. Lucky she did, now that I look back on it. The only thing we had in common was that I was in heat and she was there."

Rachel burst into laughter, caught off guard by his frankness.

"I'd have kids, too, now, if she'd married me," he said. "They'd be a little older than yours." He shrugged. "Well, that's just as well, too. If they were anything like me when I was a kid, I'd be arresting them."

"Didn't you *ever* get married?"

"No."

She studied him openly. He looked like a husband; why hadn't he married? "Because of your job? The danger?"

"No."

Clearly, he did not want to explain. "What does a policeman do in a place like Cedar Point?" she said.

"We take turns blowing the siren."

"Seriously, I mean. It doesn't seem like the kind of place where there would be much crime."

"There's enough. You're right, though—there's not a lot. I suppose that's why I stay here. The job doesn't strain me." He glanced at her again, smiling this time. "I don't have a hell of a lot of ambition," he said. He faced forward again. "I did once. I wanted to be a great writer. I think I was right on the brink of it. But then—" His expression saddened.

Rachel leaned slightly toward him. "What happened?"

"My pencil broke."

She drew back, smiling thinly, feeling tricked.

"Sorry, bad joke," he said.

"I just thought you meant it."

They turned onto Cedar Point Road, and Rachel saw the Eldorado. It was still in the ditch. There were flares burning at the front and rear. Looking around, she remembered the terror that she had experienced the night before. She wondered if she would ever be able to pass this spot without, in her mind, hearing that girl's screams and seeing the iciness in the eyes behind the masks and, worst of all, seeing the lifeless face of the little boy.

Sam Lomax stopped his car on the shoulder behind the Eldorado, and he and Rachel got out. She stood by, waiting, while he extinguished the flares, then put them into the trunk of his car. She was fascinated by the way he handled his bigness. He moved so easily, so lightly. Maybe he had been an athlete when he was younger. Maybe he was still an athlete of a sort, a weekend tennis player or baseball player or something like that. Lord, he *was* graceful.

"All set," he said. "Will you be okay?"

"Yes, fine." She extended a hand. "Thank you."

He took the hand and held it momentarily, smiling the warm, open smile. "If you ever need a cop again, I'd appreciate the business," he said. "No bad jokes next time—I promise."

"It wasn't a bad joke, it just surprised me." She opened the door of the Eldorado. "Thank you again."

"My pleasure."

When Rachel closed the door, Sam Lomax walked back toward his own car. She started the Eldorado's engine and eased it out of the ditch and made a U-turn. Sam Lomax, standing beside his car, waved casually. Rachel nodded and smiled and drove on toward the private road. In the rearview mirror she saw Sam Lomax getting into his car. She had a feeling of loss. It was ridiculous of course. How long had she known the man, an hour? How could she possibly feel a genuine discontent about parting from someone she had known for so short a time? Still, it would be nice to talk to him again sometime. He had made her laugh.

She turned the Eldorado into the private road.

The ordeal was over. Not *quite* over. There would be Paul's look of long-suffering disgust to face when he returned. But she was used to that at least, if not yet hardened to it. What was important was that the little boy was not dead. Not even seriously injured. She could shed the feeling of guilt and expunge the memory of the girl's screams from her mind. Not that it would be easy. But in time. . . .

She would do something about decorating and furnishing the rest of the house. That would help. It would keep her busy, keep her from thinking.

Four

RACHEL chose Saturday to begin the search for appropriate furnishings to fill the vacant rooms of the house. She planned to take B.J. and Holly with her to force on them a recess from, respectively, their tapes and books. But by midmorning, when she was ready to set out, B.J. was no longer on hand. He had been called for by a classmate at school—a boy named Kirk Franklin, according to Holly—and the two had driven off in Kirk's car. Rachel was pleased; at last, one of her children had found a friend in Cedar Point.

"What exactly are we after?" Holly asked as they left Catawba in the Eldorado.

"Furniture, to begin with."

"Weird stuff, like the house?" Holly asked.

"Victorian, yes. Or as close to it as we can come," Rachel replied, trying to keep her attention on Cedar Point Road's many bends. "There are . . . let's see . . . a couple more sitting rooms to furnish—that's downstairs—and the library and those smaller rooms. And I've got to do something about that foyer and get some more pieces for the dining room. I'll worry about the upstairs later."

"Where do you find stuff like that?"

"Yellow pages, where else?" Rachel replied. "There's a place called Tuck's Barn that claims to have antiques, every era. We'll start there."

"I know where it is," Holly said. "It looks like a barn. It's painted red."

When they left the area of estates and entered Cedar Point's upper-middle-class section, the road straightened out. Here the landholdings were mostly a half acre to an acre in size and the houses, although fairly large, were standard Colonials and split-levels. Eventually the road became a street. Now the houses were relatively small and lined up side by side. This was the middle-class area, the lowest rung on the Cedar Point ladder, and the prelude to the business section, which, possibly owing to its limited size, was spoken of as the village.

"It's past the high school," Holly told her mother, directing her to Tuck's Barn.

The village was an approximately eight-block stretch of one- and two-story business buildings. A few of them were new, but most were old, with new fronts. The police headquarters, a low, wide red-brick structure, came first. Rachel wondered idly if Sam Lomax was on duty. Would it be out of place for her to stop and thank him again for— For what? For making her laugh? She could say that she had been wondering if he had any further information about the boy. No, that was too obvious. If he had anything to tell her, he would have been in contact with her.

A few more blocks of homes separated the main business section from the high school, a building that looked much like police headquarters, only larger. Then came a secondary business area, with a half dozen or so shops and Tuck's Barn. Tuck's Barn did indeed look like a barn. It was high and broad, with a gambrel roof, and painted barn-red with white trim. It even had a loft door.

Rachel parked the Eldorado in the lot at the rear, and she and Holly entered. Inside the rusticity was continued. The floor was bare cement. The walls were weathered planks. The overhead beams were rough, gnarled and splintery-looking. And the stanchions were studded with long iron spikes, from which hung a miscellany of artifacts from other times, horse collars, brown jugs, harnesses, lanterns, milk pails, weather vanes, and so on.

The barn was stocked in the manner of an ill-arranged warehouse. There were tables of china and glassware and crockery, but they were here and there rather than in a common location. The furniture was in stacks, tables piled on tables, chairs piled on tables, chests piled on chests, chairs piled on chairs, chairs and tables piled on sofas, mirrors piled on mirrors. Wherever there was an open flat spot, a lamp stood. Moving with Holly through the narrow aisles, Rachel had the uncomfortable feeling that if she even so much as touched one item every jerry-built pyramid in the barn would come crashing down.

There were no clerks or other customers in sight. Voices, faint, could be heard coming from some far reach of the barn, however. As, stack by stack, Rachel pressed the search for specimens of Victoriana, she gravitated in the general direction of the sounds. Holly, meanwhile, trailing along, provided an accompaniment of weary sighs and barely suppressed groans.

"You're not going to put this junk in the house, are you?" Holly asked finally.

"Not this junk," Rachel replied. "The junk I'm looking for is much worse."

"They sure don't have much business here," Holly said.

"What they lose in volume, I'm sure, they make up in markups," Rachel told her.

Emerging from an aisle, Rachel saw a short, balding middle-aged man with a denim apron tied around his waist in earnest and animated conversation with a pair of elderly women. It was clear that he was making a sales pitch. The women looked skeptical. Motioning for Holly to follow, Rachel approached them.

"Excuse me—"

"Yes, ma'am, just a minute," the man said.

"Do you have any Victorian?"

"Up in the loft," he told her. He pointed toward the rear of the building. "The stairs is back there. If you see anything you want, just whistle." Then he resumed his assault on the elderly women's doubts.

Rachel and Holly moved on.

"I wonder if that's Tuck," Holly said.

"Maybe. Maybe not. When your father was with American Tool and Die I know, they owned the company that made Mrs. Howard's Pies. So, Tuck might really be IBM."

Holly giggled. "Or even Dad's new company," she said.

"Could be," Rachel responded, beginning the climb up the narrow but sturdy stairway.

The lighting in the loft was poor, fuzzy and grainy. Here, too, the furniture was stacked in tall, haphazard piles. In the bad light and with chair legs and table legs sticking out at odd angles, the overall effect was that of a dense thicket. Rachel hesitated, stopped by a vague feeling of foreboding.

"Well?" Holly said.

"I don't know how we're going to find anything up here in this terrible light," Rachel said, annoyed.

"I don't either," Holly said. "Let's go."

"No. We're here. Let's see what we can see."

They entered an aisle, and Rachel began peering into the stacks, looking for the dark woods and ornate carvings of Victorian pieces. She found a sideboard that appeared to have the characteristics. But because of the dimness and the fact that it was partly obscured by a tall breakfront, she couldn't be positive. Further irritated, she moved on.

The deeper Rachel penetrated into the thicket, the stronger

became her feeling of foreboding. An unpleasant memory was forming in her mind. She could not recollect ever having been in a barn loft before, though. Maybe, she thought, she was recalling some scary moment from her childhood, a bad experience in an attic, perhaps. The sensation, however, as it became more intense, was not of an attic, but of a woods.

She saw the white shoes. Someone wearing white shoes was standing in the next aisle. A picture, the memory, flashed across her mind. She was on Cedar Point Road, approaching the masked figures in the drizzle, conscious of the surrounding woods with its tangled thickets. And there were the white shoes, worn by one of the masked children. Then the girl was screaming at her, wildly, madly.

"Holly!" Rachel called out, terrified.

"What? Where are you?" Holly answered.

Rachel almost shrieked the answer. "Here!"

The white shoes were gone.

Holly came out of the dimness. "What's the matter?"

"One of them is here!" Rachel told her fearfully. "I saw him! I saw his shoes! He's over there on the other side!"

"One of who?" Holly asked puzzledly.

"One of the ones in the masks! He's after me!"

Holly looked through the openings in the pile of tables and chairs. "I don't see anybody."

"He's gone! He *was* there!"

"I'll go look," Holly said.

"Don't!"

"How can I see if I don't look?"

"I just want to get out of here!" Rachel said, grabbing her daughter by the hand and hurrying back along the aisle. "He's crazy! They're all crazy!"

"Who?"

"All of them!"

They reached the stairs and started down. At the same time the middle-aged man in the denim apron appeared at the bottom of the steps. Seeing Rachel and Holly descending, he halted and waited.

"Somebody's up there!" Rachel told him frantically.

"What? Who?"

"It's dark, and my mother saw someone," Holly explained. She sounded apologetic.

"You should've turned on the lights," he said. "I don't keep them on; it costs money. What's up there, you say? What happened?"

"It's all right," Rachel said, moving quickly past him. Her sole interest now was in getting out of the building. "I'll come back some other time," she told the man, pulling at Holly, moving on toward the exit.

"But what happened?" the man asked, concerned, following. "Did somebody grab you?"

"She just saw his shoes," Holly said.

"What'd he *do?*"

"Nothing," Holly said.

The man gave up the chase and was left behind.

When they got outside, Rachel let go of Holly's hand. She strode rapidly toward the car, with Holly trotting after her. To a degree, the terrifying picture that had flashed across her mind was still there. The details had faded, but the impression remained, like an outline of something hard and sharp on something pliant. She felt almost as vulnerable as she had that night when the masked figures with their icy eyes had pursued her into the darkness.

Inside the Eldorado, with all doors closed, Rachel finally felt safe again. She gripped the wheel tightly and sighed deeply and stared straight ahead into the reflection of the autumn sun on the hood. The brightness, after the darkness in the loft, was restorative. She began to relax. Holly, meanwhile, sat in silence, watching her mother speculatively.

"He's the same one," Rachel told her. "I remember those shoes."

"Mother, I don't know anything about any shoes."

"One of them was wearing white shoes. Those same white shoes."

[46]

"Oh. I didn't remember you mentioning that."

"I didn't mention it," Rachel said. "I didn't remember the shoes until I saw them again up there in that loft."

"What were you so scared about?"

"If you'd been there that night— I don't know. The first thing I thought was that he was after me. It was so dark up there. I didn't know what he might do."

"It wasn't so dark. Anyway, you said that policeman said it was just a joke."

"I know. . . . But *he* wasn't there either. If you could have *seen* them, the way they came at me—I couldn't help it. I saw those white shoes, and I thought he was after me."

Holly was silent again for a moment. Then she said, "What are we going to do now? Wait for him to come out?"

"No!" Rachel answered. She began looking for her car keys in her purse. "I just want to get out of here."

"I'd like to see who he is," Holly said. "I didn't see anybody up there. I didn't even hear anybody."

Rachel started the engine. "You were somewhere else," she said. "Where were you?"

"Looking at an old desk," Holly replied. "I wonder why that man didn't see him. He didn't know what you were talking about. But somebody in white shoes, this time of year, how could he miss somebody like that?"

"He was talking to those women," Rachel said, backing the Eldorado out of the parking space. "He didn't see me either, remember, until I spoke to him. A whole herd of elephants in white shoes could have marched through there without *him* knowing it."

"It just seems funny."

"Believe me, there was nothing funny about it," Rachel said, as they left the lot. She headed back in the direction from which they had come. "I saw an art store," she said. "We'll stop there."

"What are you going to do about the furniture, go somewhere else?"

"I don't know. I don't want to think about it right now."

"Dad's getting kind of itchy about it."

"I know that."

"If you don't want to do it yourself, why don't you get somebody to do it for you?" Holly suggested. "Don't they have people like that?"

"Decorators, yes. No, I want to do it myself."

"You don't do it, though," Holly said.

"I will do it," Rachel told her testily.

"Okay, okay."

Rachel parked the car across from the art store, McMillans's, and she and Holly got out and made their way through the light traffic to the other side of the street and entered. McMillan's was narrow and deep, with an art supplies section at the front and a gallery at the rear. Holly stopped at a display of books, collections of reproductions of various artists' works, and Rachel went on back to where the paintings were on display.

The smaller paintings were hung on the two long walls and the larger ones were lined up back to back on easels along the center of the gallery. Joining the two other browsers, a younger woman and an older woman, Rachel began perusing the wall-hung paintings. They were for the most part undistinguished. Her guess was that they had been done by art students as academic exercises.

The one kind of painting that Rachel looked for specifically was what she thought of as the ancestor portrait. It was Paul's choice. When she asked him if he had anything in particular in mind for the room that would be his office away from the office, he told her he wanted pictures like the ones in the boardroom at Cumberland Steel. Those were portraits of the male heads of the family that had founded the company, stern-visaged industrialists in the business suits of their times. Paul's purpose, of course, was to give the unknowing the impression that he came from a long line of businessmen. What she ought to do, she thought, was get dozens of fake portraits of Paul in old-fashioned business suits and hang them all over the house, so that he would see his "ancestors" wherever he looked.

When Rachel reached the end of the first wall of paintings, she saw a small office at the far rear of the gallery. A tall, spare, fragile-looking young man was standing beside a desk, talking on the phone. Their eyes met for a moment and he nodded and she smiled; then she turned her attention to the larger paintings on the easels. As she made her way leisurely along the line, she saw that Holly had joined her in the gallery and was inspecting the works on the wall.

A large painting of a servant girl in a medieval kitchen setting struck Rachel as suitable for Catawba. The time was early morning and the shadows in the kitchen were deep and dark, accented by reflections of red and yellow from the fire in the huge fireplace and spillage of pale sunlight coming in through an open window. Rachel studied the detail work, the perspective, the highlighting, the shading of the shadows, then stepped back for a full-view look at the painting.

As she backed away, she saw the white shoes again. Whoever was wearing them was standing at the opposite side of the wall-like lineup of paintings on easels. Her initial reaction this time, however, was not terror, but anger. She was being harassed by the white shoes, and she was indignant about it. She hadn't done anything wrong—it was an accident. The white shoes had no right to torment her! It had to stop—now!

"There he is again!" Rachel told her daughter, pointing at the shoes.

Holly, a few paces away, withdrew her attention from the wall of paintings. "What did you say, Mother?"

Rachel pointed again. "There—"

The white shoes were gone.

"He was there! I saw him!" Rachel said.

"Who now?" Holly asked.

"The same one. The one with the white shoes."

"Where?"

"On the other side," Rachel told her. Again, she pointed. "I

[49]

saw the shoes. He ran out," she said angrily, hurrying toward the front of the store. "He followed us in here; then, when I saw him, he ran!"

"Mother . . . wait a minute . . ." Holly pleaded, trailing after her.

Rachel reached the art supplies section. There were two young men standing at the counter, talking with a clerk. Neither of them was wearing white shoes.

"Mother, will you just hold it a second?" Holly said edgily, catching up to Rachel.

"I tell you, I saw him!"

"Okay. But if you did, he's gone."

Rachel went to the counter. "Excuse me, I'm sorry, but did you see who just went through here?" she said, breaking in on the conversation between the young men and the clerk. "He had on white shoes."

They looked at her curiously.

"I didn't see anybody," one young man said.

"What kind of white shoes?" the other young man asked.

"Just white."

He shook his head.

"Somebody went through, I think," the clerk told Rachel. "But I didn't look. We were talking here. . . . And people are coming in and out all the time. Is something wrong?"

"No . . ." Rachel replied drearily, turning away.

"Mother, you're making a scene," Holly said tightly.

"I don't give a damn—I *saw* him!" Rachel strode back toward the gallery. As before, Holly followed. "And somebody else in here had to see him, too," Rachel said. "I didn't make him up."

"All right. But what difference does it make? He's gone."

Rachel reached the older woman, who was examining the paintings on the other wall. "Please, could you help me?" she said. "There was someone in here just a few minutes ago with white shoes on—did you see him?"

The woman faced her, looking surprised.

"He was standing over here on this side," Rachel said. "You *must* have seen him."

The woman shook her head. "I really wasn't looking—"

"You *had* to see him!" Rachel said sharply.

The woman backed away a step.

"I'm sorry," Rachel said. She felt foolish. "I'm *very* sorry," she said, quickly moving on.

The fragile-looking young man was still in the office and still talking on the phone. He now had his back to the gallery, sitting on a corner of the desk. He seemed to sense Rachel's approach, however, for he turned his eyes toward her as she neared him. When she reached the desk he broke off the phone conversation.

"Yes, ma'am?"

"Just a few minutes ago," she said, "there was someone in here with white shoes on. He might have been a teenager. Whatever he was, he was standing there by the big paintings. Did you see him?"

The young man frowned thoughtfully. "White shoes. . . . Is he a doctor?"

"I don't know what he is," Rachel said crossly. "Did you see him?"

"I thought he might be a doctor because of the white shoes."

"Oh. That's not important. All I want to know is, did you see him?"

"Well, I might have," the young man said. "What did he look like?"

Rachel sighed frustratedly. "I don't know. I only saw his shoes."

"I don't remember any white shoes. But you know, we see a lot of people. If I had a little something more to go on—"

"All right, thank you," Rachel said.

"If he comes back, is there some message, or—"

"No."

Rachel walked back toward the front of the store. The older woman was gone, and the younger woman had apparently left earlier, because she was nowhere in sight. In the meantime, two other browsers had arrived, an elderly man and a college-age young woman. Holly was waiting for Rachel at the front of the gallery. She looked pained.

"What did he say?" Holly asked.

"He was looking the other way; he couldn't have seen him," Rachel told her.

Together, they walked through the art supplies section, heading for the exit. The clerk and the two young men had resumed their conversation. They paid absolutely no attention to Rachel and Holly, making it possible for Rachel to understand how they could have missed seeing whoever it was in white shoes. It made very good sense, in fact, now that she thought about it, that none of the others had seen him—the clerk and the two men involved in their conversation, Holly and the older woman with their eyes to the paintings on the walls, the young man on the telephone in the office with his back to the gallery. It was completely understandable.

"Are we finished?" Holly asked hopefully when they were in the car again.

"We're finished looking," Rachel replied, starting the engine. "I'm going to the police."

"Oh, Mother, can't you just drop it?"

"Holly, whoever that was, he was following me," Rachel told her, pulling out into traffic. "Don't tell me it was just coincidence that he happened to turn up at both places. I don't know what he thinks he's doing, but I'm going to put a stop to it. I can't have him trailing me around and popping up and scaring me everywhere I go. I'll be a raving lunatic."

Holly offered no further comment.

"The problem is, you weren't there that night and you don't know how they looked when they were chasing me," Rachel said. "It was awful."

Forbearing silence.

"I suppose you think I was drunk, too," Rachel said resentfully.

"Who said you were drunk?"

"That's what your father's lawyer friend thinks."

Holly shrugged.

"Well, I wasn't drunk, and I wasn't imagining," Rachel told her. "I don't know what they intended to do to me, but it was something vicious and terrible. I could see it in their eyes. I could tell by the way they came at me. And I saw those white shoes, too, no matter what anybody thinks."

More silence.

Rachel turned the Eldorado into the no parking area in front of police headquarters and stopped and switched off the engine.

"Are you coming in with me?" she asked her daughter.

"I don't know what I could do. I didn't see any white shoes."

"If anybody says anything about the car being here," Rachel said, getting out, "tell them it's an emergency." She closed the door hard, expressing her annoyance at Holly's attitude, then marched toward the entrance to the red-brick building.

Inside, a heavyset middle-aged woman in uniform was seated at a metal desk, typing. Assuming that she was there to act as a receptionist, Rachel told her that she wanted to speak to Lieutenant Lomax. The woman picked up her phone, dialed, asked for the lieutenant, listened, then hung up and informed Rachel that Lieutenant Lomax was not at headquarters at the moment.

"Do you know when he will be here?" Rachel asked.

The woman shook her head. "Would you like to talk to someone else?"

"No. It's about an accident I had. Well . . . it wasn't an accident, as it turned out. I was driving along—it was Halloween night—and I thought I hit a little boy. But I didn't—it seems. Now, though—"

"Are you Mrs. Barthelme?" the woman asked. She was smiling slightly.

"Yes. Do you know about it?"

"I processed Lieutenant Lomax's report," the woman said. Her smile had become fixed. It was now a smile of suppressed amusement.

"If you'll just tell the lieutenant that I stopped and that I want to talk to him again," Rachel said coolly. She turned and left.

On the way back to the car Rachel seethed. She felt as if she had been laughed at. She could guess what the lieutenant had put in his report that had amused the woman so much: that the so-called accident had been nothing but a drunken fantasy. If that was what he thought, she could also guess how he would react when she told him that she was now being followed by a pair of white shoes.

Damn it, he couldn't say she was drunk again, though. She was dead sober, and she had Holly as her witness. The pity was that Holly hadn't seen the white shoes. The lieutenant would probably conclude this time that Rachel didn't need to be drunk to have fantasies.

Five

SUNDAY was another bright, clear day. Standing at the bay window in the master bedroom, still in her pajamas, Rachel watched Mrs. Woolsey get into her sister's car, which had stopped on a curve of the drive, just short of the entrance. After a few moments the car departed. Sunday was Mrs. Woolsey's day off. Until Monday morning Rachel would have the responsibility of the baby all to herself. She felt like a sitter. It was Mrs. Woolsey who was performing the functions of the mother. Rachel merely filled in for her once a week.

It had been Paul's idea to have a full-time woman:

You've put in your time, Rachel. You've raised two kids. The new baby isn't your fault—it's mine if it's anybody's. So why should you be the one to pay? Get a woman in. Let her take over the dirty work. Keep your time your own.

He was right. She had put in her time. She had brought up

B.J. and Holly, staying with a man she no longer loved—or even liked—to do it. She had earned her freedom. But the new baby had robbed her of it. So she deserved the compensation that Paul had offered: the full-time woman and the right to have her time to herself.

Like most compensations, though, this one was a poor substitute for the actual loss. The marriage was still a prison. No matter how she used her time, where she went or what she did, the prison walls were always with her. And of course, eventually the compensation would cease to have any value at all. The baby would grow out of being a baby; she would become a person. Then, Mrs. Woolsey would no longer be acceptable to her as a stand-in. She would demand the attention of her real mother; the responsibility, seven days a week, would be Rachel's alone.

When the sister's car passed from sight, Rachel went back to bed. The baby, full with morning milk, would probably sleep until close to noon. And Rachel had nothing better to do than to sleep, either. She had finished the *Times* puzzle and wouldn't get the new one until tomorrow. With B.J. and Holly still asleep there was no one left in the house to talk to. If she stayed awake, she would think, and that would lead to brooding. Thank God, she hadn't yet become an insomniac.

Sleep now did not come easily, though. Rachel found that she was listening for the phone to ring. She had waited for the sound all Saturday afternoon and evening, too, expecting the lieutenant to call her. But the only call, late in the evening, had been for B.J., from his new friend, Kirk Franklin. Consequently, she had decided along toward midnight that the lieutenant had chosen to ignore the message that she left for him. Evidently, however, since she was again listening for the phone to ring, she had not given up completely on the hope of hearing from him.

It might be just as well, though, that he hadn't called. Now that she'd had some time to think it over, she was no longer so certain that the person in the white shoes really had been following her. It might have been mere coincidence that twice they were in the same place at the same time. He could have been looking for furnishings and paintings, too. And, besides, what proof did she have that his white shoes were the same white shoes that she had seen the night of the accident? There was more than one pair of white shoes in the world. Although how many people wore white shoes in winter? . . .

What made it hard to believe that he had been trailing her was that there was no rational reason for it. If he and his friends had played a joke on her, wouldn't they leave it at that? They would, surely, unless they were sadists and wanted to play another bad joke on her. That was possible. But improbable. The only other reason she could think of for his following her was that the girl's little brother had really been killed and the girl and her friends were after her for revenge. That was equally implausible, though. Because, of course, no little boy had died.

So it was probably fortunate that she hadn't heard from the lieutenant. If he had called, he would have asked Rachel all the questions that she had just asked herself and reached the same conclusion. Or worse. Since Holly had not seen the white shoes, he might think that she had imagined the whole thing, beginning with the accident. What Rachel ought to do was let the entire matter drop, not mention it again, not even think about it again. Blot it out of her mind.

Even so, she continued to listen for the phone to ring until she finally fell asleep.

The baby's crying woke Rachel. Groggy, she raised up and looked at the clock on the bedside table. It was a little after eleven. What was the significance of that? Oh, yes, feeding time. Still somewhat fuzzy-headed, she got up and went to the nursery. Speaking softly and reassuringly to the baby, she lifted her from the crib and put her down gently on the Bathinette, then began changing her diaper. Throughout the process the baby continued to cry, obviously hungry.

With the baby wrapped in her blanket and cradling her in her arms, Rachel left the nursery. As she descended the stairs, the crying stopped. Rachel guessed that the baby had been distracted by the motion. She also heard voices, one of which she recognized as her son's, coming from the sitting room. The other was also a male voice, not quite matured, leading her to assume that it belonged to her son's new friend.

Wanting to meet the Franklin boy, Rachel went to the entrance to the sitting room. B.J. was lying on a couch, his head resting on the arm. The boy who Rachel guessed was Kirk Franklin was seated in the club chair that had the telephone table beside it. He was leaning forward as he spoke, using his long, lean hands to emphasize his words. He appeared to be trying to sell B.J. on some point on which B.J. had doubts.

"—not just a dozen or a hundred, but millions, so it didn't sneak up on anybody, it's government policy," the boy was saying.

At that moment he caught sight of Rachel and interrupted himself and, staring at her, rose. He was tall, taller than Rachel, and spare. His face was narrow, and his dark hair, though bushy, was cut short. It was his eyes, however, that held Rachel's attention. In spite of the fact that he was smiling genially, his eyes were icy-cold. She was reminded of the eyes behind the openings in the masks.

B.J. was on his feet now, introducing the boy. He was, as Rachel had surmised, Kirk Franklin.

"Do you live close?" Rachel asked him, moving further into the sitting room.

"Across the road." He was peering at the baby. His voice had a soft, fuzzy quality to it.

The baby began crying again.

"Is she ill?" Kirk Franklin asked.

"No, no, just hungry." Rachel addressed her son. "I didn't get any calls, did I?"

"Nope. Dad called, but he talked to Holly."

"Did he want something?"

"I don't know. I didn't talk to him. He'll be home on Wednesday, he thinks, Holly said."

"All right. Well. . . . Nice to meet you," she said to Kirk Franklin, backing away. "I've got to get some food into this child."

He smiled again. But his eyes remained icy.

Carrying the crying baby toward the kitchen, Rachel still felt somewhat chilled by the bad memory that the look in Kirk Franklin's eyes had stirred in her. She hoped that the boy had not been aware of her distress. She had tried not to let it show. She didn't want Kirk Franklin to think that she was reacting to him personally. He was B.J.'s only friend in Cedar Point so far, and she wanted him to feel welcome in the house.

When she reached the kitchen, Rachel got one of the bottles that Mrs. Woolsey had prepared from the refrigerator and put it on to warm. She walked and rocked the baby as she waited. The baby would not be mollified, however. Rachel felt a stiffness across her shoulders and at the back of her neck. The baby's wailing was like a rasp rubbing against the raw ends of her nerves. What had happened to the patience she had when the older children were this age? Gone.

The frantic screaming stopped instantly when the baby felt the nipple touch her lips. Her mouth became a vacuum, sucking. A gurgling sound came from her throat; then she settled into the curve of Rachel's arm and, eyes closed, concentrated ravenously on filling her belly with the warm liquid. Rachel wished that her own needs and tensions could be satisfied so simply. Even with the crying stopped she was still taut. The stiffness across her shoulders and at the back of her neck had become a dull ache.

She wondered why Paul had called. It wasn't like him to check in when he was out of town. Like a child, he always assumed that as long as he knew where he was, that was all that mattered. He had probably been in need of information that he had left behind in his desk in the room that would eventually be his office away from the office—if Rachel ever got it furnished and decorated. That was why he had talked to Holly instead of Rachel; there had been no need to wake

Rachel since Holly could get the information for him just as well.

The sucking slowed, then ceased. As Rachel slipped the nipple from the baby's mouth, her eyes opened. Thankfully, she remained quiet. Rachel put the bottle aside, then, cradling the baby in both arms again, left the kitchen and walked slowly back toward the foyer. Gradually, the baby's eyes closed again. With luck, by the time Rachel reached the nursery with her she would be asleep once more.

In the foyer, turning toward the stairs, Rachel heard Kirk Franklin's voice coming from the sitting room.

"—killing isn't wrong," he said. "Isn't that the proof?"

She halted, startled by what she had heard.

"I see what you mean," B.J. said.

Rachel detoured, going toward the sitting room.

"It's only punished under those certain circumstances," Kirk Franklin said. "Not because it's wrong, but for the protection of the ones on top, the people who have the power to punish."

Rachel reached the doorway. "What are you two talking about?" she asked. "Killing what?"

The boys were where they had been before, Kirk Franklin in the chair and B.J. on the couch. Kirk raised his eyes to Rachel, and B.J. turned so that he could look over the arm of the couch at her.

"People," Kirk replied matter-of-factly.

"Killing *people?*" Rachel said, appalled. "That's not *wrong?*"

"We're just talking, Mom," B.J. said.

"About killing *some* people for the good of others," Kirk told her. "It's done every day. In Africa and Asia right now, in fact, about ten thousand people a week. They starve to death."

"Oh, starve . . ." Rachel said, relieved. "That's not the same as killing people. That famine, you mean? That can't be helped. That's the weather, isn't it? If there isn't food, there isn't food."

"There's food, Mom," B.J. said. "It just isn't where the starving is."

"Well, you can't just pick up that much food and move it."

"Yes, you can," Kirk said. "It *could* be done. There are enough ships and planes to move it. But it *isn't* being done. That's what we mean. Those people aren't just starving; they're being killed off." His manner was still matter-of-fact.

"That's ridiculous," Rachel said heatedly.

"Then why aren't we feeding them?" B.J. asked.

"I don't know. I don't know that much about it. But why would we kill them?"

"For our own good," Kirk told her. "If we didn't kill them, they'd multiply. The way things are, the world population grows by about seventy-five million people a year. If we kept them alive, they'd breed. That would just make the problem worse."

"I don't believe it!" Rachel said. The baby twitched in her arms, startled by the sharpness of her tone. Rachel began rocking her to settle her down. "Do you mean to tell me that everybody who has food got together and decided to *kill* everybody who hasn't?"

"Not everybody," Kirk replied evenly. "But the people who run things *do* get together. They have conferences and summits. They don't decide to kill anybody and announce it, if that's what you mean. They don't do anything about the starving either, though—except make up a committee to study it. So it amounts to the same thing. Not doing anything is doing something."

"It's the way the world works, Mom," B.J. said. "It's nothing new. It's been going on for a long time. People kill people."

"I still don't believe it," Rachel said. "But if it's true, it's wrong. Why isn't it wrong?"

"I just said—population," Kirk told her. "Letting those people starve today, you keep them from reproducing. That way you keep more from being born and starving tomorrow."

"You make it sound noble!" Rachel charged.

"It is, in a way," Kirk replied. "It's doing a dirty job. Nobody likes to do a dirty job. So, doing it, you could say, is noble."

[60]

"What we were talking about is the dishonesty," B.J. said. "They don't say they're doing it."

"If it's got to be done, why don't they come out and say so?" Kirk said. "We all know there's a population explosion. We all know something has to be done about it."

"That's a fact, Mom," B.J. said. "There are just too many people. And it's getting worse."

"It's the kids being born and the ones who are already around who aren't any good to anybody," Kirk said. "They're taking up space and eating up food."

"What people who aren't any good to anybody?" Rachel asked tightly.

Kirk hesitated. Not, Rachel thought, because he didn't have an answer, but because he was becoming wary of her hostility. "Crazy people, for one example," he said. "What good are they to anybody, even themselves?"

She was stunned. "You want to *kill* them?"

The baby began to struggle and whimper. In her shock and anger, Rachel was clutching her fiercely.

"Mom, we're just talking," B.J. said. "Don't get so upset. It's just a discussion."

"I'm not upset. I just think you're wrong. It might look like policy, letting people starve, but it couldn't be." She forced a thin smile. "I can't talk about it now," she said, turning away. "I've got to get the baby to bed."

As she was climbing the stairs with the baby, she heard B.J. speaking again. She wondered if he was apologizing to Kirk Franklin for her behavior. She was irked at herself for having let her anger show. But, damn it, Kirk had been so blasé about taking life, as if it had no more meaning to him than transferring people from one place to another, from Pittsburgh to Walla Walla. Still, as B.J. had pointed out, it was only an academic discussion. She shouldn't have taken it so seriously.

In the nursery she put the baby down gently, then tiptoed out and climbed the stairs to the upper floor. There she went to the door to Holly's room and knocked. The response was immediate.

"Who is it?"

"Me, dear."

"Come on in."

Like the downstairs sitting room, Holly's room looked as if by magic it had been transported intact from the Manhattan apartment. Books were stacked on every flat surface, including the floor. Quotations, presumably from the books, were penciled on the walls (Sorry, I forgot to give you the mayonnaise—Brautigan. I am a nun now, I have never been so pure—Plath. The stars are matter; We're matter; But it doesn't matter—Van Vliet). Holly was lying on the floor on her fake bear skin rug, propped up on her elbows, reading.

"How can you breathe the air in here?" Rachel said, stepping over her daughter and going to a window.

"What's the matter with it?"

"It must be a thousand years old."

"I'm recycling it," Holly told her.

Rachel tugged at the window. It was stuck. She pulled with her full strength and grudgingly it gave an inch and then refused to open any further.

"Well, at least that's something," Rachel said, turning back to Holly. "Hon, why don't you get out more? This isn't healthy, spending so much time up here in your room."

"Why not?"

"Well. . . . Fresh air."

"I get plenty of fresh air all week, going to school and back."

"You go in B.J.'s car."

"I'm out in the air on the way from the house to the car and from the car into school."

"All right . . . I can't force you," Rachel said, sighing. "B.J. said your father called. What did he want, something from his desk?"

"No."

"What did he want?"

"Just to see if everything was okay."

"That doesn't sound like your father. He never calls for that. Did he want to talk to me?"

"No."

"You mean he called *you* to find out if everything was all right?"

"I guess."

"What did he want to know, if I was still drunk?" Rachel said tightly.

"He just asked if you were okay and what you were doing."

"What did you tell him?"

"Nothing. I just told him that we went looking for some furniture and pictures . . . and about you seeing somebody in white shoes."

"What did he say about that?" Rachel asked resentfully. "I suppose you told him that nobody else saw the shoes."

"I said I didn't. What *could* I say? I *didn't* see them. Nobody saw them. I mean, you saw them, I guess, but nobody else did."

"What do you mean, you *guess?*"

"I don't *mean* anything," Holly replied, becoming belligerent. "You asked me what he asked me and what I told him and I told you, that's all. If you didn't want to know, why did you ask?" She slammed the book closed. "Boy, how did *I* get in the middle of this!"

"I'm sorry," Rachel said. "You're right, it isn't your problem. Actually," she said lightly, trying to take the tension out of the situation, "there isn't any problem. Just a misunderstanding. Your father talked to that lawyer, I suppose, and got the wrong idea and got worried." She moved toward the doorway. "That's what happens when people get their information from people who don't know what they're talking about. Don't close that window," she said, leaving. "Let the room air out."

"How long?"

"At least until I get to the stairs," Rachel replied, pulling the door closed.

Returning to the master bedroom, Rachel freed her anger, letting it rise. Obviously, the lawyer, Jack Flanagan, had told Paul that Rachel's version of what had happened at the accident had been a drunken hallucination, and Paul had believed him. That was no surprise. Paul was always ready to believe anything about her that made her look foolish or imcompetent. He seemed to get some sort of satisfaction out of it. Maybe it bolstered his concept of himself as a paragon of common sense and proficiency.

As she approached the bedroom, she heard the baby crying. Groaning, she turned toward the nursery. Was it going to be another Sunday like the last Sunday, with the baby awake almost the whole day? Why was it that she would sleep for Mrs. Woolsey but not for Rachel? Was she aware that she was being handled by someone different? Maybe Rachel was too tense. Perhaps a baby could sense a thing like that. Especially after being taken care of all week by a woman like Mrs. Woolsey, who was about as uptight as a slab of raw liver.

The baby was red-faced and writhing when Rachel reached her. But she became quiet almost immediately when Rachel lifted her from the crib and held her against her shoulder. Rachel spoke softly to her, patting her gently, then walked with her, back and forth across the room. After only a few minutes she was asleep again. Carefully, Rachel put her back into the crib and tucked the blanket around her, then left.

In the bedroom, Rachel switched on the television set and began channel hopping. The choice was between football and movies. She turned off the set and sat down in the wing chair, looking out the bay window. It was early afternoon now, a bright day with a nice sun. Clearly, she wasn't going to hear from Lieutenant Lomax. Jack Flanagan wasn't the only one who thought she was a crackpot.

She thought about Paul's call again. If he really wanted to know how she was and what she was doing, why hadn't he talked to her? By making the call directly to Holly, he had as much as implied that Rachel couldn't be relied on to answer competently for herself. Now he probably had Holly—and B.J., too—thinking that she was a muddlehead, too. Oh, fine. That was all she needed, to have her children against her.

The baby cried out.

"Shut up!" Rachel shouted, jumping up.

There was a knock at the door.

"Yes, coming," Rachel said, crossing the room. She felt penitent about shouting at the baby, even though the baby couldn't possibly have heard her.

B.J. was at the door.

"I heard her. I'm going to her," Rachel told him testily.

He looked past her into the room. "Who were you yelling at?"

"The baby. She won't stay asleep."

"Oh. I didn't come up about her," he said. "Do you want the bottle warmer on?"

"What?"

"It's on," B.J. said. "Kirk and I went into the kitchen, and he saw it. Do you want it on?"

"No. I turned it off," she said, going toward the nursery.

"Well, it's on."

"How could it be? I remember turning it off."

"I guess it turned itself back on," he said.

"Don't be smart. Turn if off," she said, going into the nursery.

As before, the baby was red-faced and thrashing, and as soon as Rachel picked her up and placed her against her shoulder, she became quiet. Again Rachel walked with her and talked to her. Before very long she was asleep. But when Rachel tried to put her down in the crib, her eyes flew open and the yowling began once more. Sighing drearily, Rachel resumed the walking and talking.

"What *is* the matter?" Rachel asked her.

The baby stopped crying and emitted a raspy breath and closed her eyes.

Nevertheless, Rachel continued the walking, back and forth, back and forth, wanting to be certain that the baby was truly sound asleep before she tried to put her down again. Damn Sundays. Maybe she ought to hire Holly to take care of the baby on Mrs. Woolsey's day off. No, then they would think she wasn't capable of caring for her own child even one day a week. Holly already thought she was seeing things, white shoes. And B.J. probably thought she talked to herself in her room—shouting—and couldn't be trusted to turn off the bottle warmer after she used it.

Standing at the crib, Rachel eased the baby from her shoulder. The moment that contact was broken, the crying began again. So, holding the baby close once more, Rachel resumed the pacing. Maybe she ought to call a doctor. No, that would be panicking. She could call Mrs. Woolsey. No, let the woman— Colic! Of course! This was exactly the way B.J. had acted when he had the colic when he was a baby. What had she done about it? Medicine? No. Cold air. Yes, she had taken him on long walks in the carriage in the cold air.

Taking the baby with her, Rachel left the nursery and went to the landing and called down to B.J. When he appeared, she asked him to get the carriage and put it out in front. Then she returned to the nursery with the baby and bundled her into a heavy sleeping bag. The baby was now wide awake, but through all the handling—and the stuffing as she was put into the bag—she remained contentedly quiet.

As Rachel descended the stairs with the baby, she heard rattling sounds from the kitchen. B.J. and Kirk Franklin getting lunch for themselves, she assumed. In the entryway she dragged a long, heavy coat from the closet, then left the house. After she had fitted the baby in its cumbersome sleeping bag into the carriage and herself into the coat, she set out along the drive, pushing the carriage.

Nearing the private road, Rachel heard a car approaching. A moment later it appeared. It was the lieutenant's car. He did not see her, apparently, for he drove on by, going toward the parking area at the rear of the house. Following, pushing the carriage at a rapid clip, Rachel felt a flush of elation. She had been more let down than she had admitted to herself by the lieutenant's failure to call. It had been as if a friend had failed her.

Lieutenant Lomax was on his way toward the front of the house when Rachel reached the rear. His car was parked beside Kirk Franklin's MGB-GT. He broke into a wide, warm smile at the sight of Rachel. She was again impressed by his bigness and look of docile bearishness.

"Where are you headed—north?" he said. "You look like you're expecting a cold spell." His own coat was flapping open.

She laughed. "Maybe I am overdoing it. It's nippy, though. And I imagine I'll be out quite awhile. The baby has been crying," she explained. "It's colic, I think. I'm hoping that the cold air and the walk will settle her down. It usually works—as I remember."

"You aren't going to walk along the road, are you?" he said. "That's dangerous."

"Well, I don't know. . . ."

"Let's try the woods," he said. "The paths are tramped down. There's a lot of traffic through there in the summer— the kids. Besides, you've got all that property, you might as well use it."

"I guess we could."

"I'll push," he said, taking over the carriage.

They crossed the cleared area at the rear of the house and entered the woods. The path was, as the lieutenant had described it, flat and wide.

"This is amazing," she said. "I expected it to be overgrown. It's like a park. How does it stay this way?"

"Mother Nature's little helpers," Lieutenant Lomax told her. "You have a crew of workmen who take care of it. They do the trimming—and whatever else they do. Not just your property, all of the property in this section. You have a property owners' association. It hires the workers, and you all pitch in and pay for it."

"Paul didn't mention that."

"Did he get back?" Sam Lomax asked. "I didn't see his car."

"No, he's still away."

"Does he travel a lot?"

"Now he does. He's in charge of buying into foreign companies for the company he works for." She looked into the carriage. The baby's eyes were closed. "It's working," she said. "She's asleep."

"I got your message that you wanted to talk to me," he said.

"I wondered. That was early yesterday."

"You didn't say it was urgent."

"Well, actually, I suppose it wasn't urgent. I don't know. A strange thing happened—twice." She told him about seeing the white shoes at Tuck's Barn and at McMillan's and her feeling that whoever was wearing the shoes was following her. "When I stopped at your headquarters to see you, I was scared," she said. "But since then, I've had a chance to think about it, and maybe it was just coincidence."

He seemed perplexed. "I don't see how the white shoes come into it," he said.

"Oh—I forgot to mention that. One of those children in the masks was wearing white shoes. I know I didn't tell you that before. But I didn't remember it until I saw the shoes again." She sneaked a look at his face to see how he was reacting. He still appeared puzzled. "I know how it sounds . . . as if I made up the white shoes," she said.

"No, that happens in situations like that. People remember things later."

"Then you believe me?"

The question appeared to surprise him. "Why wouldn't I believe you?"

"Well, I don't think my daughter does. Of course, I can't blame her. She didn't see the shoes either time. As I told you, no one else saw them."

"They could have seen them, peripherally, and paid no attention to them," he said. "You were the only one among the possible observers who had a personal interest in the shoes."

"Is that detective talk?"

He laughed. "It probably came out of a textbook," he said. He pointed. "Let's go this way." They had reached a fork in the path, and he was indicating the branch to the right. "Let's see . . . white shoes. . . . Who would be wearing white shoes this time of year?"

"The man at McMillan's thought I was talking about a doctor."

"That fits. Not necessarily a doctor—if he was a kid—but somebody connected with a hospital, an orderly, a kitchen worker."

"You know what was funny?" Rachel said. "I kept expecting that little boy to turn up at the hospital here in Cedar Point, but he didn't. Is there any connection there?"

He was silent for a moment. "Let's say they took the boy to the hospital," he said, "but with one of them who knew his way around, they didn't go through regular channels. The boy was fixed up, say, and they took him home. That's possible."

"Of course it is."

"But why?"

"Maybe the sister was afraid that her parents would blame her for what happened and she didn't want to be punished," Rachel suggested.

"All right. Let's take it to the next step. Why was the kid in the white shoes following you?"

"I think they intend to try to do something to me," Rachel said.

"What for?"

"Revenge. That's the only thing I can think of."

"Revenge for what? As it stands, we have a kid with, say, a few scratches. I can believe that with a few scratches they could whisk him in and out of the hospital without going through the regular routine. But anything serious—" He shook his head. "And if he wasn't seriously hurt, where's the basis for the revenge?" He pointed again. "That way."

They angled to the right.

"I guess I still believe he was dead," Rachel said glumly. "I can't get that pale, little, babyish face out of my mind."

"That puts us right back where we started," Sam Lomax said. "If he's dead, where is he?"

Rachel sighed frustratedly. "Evidently it was just a coincidence."

"The shoes?"

"Yes."

"I don't know. There's something about this. . . . I have the feeling that something's not quite right about it. For instance, what was a bunch of big kids like that doing out trick-or-treating?"

"Taking the little boy around."

"The whole bunch? One or two, the sister maybe. But according to you, they were all wearing masks. It doesn't fit."

They had reached the shore of the lake. Between them and the choppy, icy-green, foam-flecked water was a wide barrier of dark, jagged rocks. A broad swath of sunlight reached out across the lake and dropped off at the horizon. A steamy mist rose from among the rocks as the sun's warmth turned exposed leavings of lake water into vapor.

"That's good fishing right out there," Sam Lomax said.

"Do you have a boat?"

"With some friends," he replied. "Want to sit on the rocks?"

"All right."

Rachel looked into the carriage to make sure that the baby was still asleep. Then, with some difficulty—once losing her balance and nearly falling into a crevice—she followed the lieutenant out onto the rocks. They sat on separate boulders, but side by side, with the vapor rising around them, facing out across the water. In front of them, a short distance away, stubby waves broke against the rocks, making hard slapping sounds and sending up splashes of foamy spray.

"Wasn't that Bo Franklin's kid's car I saw in your parking lot?" Sam Lomax said.

"His name is Franklin—Kirk. I don't know what his father's name is."

"That's Bo's boy."

"Do you know him?"

"Not the kid, except by sight. I know Bo, though. Every once in a while, every few months or so, somebody threatens to kill him and we go over to the Franklin place and stand around until it blows over."

"Kill him?" Rachel said. "Why?"

"A man like him makes enemies."

"Who is he?"

He looked surprised again. "You know . . . the Bo Franklin you hear about all the time. He's one of those most-richest guys, tenth or ninth or something. He builds ships, he's got a pro football team— Let's see, which one is it? I forget. I'm a baseball man. He's in oil, naturally, and mining, I think, and probably just about anything else you could name."

"I have heard of him, come to think of it," Rachel said. "I don't care how rich he is, though, I think his son is a little weird."

"How's that?"

"He thinks it's all right to let people starve because it cuts down the population."

"What people?"

"Where they're having those famines. Africa and Asia. He says we deliberately don't send food to them to keep them from breeding. Because if they live and have children, there'll be more of them for us to feed."

Sam Lomax looked out across the water again. "He might be right," he said. "I haven't thought a lot about it, but I can see what he means."

"I understand it, too, of course," Rachel said. "But he thinks it's right. That's sick. I hope B.J. finds some different friends soon."

The lieutenant shrugged.

"It gets warm out here, doesn't it?" Rachel said, unbuttoning her heavy coat.

Sam Lomax reached around and held the coat while she wriggled free of the sleeves. As she was bunching it up around her waist to keep it out of the shallow depressions in the rocks where lake water had collected, she sensed that he was watching her. When she faced him again, he was looking at her admiringly, in a manner that brought a sudden pleasant heat to her body that was not in any way related to the warmth of the sun. For a second Rachel looked back at him in the same way, boldly, but then self-consciousness overcame her, and she lowered her eyes.

Silence.

Rachel shook out her hair, then pulled her fingers through the strands.

Still, he did not speak.

"Well, I ought to be going back," she said, looking over her shoulder toward the path where the carriage was standing.

"My name is Sam," he said.

"I know. You mentioned that when you came to the door. But, somehow, it feels awkward calling a policeman by his first name."

He let that pass. "Have you ever gone fishing?" he asked.

"On a boat? No. I've been out on boats. My father was a lawyer, and a lot of times his clients would have us out. But we never did any fishing. And . . . my husband isn't outdoorsy. I'm not either, really. That's *one thing* Paul and I have in common, at least."

He grinned. "You take things pretty seriously, don't you?"

She thought for a moment. "Yes, I suppose I do. Don't you?"

"Not much," he replied. "Oh, important things, like an onion or an olive in my gin. I have days when I suffer over that. Big decision. But not much else."

"I wish I could be that way. You're right, I do take things too seriously. It's painful sometimes." She began pulling the coat up. "Now I'm getting chilly."

Sam Lomax stood up, offering her a hand. "I've got to check in anyway," he said.

"Oh, are you on duty?" she asked, accepting the assistance and rising. "On Sunday?"

"It's just a day," he said.

They climbed back across the rocks, and Sam turned the carriage around, and they set out for the house.

"I'll look into that hospital angle," he said. "Frankly, it doesn't have a lot going for it. But it won't hurt to check it out."

"I can't think of anyone else who would be wearing white shoes," Rachel said. "Will you let me know what you find out?"

"All right. Don't expect anything right away." He smiled at her. "I work slowly. I have a theory that if I leave people's problems alone they'll go away—if not the problems, the people." He motioned toward the upcoming fork. "Left here."

"Where do all these other paths go?" she asked.

"Here and there. None of these properties is fenced. You probably have something in your deed about no fencing. This is one big long stretch, all along the lake. That's why it needs a crew to take care of it."

"It's sort of like having our own forest preserve."

"It isn't sort of like; it is."

When they reached the house, Sam walked to the front with Rachel. While she carried the baby, he pulled the carriage up the steps, then pushed it into the foyer. There they stood facing each other, Rachel with the baby still in her arms. There was a moment of hesitation. Rachel wanted to touch Sam. She sensed that he felt the same way about her. But nothing happened. Perhaps, she thought, it was because the baby was between them.

Whatever the reason, Sam finally ended the impasse, smiling mechanically and backing away.

"You'll let me know . . . about the hospital . . ." Rachel said.

"If there's anything to it."

"Either way, I'd like to know. You could call me, you don't have to drive all the way out here . . . if you don't want to. . . ."

"I'll be in touch," he said. Then he departed.

Rachel walked back to the foyer and crossed toward the stairs. As she neared the steps, she became aware of movement at the top. Looking up, she saw Kirk Franklin descending, emerging from the dimness. In that faint light his lean, narrow face had an odd appearance, as if it were ceramic, glazed. His eyes stopped her, held her. The icy coldness that she remembered was there. She could almost see the mask in front of his face.

"He's a cop, isn't he?" Kirk said, speaking softly.

"Yes."

"I've seen him at the house," he said, still descending. "When somebody writes my father a threatening letter, he comes and asks questions."

"Well, that's his job." Rachel moved back a step. "Where is B.J.?"

"Up in his room. I left my tape player in my car. I'm going after it."

"Oh. . . ." She retreated farther, making way for him.

Kirk reached the bottom of the steps. He looked straight into Rachel's eyes, transfixing her. "If you think about it . . . if it's all right to kill people by the millions," he said, "why isn't it all right to kill them one by one?"

The question caught her completely by surprise. "What?"

"About what we were talking about before," he explained. "About killing people by the millions, letting them starve. If that's okay, why not one by one? It's a crisis, the population explosion. When there's a crisis, they say every little bit helps. They ask everybody to pitch in and do their part. So killing somebody, just one person, or two or three, that would be a help, wouldn't it?"

"Now you're really getting ridiculous," Rachel said. In spite of her determination to control her irritation, she was letting it show again. "It's too ridiculous to even argue about. Anyway, I haven't had a chance to think about it."

Kirk shifted his gaze to the baby. "I like the way they breathe," he said.

"They also yell," Rachel told him. "And if I don't get this one upstairs and out of this heavy bag, she'll show you."

Without another word, Kirk moved on, going toward the entryway.

Climbing the stairs, Rachel scolded herself again for the way she had reacted to Kirk. Doubtless he had seen how she had drawn back from him, frightened. That was why he had made that idiotic statement about killing by the millions and killing one by one, to taunt her. Teenagers were like that.

When they saw an opportunity to use the needle, they showed no mercy.

She had to try harder to accept Kirk. She didn't want to hurt her son by driving away his only friend. And it was foolish to think of Kirk as one of those teenagers in the masks. His eyes were no proof. A lot of people had cold eyes. Besides, he wasn't the type to be out on Halloween trick-or-treating. That was for kids. Kirk was too mature.

Six

RACHEL awakened Thursday morning to the sound of Paul talking on the bedroom phone. She listened for a while with her eyes still closed. He was reporting on his Rome trip to someone to whom he was deferring, probably Arthur Jahnke, the president at United Machinery, or William Hoag, the chairman. She gathered from what she heard that the trip had been successful. Paul's only reservation was about the dependability of the man with whom he had been negotiating.

When finally, unable to go back to sleep, she opened her eyes, she saw that Paul's side of the bed had been slept in. Evidently he had arrived sometime during the night. She saw also that the room was half dark. Turning over, she looked at the clock. It was a little after six. Outside, the sky was just beginning to brighten. The light in the room was spillover from the bathroom. Paul was seated in the wing chair, the phone to his ear, wearing a robe, a towel hung around his neck.

The telephone conversation ended.

"Hi," Paul said to Rachel, returning the phone to the bedside table. "How are you feeling?"

"All right. When did you get home?"

"Three, three thirty, around then." He went to his chest and opened the top drawer. "My secretary made an appointment for you with a doctor for next week," he said, getting sox from the drawer. "The details are there on that memo on the table." He closed the top drawer and opened the second drawer. "He's supposed to be good. The company has him on retainer," he said, taking a shirt from the drawer. His name is—" He closed the second drawer and opened the third. "Hell, I forget. But he's done a lot of good for some of our people, they tell me."

Rachel rose to one elbow. "What gave you the idea that I need a doctor? I feel fine."

"Cut it out, Rachel," he said, getting underwear from the lower drawer. "He's a psychiatrist."

"A psychiatrist!"

"Don't blow your stack," he said. "This isn't the Middle Ages, for Christ's sake. Hell, these days people brag about going to a psychiatrist," he said, going into the bathroom.

"I don't *need* a psychiatrist!" Rachel shouted after him.

"Okay, if you don't need him, he'll tell you," he answered from the bathroom. "He's a busy guy; he's a name; he won't keep you hanging on if you don't need him."

"What started this?" Rachel demanded, sitting up now. "That lawyer? What did he tell you? That I'm a drunk, that I'm crazy? What did he say?"

"He gave me the facts, that's all. There wasn't any kid. You didn't hit anybody."

"That's a lie!"

"Have they found the kid?"

"No. He just wasn't hurt, that's all."

"Yeah. Well, according to you, you killed him." He returned from the bathroom wearing the shirt and sox and the underwear and buttoning the shirt. "Frankly," he said, going toward the closet, "Jack Flanagan thinks you made it up because you had an accident with the car and didn't want to get bawled out. But I know you better than that." He disappeared into the closet.

"I did *not* make it up!"

"And you saw the shoes, too, right?"

"Yes!"

"What about Holly and all those other people?" he said, emerging from the closet with a suit and tie. "How come they didn't see any shoes?"

"Because they weren't looking! Lieutenant Lomax believes me!"

"Who the hell is he?" Paul asked, pulling on the trousers.

"He's investigating the case."

"The case?" Paul laughed sourly. "Maybe we'd better send him to a shrink, too," he said, slipping the tie under his shirt collar and going back toward the bathroom.

The phone rang.

Paul stopped and picked up the receiver, then became involved in another business conversation.

Rachel angrily threw back the covers and got out of bed and put on her robe and went into the bathroom and began combing out her hair. She could hear Paul talking on the phone, discussing the Rome trip again. Damn him! And damn his lawyer. And damn his doctor, whoever he was. She wasn't ill, and she wouldn't be treated. Especially not by a company doctor. The only reason Paul chose him was that the bill would go to United Machinery.

When she returned to the bedroom, Paul was in the wing chair, still talking. Apparently the conversation was going to go on and on. Leaving, Rachel slammed the door. But as she descended the stairs, her indignation began to subside. What did she care what Paul and his lawyer thought anyway? She would probably never see Flanagan again; she had no intention of ever getting together with Paul and him and his wife, as he had suggested. And since Paul thought she was a scatterbrain as it was, it wouldn't matter much if he now started thinking of her as a loony. He couldn't force her to go to a psychiatrist.

Mrs. Woolsey was in the kitchen, preparing breakfast for B.J. and Holly. "Ooooooooo—look who's here!" she said brightly as Rachel appeared.

"Just barely," Rachel told her.

"I'm making oatmeal for the kids," Mrs. Woolsey told her. "Do you want some?"

"No, I don't think I'm quite up to that," Rachel replied, running water into the kettle. "I'll just make some coffee; then I'll get out of your way." She put the kettle on a burner and turned on the heat. "How is the baby? No further sign of that colic?"

"Happy as a crab," Mrs. Woolsey said. "Do you know what I think? Did you burp her after you fed her that day?"

Rachel tried to recall. "I'm not sure," she said.

"That explains it. She just needed a good burp."

"You're probably right," Rachel said, spooning instant coffee into a mug. "Why didn't I think of that?"

"You're out of practice, dear," Mrs. Woolsey told her, stirring the oatmeal. "I had a neighbor back in the old days, Mr. Carmichael. He was a bricklayer. One day a whole load of bricks fell on him. His poor wife, it looked like he was going to pass on. He was nineteen months in the hospital, believe it or not. Mrs. Carmichael got a job in a Chinese laundry. That was the first I ever heard of anybody working in a Chinese laundry that wasn't Chinese. But they kept her in back where the customers couldn't see her. It was a *bad* time."

Rachel poured boiling water into the mug.

"Those kids better come down or this oatmeal's going to be like mortar," Mrs. Woolsey said.

"Mrs. Woolsey, what's the connection between me and Mr. Carmichael?"

"Oh. Well, when he got out of the hospital and went back to work, he couldn't lay a straight wall. He was out of practice."

"I see."

Carrying the mug of coffee, Rachel left the kitchen and went to the sitting room. As she was settling in the chair beside the phone table, she heard pounding on the stairs, indicating that B.J. was on his way down for breakfast. It was a noise that she always appreciated hearing. The house was so stoutly

[78]

constructed that even after all the years it still had developed no creaks. Ordinary footfalls raised no sounds. It was possible to move about the house from back to front and top to bottom in complete silence. And at times the silence became next to unendurable to Rachel. It gave her the feeling of being in solitary confinement. B.J.'s pounding, thus, was reassuring, a message to her that she was not alone.

Paul, carrying his attaché case and a mug of coffee, came into the sitting room a short while later.

"I want to get this settled before I leave," he said, sitting down on a couch and resting his mug of coffee on the low table in front of it. "I don't want it on my mind."

She recognized his attitude. He was now being logical and reasonable.

"Fact one—" he began.

"Fact you," Rachel snapped.

"What?"

"Skip it."

"Fact one," he went on, "you need help. Rachel, you're not functioning. What do you do? Mrs. Woolsey takes care of the house and the baby. B.J. and Holly take care of themselves. You do the *Times* puzzle once a week, and you take care of the baby on Sunday. Am I right?"

"What am I supposed to do? What else is there to do?"

"That's for you to decide," he said. "You could join a group. There are probably a million things. The point is, you do nothing. Let's take the house, for instance. What have you done about the furnishing and decorating? Nothing."

"I started to."

"But you didn't follow through. Instead, you saw shoes. You don't *want* to do anything. You don't have the motivation. That's not natural. So, fact two, something has to be done about it. And the only thing I know to do about it is for you to see this psychiatrist."

"That little boy *was* there, and I *did* see those shoes."

"Let's forget that," he said. "We're talking about functioning."

"Paul, don't you know what's really wrong? It's us. It's our marriage. It's dead."

"Rachel, when it rains, it rains on both teams," he said.

She squinted at him. "What in hell does that mean?"

"Take two football teams. It's raining, and they're playing in the mud. One team loses and blames it on the mud. But both teams were playing in the mud, so the mud isn't to blame."

Rachel stared at him blankly.

"I know what our marriage is," he said. "I know it's dead. Nobody knows that any better than I do. But it's dead for me, too, Rachel, not just for you. We're *both* playing in the mud. Only I'm functioning. You're not."

"Rah for you," she said dismally.

"I'm not patting myself on the back. I'm just stating fact," he said. "Our marriage has been dead, as you call it, for years. And in those same years I've accomplished more than I ever did before. Doesn't that tell you something?"

"Our marriage wasn't ever your main thing," she said. "You're still doing your main thing. My main thing"— she gestured hopelessly—"went bankrupt."

"Okay, then let this psychiatrist help you get started up again. At the very least, let him try to help you cope. For the kids' sake. For your own sake." He rose, picking up his mug of coffee. "Especially for the kids' sake," he said, moving to the telephone table.

"Don't try to—" Rachel began. She saw Holly standing in the doorway. Apparently she had been there for a while. "What do you want, dear?" she said crossly.

Holly addressed Paul. "Dad, I need some money."

"Okay." He put his coffee mug down and got out his wallet and tossed it to Holly as she crossed the room toward him. "Take what you need." He picked up the receiver. "Are we all set?" he said to Rachel.

She didn't answer.

Paul put the receiver down.

Holly, having taken several bills from the wallet, handed it back to her father. "Thanks."

"That's okay, hon."

Holly departed.

"All right, how about it?" Paul said to Rachel.

"Did you know she was standing there?"

"No. But what difference does it make? Those kids aren't blind; they know the score." He put his hand on the phone again. "Okay?"

Well, why not? Maybe, with the psychiatrist's help, she could learn how to cope with the death of the marriage. And if her behavior was affecting the children. . . .

"All right," she said, sighing defeatedly.

"That's more like it." He lifted the receiver and began dialing. "B.J. tells me he's going around with Bo Franklin's kid," he said. "How about that!" He was pleased.

"I don't really care much for him," Rachel said, rising. "He has the idea—if he really means it—that killing people—"

But Paul was no longer listening. He had reached his secretary on the phone at her home, and they were arranging his day.

Rachel left the sitting room. As she was crossing the foyer, on her way to take the empty coffee mug to the kitchen, she saw Holly and B.J. standing near the top of the stairs. They were talking intently in low tones. Becoming aware of Rachel, they immediately fell silent, then, acting contritely, went on up the steps. Clearly, they had been discussing Rachel. She wondered how much Holly had heard of the conversation between her and Paul. Just enough to get the wrong impression, she supposed.

Seven

THE two outsiders, Sam Lomax and Kirk Franklin, were on Rachel's mind much of the time during the next several days.

Even though Sam had told her that he was a slow worker, it seemed to Rachel that he had had plenty of time to investigate the possible link between the white shoes and the hospital, and she expected a report, delivered personally. Whenever she heard a car approaching the house, she hurried to a window, hoping to see that it was Sam's. But it was always B.J.'s or Kirk Franklin's or a tradesman's truck or, in the late evening or night, Paul's car.

Often she recalled the walk in the woods with Sam and the moments they spent together sitting on the rocks. To Rachel the rocks had been an island, and she and Sam the only inhabitants. There was no baby, no failed marriage, no awareness of the anguish that had been left behind on the mainland. It was a new, fresh existence, without memories.

Once, in her mind, she merged that fancied new existence with an old reality. She was alone in the sitting room at the time, working on the *Times* puzzle. Somehow she imagined that she was back in the apartment in Manhattan and that Sam Lomax was with her. It was a contented, comfortable situation. And feeling perfectly natural, she spoke to him.

"What's a French saint? A name, I guess. Eight letters, and it begins with *C.*"

"Catherine?"

"No, I thought of that. That's nine letters."

"Got me."

"Unless Catherine is spelled differently in French," Rachel mused. "I don't think there's an *H* in it in Spanish. Could it be the same in French?"

It was Mrs. Woolsey who answered. "Could what be what, dear?"

Startled from the daydream, Rachel discovered that the woman-of-all-work had entered the sitting room with the vacuum cleaner.

"Nothing," Rachel replied, embarrassed. "I was thinking out loud."

"I talk to myself, too," Mrs. Woolsey said. "It's a sign of age. My sister's the same way. She says if all the conversations she's had with herself was laid end to end, they'd make a book."

In another instance, Rachel imagined that Sam Lomax was sharing her bed with her. Awakening in the late night or early morning darkness, cold, with her legs pulled up, huddling, she sensed that he was behind her. Partly conscious, partly still asleep, she sought his warmth, backing up to him, buttocks first. But she found only a colder coldness. Her need had to settle for the limited satisfaction that an added blanket could provide.

Kirk Franklin's presence, though, was not in the least illusionary. He had become Holly's friend as well as B.J.'s and was now almost a member of the family. Each day, soon after Holly and B.J. got home from school, Kirk arrived. And the three were usually together—in the house or out—until late at night. They ate together in the kitchen, served by the cheerfully accommodating Mrs. Woolsey. They played tapes together in B.J.'s room and read books and strangely named tabloid-size newspapers together in Holly's room. And whenever Rachel approached them when they were together, they always stopped what they were doing and gave her their full and respectful attention, as if they thought of her as something very fragile that might shatter if not handled with the utmost caution.

She couldn't object to her son and daughter about Kirk's being on hand so much, of course. She knew how important it was to children to have friends, especially a best friend. Obviously that was what Kirk was to them. Besides, she had no legitimate complaint to lodge against him. It was not his fault that she felt intimidated by him, chilled inside when his icy eyes met hers. So she simply avoided him as much as possible when he was in the house. Her hope was that before long the friendship would burn itself out. That, as she recalled, was usually the history of children's passionate relationships.

But then Kirk gave her a valid reason to protest.

Late on a Saturday night, lying awake in bed, counting her troubles, Rachel heard the baby whimpering. Deciding—since she was awake anyway—to let Mrs. Woolsey go on sleeping, she rose and put on a robe and went to the nursery. There she could find no reason for the baby's distress; she was dry, her clothing was not restricting her in any way. The whimpering continued, nevertheless. So Rachel gathered her in her arms and sat down with her in Mrs. Woolsey's rocker to try to lull her back to sleep.

A few moments later a tall, thin shadow penetrated the room. Looking up, Rachel saw Kirk Franklin in the open doorway, with the light from the hallway behind him. Annoyed, she glared. Because his face was in darkness, she could not see how he was reacting. But he did not turn away.

"Isn't it getting pretty late?" Rachel said.

"I was just going." He spoke casually, apparently unaffected by her glare.

Rachel fixed her attention on the baby again, hoping that if she pointedly ignored Kirk, he would move on.

"About what we were talking about—" he said.

"Shh! I'm trying to get her to sleep."

"—about killing—" he said.

Rachel raised her eyes again.

"I know a man who's killed people," he said, still speaking evenly, easily. "Hundreds of people, probably. I don't know the number. But a lot." He entered the room. "And nobody has ever done anything about it," he said, moving idly toward the windows. "Or ever will."

Rachel suspected that he was being schoolboy romantic, trying to shock her. "If you know about it, why don't you go to the police?" she said.

"The police don't care," He stopped at the Bathinette and picked up Mrs. Woolsey's scissors. "It's not a crime."

"Kirk, don't be silly."

"It isn't," he insisted. He turned toward her, and in the faint illumination from the night light she saw the iciness in his eyes. "Want me to tell you?" he said. "When I was still a kid, one day my father had a lot of people out. His lawyers and his public relations men. Everybody was around the pool. Me, too. I listened to them. It was a meeting about some strikes at my father's mines." He began opening and closing the scissors, making soft shearing sounds. "Do you know what black lung is?"

"It's something that miners get, isn't it?"

"Yes. It kills them." The scissors blades continued to open and close, open and close. "The miners wanted something to stop them from getting it. I don't know what. Nobody talked about that. All they talked about was how to beat them."

"Kirk, you're going to cut yourself," Rachel said nervously.

"I'm careful." The blades slowly opened. "They worked up a plan," he said. Slowly, the blades closed. "The lawyers were going to do things in court—I didn't understand it. And the public relations men were going to pay some of the miners to go around and tell the other miners that if they didn't stop the strike, my father would shut down the mines and nobody would have any jobs." The blades opened.

"That's just the way they do things," Rachel told him. "Please put those scissors down."

"It was exciting," Kirk said, returning the scissors to the Bathinette. "It was like a big game. Everybody was talking about how we had to beat them. I got excited, too. It was our team against their team. It was really real, I could feel it, out there on the field, the miners on their side and us on our side. I really thought my father was great. He was like the coach, running things."

"Kirk, what's the point?" Rachel said.

"We won," he said. "We beat them."

"Yes. . . ."

"And now a lot of them are dead."

"Is that what you're talking about? You're saying that your father *killed* them?"

"They're dead. They got black lung."

"I see the connection," she said. "But really. . . . It isn't the same as killing people."

"Why not?"

"Because it isn't. It was business. Are you disappointed in your father, is that what it is?"

"No. He's okay. I didn't say he did something wrong. I was just telling you what he did." He walked back toward the doorway, still at ease, speaking unemotionally. "If he did something wrong, the police would care, wouldn't they? If it was wrong, he'd be in jail. Well," he said, pausing in the doorway, a tall, dark shape once more, "he's not in jail. So he didn't do anything wrong."

"Kirk, you've twisted what happened to make it fit your theory," Rachel said. "That doesn't make your theory right."

"She's asleep now," he said.

Rachel looked down at the baby. Her eyes were closed, and she was breathing evenly. When Rachel looked up, Kirk had gone.

For a time she remained in the chair, holding the baby and rocking and assessing what had just occurred. Evidently Kirk Franklin believed, or professed to believe, that taking life was of no consequence. It was probably a pose, a bitter reaction to what he saw as his father's insensitivity. But even so it was dangerous. He could infect B.J. and Holly with his thinking. In fact, he already had B.J. saying things that he had never said before. *That's the way the world works. People kill people.* Something had to to done.

After putting the baby down, Rachel got the *Times* puzzle from the bedroom, then went to the downstairs sitting room to work on it and wait for Paul to arrive. A little after midnight she heard a car on the private road, and soon after that he came into the house. He looked exhausted when he entered the sitting room.

[86]

Rachel told him that she was concerned about the children's friendship with Kirk Franklin and wanted to talk to him about it. He reminded her that he had to get up early the next morning because he and B.J. and Holly were going to the Bears game with Arthur Jahnke and his children and asked that the discussion be postponed. But Rachel refused to be put off, doubting, in view of the fact that he was so seldom at home, that there would soon be another opportunity.

With Paul seated stolidly in the chair beside the telephone table, arms crossed in an attitude of resistance, Rachel told him in detail about the two conversations she had had with Kirk. As she spoke, she saw that his attention was wandering—he was probably thinking about business. But she kept doggedly on, then concluded by telling him that she wanted to ask B.J. and Holly to curtail their contact with Kirk, requesting that he support her in her stand.

"For why?" he responded. "Because he has some kooky ideas? Hell! Kids that age think that way. Everything's simple. Black and white."

"I don't want B.J. and Holly thinking that way."

"What if they do? They'll grow out of it. Kirk Franklin will, too, once he has some responsibility. What you should have asked him was: What would *he* have done if the shoes had been on his feet instead of his father's? You know, big as he is, Bo Franklin isn't God. He has a board to answer to. What could he do, let the miners walk all over him? You do that just *once,* and you're dead. Give them an inch, and they've got your number. Kirk will find out."

"Paul, you don't seem to understand. This isn't just a little thing with Kirk; it's an obsession. He came right into the nursery to talk to me about it."

"Who brought it up?"

"He did."

"Right out of the blue?"

"Well, he said he was picking up the discussion where we'd dropped it before, but he—"

"Was he?"

"Yes, in a way, I suppose, but—"

"Then what's the problem?"

"Could I finish a sentence?"

He shrugged. "Go ahead."

"He frightens me," she told him.

"Oh. It's not the kids you're worried about. He scares you— is that it?"

"Partly."

"What's he been doing, dressing up in white shoes and a mask?"

She turned away. "All right, let's not talk about it anymore. You've made up your mind not to take it seriously, so there's no point in discussing it any further."

"What has he done that scares you?" Paul asked.

"It isn't what he's done."

"In other words, it's in your mind."

"Yes!" she snapped. "I'm crazy! I imagine things!"

"All I want is some facts. What the hell has he done?"

"Nothing!" she shouted. "Leave me alone!"

"This was your idea, not mine," he said, rising. "Rachel, see the doctor. Level with him. Let him help you. If you keep *this* up, you really *will* drive yourself nuts."

Furious, she remained grimly silent.

"Christ!" he said disgustedly, striding heavily from the room.

Rachel covered her face with her hands and cried. She felt completely isolated. Her husband thought she was a mental case. Her children treated her as if she were a stranger in the house and whispered about her on the stairs. Even Sam Lomax, the one person she thought she could count on, had now deserted her.

Crying, she fell asleep on the couch and stayed the night there.

Mrs. Woolsey was picked up early the next morning by her sister. Paul and B.J. and Holly left a while later to drive to the Jahnke house for breakfast, then on into Chicago for the

Bears game. When they all had gone, Rachel went to the nursery to make sure that the baby was still sleeping—she had dozed off before finishing her morning bottle. Then, satisfied that she would not be awake again for some time, she moved on to the bedroom. There she drew the drapes and went to bed. After the restless night on the couch she had no trouble falling asleep.

Cries awakened Rachel at noon. Somewhat groggy, she went to the nursery and changed the baby's diaper and dressed her in fresh clothing, then took her down to the kitchen and put a bottle on to warm. The baby, of course, continued to howl, and Rachel, reacting to the cries, began to feel the tautness at the back of her neck and across her shoulders. Was it going to be *another* bad Sunday?

Hunger turned out to be the baby's only complaint this time, however. She began gorging herself the instant she got hold of the nipple and sucked without pause until the bottle was drained. Sated, she became a limp, amorphous bag of warm milk in Rachel's arms. After checking to be certain that she had turned off the bottle warmer, Rachel rested the baby against her shoulder and left the kitchen with her, patting her gently on the back. A few moments later, as they were ascending the stairs, the bubble came up. The baby sighed ecstatically. Rachel felt equally relieved, considering the belch an auspicious augury.

In the bedroom Rachel put the baby on a blanket on the floor. She watched her for a few minutes, amused, as the baby rolled her eyes about and every once in a while raised an arm or leg awkwardly. Finally, Rachel left her, going into the bathroom to shower. When she emerged, the baby was on the verge of dropping off to sleep again. Dressing, Rachel talked to her, telling her that she was reaching the age where she ought to begin staying awake for longer periods. But the baby would have none of it. She fell asleep before Rachel had the chance to tell her even a fraction of what she knew about tiny babies.

After returning the baby to her crib, Rachel descended to

the main floor and went to the kitchen. She prepared herself a lunch. Eating, she again thought about Sam Lomax and the pleasure she had felt sitting beside him on the rocks. This was Sunday; it would be nice if he would stop by again. It was a little too cold to go for a walk in the woods, but they could sit in the sitting room and talk and have a drink. He liked martinis, with an olive one day, with an onion another day.

"How do you know an onion day from an olive day?" she asked him.

"I play it by ear," he told her. "I reach in my ear, and if I find an olive, that's it. Or vice versa."

Rachel laughed. "We really are opposites," she said. "I'm so serious about everything, and you joke about everything."

"You know what they say about opposites."

Finished with lunch, Rachel set out for the sitting room, where she had left the *Times* puzzle. In the foyer she halted, struck by the bareness and reminded of Paul's charge that her failure to do something about the furnishing and decorating meant that she had ceased to function and needed treatment. He was wrong. It wasn't that she couldn't do the job; it was just that she didn't give a damn. Apathy.

It would do no good to tell Paul that. He wouldn't believe her. Or he would say that apathy was a sickness. When something had to be done, it had to be done, he would say. That was the way he operated. Do it. Do it. Do it. All right—if he could do it, she could do it. She would make a list of everything that was needed, every stick of furniture, every painting, every rug, then, tomorrow, she would go back to Tuck's Barn and McMillan's and give them the list and say: This is what I want, no ifs or buts, just pile it on a truck and bring it out.

She moved on to the room that was to be Paul's office away from the office and got a pen and sheet of paper from the desk, then climbed the stairs to the top floor and entered the first empty room. What would it be, a bedroom? What else? She might make it a small library for Holly's excess books. But that would necessitate hiring a carpenter to put in shelves.

Well, so what? She could hire a carpenter; it didn't take a great talent to do that.

A library it would be. Shelves. A bright, colorful rug. A pair of club chairs. Some modern paintings, Klee reproductions. But perhaps she ought to consult Holly on the paintings. On the furnishings, too, for that matter. It was just possible that Holly didn't even want an extra room for her books. Maybe she liked to have them around her, close by, stacked up, little walls within the walls of her room. So this room would have to wait until she could talk to Holly about it.

In the next empty room she decided immediately that it would be a spare bedroom. Double bed. No, it was too small for that. Single bed. Or three-quarters? Maybe she would do the room in Colonial. In a Victorian house? Hell, the whole damn house had to be Victorian. What she ought to do with the top floor was count the rooms and order a bed and a chest and a chair and a table and a painting for each one. Like furnishing an institution.

Depressed by the prospect, Rachel stood at a window looking out at the surrounding woods. It was a gray day. She saw movement. Someone walking along one of the paths. Another movement. Two people. They were partially hidden by the trees, but she continued to get glimpses of them. They were moving quickly, darting. Another one. Three. The children? Another one. Four. She saw a flash of white. White shoes!

Alarmed, Rachel pressed against the window, staring intently, looking for the flash of white again. Another figure darted by. That made five. Then nothing more. Just the trees. She stayed at the window, looking for the flicker of white. But there were no further signs of movement. Where were they? Five of them. Although she might have counted some of them twice.

Rachel hurried from the room, then, in the corridor, halted. Where could she hide? No—wait. Why should she hide? They wouldn't come into the house after her. Or would they? Did they know she was alone? Paul's car was gone, but B.J.'s was in the garage. Two cars—hers and B.J.'s—they would think someone was with her. Unless they knew that B.J. had left with his father. Maybe they had been watching the house. That would explain what they were doing in the woods, watching from hiding.

Rachel ran down the stairs. She had to call Sam Lomax. She most certainly had good reason. It was no coincidence this time that the white shoes had turned up again. Whoever was wearing them was after her. And Paul couldn't claim this time that she had imagined them, either. She had seen them as plain as— Actually, she hadn't seen them. But what else could that flash of white have been? A scrap of paper, Paul would say. Kids in the woods, one of them with a bag of candy . . . a white bag . . . then, finished with the candy, the white sack dropped on the path. . . .

She stopped at the second floor landing. If she telephoned Sam Lomax and he came to the house and looked in the woods and found a discarded white paper sack on the path, he, too, would begin to wonder about her sanity. She didn't want to do anything that would give him a reason to doubt her. And truthfully, she hadn't seen shoes in the woods, only a flash of white.

Rachel went on down the stairs. She couldn't continue the furnishing and decorating project. With the idea in the back of her mind that those creatures were out there in the woods, she wouldn't be able to concentrate. And anyway, the baby would be waking up soon, demanding another feeding. Tomorrow, though, when Mrs. Woolsey would be on hand to care for the baby, she would give the chore her full attention. If she stuck to it, she could finish it in one day. God, what a relief it would be to have it over and done with.

In the sitting room, Rachel settled in a club chair with a spiral-bound book of *Times* weekday puzzles, her reserve, turned to when she had finished the Sunday puzzle. The rest of the afternoon passed painlessly. She became aware of dusk only when she began having trouble reading the definitions for the words of the puzzle she was working on. Reaching up to switch on the table lamp, she stretched her cramped muscles at the same time. When the lamp went on, the sudden glow made her conscious of the darkness that surrounded her. She felt spotlighted and uncomfortably vulnerable.

Rising, Rachel went to the bay window. The night was especially dark, the moon hidden by clouds. Looking beyond the porch, she could see the drive and the fountain but not much else. The forest was a dark wall. There was no chance at all that she would be able to see them if they were hiding out there.

The baby began crying.

Responding, Rachel left the sitting room and went to the kitchen, turning on lights along the way. After putting a bottle on to warm, she ascended to the second floor by way of the back stairway. When she reached the nursery the baby was red-faced, howling irately. Talking to her softly and soothingly—but to no effect—Rachel changed her diaper, then rewrapped her in her blanket and, using the front stairs, carried her down to the kitchen.

The feeding routine was repeated. Once connected to the bottle, the baby became quiet. As the feeding progressed and Rachel felt more and more pressured by the necessity of sitting still, her shoulders and neck began to ache as usual. In her mind she could see the children leaving the woods and moving stealthily toward the house. At last, though, the bottle was drained. She put it aside, then, getting up, raised the baby to her shoulder and began patting her back gently to bring up the bubble.

Rachel heard a series of soft, rapid footfalls. The sounds came from the direction of the foyer. Frightened, she stopped patting the baby and cocked an ear, listening. Silence. She was certain, though, that she had heard the sounds. Someone besides her was in the house. Quietly, she went to the kitchen doorway and switched off the light, concealing herself in darkness, then peeked into the hallway, which was still lighted.

There was no one in sight. Rachel listened again. There were no sounds. But that meant nothing; a behemoth could go sneaking through the house, if a behemoth could sneak, without raising a single squeak, so sturdily was the place constructed. She could have been mistaken about the sounds being footfalls, though. They could have been— Something flapping? What could have caused it to flap, though?

"Who is that?" she called out. "Who's there?"

No answer.

The baby began wriggling. Rachel resumed the patting, quieting her.

"I know you're there!" she called. "I heard you! Who is it?"

Nothing.

Rachel turned off the hallway light. Then, still massaging the baby's back—now more for the purpose of calming herself than to dislodge the bubble—she crept silently toward the foyer. She was so tense that she had the feeling that her joints had gone stiff. What if it was them and they had come for her? What did they intend to do? What would *she* do? She had to think about the baby. They wouldn't hurt the baby, though. It was Rachel they were after.

Damn it, she was being foolish—it couldn't be them. They wouldn't dare come into her house after her. They couldn't be so reckless. Why were they so determined to get at her? She hadn't done anything to them—except possibly graze the little boy with her car. And that hadn't been intentional. Did they think she had done it on purpose? Was that the explanation? Did they believe that she had deliberately aimed her car at them?

Rachel reached the foyer. There was no one in sight. She peered into the entryway. The front door was closed. Leaning forward, squinting, she stared past the stairs into the dark corridor that led to the main floor rooms that were not in use.

[94]

The baby's burp came up, startling Rachel, causing her to clutch the baby tightly in fright. The baby struggled, then, when Rachel relaxed her hold, emitted a bubbly, contented sound.

Still shaken, Rachel looked up the stairs. She thought she saw a quick movement of a shadow on the wall at the landing, but she wasn't positive.

"I saw you!" she cried out. "I know you're up there!"

No response.

The baby was making mewing sounds and pushing awkwardly against Rachel's shoulder.

Rachel called up the stairs. "Do you think I tried to hit you? Is that why you're doing this? You're wrong. I didn't. I was just driving along the road. All of a sudden you were there. I didn't see you."

There was no reply.

"I wouldn't *do* a thing like that!" Rachel said, persisting, advancing to the foot of the stairs. "I don't drive my car at people. Honest to God, *I did not see you!* It was raining. I didn't see *any*thing. There's a turn at that spot. I just made the turn—I wasn't even going fast—and there you were."

Silence.

Rachel sighed drearily. She held the baby tightly, rocking her, and began to cry, frustrated. "There's nobody up there," she told the baby. "There's nobody in the house—just us. I went off the damn deep end again, I guess. I really am a nut. Oh, *Jesus,* why do I *do* this? Why don't I *think* first? I just plow right in . . . and make a damn fool of myself."

The baby struggled, objecting to Rachel's repressive hold on her.

"I'm sorry," Rachel said. "I don't even—"

There was a crash, something shattering. The sound came from the kitchen.

Rachel ran back to the hallway and shrieked into the darkness. "Get out! Get out of my house!" Then she fled to the sitting room.

At the phone table, terrified, still clutching the baby, she snatched up the phone and dialed police headquarters. An officer came on the line, identifying himself. Frantic, watching the sitting-room doorway, expecting the intruders to appear, Rachel asked for Sam Lomax. The officer informed her that he was not available.

RACHEL (furious): Did he tell you to tell me that?

OFFICER: Lady, I don't even know who you are.

RACHEL (no longer angry, but still terrified): There's somebody in my house! Tell Sam—he knows! I'm the only one here—just the baby and me.

OFFICER: Somebody broke into your house? What's your address, lady?

RACHEL: Catawba! On Cedar Point Road. Will you hurry?

OFFICER: Get out of the house if you can. I'll get a car over there.

Rachel hung up. But she could not leave the house. She was trapped in the sitting room, certain that the intruders were advancing on her through the darkness beyond the doorway. Holding the baby tightly again, she hid behind the club chair beside the phone table, peeking out, wanting to see them before they saw her when they came into the sitting room after her. Trembling, she listened for their sounds.

The house was silent. But she could sense their movement. In her mind she could see them, wearing their grostesque masks, moving soundlessly across the dark foyer toward the sitting room. They were a death squad of righteous avengers. She wanted to cry out to them, to tell them once more that she had not meant to kill the little boy, but her throat was closed, constricted by fear. They were mere steps away from the sitting room doorway now, moving closer . . . closer. . . .

She heard a siren. Then flashes of red light, reflections, were playing off the walls. Rachel sprang up and ran to the bay window. A police car was turning into the drive, its light

[96]

flashing, the sound of its siren waning. It stopped at the porch. Two officers got out, and one raced up the porch steps, while the other stayed with the car, standing beside it. The officer on the porch pounded on the door. Rachel rapped on the window, drawing his attention, then signaled to him that the door was not locked. As he entered the house, she hurried from the sitting room.

The officer had the lights on when she got to the foyer. "Did you call us?" he asked.

Rachel, clutching the baby, looked around fearfully for the intruders. "They were right here!" she told the officer. "I don't know where they are!"

"Where did you see them?"

"I didn't see them. I heard them. There was a crash in the kitchen." She pointed. "That way!"

"Stay here," he told her.

He went to the hall and turned on the light, then, with Rachel watching from the foyer, moved on toward the kitchen. When he reached the kitchen doorway, he halted, and Rachel heard him speak, but she could not make out the words. A moment later the kitchen light went on; then the officer entered the kitchen, and Rachel could no longer see him.

Faintly, she heard a car approaching the house. She hoped it was bringing Sam Lomax. Then the officer who had gone into the kitchen reappeared and motioned to her. Holding the baby protectively, with her arms covering as much of her small body as possible, Rachel entered the hallway and walked warily to where the officer was waiting.

"There's nobody in here," he told her. "But watch where you step. There's glass on the floor."

"Did they break a window?"

"No, it looks like a baby's bottle," he told her. "I found a nipple."

"Yes! I left it on the table."

"They must've knocked it off in the dark," the officer said.

Rachel saw that the dial on the bottle warmer was glowing. "look/" she said, pointing. "they turned that on/" she heard paul's voice coming from the direction of the foyer. "that's my husband," she told the officer, leaving the kitchen. hurrying back along the hallway, she realized disappointedly that the car that she had heard approaching had been paul's, not the lieutenant's.

the second officer and b.j. and holly were with paul in the foyer.

"what's going on here0" paul asked rachel testily.

"they came right into the house," she told him. "i saw them earlier in the woods. I didn't dream that they'd come into the house. But they did—as soon as it got dark."

"Who was it?"

"The same ones. I saw the white shoes."

Paul's expression became skeptical. "What did they do?"

"They were after me," she told him. "They were out in the kitchen. They broke the baby's bottle. They turned on the bottle warmer. Maybe they broke the bottle by accident—I don't know. It was dark in there."

The first officer appeared from the hallway. "It looks like they're gone," he said, addressing Rachel. "Just to be sure, though, we better check out the rest of the house."

"Did *you* see them?" Paul asked him.

"No."

"Just hold it," Paul said to him. He faced Rachel again. "Did you *see* them?" he asked her. "Did you actually *see* them?"

"I heard them," she told him. "But I *saw* them earlier. They were in the woods. I told you, I saw those white shoes again."

"Did you see the guy? What did he look like?"

"I didn't see *him,* I saw the shoes. The trees were in the way."

"What does that mean, the trees were in the way?"

"He was hidden. I only saw his shoes."

"What did you hear—in here?" he asked.

"I heard footsteps. If they weren't in here in the house, how did that bottle get broken?" she said angrily. "I didn't break it!

And who turned on the bottle warmer? I turned it off after I used it."

"Mom," B.J. said, "you left it on the other day, remember?"

"I know I did. That's why, today, I was very careful to turn it off."

"Let's get this straight," Paul said. "This guy in the white shoes stood around out there in the woods; then, when it got dark, he sneaked in here and broke a bottle and turned on the warmer. What kind of sense does that make?"

"They were after me!" Rachel told him fiercely.

"They? The whole bunch again? Did they have their Halloween masks on this time?"

"I didn't *see* them!"

"But you heard them. You heard them walking around. How many did you hear?"

"I don't know!" she shouted.

The first officer spoke. "Do you want us to look around?" he asked.

Paul threw up his hands. "Look!" he said. He strode off, going into the sitting room.

The first officer addressed Rachel. "We'll look around," he told her.

"Please . . . I wish you would. . . ."

The first officer went up the stairs and the other officer entered the corridor that led to the rooms that were not in use.

"Mother, do you want me to take the baby up?" Holly asked.

Rachel discovered that the baby had fallen asleep in her arms. She handed her over to Holly, then, trailed by B.J., went into the sitting room. Paul was at the bar, near the bay window, mixing himself a drink.

"Thanks for making me look like an idiot," she said to him.

"They must already have quite a book on us at that police station."

"What am I supposed to do when somebody breaks in here, just ignore it, because it won't *look* well at police headquarters?"

"Where were you when you heard them walking around?" he asked.

"I didn't hear them walking around. I heard footsteps."

"All right, footsteps. Where were you?"

Rachel sat down on a couch. "In the kitchen."

"What did you do?"

"I turned out the light—so they couldn't see me—then I went into the foyer. But they weren't there. I think they were upstairs. That's when I heard the bottle break."

"Did you hear them upstairs?"

"No. I saw a shadow . . . maybe . . . I'm not sure."

"Okay, they're in the kitchen now, breaking the bottle," he said, leaning against the bar. "How did they get there? You just came from the kitchen, you said. How did they get past you?"

"They went down the back stairs."

Paul shrugged, conceding that that was possible. He sipped his drink.

"Mom, I'm not arguing," B.J. said, "but if they came into the house after you, how come they didn't get anywhere near you? The way it sounds, they were trying to stay away from you."

Holly came into the room, returning from taking the baby up to the nursery.

"I don't know," Rachel replied to her son. "Maybe they didn't know where I was. They were probably looking for me. There's one thing I'm sure of, though. That bottle is broken, and I didn't break it."

"You put it on the edge of the table, and it fell off," Paul said.

"I didn't!"

"Sure, and you didn't leave the warmer on, either. Rachel, for God's sake, think," he said disgustedly. "Why would anybody break into a house to turn on a bottle warmer? It's so goddamn ridiculous."

"The cops are back," B.J. said.

The officers were standing in the foyer, talking in low tones.

"Everybody stay here," Paul said, putting his drink down.

He left the sitting room and joined the officers in the foyer; then, after a moment, he and the officers walked toward the entryway.

"I guess they didn't find anybody," Holly said.

"Of course not," Rachel said. "They wouldn't stand around waiting for the police to catch them. They went out the back door and back into the woods."

There was the sound of the front door opening, then closing. But Paul did not return. Rachel got up and went to the bay window. Paul and the two officers were standing beside the police car. Paul was doing the talking, gesturing a great deal. Listening, solemn-faced, the officers nodded mechanically. Rachel supposed that her husband was telling them about her fantasies, the accident that did not happen, the white shoes that were invisible to everyone but her. And, she assumed further, the officers were accepting his explanation. He was very convincing when he was selling.

"How was the baby today?" Holly asked.

"Good," Rachel replied. "But of course, she didn't know what was going on. Children, you better get to bed," she said. "School tomorrow."

"Are you okay?" B.J. asked.

"Yes, I'm all right."

They said good-night to her and left. A short while later the officers departed. Rachel went back to the couch to wait for Paul to return.

"Did you convince them that I'm a raving lunatic?" she asked, when he came striding back into the sitting room.

"I told them that you've been under a lot of pressure," he answered, going to the bar.

"What pressure?"

"Everything." He picked up his drink. "Leaving New York, moving out here, the new baby, everything," he said, walking back toward the telephone table. "It's nothing new to them; they understand." He picked up the phone and began dialing.

"Can't you leave that damn toy alone for a second!" Rachel said angrily. "I'm trying to talk to you."

He put the phone down, but kept his hand on it. "I've got to call my secretary," he said. "I'm going to London tonight, and I've got to talk to her before I leave."

"Tonight? You didn't say anything about going anywhere tonight."

"I wasn't planning on it. It came up out of something that Art Jahnke and I were talking about at the game today. Okay? May I call her now?"

"Don't you give a damn about what's happening *here?*"

"Rachel, don't put me through that again," he said. "I've got eight million things on my mind. Don't screw me up; don't throw me that curve again. I got you a doctor. He can help you—*if you let him.* I told you this before: I am not a lawyer, I am not a doctor, I can't do a thing for you. So, for Christ's sake, let me up, get off my back."

She gestured defeatedly. "Go back to your toy."

"Will you go to the doctor?"

"Yes . . . I said I would . . ." she replied, rising and departing.

"Now you're making sense."

He was dialing again as she left the room.

Ascending the stairs, Rachel almost had to drag herself from step to step, so heavy was the weight of the depression that she was carrying. What was most debilitating was that she, too, was having doubts about what she had told Paul and the police and the children. Perhaps it hadn't been white shoes that she had seen in the woods. Maybe it hadn't been footfalls that she had heard in the house. Perhaps she *had* set the bottle on the edge of the table and it had fallen off. She was sure she had turned off the bottle warmer after the first feeding, but in all honesty, she wasn't positive that she had turned if off after the second. Maybe nothing that she thought had happened had really happened at all.

But she wasn't crazy. She was nervous and excitable, and she had a lively imagination. But she wasn't crazy.

Eight

BEING early afternoon, there was relatively little traffic on the expressway. Rachel had been able to keep the Eldorado in the same lane, the far right, the slow lane, for so long that she now had the feeling that it was on a track, like a train, that she was no longer the driver, merely a passenger. She was aware, too, of the desirability of that. It would be a relief to be a captive in a car that could not turn, that could only go straight ahead, on and on, leaving troubles behind. A captive could not be blamed for fleeing; a captive could not be held responsible.

As it was, though, the troubles were with her, brief explosions going off in her mind:

She was intimidated by psychiatrists; they were authority figures, like school principals and fathers and presidents. She knew that logically there was no reason to be in awe of them; they were, after all, only human beings like herself. But face to face with them logic always gave way to emotion. . . . B.J.'s and Holly's relationship with Kirk Franklin, rather than moderating, was becoming more intimate. Rachel kept coming upon them—and the new member of the clique, Jewel Brill—with their heads together, talking secretively. And even though she had no legitimate reason to, she always felt that they were talking about her and her condition. . . . Sam Lomax still had not contacted her. He probably hadn't done a thing about investigating the possible connection between the white shoes and the hospital; he probably hadn't even intended to; more likely than not he had told her he would simply to mollify her; a placebo for her anxieties. . . . It could have been Kirk Franklin who was in the house that night when she heard footfalls and thought she saw a shadow. Kirk was familiar with the interior of the house; he knew about the back stairs. Why, though, would he slip into the house just to break the baby's bottle and turn on the warmer? Or, for that matter—as Paul had pointed out—why would *anybody?* . . . Had the officers who came to the house that night told Sam Lomax what had happened? Maybe they had warned him: *Don't get mixed up with a daffy dame like that, she's trouble, she's got a wire loose.* . . . Jewel Brill, in a different way, was as frightening as Kirk. Whereas he appeared to be more at ease than was humanly possible, she seemed to be wound up too tight. But maybe Jewel thought that about Rachel, too. . . . It was Kirk who had pointed out that Rachel had left the bottle warmer turned on the first time. She could remember B.J.'s exact words when he told her about it: *It's on. Kirk and I went into the kitchen, and he saw it.* The question was, did Kirk really discover that the bottle warmer was on, or did he turn it on himself and then point it out to B.J., planting the idea that Rachel had left it on out of carelessness. Why would he pull a trick like that, though? It wasn't a big, important thing, a bottle warmer left on. . . . Maybe Sam was ill. Or on vacation. Maybe he'd gone somewhere to fish. . . . There was something about Jewel Brill's voice—her way of speaking, rather; the tightness, the way she hardly opened her mouth—that reminded Rachel of someone. A long-ago schoolmate, maybe. . . . If Sam had gone away somewhere on vacation he could have at least sent her a postcard. Although they weren't that close. The only closeness, probably, was in her mind. . . . Damn it, she was an adult now; she had no reason to be afraid of authority figures. They could no longer punish her, send her to her room, suspend her from school, have her beheaded without a trial.

The turnoff that would take her into the Loop was coming up.

The office of the psychiatrist, Dr. Blalock Edwards, was in

the same Michigan Avenue building as the offices of United Machinery. Riding up in the elevator, which had a string orchestra concealed in its walls, Rachel mused on the convenience of having the psychiatrist so close at hand. A legal problem, twentieth floor, legal department; a money problem, fortieth floor, financial department; a vice-president who is exposing himself to the girls in the steno pool, fiftieth floor, Dr. Blalock Edwards' department.

She was early for the appointment; she could not bring herself to be late for meetings even when she dreaded them. The nurse in the outer office, a pleasant young woman, invited her to sit and pointed out a selection of magazines in a rack on a wall, then resumed the chore that she had been performing when Rachel entered, typing names and addresses on envelopes. Rachel elected simply to sit.

The furnishings were all metal. Rachel wondered if the psychiatrist had a purpose in giving his outer office a stainless-steel look. If so, she couldn't guess what it would be. She wondered next if the nurse was really a nurse or merely a typist in a white uniform and white stockings. What need did a psychiatrist have for a nurse? Maybe he had patients with stigmata, and when they began to bleed, she was called in with wads of cotton to stop the flow.

Eventually a chicly dressed woman emerged from the inner office and departed. A few minutes later, Dr. Blalock Edwards came out. He was middle-aged and plump and clean-shaven, with an uncommonly pink complexion that made him look as if he had just stepped out of a steam room. He introduced himself to Rachel in an impatient, perfunctory way, then escorted her into his sanctum.

His office was rich. The carpeting was so deep and thickly padded that walking on it was almost like walking across a mattress. The furnishings were dark woods with intricate carvings and dark leathers. Here and there there were touches of gold: in the heavy draperies, in the bases of the lamps, in the implements on the desk. Rachel thought: This is the throne room; therefore, I am in the presence of the emperor.

"Sit anywhere," he said, settling into the high-backed swivel chair behind the broad desk.

She chose a drum chair.

"I have your data here," he said crisply, indicating a paper on his desk. "It came down from UM."

"From where?"

"United Machinery."

"Oh."

He was no longer the emperor. She saw him now as the man in charge of the shipping department.

"The problem is what?" he asked.

"It seems I can't cope."

"Can't cope with what?"

"A dead marriage."

"That's not unusual." He was bored. "Have you thought about divorce?"

"I've thought about running away," she told him. "I suppose I had divorce in mind. Mostly, I just want to run away."

"Why don't you?"

"I can't now. I have a new baby. The other two children are old enough to take care of themselves, I could leave them. But not a baby."

"Uh-huh. I see that your husband made this appointment for you, so I assume that he knows about this. What does he think about it?"

"He doesn't," she replied. "He's busy."

"There's nothing unusual about that either. In what ways do you have trouble coping?"

"I'm depressed. I just don't give a damn. We have a new house; it's big; it needs furnishing. We have the furnishings from the apartment, but the rest of the house is empty. I can't get myself to do anything about it, though. Apathy."

"How do you feel about the house?"

"It's a monster."

[106]

"You liked the apartment, I take it."

"Yes. It was perfect. It was in Manhattan, too—that helped. Here I'm out in the middle of nowhere. All my friends are back in New York. But that's not really the reason. I could make new friends—if I'd do it. That's the thing. I don't care whether I do or not. I don't care."

"When your husband reacts to this, what does he do?" the doctor asked. "Does he yell? Does he pout? Is he sympathetic, is he indifferent? What?"

"He wishes I wouldn't bother him with it. He thinks I'm a little . . . a little off. . . ."

He looked puzzled. "Off what?"

"Loony," she explained. "For instance, I had this accident—" She stopped herself. "No, that's something else."

"Go ahead, what about it?"

So she told him about the accident, about the little boy and the children in the masks, then about Paul deciding, based on what the lawyer, Jack Flanagan, had told him, and on the fact that no dead or even injured boy could be found, that she had imagined the whole affair.

"Your new baby—it wasn't planned," he said when she finished. "Is that right?"

"*Very* right."

"Mrs. Barthelme, are you aware that an unplanned child is sometimes referred to as an accident?"

"Yes. . . ."

"When you were describing the little boy just now," he said, "you referred several times—three, to be precise—to his babyish face. It seems to me that if he was old enough to be walking along the road, he was no longer a baby."

"I didn't say he *was* a baby. I said he had a babyish face. He did."

"Mrs. Barthelme, how do you feel about your baby? Are you comfortable with it?"

"She's a she," Rachel told him. "No, I can't truthfully say that I'm comfortable with her. But that's because I don't have her much. We have a woman who takes care of her—except on Sundays."

"Do you resent the baby?"

Rachel drew back. "Why would I resent her?"

"You told me, I believe, that you intended to leave your husband—but then the baby came along."

"But that wasn't the baby's fault," Rachel argued. "I wouldn't blame her." She shifted in the chair, not liking the way the conversation was going. "Aren't we getting off the track?" she said.

"We might be. I'm just doing a little exploring. The key words, perhaps, are 'baby' and 'accident' and 'death.' Now—"

Rachel interrupted. "I didn't say anything about death."

"You said the little boy looked dead."

"Oh . . . yes. . . ."

"Let's say that the little boy represented your baby," he went on. "Do you see the connection? Your baby was an accident—that is, unplanned. And your contact with the little boy was through an accident—the business with the car. Now, if we've got this right, when you looked at the little boy—your baby, that is—you wanted to see him dead."

"That's stupid!" she snapped.

Umbrage had no discernible effect on him. "Let's take this in order," he said. "You're here because you're unable to function. The disability is a result of depression. The depression stems from the fact that you feel trapped in a no longer satisfying marriage. The factor that keeps you locked into this situation is the baby. Therefore, you feel, if the baby were eliminated—dead—you would be free."

"That makes perfect sense," she told him. "But it happens to be wrong. I *don't* want the baby dead. I don't want *anybody* dead."

"Not consciously, I'm sure. But, Mrs. Barthelme, this isn't at all unusual. When you had your other children, did you go through a period of postpartum depression?"

"Yes . . . very brief periods."

"What you're experiencing now," he told her, "is *acute* postpartum depression. It's textbook. The severity is a consequence of the pressure that you have on you now that you didn't have when you had your first children—the ailing marriage and the desire to run away."

"I don't know about that. Maybe you're right, partly. But I don't want the baby dead, that's what I'm saying."

"Mrs. Barthelme, I have another client who is experiencing the very same thing," he said. "She can't have anything sharp in her home . . . knives, scissors, razor blades. . . . She's afraid that she's going to murder the child. I'm telling you this because I want you to understand that your own feelings aren't at all uncommon. As I say, it's textbook."

"And, Doctor, what I'm trying to get *you* to understand is that I didn't imagine that that little boy looked dead," Rachel countered. "I didn't imagine that he had a babyish face either. He had a babyish face, and he looked dead. I didn't imagine any of it. It all happened."

"Very possibly. Yet what is known disputes that, doesn't it?"

"What do you mean?"

"According to what you told me, the police couldn't find any evidence to indicate that those youngsters in the masks were there. Nor was the boy ever found."

"What are you saying? That I lied about it all?"

He raised a hand, objecting. "Not lied. It's possible for people in an agitated state to see what they want to see. To actually see it, even if it isn't actually there."

"Why would I *want* to see a bunch of children in masks?"

"I don't know, Mrs. Barthelme. In time, I hope, you'll be able to tell me. After that, I think you'll find we'll begin to make some progress."

"This is ridiculous," she protested. "What you're telling me is that before you can help me, I have to admit that something is true that I know isn't."

"Well, we have another minute. Let's explore it. You were

driving home from the airport, you say. It was Halloween. Were you seeing children in masks and costumes along the way?"

Rachel thought back. "Some."

"Perhaps, then, you had a picture in your mind of children in masks. Next, we have the accident, the car out of control. You were frightened. Isn't it possible that in this agitated state, you gathered up these children that you'd been seeing along the way and—in your mind—transported them to the scene of the accident? And isn't it possible, too, that this created for you the opportunity to kill your baby—the cause of your distress— without, of course, actually doing it?"

"Incredible!" Rachel said. "That's so ridiculous, it's absolutely and totally incredible."

"If you think about it . . ." the doctor said, rising. "Next time we'll go into it a little deeper."

Rachel remained seated. "I'll tell you what's wrong with your theory," she said. "I've seen one of those children who had the masks on since then. He was following me. I recognized him because he was wearing the same white shoes that he was wearing that night. I've seen him three times—in a furniture store and in an art store and in the woods outside our house. How do you explain *that?*"

He was unimpressed. "We'll get into that next time, too."

Grudgingly, Rachel rose and followed him to the door. "I don't see any reason to come back," she said. "This isn't doing any good."

"It takes time," he told her. "But that's your prerogative, to return or not. If you change your mind, my nurse will set up another session." He opened the door. "Nice to meet you, Mrs. Barthelme," he said, smiling amiably. "My regards to your husband."

"Are you going to report to him?"

"Do you want me to?"

"Why would I?"

"To get attention from him, perhaps. I got the impression from what you told me that he's been neglecting you."

[110]

"I don't care about that. But I don't want you to tell him that rubbish about me wanting to hurt the baby."

He raised a finger admonishingly. "Ah-ah—you misquote me, Mrs. Barthelme. I didn't say hurt. I said kill. Hurting would be directed against the baby. Killing would be directed against the problem. Do you see the difference?"

"Oh, tell him anything you want!" Rachel said, storming out.

She fumed silently while she rode down in the elevator and while she waited in the parking garage for the Eldorado to be brought to her. But when she was in the car, out on the street, with the windows closed, sealed in, she let her frustration explode.

He was a damn petty tyrant! The only thing he knew was what was in his textbooks! That goddamned smugness! *Mrs. Barthelme, this isn't in the least unusual.* The hell! Telling her that she hallucinated it all, just because that fit his textbook example! He wasn't a psychiatrist; he was a goddamn expediter! No wonder they loved him at United Machinery. He kept the assembly line moving!

By the time she was back on the expressway, driving north toward Cedar Point, she had stopped raging at the doctor and started arguing with him.

RACHEL: If I wanted to kill the baby, I'd know. I'd feel something.

EDWARDS: Not if you suppressed the feeling. And if you have been suppressing it, that would explain the fantasy, hitting the child with the car, seeing the child dead. You carried out the killing in your mind. Your guilt feelings were relieved—somewhat—and no actual harm was done to the baby.

RACHEL: I *did* see the white shoes!

EDWARDS: Mrs. Barthelme, you're being stubborn about that. You're clinging to it. Apparently you're trying to persuade yourself that if the white shoes really exist, then that will prove that all the rest of it really happened. But none of the others saw the white shoes. Not in any of the instances. But for the sake of argument, let's say that you actually did see the white shoes, at Tuck's Barn, at McMillan's, even in the woods. Isn't it odd, don't you think, that you didn't mention the white shoes to anyone until you saw them at the Barn? You didn't remember until that very moment, you say, that one of the children was wearing white shoes that night. That was very timely of your memory to come up with that recollection just when you needed something to back up your story about the accident.

(Arguing with him was pointless, too.)

RACHEL: Shut up, you son of a bitch!

When Rachel reached Catawba, Mrs. Woolsey told her that a Lieutenant Lomax from the police department had stopped at the house while she was gone.

Rachel was elated. "What did he say? Does he want me to call him? Is he coming back? What?"

"He didn't say anything," Mrs. Woolsey replied. "He just said was you here, and I said no, and he said thanks and went on his way. Maybe he come about the dogs. But he could have asked me that."

"What dogs?" Rachel asked.

"Don't they send the cops around here to see if you've got dogs, so they can make you get a license? They do that where my sister lives."

"I don't know. . . . I'm sure it wasn't about that."

"If you had a dog and you knew they was coming, you could hide it in the woods," Mrs. Woolsey said, as Rachel left her, going up the stairs.

When she got to the bedroom, Rachel went straight to the phone and called police headquarters. The officer who answered asked her for her name, then had her hold. A few seconds later Sam Lomax came on the line:

SAM: Hi! I stopped to see you today.

RACHEL: I know. I thought I'd better call you. I was beginning to wonder. I thought I'd hear from you before now.

SAM: I've been out on the Coast.

RACHEL: In California? What for?

SAM: An extradition thing. How are you? I understand you had us out to your house again the other night.

RACHEL (warily): What did they tell you?

SAM: Nobody told me anything. I saw the report, but I haven't had a chance to talk to the officers—I've been busy catching up. What happened?

RACHEL: What does the report say?

SAM: It says you called in about an intruder, but nobody was found.

RACHEL: Is that *all?*

SAM: About. Was there more to it?

RACHEL: I think it was the same one, the one with the white shoes. I saw something white in the woods that afternoon. I'm sure it was him. I guess, if you've been gone, you haven't been able to do anything about the hospital, have you?

SAM: I had somebody on it. It turned up dry, though.

RACHEL: What do you mean?

SAM: They have a couple teenage boys working there, but they don't wear white shoes. They say, too, that it wouldn't be possible to bring somebody in and work on him—that boy, for instance—without getting it on the record. Of course, they'd say that. I've never seen an institution yet, including us, that didn't think its procedures were infallible. As it stands, though, I can't make any connection between the white shoes and the boy and the hospital.

RACHEL (defiantly): There *is* a boy with white shoes.

SAM: I didn't say there isn't. I just said the hospital angle came up dry. That's why I stopped at your house today. I wanted to tell you about it.

RACHEL (urgently): Sam, I'm really afraid. I know—nobody believes that there is a boy with white shoes or that somebody was in the house the other night. They think I'm crazy! Not just upset, really *crazy!* Honest, I'm not!

(silence)

SAM: As soon as I get caught up—in a day or two—I'll stop by again and we'll talk about it and see what we can come up with. In the meantime, we patrol that area. I'll make sure that we keep an eye on your house.

RACHEL: I wish you would. I'll feel better. When will I see you?

SAM: Just as soon as I get out from under here. (pause) Hold on a second—

(murmur of voices in the background)

SAM: I've got to cut off now, Rachel—something's come up. But take it easy. I'll alert that patrol.

RACHEL: Thank you. Good-bye, Sam.

She felt considerably better. He hadn't been avoiding her, after all. In fact, he wanted to see her; he had stopped at the house today—when he could have just telephoned—and he was going to stop again in a day or so. What was even more important, though, was that he hadn't written her off as a lunatic, the way the others had.

But, then, he didn't have all the details.

That thought diluted her hopefulness.

Nine

RACHEL became aware of a buzzing. It was intermittent: the buzzing, then silence, then the buzzing again. Emerging from sleep, she realized that she was hearing the phone ringing. As she groped in the dark for the phone, the silence that followed the last ring became prolonged, indicating that the caller had hung up or that the call had been answered by someone else on another extension. Still only half awake, Rachel picked up the receiver anyway.

She heard Paul's voice on the line:

[114]

PAUL: —raining. But it does a lot of that this time of year. I think it has something to do with it being an island. I was in Paris for a couple hours yesterday, and the weather was fine there. Crisp but good. How is it there?

Holly came on, apparently from a downstairs extension.

HOLLY: About the same. It was sunny today, but a little colder.

PAUL: Did she go to see the doctor?

HOLLY: Mrs. Woolsey said she left this afternoon and said she was going into the city, so I guess she did. She was still gone when we got home from school. We tried to think of some way to ask her if she'd been to the shrink when she got back, but we couldn't. That must have been where she was, though.

PAUL: I hope so. How has she been?

HOLLY: The same. Ups and downs. You know, just as normal as anybody sometimes, then down, like she's on something. Kirk says his mother went through the same thing. Now she drinks.

PAUL: Christ! We don't need that. I wish I knew what the doctor told her. Maybe it's too soon—

Furious, Rachel broke in.

RACHEL (shrilly): He told me I'm a loony! I make things up! I kill babies! I make them up in my mind and run them down with the car! Hide all the knives! I can't have anything sharp around! I'm Jack the Ripper! Are you satisfied?

PAUL (wearily): That's right, make a scene out of it. Rachel, for God's sake, I just called up to find out how you are. Turn off the hysterics.

RACHEL (shrieking): If you're so damn interested in *me,* why not ask *me?* What's Holly supposed to be, my keeper?

PAUL: I can't ask you because I can't talk to you. Every time I try, either you scream or you clam up. There's just no point to it anymore.

RACHEL: You *never* try to talk! You tell! You tell me this, you tell me that! That's not talking!

PAUL: Okay, okay. Now, it's your turn, you do the telling. Tell me what the doctor told you.

RACHEL: I told you! I make things up! All of it—I made it up! The accident, the little boy, the masks, the white shoes, none of it ever happened! Are you happy? That's what you wanted him to tell me, isn't it? That settles it! Out of the "in" basket and into the "out" basket! I'm stamped and stapled! I'm a certified lunatic! Are you happy?

PAUL: Holly, are you still there?

HOLLY (softly): Yes.

PAUL: Thanks for staying up, hon. You'd better go to bed now.

RACHEL: No, stay on, Holly. Maybe you can pick up a few more tidbits for Kirk!

HOLLY: Good night.

(a rattling sound as the receiver was put down)

PAUL: Rachel, don't blame her. I asked her to stay up. I told her I'd call. I wanted to find out if you kept that appointment. I wasn't sure you would. Now. . . . Are you going back to him?

RACHEL: No! He doesn't need me there to analyze me. He doesn't listen. He's like you; he tells. He gets his answers out of his textbooks. Hell, he can mail my analysis to me.

PAUL: I think you ought to go back. Give him a chance. He's had a lot of success with our people, they tell me. Jack Flanagan swears by him. He straightened out Jack's wife.

RACHEL (acidly): Was she crooked?

PAUL: Well, do whatever you want to. Go back or don't. But for the kids' sake, you'd better do *something*. They're upset enough as it is.

RACHEL: If they're upset, it's because you have them spying on me.

PAUL: Yeah, right, it's my fault. Okay, Rachel, let's drop it. We're just starting up the old round-and-round again. I've got only one more thing to say. I've got too many things on my mind these days. I can't have this thing hanging fire forever. That's it.

RACHEL: What'll you do? Fire me or retire me?

(a few seconds of silence; then the line went dead)

Rachel dropped the receiver into the cradle and lay back. She was too angry to cry. Besides, she was tired of crying. She was tired of being treated like an unstable and possibly dangerous lab specimen, too, watched and studied by her husband and children—and probably by her children's friends, Kirk Franklin and Jewel Brill, too. It was time to put an end to it.

She got out of bed and put on a robe, then left the bedroom and headed up the stairs and toward the top floor. The thing to do was to set Holly straight on why she was up one day and down the next: because she was stuck in a dead marriage and she couldn't get out of it because she had a new baby. Mothers didn't run out on new babies. They stayed and saw it through—and had down days and up days, but more down than up.

She knocked at Holly's door. No answer. She knocked again, louder. Still no response. Rachel opened the door and looked in. Holly was not there. Assuming that she was still downstairs, Rachel closed the door and walked back toward the stairs. As she reached the landing, she heard the murmur of voices from B.J.'s room. She went to her son's door and knocked.

"Yeah . . ." B.J. answered.

Rachel opened the door. B.J. was in bed, propped up on an elbow. Holly, still fully dressed, was seated cross-legged on the floor. They looked at Rachel as if they expected her to do something wild and irrational. The look refired her anger. All thoughts about explaining why she had periods of depression left her mind.

"I don't want any more spying!" she said fiercely to Holly.

"Mother, I didn't spy on you. Daddy asked me to see if you went to the shrink, that's all."

"Don't use that word!"

"What? Shrink? Everybody says shrink."

"Don't use it!"

Holly lowered her eyes, looking away.

"What was she supposed to do?" B.J. said to Rachel. "He asked her to find out. What did you want her to do, tell him she wouldn't? I don't know why you're so hopped up anyway. He was just worried. What's wrong with that?"

"He's not worried. Not about me. He just wants to make sure that everybody knows. What has he told you?"

Silence. B.J. looked away, too.

"You tell him about me, but you won't tell me about him!" Rachel said resentfully. "You tell everybody about me. You tell Kirk and Jewel. I see you whispering together. Who else do you tell? Does the whole school know?"

Another silence. They were enduring her.

"Somebody say something!" Rachel raged.

B.J. spoke, evenly, looking at her again. "Kirk's mother had the same trouble, that's all," he said.

"Trouble? What trouble? What do you call it when you talk about it?"

He shrugged. "We don't call it anything."

"Sick—that's what you call it!"

He shook his head.

"Sick is when somebody's gross, Mom," Holly said.

Rachel's anger ran out on her. She couldn't continue to castigate them when they wouldn't fight back. "All right—I'm sorry," she said drearily. "It's not your fault. But, please," she said, addressing Holly, "if you want to know where I go, don't ask Mrs. Woolsey, ask me."

"You weren't home," Holly said.

"You could have waited and *then* asked me."

"All right."

"You'd better go to bed," Rachel told her. "It's awfully late."

Holly rose. "Good night, Mom," she said, departing.

"Good night, dear."

"B.J.," Rachel said, when Holly had gone, "haven't you met anybody but Kirk at that school? You're always with him. I don't want to try to choose your friends for you, but it seems to me that you could find someone else that you'd like just as well."

"What's the matter with Kirk?"

"Nothing. He has some strange ideas about certain things— but that's his privilege. I just think you're missing out on a lot of fun. All you and Kirk do is sit around and talk and play tapes."

"If it's his privilege to have his own ideas, how come you want to blackball him for it?" B.J. asked.

"I don't want to do any such thing. He's welcome here."

"Okay."

"I just wish you'd find other friends besides."

"I'll look around," he said.

"Good." She moved to the doorway. "B.J., don't misunderstand, I'm not accusing him of anything," she said. "But does Kirk have a pair of white shoes?"

"I don't know."

"You've been in his house, haven't you?"

"Sure."

"In his room?"

B.J. nodded.

Rachel had the feeling that a barrier had suddenly gone up between her and her son. "Did you see his shoes?"

"I didn't look."

"I was just thinking—" He had shut her out. "Never mind," she said, leaving. "Good night."

" 'Night."

Descending the stairs, she despaired. She had done it all wrong. Instead of mending the break between herself and her children, she had made it worse. She had sounded like a paranoiac again, accusing them of spying on her and whispering about her behind her back. Both were true, of course. Holly had spied on her. And B.J. had admitted that he and

Holly and Kirk and Jewel had been talking about her when they had their heads together. So she wasn't paranoid. But she should have handled it differently. She shouldn't have lashed out at them. Now they were probably even more convinced than before that she was unstable.

She shouldn't have asked B.J. if Kirk had a pair of white shoes either. If Kirk was the one with the white shoes, he wouldn't leave them sitting around where B.J. could see them. Because by now, through his conversations with B.J. and Holly, Kirk undoubtedly knew that Rachel had remembered that one of the children in the masks had been wearing white shoes. So, what she had done by asking B.J. if Kirk had a pair of white shoes was make B.J. think that she was looking for an excuse to break up his friendship with Kirk.

What a mess!

Reaching the bedroom, Rachel got back into bed and switched off the light. Wide awake, she stared into the darkness. Her mind churned with thoughts. Perhaps B.J. was right; she *was* looking for an excuse to end his friendship with Kirk. She had no solid evidence that Kirk was one of the ones in the masks—except his icy eyes. But did eyes alone have an expression? Or did they depend on the expression on the face to give them character, iciness or warmth? The faces behind the masks had been completely hidden from her. Maybe, because she was frightened, she had imagined the icy look of the eyes.

That was what Dr. Blalock Edwards would say. He would riffle through the pages of his textbook mind and find that she had hallucinated the icy eyes just as she had hallucinated the rest of it. Seeing the same coldness in Kirk's eyes, he would say, was just another attempt to give substance to her original story. And, he would tell her, she would find peace of mind only when she admitted to herself that the creatures in the masks had never existed. Recant, Rachel!

Rachel felt fury rising again, directed this time at the psychiatrist. Unable to lie still because of it, she got up and went to the windows and, from the darkness of the bedroom, stared out at the darkness of the woods. She was angry at the doctor, she suspected, because she was afraid that he might be right about her. If he was, she was in a bad way, incapable of distinguishing fantasy from reality. Her husband and her children thought that about her. If it was true—

From the nursery came a sound of the baby complaining restlessly. Maybe she had become tangled in her blanket. Rachel left the bedroom to tend to her, hurrying, wanting to reach her and quiet her before her sounds awakened Mrs. Woolsey needlessly. In the nursery, at the crib, she found that she had been right about the reason for the baby's distress: The blanket was tangled in her legs. Rachel pulled it free, then lifted the baby from the crib and took her to the Bathinette to change her diaper.

As Rachel was removing the wet diaper, she became aware of Mrs. Woolsey's scissors lying on the Bathinette. She felt a quick catch in her breathing, remembering what the psychiatrist had told her about another patient. *She can't have anything sharp in her home . . . knives, scissors, razor blades. . . . She's afraid she's going to murder the child.* Rachel's hands shook as she completed the changing. Out of a corner of an eye she could see the shiny reflection from the night-light on the long, closed blades of the scissors. The scissors were daring her to pick them up, challenging her to prove that she could hold them in her hand and not plunge them into the child on the Bathinette.

Rachel could not shut the idea out of her mind. It would be so easy. The baby wouldn't even know what had happened. She wouldn't feel any pain. One quick thrust, and it would be over. No, damn it, it *wouldn't* be easy. She couldn't ever do such a thing. It was insane, just thinking about it. Insane. Not guilty due to temporary insanity. The psychiatrist would testify to that. Would they put her away? Or would they set her free, because, after all, the insanity had been temporary and she was well again now. Christ! She had to stop this!

Rachel hustled the baby back to the crib and tucked the blanket in around her, then fled, going back to the bedroom.

She got back into bed and, as she had done when she was a child and was afraid of the monsters that were prowling through the house in the dark of night, covered her head. But she could still see the scissors, with the light glistening on the blades. She saw herself standing over the baby with the scissors raised. Horrified, afraid to watch herself as she drove the scissors into the child, she threw back the covers and scrambled out of bed and began turning on lights.

The darkness in the room went away, but not the darkness in her mind. She could still see the scissors blades, long and slender like a dagger, reflecting the soft glow from the nightlight. She paced the room, from the bed to the windows, from the windows to the bed, her hands clenched into knotty fists. She remembered: When she was a child she had climbed a ladder to the roof of the two-story house in Winnetka. Standing on the roof, frightened by the height, she had felt an uncontrollable desire to hurl herself over the edge. To defeat the compulsion, she had to flatten herself out on the roof and scream for help. When they rescued her, her fingertips were bloody from trying to get a grip on the rough roofing.

It was the same compulsion, just as irresistible, that had drawn her to the scissors. But she wasn't a child now; she couldn't throw herself on the floor and scream for help and expect to be rescued. She had to remove the source of the temptation, the scissors. From now on, the scissors—all sharp things—had to be kept out of the nursery. In the morning she would issue an order to Mrs. Woolsey: As of today, nothing sharp in the nursery, especially scissors.

Calmed somewhat, Rachel turned off the lights and went back to bed. She couldn't close her eyes. What if she walked in her sleep and went into the nursery? The scissors were there. No, that was preposterous. She hadn't ever walked in her sleep in her life. But she hadn't ever felt so unsure of her control over herself before either. If she did something to the baby during the night, even if she didn't know she was doing it—

Again, Rachel got up. She left the bedroom and went to the

door of Mrs. Woolsey's room and knocked softly. There was no response. Quietly, she opened the door and entered the room and crossed to the bed and turned on the table lamp. Mrs. Woolsey, a lumpy mound under the covers, stirred, but did not awaken. Rachel whispered her name. The woman remained motionless, breathing noisily. Rachel put a hand on a lump that she guessed was a shoulder and shook it gently but urgently. At last, Mrs. Woolsey's eyes opened. She blinked into the light, looking disoriented.

"I'm sorry—" Rachel said. "Are you awake?"

Still blinking, Mrs. Woolsey replied with mumbles.

"We have to get everything sharp out of the nursery," Rachel told her.

"Is the baby—" Mrs. Woolsey began, starting to rise. Then she seemed to lose track of the thought.

"The baby's all right," Rachel said. "I just changed her. I saw your scissors when I was in there. You left them on the Bathinette. I think that's dangerous."

Mrs. Woolsey was sitting on the edge of the bed. She was more awake than asleep now. "My scissors . . ." she said uncomprehendingly.

"I don't want anything sharp in there anymore," Rachel explained. "I don't think it's safe. So many things can happen by accident."

"What happened?"

"Nothing. Nothing happened. I just don't want to take any chances. I was thinking about it, worrying, and I couldn't sleep."

"Do you want me to make you some hot milk?"

"No. Thank you. I want you to get the scissors."

"Now?"

"Yes. Please. I can't sleep."

Mrs. Woolsey stared at her befuddledly, then looked away for a moment, then began peering at her again in the same baffled way.

"It worries me—what might happen," Rachel said. *"That's why I can't sleep."*

"Oh." Mrs. Woolsey pushed herself up from the bed and her tentlike nightgown settled down around her. "You want me to get the scissors?"

"Please."

The woman plodded toward the doorway. She halted. "My slippers," she said. "The floors get cold."

Rachel picked up her slippers from under the edge of the bed and took them to her and put them down in front of her.

"From now on," Rachel said, "I'd appreciate it if you didn't keep anything sharp in there."

Mrs. Woolsey grunted. With the slippers on, she padded out. Rachel followed her and stood in the hall while she went into the nursery. When she emerged a few moments later, she was holding the scissors.

"I use them in there to cut up cotton squares," Mrs. Woolsey said.

"I know. But just keep them somewhere else from now on—please."

"Well. . . . All right. I'll put them—"

"No!" Rachel said. "Don't tell me!"

Mrs. Woolsey stared at her again. There was apprehension mixed in with the puzzlement this time.

"If I knew where they were, I might use them and forget to put them back," Rachel said. "I don't want to lose your scissors."

"Uh-huh."

"Mrs. Woolsey, I'm really very sorry about this. I apologize. But I just couldn't sleep."

"I know how that is," she said. "Only—" Evidently she decided to keep the statement or question that had been in her mind to herself. "Is that all?" she asked.

"Yes. And thank you again."

"No trouble."

When Mrs. Woolsey had gone back to her room, Rachel went to the stairs and descended. With the scissors removed from the nursery, her anxiety had diminished considerably.

[124]

But she was afraid that if she returned to her bed and closed her eyes to try to sleep, she would see other sharp things in her mind. So the best thing to do was to stay awake as long as possible, until she became so exhausted that sleep would be able to take her without her knowing about it.

In the sitting room she settled in the chair beside the telephone table with the Sunday *Times* puzzle. She finished it just as the first light of morning was beginning to brighten the room. Then she went to the book of weekday puzzles.

Rachel was awakened by a heavy pounding sound. She realized dimly that she was hearing B.J. coming down the stairs for breakfast. Opening her eyes, she found that she was huddled in the fetal position in the sitting-room chair, and she remembered the circumstances that had caused her to spend the night there. The recollection was painful and persistent, keeping her from going back to sleep.

Slowly, she unkinked her body and got up, then set out for the kitchen, moving silently, since she was still barefoot. As she proceeded along the hallway, she heard Mrs. Woolsey speaking. As always, the woman sounded cheerful. Rachel winced at the prospect of facing so much good humor so early in the morning and with her own spirits so low.

"I was going to ask her why she didn't go in and get the scissors herself, why'd she wake me up," Rachel heard Mrs. Woolsey say. "But after she told me she didn't want to know what I was going to do with them, I thought I better not. What you don't know won't hurt you, they say."

Then Rachel was in the kitchen doorway and Mrs. Woolsey—and B.J. and Holly, seated at the table, finishing breakfast—became aware of her.

"We didn't hear you," Mrs. Woolsey said brightly. "You came up like a mouse." She was at the sink, washing out a pot. "Can I put on some mush for you? Or oatmeal? Or would you like some pancakes?"

"No. I'll just have coffee," Rachel said.

"Then sit down," Mrs. Woolsey said. "I'll make it." She put

the pot aside and picked up the kettle. "I'll never get used to instant coffee," she said, running water into the kettle. "I miss the perking. *Pooka-pooka-pooka.* It made a nice sound."

Rachel sat down at the table with B.J. and Holly.

"Are you all right, Mother?" Holly asked.

"Yes. Of course. A little stiff. I fell asleep in the sitting room last night in a chair. I was doing a puzzle."

"You ought to go back to bed," Holly said.

"I probably will."

"We'd better go," B.J. said to his sister.

"Okay."

"Sleep is the stuff that dreams are made of," Mrs. Woolsey said, spooning coffee into a mug. "That's from a poem. One of them old poets. Did you kids ever hear that in school?"

"I don't remember it," Holly replied, rising.

"I think it's Shakespeare," B.J. told Mrs. Woolsey.

"No. 'How thankless is a serpent's tongue'—that's Shakespeare."

"Are you sure you're okay, Mother?" Holly asked.

"Yes, dear."

"Okay."

Holly and B.J. departed.

"They're good kids," Mrs. Woolsey said. "If you wasn't told, you'd never know they was brought up in New York." She poured boiling water into the mug.

"Mrs. Woolsey, I want to apologize again about last night."

"Don't think a thing of it. I know how it is. Your machinery's not in order yet, that's all."

"What?"

"Your machinery's not in order yet," Mrs. Woolsey said again, delivering the mug of coffee. "That happens after a new baby. It takes time for the machinery to settle. My niece Barbara had it. She's my sister's oldest girl. My sister had to take the baby. It almost caused a divorce. She wouldn't make her husband nothing but meat loaf."

"Are you talking about postpartum depression?"

"I don't know about that," Mrs. Woolsey replied. "But I know machinery. When it gets twisted up, it goes to your head. Barbara wouldn't do a thing all day. She didn't do the wash; she didn't do the cleaning. Then, when Mike was due home, she'd put on a meat loaf. The poor boy was about ready to strangle her by the throat."

"Did she get over it?"

"The priest fixed her up," Mrs. Woolsey said, going back to the sink. "He had her saying her beads. And he had a talk with Mike. He told him to eat meat loaf and keep his mouth shut. It went away. The Lord moves in mysterious ways."

Rachel sipped the coffee.

"Don't you worry," Mrs. Woolsey said. "I got the scissors put away. You couldn't find them with a fine-tooth comb."

"That's not it. I just don't want anything sharp around the baby. It's not safe."

"I know. . . ." She was scrubbing the pot again.

Rachel left the kitchen, taking the mug of coffee with her. She felt isolated, completely alone in her belief in her sanity. She understood now why she had been so drawn to the scissors and so fearful of harming the baby. She had been reacting to the power of suggestion, the psychiatrist's story about his other patient. But she knew, too, that it would be pointless to tell that to Mrs. Woolsey. Because Mrs. Woolsey was an expert on machinery and was convinced that Rachel was going through a period of breakdown.

What troubled her more was what Holly was undoubtedly thinking. Rachel remembered what she had shrieked at Paul over the phone and that Holly had overheard: *I kill babies! Hide all the knives! I can't have anything sharp around!* Linking that with what Mrs. Woolsey had told her, Holly would reach the conclusion that Rachel had been afraid that she would murder the baby if the scissors were left in the nursery.

Holly, of course, would now tell B.J. what she had figured

[127]

out. And Paul would be told when he returned. Even Kirk and
Jewel would probably learn about it. The whole damn world
would soon know that Rachel Barthelme was, for sure, crack-
ing up. And when everybody knew it, it would be true. That
was the way with a misunderstanding; as soon as it gained a
majority, it became a truth.

Ten

AS soon as I get caught up here—in a day or two—I'll stop by again.
Rachel was sure that was what Sam had told her on the
phone. But he still hadn't arrived at the house or called again,
even though three anxious days had gone by (plus Thanksgiv-
ing, but she hadn't expected him on the holiday). Now it was
Sunday morning, and Mrs. Woolsey had departed as usual
with her sister, and Rachel was lying awake in bed listening for
the baby's first cries and preparing herself for another day of
disappointment.

When the baby finally began whimpering, she sighed
resentfully and closed her eyes, determined to stay in bed
another few minutes. The rebellion did not last long,
however. From the corridor came the sound of hurried movement and whispering. A few moments later, the baby's whimpering ceased. Puzzled, Rachel got out of bed and put on a
robe and went to the nursery.

Holly was there, fitting the baby into a dry diaper. With her
was Jewel Brill, who had slept over.

"What's going on?" Rachel said.

"Oh—I wanted you to sleep," Holly replied. "We're going to
take care of the baby today."

"That isn't necessary."

"We want to," Holly said.

"It's for practice," Jewel told Rachel. "We want to know what to do in case a pill ever fails."

Rachel looked at her with raised eyebrows. Jewel was slender, blond and sharp-featured, with a distinctive, husky-sultry voice. She had the manner of a professional needler. Her expression at the moment—sly—told Rachel that the remark about the pill had been made for the express purpose of provoking a shocked response. So she let it pass.

"All right, you can take the first feeding," Rachel said to Holly. "After that, though, I'll take over."

"Mom, it's okay, we can do it. We don't have anything else to do, anyway," Holly said, lifting the baby from the Bathinette. "You need the rest. Go back to bed, why don't you?" She moved toward the doorway, trailed by Jewel. "If we have any trouble, I'll check with you. Just relax."

Rachel followed them out and watched them start down the stairs, then returned to the bedroom. She felt crushed, knowing the reason for her daughter's sudden interest in the baby. It wasn't because Holly thought Rachel needed the rest; it was because she thought she couldn't be trusted with the child. Holly was thinking about Rachel's wild statement to Paul on the phone—*I kill babies!*—and her middle-of-the-night visit to Mrs. Woolsey's room to get her to remove the scissors from the nursery.

Rachel dressed and set out for the kitchen. She wasn't going to stay in bed all day, giving support to the idea that she had become a mental invalid. There were a lot of things she could do besides taking care of the baby. For one thing, she could complete the list of furnishings that were needed for the house. What had she done with the list that she had started? Well . . . she would start a new one.

In the kitchen the two girls were seated at the table. Holly was holding the baby, feeding her. Jewel was peeling an orange. Rachel glanced at the bottle warmer. It was off. She wished that just once someone other than her would leave it on after using it. That seemed to be so crucially important to everybody, whether the bottle warmer was turned off or left on. She was glad she hadn't told the psychiatrist about her problem with it. His textbook probably would have told him that she thought of it as a mysterious death ray that was zeroed in on the baby.

"I'm going to get this damn furnishing business finished today for once and all," she said briskly to Holly. "Is there anything particular you want for your room?"

"Mom, the stores are closed."

"I know that," Rachel said, running water into the kettle. "I'm going to make up a list today. Then, tomorrow, I'll go into the village and do the buying and get it over with." She put the kettle on a burner and turned on the heat. "I was thinking about one of those third-floor rooms. Would you like to have a library in there?"

"What for?"

"A place where you could read in privacy," Rachel said, getting a coffee mug from the cabinet.

"I can do that in my room. That's where my books are."

"You could put the books in the library."

"I like to read in bed."

"Put your bed in the library," Jewel suggested. "Then you can tell people you sleep in the library and commute to the bedroom. It'll make you interesting."

Holly snickered.

Rachel looked at Jewel. She was separating the segments of the orange, pulling them apart very slowly and deliberately—sadistically.

"All right, if you don't want a library," Rachel said to Holly. She spooned instant coffee into the mug.

"I don't care. Make a library if you want to."

"No. Not if you don't want it."

Holly rose and put the baby bottle, now empty, in the sink, then rested the baby against her shoulder and began patting her.

"Where did you learn that?" Rachel asked, pouring boiling water into the mug.

[130]

"Watching Mrs. Woolsey."

"There's a certain technique—" Rachel began.

But at that moment the baby burped.

"What?" Holly said.

"Nothing."

"Let's take her into the front room and let her play," Jewel said to Holly.

"Okay." Holly turned to Rachel, looking at her appraisingly. "Mom, will you be all right?"

"What do you think might happen to me?" Rachel asked her acidly.

"Nothing."

When the girls had gone, taking the baby, Rachel dropped a slice of bread into the toaster, then sat down at the table with the mug of coffee. She knew now that it wasn't Jewel Brill's way of speaking that reminded her of someone else; it was her voice, the throatiness. Whom, in the past, had she known who had a voice like that? Someone at college? A friend of a friend in New York? Whoever the person was, Rachel's meeting with her apparently had been fleeting, but in some way memorable.

The toast popped up. As she was buttering it, Rachel heard the phone ring. Maybe, at last, Sam was calling. Hopeful, she left the kitchen and hurried along the hallway toward the sitting room. The phone was no longer ringing; evidently Holly had answered it. As she entered the foyer, she saw Jewel closing the heavy doors to the sitting room.

"What are you doing!" Rachel said sharply. "I heard the phone."

Jewel blocked the way, standing in the narrow opening, looking at Rachel mockingly. "It's for Holly," she told her.

"Oh. . . . I thought—" She couldn't demand that Jewel open the doors. Holly had a right to have a private telephone conversation. "I was expecting a call," she said. Then she retreated.

The call was from Paul, Rachel decided, as she walked back

to the kitchen. He was calling to check on her. Holly had asked Jewel to close the sitting-room doors because she didn't want Rachel to hear what she was telling her father. What *was* she telling him? What didn't he know? She could find out easily enough by listening in on an extension. But the hell with it. She had no desire to hear any more evidence against herself. And disputing it would be a waste of effort. They knew what they knew.

When she finished breakfast, Rachel tore a sheet of paper from the pad that Mrs. Woolsey used to make up grocery lists and got a pencil from a drawer, then left the kitchen again. Reaching the foyer, she saw that the doors to the sitting room had been rolled back. Holly and Jewel were sitting cross-legged on the floor, watching the baby, who was lying on her back on a blanket, kicking her legs awkwardly.

Rachel stopped in the doorway. "Is your father still in London?" she asked Holly.

"No, Paris. He—" Holly realized that she had been tricked. "He'll be home in a couple days, maybe sooner," she said, looking away.

Having established that the call had been from Paul, Rachel dropped the matter. "Don't wear her out," she said, referring to the baby.

"We won't."

Rachel felt Jewel's eyes on her. Facing her, she found that she was looking at her in the same mocking way as when she had barred the opening to the sitting room to her earlier, as if she knew a secret about Rachel that she considered to be incalculably amusing. Rachel assumed that she knew the reason for the look: Jewel, having been told about her by Holly and B.J., looked upon her as a lunatic and thought that was funny. She glared venomously at the girl, then turned away.

On the way up the stairs, Rachel met B.J. coming down. "Hi, Mom!" he said breezily. "Are you all right?"

She passed him. "No!" she snapped. "I ate the baby, and she gave me heartburn!"

From behind her, he asked innocently, "What did I say?"

Rachel did not answer.

When she reached the top floor, she went to the room that she had planned on making into a library for Holly. Now she had to think of something else to do with it—unless she just made a bedroom out of it, as she intended to do with the other rooms on the floor. Undecided, she stood at the windows, looking out toward the woods. The day was typically end-of-November, misty gray, soggy, decayed-looking.

She *did* see white shoes when she looked out the windows the time before, damn it. And she would bet that it had been Kirk Franklin who was wearing them. And Kirk Franklin who had slipped into the house that night, too. Maybe there was some way that Sam could find out if Kirk had a pair of white shoes. He could have one of his men tail Kirk until he caught him with the white shoes on. Oh, Christ! Pipe dreaming.

The phone was ringing again.

Rachel ran from the room. By the time she reached the landing the ringing had stopped.

"Is that for me?" she called down the stairs.

Silence.

She hurried down the steps to the second-floor landing, then shouted down to the first floor. "Holly! Is that for me?"

After a moment Holly appeared at the bottom of the stairs. "Do you want me?" she asked.

"Yes. Is that call for me?"

Holly shook her head. "It's Kirk—for B.J."

"Oh. . . . All right. I just wondered. I'm expecting a call."

"Who from?"

"What difference does it make? Are you screening my telephone calls now?"

"No."

"I think you'd better bring the baby up," Rachel said.

"I took her up a couple minutes ago." Holly peered up at Rachel as if she were attempting to make a judgment about her. "Are you going to be up there?"

"I might be. I might not. Do you want my itinerary for the day, where I'll be, when, why?"

"No," Holly answered evenly.

They were being so goddamned patient with her! "Then stop treating me like a lunatic!" Seething, she strode away.

In the bedroom, Rachel wadded the sheet of paper from Mrs. Woolsey's pad into a tight ball and hurled it at the wastebasket. It soared past the target. Infuriated by the miss, she threw the pencil after the wad of paper—and missed again. With nothing more in hand to throw, she slumped dejectedly and trudged to the wing chair and dropped into it. For a second her rage came back. She hammered savagely on the arms of the chair with her fists and kicked the air. Then, spent, she sagged again.

In time the anger drained away, leaving frustration. To get her mind off her feeling of powerlessness, she set to work on a book of partially completed crossword puzzles. She reserved a portion of her attention for the private road, however, hoping to see Sam Lomax's car approaching. But the only car that appeared was Kirk Franklin's.

When the outside light began to fade, Rachel put the puzzle book aside and left the bedroom and descended the stairs. Holly and B.J. and Jewel and Kirk were in the sitting room, sprawled, talking quietly, backed up by a tape of a sweet-voiced folk singer. Rachel moved on to the kitchen and opened a can of minestrone and put it on to heat. When the soup began to bubble, she ladled out a bowlful and sat down at the table with it.

As she was finishing, Holly and Jewel came in with the baby.

"I'll take over now," Rachel told her daughter.

"No, that's okay, Mom."

"I said *I'll* take the baby."

Reluctantly, Holly handed her over.

"There's some soup in the pan, if you're hungry," Rachel said, getting a bottle from the refrigerator.

"Not now," Holly replied.

Jewel went to the stove and looked into the pan. "What is it, vegetable?"

"Minestrone," Rachel said. She put the bottle in the warmer and turned it on.

"Maybe later," Jewel said.

"Do you want me to wait for the baby?" Holly asked Rachel.

"*I* will take care of her. Believe me, I *know* how. She's not my first baby."

"Okay . . . okay. . . ."

The girls left.

The baby was squirming, chewing on a fist, so Rachel walked with her, jiggling her gently, while she waited for the bottle to warm.

"Turn the warmer off when you take the bottle out," she said aloud to herself. "Remember now, as soon as you take the bottle out, turn the warmer *off*. Don't forget, don't leave it on."

The baby began to cry softly.

"Shh-shh-shh. . . ."

The squirming became more vigorous.

Rocking her, Rachel chanted to her soothingly. "Turn the warmer off . . . don't forget . . . turn the warmer off . . . don't forget . . . turn the warmer off . . . don't forget. . . ."

At last, the bottle was ready. Rachel put it on the counter, then, focusing her entire attention on the task, turned the warmer switch to the off position. "It's off," she said out loud. "Nobody can say I left it on because it's off. It's off." Satisfied, she retrieved the bottle and sat down at the table with the baby and began the feeding.

When the bottle was empty, Rachel placed it in the sink, then looked at the warmer again to make sure once more that it was off. "See?" she said to the baby. "See where the dial is pointing? It's off. O-F-F—off. They can't say I left it on this time, can they?" With that established, she raised the baby to her shoulder and left the kitchen with her, patting her gently to bring up the bubble.

Rachel returned to the bedroom. She put the baby on the bed and watched her for a while as she exercised and made soft sounds of contentment; then she made herself comfortable again in the wing chair with the book of crossword puzzles. Before long, though, she became aware of a disturbing odor. It was a charred smell. Rising, she left the bedroom and went to the head of the stairs.

"Holly!" she called. "What's going on down there?"

Holly appeared from the hallway that led to the kitchen. "It's okay, Mom," she said.

"What's okay? What's that smell?"

"It's nothing."

"Don't tell me it's nothing," Rachel said crossly. "What are you doing down there?"

"We're not doing anything, Mother," Holly replied forbearingly. "You left the heat on under the soup. It was burning."

"I didn't!" Rachel shrieked. "I turned if off!"

"Well, it was on."

"I turned it off!"

"All right, Mother, you turned it off."

"Stop babying me!" Rachel shouted. "I'm not crazy!"

Holly winced. "Nobody said anything like that. I just said you left the burner on. That can happen to anybody."

"I didn't!" Rachel screamed.

She ran back to the bedroom and slammed the door behind her. The sudden loud sound caused the baby to jerk convulsively, then cry out in fright.

"Shut up!" Rachel bellowed at her.

That, of course, frightened her more. She began howling frantically.

"Shut up! Shut up!" Rachel screamed.

The door opened, and Holly came scurrying in. She scooped up the baby and fled with her.

"I am not crazy!" Rachel shouted after her daughter. She went to the door, which Holly had left open, and slammed it again. "I'm not crazy! Damn you all! I'm not crazy!"

Rachel threw herself on the bed. She sobbed heartbrokenly until no more tears would come. Then, wholly exhausted, she slipped off into a numbed kind of sleep.

Eleven

A SENSE of the sun awakened Rachel. Not sure where she was, she raised her head to look. Sunlight, coming in through the bedroom windows, hit her directly in the eyes, causing her to flinch and put her head down again. Monday morning. With her eyes closed she began remembering Sunday. The thoughts were painful, especially the recollection of Holly dashing into the room to rescue the baby. That had been the worst hurt, the realization that her daughter actually believed that she might harm the child. After all the loving and tenderness she had given Holly, didn't Holly know her any better than that?

DR. EDWARDS: Well, you must understand, you're a stranger to your daughter now. She's never seen you this way—irrational.

RACHEL: It's not irrational. They think I'm crazy, and I'm not. I'm protesting. What's more rational than that?

EDWARDS: There's that line about protesting too much.

RACHEL: You mean I *am* crazy?

EDWARDS: I mean that certain things have happened, and you have one version of how they happened and common sense has another.

RACHEL: I *did* turn off that burner.

EDWARDS: What you turned off was the bottle warmer.

RACHEL: I turned off the burner, too.

EDWARDS: How did it get turned back on?

RACHEL: Kirk Franklin sneaked in there and turned it on. Or Jewel turned it on when she looked into the pan to see what kind of soup it was.

EDWARDS: Why?

RACHEL: How do I know why? Why was that boy with the white shoes following me around? Why did he sneak into the house and then not do anything but turn on the bottle warmer? I know it doesn't make any sense, none of it. But it all happened. As long as we're asking why, why would *I* leave the burner on? I know how dangerous that can be.

EDWARDS: One explanation might be simple absentmindedness.

RACHEL: That's not what you think, is it?

EDWARDS: Let's go back a step. You started out the day with a determination to make a list of the furnishings you need for the house. You've tried to do that before—and failed. And you failed again. Isn't it becoming obvious to you that you're never going to make out that list, that you're never going to actually *do* anything about furnishing the house?

RACHEL: It's *not* obvious. It's not true. Do you think I *like* living in this empty barn?

EDWARDS: You hate living in it. And you're afraid that living in it will become your permanent way of life. As it is now, with all the empty rooms, the house is merely a house. But once it's furnished it will become a home. To you, that will make a very big difference. Home is important to you; house is not. You might to able to run away from a house—but not a home.

RACHEL: What are you saying now? That I tried to burn the house down to keep from furnishing it?

EDWARDS: You told me yourself, just a second ago, that you know how dangerous it can be, leaving a burner on under a pan. Dangerous how? Dangerous enough to start a fire and burn down a house—isn't that what you meant?

Rachel grabbed a pillow and folded it around her head, clutching it tightly, shutting out sight and sound. The doctor was wrong, she knew; she *hadn't* tried to burn down the house. But how could she prove it? She had no more chance of proving that than she had of proving that the boy with the white shoes had been in the house. She couldn't produce the boy with the white shoes.

Come to think of it, though, she *could* finish furnishing the house. That would prove that she wasn't afraid to have it become a home. It would also prove—in a roundabout way, admittedly—that she hadn't left the burner turned on. But no list this time. It was when she began making up the list that she always blocked. She would go straight to McMillan's and then to Tuck's Barn and just buy, buy, buy, higgledy-piggledy. Neat, it wouldn't be, but it would get the job done.

Excited by the prospect of not having the house furnishing hanging over her, Rachel flung the pillow aside and scrambled from the bed. She undressed feverishly, then showered, then dressed, putting on an expensive suit that would get her attention at McMillan's and Tuck's Barn. When she had herself looking like a rich North Shore wife—pearls, and, of course, heels with the suit—she left the bedroom and went to the kitchen. There was a note there from Mrs. Woolsey saying that she had taken the baby out in the carriage. Rachel wrote a reply at the bottom of the note, telling Mrs. Woolsey that she had gone furniture shopping.

When she did not see Mrs. Woolsey and the baby on the private road, she assumed that they had gone into the woods for the walk. After that she concentrated her thoughts on buying furniture and paintings. The selection of furniture pieces would be the most difficult, because of the variety needed, beds, chairs, tables and so on. She decided, consequently, to stop at the art store first.

Reaching the village, she looked hopefully for Sam as she passed the police building. But of course, he was nowhere in sight. A distressing thought struck her: What if, at this very minute, he was calling the house? There would be no one there to answer the phone. Perhaps she ought to stop and explain to him why he hadn't been able to reach her—*if* he had called. No, God, that was too high schoolish. Besides, if he was calling—and not getting an answer—surely he would call back. Or maybe Mrs. Woolsey had returned from the walk with the baby by now. As a practical matter, the only thing she could do about it was hope for the best.

When Rachel entered McMillan's, she went straight back to the gallery. The tall, fragile-looking young man whom she had talked to before was there, examining a frame, scratching meticulously at the gilt. He turned toward Rachel as she neared the desk and smiled cordially, seeming to recognize her.

"Hello again," he said. "Did you ever find the doctor?"

"It wasn't a doctor; it was a boy in white shoes."

"Oh, yes."

"What I'm looking for is what I think of as ancestor portraits," Rachel told him. "They're the kind of thing you could hang in the house and people would think they were paintings of your ancestors. That's what I was after when I was in here before. I didn't see any on display, but I thought you might have some tucked away somewhere."

He frowned thoughtfully. "I think I know what you mean. Ancient ancestors or fairly recent?"

"Recent—the twenties or thirties, in that general area. I'm doing some decorating—I'll need more than one."

"I just might have something like that in the back room," he said, getting a ring of keys from the desk. With Rachel trailing him he walked to a door at the rear of the office area. "If we can find a sample of what you want," he said, unlocking the door, "we can have any number made up."

"Just painted? On order?"

"Oh, yes. You've seen paintings done from photographs, I'm sure. It's the same thing."

The storage room was small and jam-packed. A few of the framed paintings were hung, but most of them were lined up dominolike, face to back, in four rows.

"I can't be positive that what you want is here," the young man said, "but I have a faint idea that I saw something like that lately."

"I can look through them," Rachel suggested.

"Would you mind? I really ought to be out front. It's hard to believe, I know, but we actually get shoplifting in here—the smaller items." He moved to the doorway. "I'll leave the door open."

"Fine," Rachel said, beginning the search with a row of the largest paintings.

"Just out of curiosity," the young man said, still standing in the doorway, "do you have some special purpose for these . . . uh. . . ."

"I'm furnishing a house—a big house," Rachel told him.

"Oh!" He walked back to where she was going through the paintings. "Then you might be interested in our rental program," he said. "We put any number of pieces in your home or office—your choice or ours—and then change them every six months. The only charge is the rental fee. That varies, of course, depending on the paintings and how many."

"I've never heard of that," Rachel said, preoccupied with the search.

"Quite a few families use it. It assures one of a change of scenery, so to speak, twice a year. And, too, it eliminates the need for a large personal investment in paintings."

"I'll think about it," Rachel said.

The young man departed.

By the time Rachel finished inspecting the paintings in the first row she had the feeling that she had seen every landscape and seascape ever done and that all had been painted by the same artist using the same scene. Determined, however, she dug into the second row and, to a degree, had her persistence rewarded. She found a portrait of what appeared to be a middle-aged businessman. He looked too modern, though, to pass as an ancestor. She took the painting from the row, to have as an example in case she located nothing better, then resumed the hunt.

Nearing the end of the row, she turned up a painting that first startled her—because it was so different from what she had become used to seeing—and then stunned her—because she realized the significance of what she had found. It was a close-up view of what appeared to be an Indian ritual. All the figures in it, brown-skinned men, naked to the waist, were wearing masks—the same kind of primitive, brightly decorated masks that the children had been wearing the night of the accident.

For a second, Rachel reexperienced the terror she had felt that night. She was immobilized. But then she began to realize that the masks in the painting, rather than being a threat to her, were a vindication. They were proof that what she had said had occurred that night had really happened, that she hadn't made it up. Horror became elation. Quickly, she took the painting from the row and set it aside, then hurried from the storeroom.

The young man was chipping away at the gilt on the frame again.

"May I use your phone?" Rachel said urgently. She had already picked up the receiver and was dialing.

"Yes, of course." He was looking at her curiously.

An officer came on the line, advising Rachel that she had reached the Cedar Point police headquarters. She identified herself and asked to speak to Lieutenant Sam Lomax. The officer put her on hold.

"Did you find what you were looking for?" the young man asked Rachel as she waited.

"Yes and no. As a matter of fact, I found more than I was looking for."

SAM: Lieutenant Lomax. Rachel?
RACHEL: Sam, I found the masks! The masks I told you about. They're in a painting! I'm at McMillan's, the art store. Can you come over here?
SAM: Slow down. What about the masks?
RACHEL: They're in a painting. A painting of some Indians or somebody doing something. They're the *same* masks! I've got the painting. I want you to come and look at it.
SAM: All right. Stay there. I'll be there in a minute or two.

[142]

RACHEL: I'm in the gallery, in the back.
SAM: Got it.

Rachel hung up and, out of good feeling, beamed at the young man.

"Was that the police?" he asked, concerned.

"Yes. Oh . . . but it has nothing to do with you. It's about a painting I found in your back room. Excuse me," she said. "I'm going to get it. I want to bring it out here."

In the storeroom she held the painting up, examining it closely. The masked figures appeared to be performing a ceremony at a stone altar that was directly behind them. A pyramidlike temple stood in the far background. The masks, however, dominated the picture. They had been painted in high relief, the oils heaped onto the canvas. There was a name—Otu—in the lower center section of the painting. Rachel assumed that it was the name of the artist, although it was not where a signature was usually located.

The young man entered.

"That's not at all what I thought you had in mind," he said.

"It isn't. This is something else." She indicated the other painting that she had taken from the row. "That's sort of what I was thinking about," she told him. "Only the clothing gives it away. It's too up-to-date."

"Men like that, businessmen from the twenties and thirties?"

"Yes, exactly."

"That can be done," he said.

Carrying the painting with the masks, Rachel headed back toward the gallery, and the young man trailed after her. As they exited from the storage room, Rachel saw Sam approaching the desk. The sight of him, his bigness, his confident casualness, excited her. She called to him, a little more loudly than was necessary, and seeing her, he broke into the broad smile that had such a warming effect on her.

Rachel stood the painting on the desk, holding it upright. "There!" she said exultantly to Sam.

"Those are masks, all right."

"They're exactly the same," she told him. "I couldn't *ever* forget masks like that."

"They make an impression," he said. "What did you do, just walk in here and see this?"

"No. I found it in the back room. I was looking for paintings for the house and just happened to come across it."

The young man introduced himself to Sam. His name was Roger Gleason. "Is the painting stolen?" he asked. "If it is, we're not at fault. We buy these paintings in batches from our supplier. I can show you the invoice."

"No, this isn't a theft; it's something else," Sam told him. He looked at the painting again. "What is it, some kind of ritual?"

"Those are ceremonial masks, I would guess," Gleason replied. "The figures are— Well, they might be Incas. South American Indians, I imagine, but I'm no expert on primitives."

"I wonder what the ceremony is."

"God only knows," Gleason said.

Sam pointed to the name Otu. "Is that who painted it?"

"Otu . . . Otu . . ." Gleason said, looking away. He shook his head. "It doesn't ring a bell. But so many of these are done by students and unknowns in general. . . ." He shrugged.

"Mrs. Barthelme says she found it in the back room. When did you last have it out on the floor?"

"It's never been out."

"Are you sure about that?"

"Positive," Gleason said. "I put the canvases out myself. I *know* I wouldn't put this one out. It's just not for our clientele."

"What do you mean?"

"It's too . . . too . . . too disturbing," Gleason explained. "The nakedness, for one thing. And *brown* bodies. Frankly, I didn't know we had it."

Sam addressed Rachel. "That makes a little problem," he said. "What were you thinking, that they saw this painting and made copies of the masks? How could they do that if it hasn't ever been out where they could see it?"

"I didn't really think," she replied. "I just saw the masks and they were the same. . . ."

Sam gestured in the direction of the storeroom. "Do you let kids go in there, teenagers?" he asked Gleason.

"Never!" he replied. "That is, unless they're with an adult."

"How about in the past couple weeks or months or so?" Sam asked. "Have any teenagers been in there with any adults?"

"Oh, my, let's see. . . . That's a big order. A number of customers have been in there. I don't specifically recall, though, that any of them had teenagers with them." He shook his head. "I just don't know. Maybe yes, maybe no."

Sam turned his eyes to the painting again. "Well, it's possible," he said. "A kid could have seen these masks and remembered them and made up something like them." There was doubt in his tone, however.

Rachel felt as if she had been suddenly stepped on, flattened.

"What do you think?" Sam asked her.

"I don't know what to think now. I was so sure. . . ."

"Don't give up on it," he said, surprising her. He spoke to Gleason again. "Could you put this away for me?" he said, indicating the painting.

"For how long?"

"I'll be in touch with you," Sam replied. "Or if anybody asks about it—or even mentions it—will you let me know?"

"Yes, of course."

Sam touched Rachel's arm, directing her toward the front of the store. They passed through the gallery and then through the art supplies section in silence. Rachel castigated herself in her mind for not thinking before telephoning Sam. She could have asked Roger Gleason the questions that Sam had asked him and determined that the painting had not been on display for the children to see. But no, she had acted first and thought later, making herself look like a fool again.

"Is it too early for you for a drink?" Sam asked when they got outside.

"No. . . ."

"There's a place up the street," he said. "It ought to be quiet for a while—until the after-five crowd arrives. We can talk."

"All right."

"This has worked out fine," he said as they set out. "I was going to stop at your house tonight. You've saved me a trip."

"Were you? I was beginning to wonder. When I talked to you on the phone, you said a day or two. But that was a week ago."

"I apologize for that. I've been snowed under. I should have called you, though."

"No, that's all right."

The place that he had mentioned turned out to be The Malt Shop. Its cuteness ended with the name, however. Inside, it was an ordinary saloon, with a long bar along one side and a row of booths along the other. There was but one customer when they entered, an elderly man who had his cane hanging over the raised edge of the bar. He and the bartender—middle-aged and barrel-bellied—were in quiet conversation.

"What would you like?" Sam asked Rachel.

"Scotch and water—plenty of water."

He addressed the bartender. "Scotch and water—plenty of water—and an onion for me."

"Coming up."

Sam guided Rachel to the final booth in the row, then took her coat and hung it up with his own floppy brown raincoat.

"What makes this an onion day?" she asked as he sat down across from her.

"Whim."

The bartender arrived with the drinks. Sam's martini was in the same size glass, a tall tumbler, as Rachel's scotch and water.

"It saves ordering that second and third," Sam explained, responding to her questioning look.

"But how can you drink that much gin?"

"I skip lunches. That leaves room."

Rachel laughed, and felt herself relaxing.

"I like the pearls," Sam said. "They're nice with that suit."

"Thank you. Sam, when you said, 'Don't give up'—about the masks—what did you mean?"

"How much do you know about cermonial masks?"

"Nothing. . . ."

"That's what I thought. What I was getting at was, if you're not an expert on ceremonial masks, they all look pretty much alike. So the fact that the masks in that painting weren't out where they could be seen—and copied—doesn't prove that those kids didn't have on something like them. See?"

"Yes. You're right." She sipped her drink. "I could almost swear, though, that they're the same."

"They might be," he said. "We don't know that one of those kids didn't see that painting. All we know at this point is that it's unlikely. I've had some pretty unlikely things prove out."

"I don't understand," Rachel said glumly. "Everybody else thinks I'm losing my mind. But you seem to believe me. Why?"

"Maybe because everybody else hasn't been a cop as long as I have," he said. "I learned the hard way, Rachel. You can't ever be positive that you have the final answer until you've eliminated all the ifs and buts."

"The hard way how?"

"I worked up a case on a guy once that sent him up for twenty years minimum. I was a lot younger then." He drank from the tumbler. "Anyway," he said, "his lawyer kept digging, working on those ifs and buts, and showed us that we'd put the wrong guy away."

"Did he get out?"

"Oh, sure. The conviction was thrown out. It has a happy ending all the way around. I got a promotion."

She blinked at him. "For what?"

"The brotherhood," he replied. "We take care of our own. When one of us boots one, we show him we're still behind him, we give him a boost up. It's the one thing that distinguishes us from the Mafia. When one of theirs makes a mistake, they put out a contract on him."

Rachel laughed again.

"About your case, though," he said, "I can see why they're having trouble believing you. I've been over the details in my mind a hundred times, and it doesn't add up, the way you tell it. But. . . . The story is just a little bit too spooky for me to toss out and forget and still satisfy myself."

"You really *have* been thinking about it," she said, pleased.

"Of course. It's still an open case."

"You seem so busy."

"Well, your case is part of what keeps me busy. I admit I haven't made any spectacular breakthrough on it, but I'm still hanging in there. Because of those ifs and buts."

"Which ones?" she asked hopefully.

"Well, the kids and the masks. Especially the masks. If you were making it up, why were the masks so elaborate? It was Halloween. Why not just plain ordinary Halloween masks? And taking it a step further, if your story is true, why were the kids wearing such elaborate masks?"

"Why?"

"I don't know. So far I only have questions. I don't have any answers."

Rachel felt let-down.

"Sorry."

"Haven't you found out *anything?*"

"Oh, bits and pieces, nothing substantial. But that's the way a lot of cases go. At first, nothing makes sense. Then you pick up something here, something there, and the bits and pieces begin fitting together. Then, when it breaks, it breaks fast. So don't give up."

Avoiding his eyes, Rachel looked toward the bar. There were more customers now; a half dozen to a dozen barstools were occupied. Evidently the afternoon crowd that Sam had mentioned was beginning to collect. Holly and B.J. would be home from school now; she ought to go home, too.

"Is there any part of it that you haven't told me?" Sam asked.

"Like what?"

"How would I know? Some little detail, maybe, that you didn't think was important."

Rachel thought back, recalling the night of the accident, seeing the white shoes at Tuck's Barn and at McMillan's and in the woods, hearing the intruder in the house.

"I can't think of anything," she said. "Except that Kirk Franklin's eyes remind me of the eyes behind the masks."

"Do you want another drink?"

She rattled what was left of the ice cubes in her otherwise empty glass. "I ought to be going home."

"Dinner to get?"

"No. Mrs. Woolsey is there."

"What about your husband?"

"He's in London. No, Paris—I think. I lose track."

"Have dinner with me," he said.

"Well. . . ."

"We can talk about the case if you need an excuse."

"No, I don't. Fine," she said, brightening. "I'd like to. I have to call home, though."

Sam pointed to a phone booth at the end of the bar.

Rachel called the house and spoke to Mrs. Woolsey, telling her that she was having dinner with a friend. When she left the booth, Sam was standing, holding her coat for her. As he helped her into it, he told her that it would be necessary for him to stop at headquarters to sign out, but that it would take only a minute or so. They then left The Malt Shop and walked back to where Rachel had parked the Eldorado. There was a ticket under the windshield wiper.

"I see the boys were on the job while I was on my gin break," Sam said, opening the door on the passenger's side.

"I don't see why I should have to pay that," Rachel said, getting in. "I was on police business."

"Tell it to the judge."

He closed the door and got the ticket from under the wiper, then got in behind the wheel. Rachel handed him the car keys, and he gave her the ticket.

"Are you really going to make me pay this?" she protested.

"You wouldn't want a dishonest cop on your case, would you?"

"No. . . ."

"There's your answer."

Sam started the engine, then pulled out of the parking space, made an illegal U-turn and drove toward the headquarters building.

"Some honest cop," Rachel said in mock reproach.

"I didn't see the sign, Officer, honest," Sam said. "The sun was in my eyes."

Rachel laughed. "Is that what they say?"

"That's what they used to say. It's been a long time since I had the traffic detail. I don't suppose the excuses have changed, though."

He turned the Eldorado into a drive that led to the rear of the police building and pulled into an empty space in the parking area and switched off the engine.

"Be right back," he said, getting out. "While I'm gone, think about what you want for dinner, steak, seafood, Chinese, whatever."

Watching him walk toward the rear entrance, Rachel smiled affectionately. She was enjoying herself already, and it had been a long while since she had last had that feeling. She even felt encouraged about the "case." It seemed possible to her that somehow Sam would be able to prove that the children in the masks and the little boy and the white shoes really existed, that she hadn't hallucinated them all, as the psychiatrist thought.

That was because Sam had so much confidence in himself, of course, not because he had, so far, turned up anything new in her favor. Still, she could almost believe now that sooner or later he would be able to put all those bits and pieces that he had talked about together and produce an explanation that would vindicate her. She had confidence in his confidence.

There was one bit or piece that he didn't have, though. He didn't know about Dr. Blalock Edwards' textbook diagnosis. She probably ought to tell him about that. Except that it was so wrong that it was totally irrelevant. It might make him doubt her. After all, he had no way of judging how wrong the diagnosis was; he wasn't her, he couldn't look at it from inside her mind. If she told him about it, he might stop looking for the other bits and pieces that were so important.

What would Dr. Blalock Edwards' textbook say about the masks in the painting? she wondered.

EDWARDS: Well, I see that you managed to put off the house furnishing again.

RACHEL: I was upset about seeing the masks. I couldn't stay there and go through the rest of those stupid paintings. Besides, Sam took me away.

EDWARDS: Sam. . . .That's an interesting development. You've been anxious about him, waiting for him to call or come to the house. Now you have him. All you had to do was discover some masks in a painting.

RACHEL: I didn't put the painting there! I didn't make the masks the same!

EDWARDS: How do we know that the masks actually *are* the same?

RACHEL: I told you! I remember!

EDWARDS: You remember? Just as you remembered the white shoes when you needed something to support your story? Isn't it possible that when you saw the masks in the painting, you decided, rather than remembered, that they were the same?

Rachel was saved from answering. Sam had emerged from the building and was walking back toward the car.

Twelve

"I KNOW a place I think you'd like," Sam said as they left the police headquarters parking area. "It's about an hour drive. You're not in any hurry, are you?"

"No, none."

Getting comfortable, Rachel pulled her legs up and sat sideways on the seat, facing Sam. She liked being a passenger in the Eldorado. When she was at the wheel, she was always a bit wary of its weight and power, conscious of the damage it could do if she lost control of it. But Sam seemed to be completely at ease, certain of his ability to contend with the monster should it get too strong an injection of its premium fuel and suddenly go berserk.

On the way, they used the relatively crowded through streets that linked the North Shore villages rather than an expressway. Consequently, with Sam's attention on traffic, the talk was mostly trivial. Rachel learned that Sam lived in one of the small houses on Cedar Point Road, renting it, sharing the cost with a fellow detective named Frank Shea. He asked her how she managed to fill all her time with her older children in school and the baby cared for by Mrs. Woolsey, and she told him that planning the furnishing and decorating of the house kept her busy—and that she liked to do crossword puzzles when she had a spare moment. And so on.

The place that Sam had chosen—Camelot—was familiar to Rachel.

"I know this!" she said, excited. "I came here with my mother and father when I was a girl."

"I thought you'd know it," Sam said, pleased.

"Did you come here, too?"

"No. My family didn't eat out. There were eight of us, and my father wasn't always working."

Inside, Camelot still had the aspects of a cloister that had so impressed Rachel when she was younger. The main room was large, with soft lighting. The walls were dark and paneled. There was an illusion of glitter, a sprinkling of gold dust, in the dimness. The conversations at the few tables that were occupied—its being early—were thoughtfully modulated. A quartet, piano and strings, hidden away in an alcove behind a small dance floor, was playing unobtrusively. And the waiters, when they moved and spoke, had the manner of loyal confidants rather than obedient servants.

Sam and Rachel's waiter accepted Sam's order for a water glass of gin as if it were one of the standard items on the menu.

"Don't those things get to you?" Rachel asked Sam.

"I inherited my father's hollow leg," he told her. "That was the sum total of the estate."

She looked around. The other diners were all middle-aged or older. "This really brings back memories," she told Sam. "How old was I when I was here last? I was in high school. No, I was out of high school, graduated, and I think we came here a night or two before I left to go east to school. That was . . . over twenty years ago."

"Twenty years ago. I was in the Navy."

"In a war? *Was* there a war? My God, let me think. Well, I guess there's *always* a war."

"There wasn't where I was," he said. "I was in San Francisco. Stationed there—on shore patrol."

"Is that how you became a policeman?"

He shrugged. "Could be."

"Shelley Berman—remember him?" Rachel said. "And Nichols and May? I always connect them somehow with school."

"College, you mean?"

"Yes. We always called it 'school.' Let's see, who else was around then? Oh, yes . . . Remember coffeehouses? Espresso? I saw Allen Ginsberg at a coffeehouse once. Oh—and Jack Kerouac. Didn't he die?"

"I don't know who he is."

"He wrote that book about hitchhiking," Rachel said. "I didn't read it, but everybody was talking about it back in those days. Who do you remember?"

"Hog Waters."

"Who?"

"He was a mechanic at the air base," Sam explained. "I busted his head in a hotel on Market Street. He was breaking into rooms, looking for his wife."

[153]

Rachel laughed. "Why do you remember him?"

"He was the first head I ever busted."

"Well, truthfully, my life wasn't all coffeehouses back then either," Rachel said. "Paul and I got married that first year at school. I got pregnant, so I dropped out. We lived in one little room. My father paid for it. He could have afforded better, but I guess it was punishment." She smiled reflectively. "It was fun, though. I didn't feel deprived."

"Rosemary Clooney," Sam said.

"Yes, I remember her."

"Peggy Lee."

"Sure. Well, she's still around."

The waiter arrived with their drinks.

"The Edsel," Sam said to Rachel.

"Uh-huh And three-D movies. Remember? With the glasses?"

"Charles Van Doren," the waiter said.

"Right," Sam said. "That quiz show. He won a bundle. Then they found out it was rigged. What was that show?"

"Twenty-one," the waiter said.

"Yeah."

The waiter departed.

"How did you know that I'd know about this place?" Rachel asked Sam.

"A wild guess."

"No. How?"

"From things you've told me about yourself. And things I've picked up."

"Have you been investigating me?"

"I wouldn't call it an investigation," he replied. "A little digging."

"Why?"

"You're an element in the case."

"My God! I've never been an element before." She looked at him resentfully. "But I'm the victim," she said. "Why investigate me?"

[154]

"Routine. I always start out by assuming that everybody on a case is lying. Just because my hunch tells me that you didn't make up that business about the accident—the kids, the masks, that stuff—that's no proof that you didn't. My judgment isn't perfect." He smiled faintly. "Especially when the lady in the case is on my mind a lot even when I'm not thinking about the case."

Rachel looked at him levelly. "Do you mean that? Or are you being charming?"

"I mean it. But I'm *always* charming."

Rachel sipped her drink, then, putting it down, kept her eyes on it.

"That's your cue to tell me, 'Nothing doing,' " Sam said.

She raised her eyes. "I can't say that. You've been on my mind a lot, too."

"It's not fatal," he said, smiling.

"I'm just thinking about what could happen—"

"Don't," he said, breaking in. He motioned toward the dance floor. "I'm game if you are."

"There's nobody out there."

"There never is until somebody makes the first move," he said, rising.

He took her hand as they made their way between the tables. On the dance floor he held her firmly and gently, and she rested her head against his chest. The music, a dusty ballad, somehow sounded distant, as if it were a recollection rather than real. Rachel discovered after a moment that she was clinging to Sam. She loosened her hold. But the urge to cling remained. It had been so long since she had last had arms around her that she wanted around her.

Other couples joined them on the floor. Rachel and Sam's range narrowed, until their movement was limited to a few square feet of space. They were now embracing more than dancing. Still, though, Sam's touch was gentle. She couldn't imagine his breaking Hog Waters' head. But that was twenty years ago. From breaking heads, perhaps, he·had learned to appreciate gentleness, just as, from sending a man to jail unjustly, he had learned not to be satisfied with conclusions until he had eliminated all the ifs and buts.

Sam whispered to her against her hair, "There's something I've got to tell you."

"Yes. . . ."

"I'm hungry."

"That's cruel," she told him, looking up at him.

"I know it. It's torture, dancing when you're hungry."

Laughing quietly, they returned to the table. The waiter—omniscient—appeared and took their dinner order, plus an order for another tumbler of gin for Sam.

Waiting for food, they played the Remember? game again. Sam remembered the Russian dog in space. Rachel remembered James Dean. Sam remembered picture windows. Rachel remembered Senator Dirksen. Sam remembered paint by numbers. Rachel remembered tube dresses. Sam remembered Hugo Winterhalter. Rachel, at last, brought the competition to an end—in shambles—by claiming to remember Gogi Grant. Sam refused to believe that there had ever been anyone named Gogi Grant.

When they had eaten and coffee had been served, they let the coffee stand and returned to the dance floor. They made very little pretense at dancing this time. The object clearly was to be in each other's arms. Rachel found that she now had no need to cling to Sam; she had somehow gained confidence in his commitment to her. The mood and the embrace had a healing effect on her. She sensed that her hurts were diminishing, that her wounds were closing, and she began to think of the embrace as a marvelous cure that, continued, could make her recovery permanent.

The music ended, and the quartet left the alcove for a respite. When Sam and Rachel got back to their table, the waiter was there with fresh coffee. But Sam waved it away and asked for the check. They spoke softly and warmly to each other across the table as they waited, saying nothing of any importance, simply sustaining the feeling of intimacy that they had brought with them from the dance floor. When the check had been paid, they left Camelot holding hands.

As they drove back toward Cedar Point, Rachel sat close to Sam, resting against him, and he put an arm around her. The Eldorado was like a comfortable and familiar room, warm and secure. Rachel thought: If Sam and I had a place of our own, it would be like this because Sam is like this. But then she realized that she didn't know him that well, she knew him only by what had occurred so far this night and from her imaginings.

"Do you go there a lot?" she asked.

"Camelot? Once before."

"Where do you go?"

"To eat? Wherever is close. Atmosphere isn't my thing."

"Not just to eat. When you have a date, I mean."

He was silent for a moment. "This is the first date I've had in a long time—if that's what this is," he said. "I don't go on dates. Does anybody anymore? I meet somebody, and we go somewhere. But I don't think of it as a date. The last time I went on a date, I was a kid."

"All right, when you meet somebody and you go somewhere, where do you go?"

"A movie sometimes. In the summer, out on the boat. To the beach. A Cubs game. It depends."

"Where do you meet these somebodies?"

"Here and there. Why?"

"I don't know anything about you," she said. "I can't associate you with any particular place—except police headquarters. Me, you associated with Camelot. That told you something about me. If Camelot is my place, what is your place?"

"Saputo's."

"What's that?"

"A bar."

"It sounds Japanese."

[157]

He laughed. "Try Italian," he said.

"All right, I will. Take me there."

"Okay."

Rachel nestled deeper into the crevice that she had made for herself beside Sam. She thought about his statement that she was on his mind a lot even when he was not thinking about the case. She was glad that he had said "a lot." If he had said "sometimes" or "occasionally," it wouldn't have been so significant. But "a lot" was a confession that he had tried not to think about her—for the obvious reason, because she was married—but couldn't get her out of his mind.

She felt slightly uneasy, though, about what he had said about his relationships with women. *I meet somebody, and we go somewhere. But I don't think of it as a date.* By her definition that was a pickup. Was that the only kind of woman who interested him, the pickup? She couldn't believe that he was that shallow. Maybe it was her understanding that was at fault. Perhaps men and women *didn't* date anymore, in the formal sense. That didn't necessarily mean that their relationships were superficial.

Anyway, his past behavior didn't matter. He was open to change. He had started out busting heads and had become gentle. So, if he were in love, if he found a woman he could not get out of his mind, he would have no trouble adapting to domesticity. She guessed, in fact, that he had already prepared himself for having a home. He lived in a house, not an apartment. He had built the nest, so to speak, and was simply waiting for the right woman to share it with him.

"Ready or not, here we are," Sam said, turning the Eldorado into a parking lot next to a long, low cement block building.

Inside, Saputo's was essentially the same as The Malt Shop, with a long bar along one side and booths along the other. There was little light and a thick, low-lying fog of tobacco smoke. The bar was crowded, at places three deep, and all the booths were occupied. Sam was clearly a regular. He was

[158]

greeted exuberantly, and spaces were opened up to him and Rachel as they made their way along the line at the bar. He obviously had a privileged status at Saputo's. For when he declined the openings, simply smiling the offers aside, the rejections were met with easy submissiveness. Rachel was reminded of the many times that she had watched a chairman of the board arrive at an office Christmas party.

They finally accepted a space offered by a flat-faced young man, Joey, who was in the company of a bosomy, sleepy-eyed young woman named Chris. Immediately, one of the bartenders, a short but muscular dark-skinned man with a droopy black mustache, was there with Sam's tumbler of gin. Sam introduced him to Rachel. He was Saputo.

"You had a call," Saputo told Sam. "What do you want, lady?" he asked Rachel. Evidently he had already forgotten her name.

"Scotch and water, please."

Saputo departed.

"Seen any more of that guy in the tennis shoes?" Joey asked Rachel.

"What? Who?"

"You don't remember me, do you? I was out at your place when you had that prowler, the guy in tennis shoes."

"Yes, now I remember you. I didn't recognize you without your uniform." She shook her head. "It wasn't tennis shoes. Just white shoes."

Saputo put her drink on the bar in front of her. To Sam, he said, "You here?"

"I'm here," Sam replied.

Again Saputo departed.

"Your old man—" Joey began, addressing Rachel. He laughed. "When we were leaving, he went out with us—did you see that? He told us you had nervous problems. We thought you were spooked. Then Sam came back from the Coast, and I got straightened out on it."

Rachel smiled feebly.

"That's some place you got out there," Joey said. He turned to Chris. "It's about fifty rooms."

"Oh, no, not that many," Rachel said.

"Where's that, out on the Road?" Chris said. "All those places are a bunch of big barns. Who was that dame that lived out there that used to come in here?" she asked Sam. "She'd get crocked, remember?"

"That sounds like a lot of people," Sam said.

"What's the idea of all those empty rooms?" Joey asked Rachel.

"I'm furnishing them now," she told him. "That's why I'm with Sam. I was picking out paintings and . . . well, something happened, and I called him about it. Then we didn't have anything else to do, we went to dinner to talk about it."

"Oh, yeah." Joey suddenly snapped his fingers. "Hey!" he said, speaking to Sam. "I saw a kid in white shoes the other day. It didn't click. I didn't connect it." He frowned, trying to remember. "I saw him . . . I saw him . . . where the hell did I see him?"

"On the street? Inside? Where?" Sam said.

"On the street. Yeah, I was in the car. I saw him out of the corner of an eye. It registered, you know. But it didn't click." He shrugged. "I don't know. Maybe it'll come to me."

"What did he look like?" Rachel asked urgently.

"I didn't look at him. He was a kid. But now that I think about it, maybe he wasn't. I just noticed the shoes. How many guys do you see in November in white shoes."

"I went with a guy that used to go swimming in the lake in the middle of winter," Chris said. "With the ice! He called himself a polar bear. They had a club."

"I heard of them," Joey said.

"His name was Robert," Chris said. "Nobody called him Bob. Robert. He used to squirt lighter fluid on his fingers and set them on fire. That was supposed to be a trick. I think he froze his brains."

"Maybe he was thawing out," Joey said.

Saputo reappeared. "Your squawker's on the line," he told Sam, taking away his empty glass and putting a fresh drink in front of him.

"Thanks."

Sam smiled fleetingly at Rachel, then, taking his drink with him, began making his way toward the far end of the bar.

She looked after him puzzledly.

"It's some guy with a tip," Joey explained. "Sam's contacts call him here. It's like his office." He addressed Chris again. "I hope it isn't something hot," he said. "I don't want him sending me out on anything."

Chris glanced at Rachel. "He's not going out on anything tonight," she told Joey.

"I'm not talking about him. I'm talking about me."

"When did he ever send you out on anything?"

"I've been with Sam a lot of times."

"With him, sure. I'm saying alone."

Joey snorted crossly. "Set your fingers on fire."

"Sam won't be going anywhere tonight on police work," Rachel told them. "He signed out just before we went to dinner."

Joey looked at her sideways.

"You got a lot to learn about Sam, honey," Chris said to Rachel. "He's plugged in twenty-four hours a day. He's like a racehorse. When the bell rings, he's off."

"That's a firehorse," Joey said.

"Racehorse. Didn't you ever go to the track?"

"The hell with the track. When they say that, they say firehorse."

"When did you ever see a firehorse?" Chris argued. "They haven't had any firehorses in fifty years. Wake up and smell the coffee."

"Which is it?" Joey asked Rachel. "Firehorse or racehorse?"

"I don't think I've ever heard that saying."

"Firehorse," he said assertively to Chris.

She gestured indifferently, withdrawing from the debate.

Rachel looked toward the far end of the bar, wishing that Sam would return.

"He's in the back room," Chris told her. "Saputo's got a phone back there. Don't worry. He'll be out in a minute. He'll have to come out for a refill."

Rachel laughed lightly. "That's amazing, the way he can drink all that gin."

"He's got his old man's hollow leg," Joey said.

"I bet he's got his old man's hollow liver, too," Chris said.

"Nah. It's like water over the dam to Sam," Joey said. "When did you ever see it show on him? I've seen him sit all night putting that stuff away and get up and walk out like he never had a drop. He's got a cast-iron stomach."

"It'll tell," Chris said. "Give it time, it'll tell."

"I heard on the radio some guy that lived to be a hundred and seven and he had a quart of whiskey every day," Joey said.

"That's whiskey," Chris said. "This is gin. Doctors tell you to take a shot of whiskey. It's medicinal. But when did you ever hear of a doctor telling anybody to take a shot of gin? It'll kill you."

"For Christ's sake!" Joey said disgustedly. "Booze is booze. What're you talking about!"

"They make whiskey with charcoal," Chris said. "It's healthy. My grandmother used to put charcoal in the ground when she planted potatoes."

"Ehhh! That's an old wives' tale."

Rachel saw Sam returning.

"She had prize potatoes," Chris told Joey.

"Who the hell ever gave a prize to a potato?" He saw Sam. "Anything hot?" he asked.

Sam shook his head. "Are you ready to leave?" he asked Rachel, putting his empty glass on the bar.

"Yes . . . if you are." She addressed Joey and Chris. "It was very nice meeting you."

"Take it easy," Joey said.

"See you, honey," Chris said.

When they were outside and walking toward the Eldorado, Sam put his arm around Rachel again. "That's my place," he said, sounding amused. "What did it tell you about me?"

"Well . . . people like you. . . ."

"Those people like me. What does that prove? I wouldn't hang out where people didn't like me."

"I suppose not."

"How did you like the small talk? Pretty boring?"

"It would probably get that way." She looked up at him. "If it bores you, why do you go there?"

"It doesn't engage me," he replied. "I don't want to be engaged in interesting conversation. I have my work on my mind, I don't want to be distracted. I can listen to that junk at Saputo's and not even hear it."

Paul was like that. He didn't want to be distracted from his work either.

Sam opened the car door, and Rachel got in. As he walked around to the other side, Rachel continued to compare him to Paul. They were not the same, she decided. Paul, putting his work first, had abandoned her to the psychiatrist. Sam was trying to help her and, in the meantime, was supporting her by believing in her. Probably, though, the main difference between them was in the way she felt about them. She felt nothing for Paul, and for better or worse, she was in love with Sam Lomax.

When they had left the parking lot and were in traffic, Rachel nestled close to Sam again, and once more his arm enclosed her. She closed her eyes and felt a slight light-headedness, a consequence of the several drinks that she'd had, she assumed. It was a pleasant sensation.

"Where are we going?" she asked.

"Home."

She realized that he meant his home, not hers. But she was ready for that. She wanted it.

Thirteen

SAM'S house was one of a dozen or so that were set close together and looked alike. They were Capes, with glassed-in front porches. Most of them were dark, and in the pale winter moonlight they looked like a row of the little wooden houses that came with Monopoly sets.

Sam switched off the motor and handed the keys to Rachel. She dropped them into her purse, then they left the car and walked hand in hand up the walk to the steps, then entered the enclosed porch. As Sam was unlocking the door, Rachel began trembling a bit, from anticipation, not because of the cold. The door opened. Sam took her hand again and led her inside. The door closed, and they advanced into the darkness.

When they stopped, Sam took Rachel's purse from her. She heard it drop on something soft. With both of them working at it, they got her out of her coat. Then Sam removed his own coat. Free of those encumbrances, they embraced, holding each other tightly and kissing roughly. Rachel's trembling eased. She felt that she had reached and crossed a barrier and that from now on the going would be easy and natural.

The kiss softened, then ended. They held each other loosely, kissing randomly and lightly, becoming accustomed to the intimacy. Then the fire flared again. Their mouths mashed together. They gnawed at each other passionately and primitively. But the ferocity could not be sustained. Once more the kissing became unhurried and gentle.

Sam unfastened the buttons of Rachel's suit jacket and slipped it back over her shoulders. She kissed his hands. Sam unbuttoned her blouse, and it joined her jacket on the floor. With his assistance she removed his jacket and tie and shirt. Reaching behind her, Sam released the catch on her bra. They embraced again, exploring each other's bareness. Rachel felt a breathlessness, as if she were aboard a rapidly descending elevator. The sensation was at once mildly frightening and highly pleasurable. It made her want more.

The undressing resumed. On his knees after removing Rachel's pantyhose, Sam wrapped his arms around her hips and kissed her belly and thighs. For Rachel, the feeling of breathlessness became acute, causing her to tremble once more in anticipation. Rising, Sam got out of the rest of his clothing. As they held each other tightly again, kissing urgently, Rachel could feel the physical response she had aroused in Sam, and she delighted in this evidence of her power. By being, she had created something from almost nothing.

Sam separated himself from her.

Rachel raised her arms to release the catch on her necklace.

"Wear the pearls," he said.

Then he scooped her up. He carried her through the darkness, turning sideways once to negotiate a doorway. With her arms around his neck, Rachel kissed him lovingly along the way. Halting, he put her down on a bed and joined her. Side by side and facing, they tangled themselves together, arms and legs, kissing bruisingly.

After a while they broke from the harsh kissing and rested, remaining twined together. Rachel moved her hands leisurely across the broadness of Sam's back. Gently, he kissed her face, her throat, her shoulders. Drawing away a bit, he kissed her breasts. Rachel bent her back, pressing a breast to his mouth. Then he was sliding downward in the bed, kissing her belly again, kissing her thighs. Along with the excitement, she felt a warm snugness, a sense of being safe.

As Sam crept upward, he lingered again at her belly and at her breasts. When they were mouth to mouth and kissing again, she discovered that his hardness had gone. Using her power, transmitting it through her touch, she brought it back. Then, taking Sam with her, she eased over onto her back.

Crouched over her, he kissed her face again and her hair. She maneuvered the hardness to the opening. Gently, gently, gently, with soft probings, he entered her.

They lay still, celebrating the joining, kissing lightly. The hardness inside Rachel pulsed. Slowly, Sam pulled back, then eased forward. The retreat and thrust were performed again. Rachel responded to the rhythm that he had set. As the easy, slow-motion movement continued, they kissed again and again, briefly and delicately.

The euphoria came gradually. There was first a tingling, as if an anesthetic were taking effect. Rachel tensed slightly. Sam's thrusts and her responses became a bit more rapid. Then she relaxed again and a feeling of sweet dreaminess came over her. By small degrees the sweetness increased, building. She felt a pleasant numbness and heard herself making quiet straining sounds.

Then Sam was driving against her. Sam's hardness was like a large knob. He was thrusting at her fiercely. An odd thought passed through her mind: He was busting Hog Waters' head. She no longer had the rhythm. A sudden spasm of ecstasy gripped her and held her, stiffening her body. The ecstasy spread, as if a floodgate had ruptured, inundating her with a lovely, warm languor. Sam flattened himself against her, pushing, groaning. As Rachel had, he stiffened. The hardness inside her expanded. Then they were kissing again, wildly, savagely.

The kisses became lazy, gentle nibbles. The hardness inside Rachel had softened; what she had given, she had taken away. She became more conscious of Sam's weight. But it was no burden. She wanted him on top of her, covering her. She wanted to keep him inside her, even though he was now soft. She did not want the coupling to be broken; it made them one. As they kissed, she caressed him lovingly.

Eventually, Sam withdrew. He lay on his back, with his arm around Rachel, holding her against him. She kissed his chest and his face and rested one of her legs between his thighs to keep as much body contact with him as possible. She wished that she could see his face; she wanted to be certain that he was happy and satisfied. Surely, he was, though; he was still holding her. When Paul was done with her, he always left her, or, at the least, separated himself from her.

She kissed his chest again. "Sam, I love you."

He murmured drowsily.

"Did you hear me?"

Another murmur.

"You're not asleep, are you?"

"Uuh-uuh," he said.

"I'm not imagining this, am I?"

"Uuh-uuh."

"I didn't imagine that boy with the white shoes either, did I? Joey saw him, too."

"Don't bank too much on that," Sam said faintly. "Joey likes to be agreeable—with everybody but Chris."

"You mean he'd *say* he saw the boy even if he didn't?"

"He might."

"Damn!"

Sam tightened his hold on her for a second. "Don't worry about it. . . ."

She rested her head on his chest. It didn't really matter much to her at the moment whether Joey had seen the boy in the white shoes. What was important was that she now had Sam. She wouldn't ever be afraid again. Sam loved her and believed in her, and Sam was strong. They would share his strength. They would share his belief in her, too. She wouldn't ever doubt herself again.

"I love this bed," she said.

No answer.

"Sam. . . ."

He was asleep.

Rachel hugged him and snuggled closer to his warmth. She would let him sleep for a while. Then she would wake him, and maybe they would make love again before she left. If only she could stay. But that was out of the question. She had to be at the house when B.J. and Holly got up to go to school. They would probably call the police and report her missing if she weren't there. It would be funny, in a way, if that happened and headquarters called Sam to direct the search for her. He wouldn't have to look very far.

She wished she knew what time it was. It was probably early, no later than midnight or so. . . .

Rachel was awakened by a gruff voice and a rough touch on her bare shoulder. She thought at first that Sam was waking her. Then she realized that Sam was still beside her and not moving. Looking up, she saw that there was now a dim light in the room, coming in through the open doorway, and that a dark shape was standing beside the bed.

"Mrs. Barthelme. . . ." The voice was gravelly.

"Who—"

"I'm Frank Shea. I live here. I don't know what you want to do, but I thought I better tell you. Your husband called in a couple hours ago, and we've got a missing persons out on you."

Rachel sat up. "My husband? Paul? He's in Paris."

"I don't know about that," Shea said. "But he called in, saying you're missing."

Rachel became aware of her nakedness. She yanked at the cover that she and Sam were lying on, pulling a corner of it over her.

"How did you know I was here?" she asked Shea. "Does Paul know?"

"Take it easy. He don't know. I saw your car outside when I got home," he told her. "I said, 'What the hell, what's going on?' Then I came in and saw the clothes all over the front room. I put two and two together."

Rachel shook Sam. "Sam! Wake up!"

There was no reaction from him.

"Forget it," Shea said. "When he konks out, he's dead. It's

that gin. He can carry it as long as he's on his feet, but put him down and he's out."

She shook Sam again. "Sam! Sam!"

"You're wasting your time," Shea said.

"What am I going to do?"

"Stay here or go home."

"I've got to go home."

"You want me to get your clothes?"

"Yes, will you, please?"

He left the room.

Rachel got a hold on Sam's hair and shook his head, angrily demanding that he wake up. The shaking had absolutely no effect. Except that he was breathing, he truly seemed to be dead.

Frank Shea returned and dropped Rachel's clothes on the bed.

"Thank you," she said. "Do you know what time it is?"

"About five."

"Good Lord!"

"I'll call in and tell them you're not missing," Shea said, going toward the doorway.

"Wait— What will they do? Will they tell Paul?"

"I'll fix it," Shea said.

When he had gone, Rachel got quickly out of bed. She covered Sam, then began to dress. As she was putting on her skirt, she heard Frank Shea talking on the phone. She could not hear what he was saying, but he sounded amused. To Rachel, there was nothing humorous about it. Now the whole police department would know that she had slept with Sam. It would be something she would have to live down after they were married.

Dressed, she left the bedroom. The front room was small and haphazardly furnished. Sam's clothes were still on the floor. Her coat and purse were on the couch. Frank Shea was seated in one overstuffed chair, holding a beer, with his feet up on the arm of another overstuffed chair. He was a big, beefy man, and he broke out in a broad grin as Rachel appeared.

"You're all set," he told her. "If they don't hear from him, they'll call out to your house in about an hour and ask him if you've showed up yet. So you can tell him any story you want—we haven't seen you—right?"

"Thank you." She began picking up Sam's clothes. "I feel silly as hell," she said.

"Forget it."

"Does Sam pass out like that a lot?" she asked.

He shrugged.

Having put Sam's clothes on the couch, she picked up her coat and began getting into it. "This is a crazy way to meet," she said. "But nice to meet you."

He gestured offhandedly with the beer can. "See you again."

"Thank you for waking me."

" 'S okay."

Rachel left the house and, shivering in the cold, got into the car and set out for Catawba. When the engine warmed up, she turned on the heater, and soon she was comfortable again. The sky was brightening; it would be light by the time she reached the house. Paul would be waiting, furious, no doubt. Well, let him be furious. She wasn't afraid. She had Sam.

Fourteen

THERE were lights on all over, Rachel saw, as she approached the house. That probably meant that B.J. and Holly—and maybe even Mrs. Woolsey—were up and waiting, too. It was understandable; they were undoubtedly worried about her, having no idea where she was. But it would make it difficult. She could hardly tell Paul about Sam in front of the children and Mrs. Woolsey. She would have to be evasive until she could talk to him in private.

Rachel parked the Eldorado in the drive. As she got out, the door of the house opened and Paul appeared, then B.J. and Holly. Paul started down the steps, while B.J. and Holly stopped on the porch. By then Mrs. Woolsey had appeared, standing in the doorway. Rachel took in a deep breath to brace herself, then closed the car door and moved on to meet Paul.

"Are you all right?" he asked her worriedly.

She answered calmly. "Yes, I'm all right."

"Where have you been?"

They walked toward the porch together.

"I'm fine," she said. "Nothing has happened to me. I had dinner with a friend, that's all."

"Who?" He was angry now. "Who in hell did you have dinner with until six o'clock in the morning?"

"Are you okay, Mom?" Holly asked as Rachel and Paul ascended the steps.

"I'm fine, dear. Why aren't you in bed? Do you realize what time it is?"

"For Christ's sake!" Paul erupted. "What the hell did you expect? We've got the cops out looking for you! We didn't know where the hell you were!"

"Paul, stop yelling," Rachel said. "I'm home, and I'm all right. And if you have the police looking for me, you'd better call them off." She addressed Mrs. Woolsey. "I told you I was going to have dinner with a friend."

"It's six o'clock in the morning!" Paul said, furious.

They straggled through the entryway into the foyer.

"Good night," Mrs. Woolsey said, heading for the stairs. "All's well that ends well."

"Children, you'd better get to bed, too," Rachel said to B.J. and Holly as she got out of her coat.

"It's time to get up," B.J. said.

Mrs. Woolsey stopped at the foot of the stairs. "Lord, it is," she said. She detoured, going now to the hallway that led to the kitchen. "No rest for the weary."

"Have breakfast; *then* go to bed," Rachel said to B.J. and Holly. "You can skip school today. You wouldn't be any good, anyway, if you've been up all night."

"I've *got* to go," Holly said. "There's play rehearsal after."

"You didn't tell me you were in a play," Rachel said, surprised.

"Yes, I did."

"Oh. Well. . . . All right, go if you want to."

Holly and B.J. left for the kitchen.

"All right, you got rid of them," Paul said angrily. "Now, what the hell is going on?"

Rachel walked toward the sitting room. "If you'll calm down, I'll tell you," she said. She dropped her coat and purse on a chair. "Aren't you going to call the police?"

"The hell with the goddamn police."

Rachel sat down on a couch. "I went in to buy some paintings today," she told him. "While I was looking through them, I found this painting with these masks in it. The *same masks* that those children were wearing the night of the accident."

"Oh, Christ, not that again," Paul said disgustedly.

"Paul, I don't care what you think, they *are* the same masks."

He went to the phone and picked up the receiver and dialed. "I should have guessed it was something like this," he said to Rachel, waiting. Then he spoke into the receiver. "This is Paul Barthelme. I called earlier about my wife. It's all right. She's home." A pause. "Yes." Another pause. "No, she's all right. Thank you." Another pause. "Yes, thank you." He hung up. "Are you going to tell me now what you've been doing out until six o'clock in the morning?" he asked Rachel.

"I'm telling you. I saw the masks, and I called Lieutenant Lomax."

"Who's— Oh, yeah, that one."

"I was upset," Rachel went on. "We went for a drink. Then, it was time for him to be off duty, and I didn't have anything to do, so we went to dinner."

"Okay. Then what?"

"Well, we went to another place, a sort of bar. There was

another policeman there, and he's seen the boy with the white shoes . . . he thinks. . . ."

"He thinks," Paul said, nodding. "Did it take him until six in the morning to think it?"

"No. We went to Sam's house."

"Sam? Who's he? How did he get into this?"

"Lieutenant Lomax. Sam Lomax."

"You went to his house. With who, the other cop? Why? You're not making any sense. Why in hell did you go to his house?"

"To be together."

He stared at her. "Oh. Oh-ho. You're shacking up with this cop, is that what you're telling me?"

"No. Yes, we did sleep together. But it's not shacking up. We're in love."

Paul sat down in the chair beside the telephone table. He stared at her again. "Jesus, Rachel. I'm sorry," he said contritely. "I didn't realize how bad off you are."

"I don't understand what you mean."

"Are you blaming me, is that what this is all about?" he said. "Are you trying to punish me, jumping in bed with some cop?"

"Paul, it has nothing to do with you. I'm in love with Sam."

"Oh, crap! Rachel, I'm going to be the president of one of the top five hundred companies in the country, and you're trying to tell me that you're in love with a cop? Jesus!" He got up. "Look, I talked to Dr. Edwards. After Holly told me what was going on here, I called him from Paris. I know you've got problems. I just didn't realize how bad it is. But that's all right. He can help you. It will take time, but he'll get you out of it."

"I don't need help," she protested. "I've been upset, yes. But I'm all right now."

"Oh, you are? One jump in the hay and, just like that"— he snapped his fingers— "you're cured? That cop ought to bottle that stuff."

"Stop that! You're trying to make something dirty out of something that's very important to me."

"It's important to you because you don't know what the hell important is," he told her. "You've got everything all screwed up. You don't know what's real. That's not just what I think. That's what the doctor told me."

"He had no right to tell you anything!"

"You told him he could, didn't you? That's what he told me. He said you said it was okay to tell me."

"Yes!" she shouted. "I don't care *what* you know—or what you think! You're wrong! And he's wrong! I'm *not* sick!"

"What do you call it then?" Paul asked her. "Imagination? Visions? You can call it hay fever, for Christ's sake, for all I care! But get it treated!"

"I am not sick!" she shrieked at him, standing.

"What do you call it when you see people and they're not there?" he shouted back at her. "Hell, people? You see shoes!"

"They're real!"

"Okay, they're real. What about waking Mrs. Woolsey up in the middle of the night and making her get the scissors out of the nursery? Is that normal?"

"That was that damn doctor's fault," Rachel told him. "He told me about some girl who can't have knives around. It was just the power of suggestion."

"Oh, brother! Do you do everything everybody mentions? Who told you to leave that pot on the stove and damn near burn down the house? Who told you to go out whoring? Do you hear voices? Is that where you get your ideas?"

"It wasn't whoring! I'm in love with him! He's in love with me!"

"How the hell long has this been going on, you and that cop?"

"It hasn't been going on."

"Just tonight, this is the first time?"

"Yes."

"And you tell me you're not sick? You go out *once* with some two-bit cop and hop in bed with him and then come home and tell me you're in love with him—and you tell me you're not *sick?"*

Rachel sat down. "It's not like that," she said. "I *do* love him. And he loves me. I don't want to go on with this dead thing we have, Paul, this marriage. I'm turning into a lump. But when I'm with Sam, I'm alive. He's what I need. He's kind and gentle and he cares."

"Yeah, he's got a big heart," Paul said sourly. "He found a pushover, and he pushed. What else does he do for kicks, mug cripples?"

"Shut up!" she screeched.

Paul raised his hands in a sign of truce. "Okay, okay—forget him," he said, going to the bar. "I don't care about that damn cop. I don't care what you did with him either—you're not responsible for what you do. But I want an end to it. You've got us all climbing the walls, me, the kids," he said, pouring from a decanter of scotch. "Stop telling us there's nothing wrong. Face it; take the cure; get yourself straightened out."

"I'm not going back to that doctor."

"Yes, you are. I'll call him in the morning and get you another appointment." He turned from the bar. "Look at this," he said, raising his glass. "Six o'clock in the morning—it's almost seven now—and I'm drinking. I didn't want a drink. I don't know what I'm doing, you've got us so screwed up around here. For Christ's sake, enough is enough."

"That doctor doesn't care," Rachel said. "All he's interested in is making me fit somebody else's case history."

"According to you, nobody cares. If I didn't care, would I be sending you to a doctor? I'd kick your ass out in the snow." He glanced toward the windows. "If it was snowing. . . ."

"I'm not going to that doctor."

"You're going."

She rose and walked toward the doorway.

"Think about it, Rachel," he said. It was a threat.

She went on, not answering.

As Rachel reached the foyer, she heard hurried footfalls on the stairs, but when she looked up, no one was there. She guessed that B.J. or Holly—or both—had been standing on the stairs, eavesdropping. That had hardly been necessary, though, with all the shouting that she and Paul had been doing. The children—and Mrs. Woolsey—had probably heard everything. And no doubt, they agreed with Paul that she was not responsible and that Sam had used her. How could they think otherwise? They didn't know Sam the way she knew him. They couldn't know how much she and Sam loved each other. They only knew the facts; they didn't know the truth.

Fifteen

WHEN Rachel reached the bedroom, she went on into the bathroom to shower. She stayed under the spray longer than usual, idly recalling moments from the evening with Sam and reexperiencing the pleasures. When she emerged from the shower, she heard sounds of movement from the bedroom and guessed that Paul was there. He was gone, though, when she left the bathroom. As she dressed, she heard a car leaving. Fine. She had hoped that he would be gone when Sam called.

B.J. and Holly departed a few minutes later in B.J.'s car. Rachel decided to have breakfast. As she left the bedroom and walked toward the stairs, she heard Mrs. Woolsey talking chattily with the baby in the nursery. But she didn't stop. She supposed that Mrs. Woolsey was thinking disapproving thoughts about her, and she wasn't yet ready to face that. First, she had to talk to Sam. She needed that reassurance. Then, with his strength to support her, she would be able to contend with anything: Paul's cynicism, Mrs. Woolsey's disapproval, even B.J.'s and Holly's disappointment.

She failed to evade Mrs. Woolsey, however. As Rachel was sitting at the breakfast table a short while later finishing a grapefruit half, the woman came waddling into the kitchen with the baby. She said nothing to Rachel. Carrying the baby, she got a bottle from the refrigerator and put it into the warmer, then, with one hand, began loading the dishwasher with her own and the children's breakfast dishes.

"I'll be out of your way in a second," Rachel said.

"No bother." Her tone was punitive.

"Do you want me to take the baby while you do that?"

"I'll keep her."

Taking her mug of coffee with her, Rachel left the kitchen and walked toward the sitting room. She was annoyed by Mrs. Woolsey's attitude but not angry. It didn't really matter what the woman thought or how she acted. Before very long, Rachel would be out of this house. She and Sam were in love, and they were the kind of people who took love seriously. In time, after the details were worked out, they would be married.

Rachel marveled at how well things were working out. A few days earlier she had been about as low as it was possible to get. Now all was bright; she was soaring. She would be able to give the baby the years of caring she owed her, and they would be happy years, because she would have Sam. All the suffering over the past few weeks had been worthwhile; it had earned her this reward, happiness at last.

In the sitting room she found that the Sunday *Times* had been delivered. Its sections were in various places in the room. She saw that a piece had been torn out of the front page. Eventually she located the magazine section on the bar. She opened it to the crossword puzzle and sat down with it in the chair beside the telephone table. Working on the puzzle, she waited for Sam's call.

Or he might drive to the house to get her, she thought. Like a knight rescuing his lady. She couldn't leave with him yet, though. First, she had to settle things with Paul. And explain the leaving to B.J. and Holly. She would still be seeing them, she would tell. She would have to make sure, too, that they understood that they were in no way to blame for the breakup. She didn't want them to have guilt feelings about it.

Why didn't Sam call?

Could he still be unconscious? She remembered Frank Shea's words: *When he konks out, he's dead.* Well, some people were like that probably. It was only a minor flaw. She couldn't expect him to be perfect. He always knew what he was doing as long as he was still on his feet, Shea had said. He hadn't seemed at all drunk. Surely he hadn't forgotten everything that had happened; that wasn't why he hadn't called yet. No, that wasn't possible. He was probably waiting until he could get a few minutes off to drive out to the house. He wanted to see her, not just talk to her on the phone.

Rachel put the puzzle down and got up and went to the windows and peered out along the private road, hoping to see Sam's car approaching. There was nothing on the road. She continued to watch for a while, then became restless. As she turned from the windows, her attention was caught by a wadded-up piece of paper at the bottom of the otherwise empty wicker wastebasket at the end of the bar. She started to move on, then remembered the hole in the front page of the *Times.*

Curious, she got the wad of paper from the basket and, walking back toward the chair, unfolded it. It was the missing piece from the *Times,* as she had suspected. It was a story about a man on Long Island, an ex-mental patient, who had set fire to his house. His wife and four children had died in the fire. For a moment Rachel was puzzled, wondering why the story had been torn from the paper. Then she remembered Paul's comment: *Who told you to leave that pot on the stove and damn near burn down the house?* She recalled something else that he had said: *You're not responsible for what you do.*

That was terrible! Did he really believe that she would burn the house down? No, not deliberately. But he did believe, evidently, that she was so far gone that she might do it without knowing what she was doing. She looked at the hole in the newspaper's front page. It had jagged edges. That wasn't Paul's way of tearing. He always used a pair of scissors or a ruler as an edge, leaving a neat hole. Apparently, B.J. or Holly had removed the story from the *Times.* Because they were afraid that it might give her an idea? Lord! The situation was worse than she had guessed. Her children were afraid of her.

Shattered by the thought, Rachel dropped into the chair. How could her children possibly believe that about her? After all these years, didn't they know her better than that? But she was a stranger to them these days, the doctor had told her. Or had he told her that? Maybe she had said it to herself in one of her imaginary debates with him. It was so hard to remember what was real and what was— No, she couldn't let herself start thinking like that, believing along with the rest of them that she couldn't distinguish reality from fantasy.

The phone rang.

Rachel snatched up the receiver. But it was Paul's secretary calling to tell her that an emergency appointment with Dr. Blalock Edwards had been arranged for her for the next day. Coolly, Rachel asked the secretary to transfer the call to Paul, intending to inform him—again and for the final time—that she would not go back to the doctor. Once more, however, Paul managed to frustrate her. He was on his way to New York for a business meeting, the secretary told her. Rachel slammed the phone down.

She seethed. Paul couldn't make her go back to the doctor. What could he do to her if she didn't? Kick her out in the snow, he had said. But he hadn't meant that. Even if he had, he couldn't do it. She wouldn't be around for him to kick out into the snow; she would be with Sam. Surely Sam was awake and up by now—it was close to noon. Maybe he had the day off and had decided to sleep late. Maybe he was waiting for her to call him. Of course!

She got the telephone book from the lower shelf of the table. There was no listing for Sam Lomax. And no listing for Frank Shea. They had a private number, no doubt. She wouldn't be able to get it from the telephone operator. By now Sam was probably at headquarters anyway. She dialed the number and, when an officer answered, asked for Lieutenant

Lomax. The officer asked her to hold. There was a buzzing.

MALE VOICE: Lieutenant Lomax's phone.
RACHEL: The lieutenant, please.
VOICE: He's tied up, ma'am. Want to leave a message?
RACHEL: Will you tell him it's Rachel, please? He wants to talk to me.
VOICE: Minute.

Rachel felt a nervous excitement. She was right; Sam *had* been waiting for her to call him. He probably thought it might be awkward if he telephoned the house and Paul answered.

VOICE: Ma'am? The lieutenant's in a meeting, but he says to tell you he'll call you the first chance he gets.
RACHEL: The first chance he gets?
VOICE: Yeah, he'll call you.
RACHEL: Did you tell him it was me?
(pause)
VOICE: Yes, ma'am. He says he'll call you. He's in a meeting.

Rachel hung up. The nervous excitement had become an emptiness. He would call her the first chance he got. That sounded like a dismissal. Paul's words about Sam flashed across her mind: *He found a pushover, and he pushed.* Immediately, she rejected the thought. Sam wasn't like that. No one could pretend the kind of caring and kindness that he had showed; it was real. Or had she imagined it—because she wanted it so much—the same way that she had imagined the white shoes and— God! She was doing it again, thinking like that damn psychiatrist!

She scolded herself for having attributed so much importance to what had probably been a casual statement. More than likely, Sam was in a meeting with a superior. He couldn't get up and walk out on it simply because she had happened to call at that moment. He had to be offhand about it, telling the young officer to tell her that he would call her back when he got a chance. It didn't mean that he wasn't anxious to talk to her. He would call soon, the instant the meeting ended.

Rachel tried to concentrate on the puzzle, but she was distracted by sounds from the foyer. Looking up, she saw Mrs. Woolsey go by the doorway pushing the carriage. Rachel rose and went to the windows. After a few moments she saw Mrs. Woolsey and the carriage emerge from the house. Mrs. Woolsey was now wearing a heavy coat and large furry mittens. Rachel watched her maneuver the carriage down the steps, then lost sight of her when she turned the corner of the house, going toward the rear. Apparently she was taking the baby to the woods for the airing.

Rachel walked back to the phone table and made sure that the phone was resting snugly in the cradle, then sat down and picked up the puzzle. She was unable to keep her mind on it, though; eventually she discovered that she had drifted off into a kind of trance and was staring blankly into space. Again, she put the puzzle aside. A watched pot never boils, Mrs. Woolsey would say. She ought to do something while she waited for Sam to call. But she *had* been doing something— working on the puzzle—and it hadn't done a thing to set the pot boiling.

Rachel returned to the windows. A few feathery snowflakes were falling. But they seemed to be strays rather than harbingers. They reminded her, even so, that Christmas was only weeks away. She ought to order cards. She wouldn't feel right about sending out family cards with the family breaking up, though. Skip cards this year. Or let Paul worry about it. That was best; let Paul handle it; his secretary could do it.

The phone rang.

Rachel ran to the table and picked up the receiver.

RACHEL: Hello.
GIRL'S VOICE (shrieking): You killed my brother! Murder!

A click and the dial tone.
Stunned, Rachel stood frozen, with the receiver still to her

ear. She heard the shriek again in her mind, then again and again, reverberating. It was as if she were reliving that moment from the night of the accident. At last, the shock began to ebb.

"I didn't mean it!" Rachel shouted into the phone.

The dial tone continued.

Frantically, Rachel tried to fit the phone back into the cradle, afraid that she would hear the shriek again. It slipped from her grasp and went skittering across the table and over the edge. Retrieving it, she slapped it into the cradle, then fled from the phone table, going toward the windows, seeking the brightest light. In her mind she heard the scream again. There was something distinctive about the girl's voice. The raspiness! Jewel Brill!

Jewel and Kirk! They were two of them. They were after her!

The phone rang again.

"It was an accident!" Rachel screeched across the room at it.

It rang again.

She looked around wildly for something to throw at it.

It rang again.

Rachel suddenly realized that this time it might be Sam calling. Leaving the windows, she approached the phone cautiously. It continued to ring. She had to answer it—it *might* be Sam. But what if it was the girl again? She would tell her she knew who she was. That would stop her.

Rachel lifted the receiver. She listened.

SAM: Hello?

RACHEL: Sam! Thank God, it's you! That girl called! Just a minute ago. She screamed at me—the same way—about killing her brother. Sam, I know who she is! Her name is Jewel Brill. She's a friend of Holly's.

SAM: Wait a minute. Hold it. Easy. Give it to me slowly. What happened?

RACHEL: I was waiting for you to call and the phone rang

and I picked it up and she screamed at me. She said I murdered her brother. Then she hung up.

SAM: What's this about her being a friend of your daughter's?

RACHEL: I recognized her voice. It's throaty.

SAM: Why didn't you recognize her voice that night of the accident?

RACHEL: I didn't know her then. She didn't become Holly's friend until after that. She's after me! Her and Kirk Franklin. He was one of them, too. I remember his eyes.

(silence)

RACHEL: Sam, believe me!

SAM: You haven't ever said anything before about that girl that night having a throaty voice.

RACHEL: I just remembered, just a couple minutes ago, when I heard her scream at me again. Sam, I'm *not* making it up!

(silence)

RACHEL: Please! Please believe me!

SAM: Take it easy. I'm thinking. What's her name again?

RACHEL: Jewel Brill. She's in school with Holly.

SAM: All right, I'll check it out. But, Rachel, don't say anything about this to anybody. Not about Kirk Franklin either. Let me do some checking first.

RACHEL: Sam, she's here in the house all the time. So is Kirk.

SAM: It's a big house, stay away from them. How are things otherwise?

RACHEL: All right— Oh! Did Frank Shea tell you what happened?

SAM: Yes. I'm sorry you couldn't wake me up. I get that way. Was it rough when you got home?

RACHEL: Well . . . yes and no. . . . I told Paul about us. He doesn't care. I should have told you, I guess . . . our marriage hasn't been anything for a long time.

SAM: I figured that out.

RACHEL: What are we going to do?

SAM: If he doesn't care, it's no problem, is it?

RACHEL: No, I mean what do we do now?

SAM: We'll talk about it. I can't right now, I've got a meeting in the works. I took a break to call you. I'll check on that girl. Keep your head, Rachel. That's the most important thing to do right now. Okay?

RACHEL: Yes. But I need to know what we're going to do. Everything is up in the air.

SAM: It'll work out. Everything does. My men are back, I've got to go now. I'll call you. Take it easy.

RACHEL: I'm trying. Sam, I love you.

SAM: Okay. I'll talk to you.

The line went dead.

Rachel hung up, feeling dissatisfied. He could at least have told her that he loved her. He probably couldn't say it because of his men being there. The whole conversation had been a disappointment. They hadn't talked like lovers; they had talked like a woman calling a policeman and a policeman answering. It was that girl's fault. Rachel's mind, when Sam called, had been on the earlier call from the girl, not on what she wanted to say to him and what she wanted him to say to her.

Well, he would be calling back soon. Then they would get things straightened out.

Rachel heard sounds from the foyer. Mrs. Woolsey and the carriage passed by the sitting-room doorway. Mrs. Woolsey did not look in; apparently she was still punishing Rachel. To hell with her. Rachel would be free of Mrs. Woolsey and her righteousness soon—if everything worked out right. Now why had she added that? Of course things would work out right. She was worrying about little things again—the fact that Sam had been so businesslike on the phone. She had to stop that.

She retrieved the crossword puzzle. After only a few moments, though, Dr. Blalock Edwards intruded:

* * *

EDWARDS: It took at the most three or four seconds for that girl to scream at you, yet you were able to identify her voice?

RACHEL: Jewel has a different kind of voice. I've heard her talking. I know her voice when I hear it.

EDWARDS: How many times have you heard her scream?

RACHEL: What difference does that make? Her voice is her voice.

EDWARDS: Is it? Does a voice sound exactly the same when it's screaming as when it's being used in normal conversation? If it isn't exactly the same, is it enough the same over a period of three or four seconds to make a positive identification?

RACHEL: The voice I heard was her!

EDWARDS: Let's assume that it was. Where did the voice come from, though? Over the phone? Or out of your mind?

RACHEL: Out of my mind? What does that mean?

EDWARDS: Let's say that the phone rang—which it did. You picked it up and you spoke. Now let's say that at that point the person who was on the line—hearing your voice—realized that he had dialed a wrong number. He immediately—as some people do—hung up.

RACHEL: That's ridiculous.

EDWARDS: Hasn't that ever happened to you? The phone rings; you answer it; there's a moment of silence; then the other person hangs up.

RACHEL: Yes, of course it's happened. But it didn't happen this time. I heard her scream.

EDWARDS: I don't doubt that. The question, however, remains: Where did the scream come from? From the phone or from somewhere in your mind? As the lieutenant pointed out, you made no mention of the girl's distinctive voice quality when you first told your story.

RACHEL: I just didn't remember until I heard her scream that at me again.

EDWARDS: Yes. You didn't remember the white shoes at first either—until you needed something to firm up your story. Perhaps you think it needs firming up again.

RACHEL: You're an idiot. I don't think that way.

EDWARDS: Not even subconsciously?
RACHEL: No.
EDWARDS: I'd be interested in knowing how you can be so certain about that.
RACHEL: Ask your textbook.

She ended the argument with that, counting herself the winner, by leaving the sitting room and going to the kitchen. There she began busily preparing a lunch for herself, wanting to finish before Mrs. Woolsey appeared, seeing no point in subjecting herself needlessly to the woman's unspoken recrimination. As she was pouring a glass of milk, however, she heard the sound of plodding footfalls coming from the hallway, announcing Mrs. Woolsey's approach. Quickly, she collected the elements of the lunch—sandwich, fruit salad and milk—and fled by way of the back stairs.

When Rachel reached the second floor, she crossed to the front stairs and descended and returned to the sitting room. After placing her lunch on the low table in front of a couch, she closed the heavy sitting-room doors, shutting herself in— or shutting Mrs. Woolsey out. With the doors closed the room was nearly soundproof. Consequently, since the phone did not ring, she passed the early part of the afternoon in monastic solitude and silence.

Eventually the quiet was interrupted by the sound of B.J.'s car arriving. When it had passed the house, going to the rear, Rachel went to the bay window and waited. Soon B.J. appeared, accompanied by Kirk Franklin and Jewel Brill. Rachel wondered why Holly wasn't with them, then remembered that her daughter had mentioned that she was involved in some way in a play at school. Rachel watched B.J. and Kirk and Jewel until they entered the house, then she went back to the club chair by the telephone table.

A few moments later the big sitting-room doors parted, sliding quietly along their tracks. B.J. appeared in the opening. Kirk and Jewel were standing a few steps behind him in the dimness of the foyer. B.J.'s expression was inquiring in a concerned but amicable way.

"Are you all right?" he asked.

"Do I look all right?"

"I guess. Mrs. Woolsey was wondering. She says she hasn't heard anything in here all afternoon."

"Why didn't she come in and find out?"

"I don't know."

"You can tell her it's safe. Sin isn't catching," Rachel said.

"She was worried."

Rachel looked past him. Kirk and Jewel were smiling softly and secretively in the dimness, smirking. They knew about her, no doubt. Rachel wanted to shout at Jewel that she knew about her, too, knew that she was the one who had made the phone call. But with effort, she maintained control, obeying Sam's order to keep what she knew to herself.

"Well, if you're all right," B.J. said, retreating a step.

"B.J., please stop asking me if I'm all right," Rachel said tightly.

"Okay."

"How is Holly going to get home?"

"I'm going back and pick her up in a couple of hours," he replied. "Do you want me to leave these doors open?"

She picked up a letter opener from the table. "Here's a sharp object. Don't you think you ought to remove it, too?"

"What do you mean?" he said. But his expression told her that he knew what she meant.

"Oh, Christ!—never mind." She glared past him at Kirk and Jewel, then looked away, dismissing them all.

When she looked back a few seconds later they were gone.

B.J. had left the doors open.

It was after ten that night when Sam finally called back. Rachel was still in the sitting room, curled up in the chair beside the telephone table, with only a single lamp on.

SAM: I can only talk a minute. I'm outside. But I wanted to let you know about that Brill girl.

RACHEL: What do you mean, you're outside?

SAM: I'm not at headquarters.

RACHEL: Oh. Where are you?

SAM: Out on a job. About the girl. I don't know a lot about her yet, but there's one thing: She doesn't have a brother. She's never had a brother. She has a sister, but she's older.

RACHEL: But that's what she screamed at me: "You killed my brother!"

SAM: She doesn't have a brother.

RACHEL: Sam, I know her voice! It was her!

SAM: Hold it—I didn't say it wasn't her. She's close to your daughter, isn't that what you told me? Your daughter probably told her what you say that girl yelled at you that night. Maybe she decided to have some fun with it—if that's fun—and called you and yelled it at you.

RACHEL: No! It was *her* that night! I know!

SAM: Then she must have rented a brother for the night. She doesn't own one of her own.

RACHEL: I don't know. . . .

SAM: Have you had any trouble with her? Would she make that phone call, do you think, to get back at you?

RACHEL: No . . . no trouble. . . .

SAM: All right. Don't quit. I haven't dropped it. I thought you ought to know about the brother business, though. Hang on, Rachel. Nothing is finished until it's done. I know, that sounds stupid, but you know what I mean.

RACHEL: Can I meet you somewhere?

SAM: I'm on a job.

RACHEL: When am I going to see you?

SAM: Just as soon as I get out from under. This is one of those times; I'm getting everything at once. It hasn't been that long since you saw me, you know. It was only last night.

RACHEL: I don't mean *see* you, I mean talk to you.

SAM: I've got to go now. Stick in there.

RACHEL: Sam—

The tone.

Rachel put down the phone and curled up again in the chair. She remembered a statement that Sam had made that had bothered her. *You probably told your daughter what you say that girl yelled at you that night.* What *you say* that girl yelled at you, he had said. His belief in her was faltering. He was starting to doubt that there actually was a girl there that night. He was beginning to think what the others already thought: that she had made it all up.

He certainly had good reason to doubt. Why *would* Jewel stand there in the road in the rain, holding the boy and screaming at Rachel that she had killed her brother, when she didn't have a brother? And if the girl wasn't Jewel, who was she, and how had she managed to disappear so completely, and where had the dead little boy gone?

No answers.

She ought to go to bed, Rachel thought. The tension that had built up during the day had almost totally exhausted her. She dragged herself up out of the chair, but the prospect of climbing the stairs defeated her. Instead of leaving the room, she went to the bay window. A hard rain was falling, and there were occasional gusts of wind. She peered out toward the woods, her vision dimmed by tiredness. Her eyes ached; her whole body ached. She was almost asleep on her feet—or maybe she *was* asleep; she wasn't sure.

There was a shimmering, silvery, liquidy movement at the edge of the woods as if a protoplasm were materializing. Rachel stared at it fixedly, assuming that it was an illusion. The image became gradually more distinct, coming closer. It now had a shape, several shapes. The silveriness had become white, glistening in the rain, marked with luminous colors. She was seeing the masks, she realized. They were floating across the space between the woods and the house, close together, as the children had been when she first saw them on the road.

She could see no bodies beneath the masks, and that confirmed to her that she had fallen asleep standing up and was

[189]

dreaming, although it occurred to her that the bodies might be there but hidden by the darkness and rain. Rachel was more interested in the overall scene than in particulars, however. The masks were approaching the house at a slow, measured step, as if the wearers could hear the music that set the pace for them, an accompaniment to a high mass for some martyred dead.

The masks reached the drive and moved on toward the porch. Even though she was convinced that she was dreaming, Rachel could not help being terrified. She was afraid that her dream was going to bring the children into the house and into the sitting room. There was nothing she could do to stop them. She could not end the dream; it was so real that she had no control over it. She could only hope that she would wake before the children reached her and fell upon her with the long, slender, clawlike fingers that she remembered.

The masks arrived at the steps and began the climb upward, and for a moment Rachel lost sight of them. Then they reappeared, on the porch, moving toward the door. Rachel could only watch, terror-stricken. Suddenly they stopped—as if they had become aware of Rachel—and the dirge in her mind stopped, too. One of the masks had turned toward Rachel and was facing her through the window. For a second there was a stalemate, Rachel staring horrified into the icy eyes behind the mask, the eyes staring chillingly at Rachel.

The masks turned away, retreating, moving back across the porch. When they started down the steps, Rachel lost sight of them once more. So fierce was her relief that it was like an electrical shock, leaving her limp. She closed her eyes and kept them closed for a long while, hoping that her tightly shut eyelids would pinch off the dream, severing it from her mind. When at last she opened her eyes, looking in the direction of the woods, she saw only the darkness and the rain.

She was fully awake again, too, she found. Evidently the closing of her eyes had accomplished what she hoped it would, ending the dream. Cautiously, she stepped closer to the window and looked out onto the porch. There was no sign that the children had been there, only the rain splattering on the porch—and on the steps a wet, clear plastic bag that she supposed had been blown there by the wind. So, obviously she had dreamed the masks.

Or hallucinated them.

Rachel decided that she would see the doctor once more. Maybe she hadn't been fair to him.

Sixteen

BECAUSE of unexpected heavy traffic on the expressway, Rachel arrived a few minutes late for the early-afternoon appointment with Dr. Blalock Edwards, so she was given immediate entrance into his operating room. The things that she remembered about him and his office—his plump pinkness, as if he had been fattened for market; the darkness and richness of the furnishings, with the touches of gold—at first made her apprehensive. But his manner had changed. Before he had been perfunctory, impatient. Now he seemed tranquil, open to dissent. It occurred to her that perhaps his attitude had changed because he felt that he had her trapped and could devour her at leisure. But even so, she welcomed the new manner. It relieved her of the obligation to fight with him.

"How did you decide that they were the same, what was the basis?" he asked after she had told him about the masks in the painting.

"I'm not sure that there was anything in particular. They looked the same, that's all. I knew it the instant I saw them."

"There were no specific distinguishing marks?"

"There might have been. I wasn't thinking about that."

"Yes, I see. Have you thought about it since?"

"No."

"Isn't that peculiar? I would think it would be important to you."

"Well, I've thought about it," she admitted. "I've thought about it the way I thought you would, asking myself questions. Did I decide that the masks were the same so I could stop looking for paintings for the house? Or was I just looking for an excuse to call Sam? Questions like that."

"Sam—he's the policeman your husband mentioned?"

She nodded.

"Those are two reasonable explanations," he said. "Either or both could be the answer. What's important, though, is that you worked it out yourself."

"I didn't. I was talking to you . . . I mean pretending. . . ."

"Using me," he said, nodding. "It was your subconscious you were talking to, though, not me. I wasn't questioning you; your subconscious *self* was questioning you. It detected some holes in your story, I assume." He began turning idly from side to side in the chair. "I'm puzzled by this incident with the policeman," he said. "It's not characteristic of you. You're a serious person. I find it difficult to see you in a casual sex situation. I wonder—"

"It isn't casual," Rachel protested. "I haven't known Sam a long time, that's true. But there was something between us right from the first. I sensed it and he sensed it."

"Did you— Both of you. Did you verbalize this sharing?"

"There wasn't any need for that. We felt it."

"Very possible," he said. "But what evidence do you have—other than what you feel—that he is as serious about the relationship as you are?"

"We're going to be married."

"Oh!" He leaned back. "That's been decided?"

"Not the details. We haven't had a chance to talk."

"I get the impression that he hasn't actually asked you to marry him."

"Men don't make formal proposals these days," she said. "Especially men like Sam. He's very easygoing about things. For instance, he doesn't date. He just meets somebody somewhere, and they go out. I didn't expect him to get down on one knee and say, 'Will you marry me?' He's not like that."

"I see. . . ." He resumed the pendulumlike swinging from side to side in the chair. "Have you been thinking about that incident on the road, the dead child, the explanation I suggested?"

"How could I help thinking about it? But something else has happened. The girl—the girl who screamed at me—she called me. Just yesterday. She screamed the same thing, that I killed her brother."

He looked surprised. "That's *very* interesting."

"And I know who she is. She's my daughter's friend. But she didn't become Holly's friend until *after* the accident. Do you see?"

"She isn't really interested in your daughter, she's after you, you mean?"

"Well?"

"Yes, that's possible," he said. "You couldn't have imagined the phone call, could you, the way you've been pretending to talk to me when I wasn't actually there?"

"No! It wasn't the same."

"Uh-huh. What else has happened?"

Rachel thought for a moment. "Nothing important, I guess. . . ."

"Your husband mentioned a pot that you left on the stove. It burned. . . ."

"That was nothing," she said. "It's like the bottle warmer. I kept leaving the bottle warmer turned on. They're making a big thing out of it. I'm not the first one who ever left a pot on the stove. I don't even think I did it. I think someone else turned the heat on under it after I left the kitchen. Holly's friend—I think she did it."

"Why?"

"She had the opportunity."

"Yes. What do you mean when you say they're making a big thing out of it?"

"Thinking I'm going to burn the house down." Rachel

looked away from him. "They're afraid of me," she said. Her voice was suddenly hoarse. "I don't know. Maybe I did leave the pot on. Did Paul tell you about the scissors?"

"Mmmm . . . in the nursery."

"You told me about that other woman, the one with post-partum depression, that's why that happened. It was the power of suggestion."

"Very possible."

"What makes it so hard is I'm not sure about anything anymore,"she told him, still not looking at him. Her voice was now little more than a whisper. "As I say, maybe—"

"I'm sorry, I can't hear you."

"I say, maybe I did leave the pot on and—"

"Mrs. Barthelme, I still can't hear you. Can you speak just a little louder, please?"

Rachel took in a deep breath and released it slowly. "Maybe I did leave the pot on," she said. "I *was* afraid of the scissors, I admit that. I don't know what I might have done. I don't think I would have hurt the baby . . . I don't see how I could . . . . But I don't know. That's what I mean when I say it's so difficult. I don't know *what* I might do."

"I understand."

"Am I crazy?" she asked him. She knew she had spoken the words, but oddly, she hadn't heard them.

"What is it?" he said. "You said something?"

"Am I crazy?"

"I'm sorry, try again, please. I know how difficult this is." He leaned forward. "Now . . . what is it?"

"Am I crazy?"

"Oh. . . ." He leaned back. "Well . . . insane, you mean. The word has so many meanings, depending on who is using it, I really don't know how to answer that. The important question is: Are you dysfunctional? That's the term I prefer."

Rachel looked at him baffledly.

"You are not, at this point, dysfunctional," he told her. "Our object is to see to it that you do not. *become* dysfunctional— agreed?"

[194]

She looked down again. "Yes."

"Before we can clean up the yard, though, we've got to get all the trash out from under the bushes," he said.

Once more Rachel raised her eyes to him.

"All that trash that's been collecting in your mind, back there in the far reaches. We've got to get it out where we can look at it, sift through it," he said. "I think we made a good start today. How do you feel about it?"

"I'm afraid."

"Of what?"

"I don't want to be crazy."

He turned the chair so that he was facing toward a side wall. "Being dysfunctional brings an image to your mind, apparently," he said. "What is it?"

"Terrible."

"What is the specific picture, though?"

"I don't know. . . . A white room, I guess . . . like a hospital room. I'm in a hospital gown. I look awful. My hair is wild. I'm like an animal. I want to get out."

"That's a common mistake," he said. "You're seeing yourself as functional—and trapped. But if you were functional, you wouldn't be in the institution, would you?" He faced her again. "It's something like the death situation," he said. "You see someone dead and you weep, thinking that death is terrible. Actually, though, you're weeping for yourself, not the dead person. You see *yourself* as dead—yet, at the same time, conscious of what is going on around you. The dead person, however, is *not* conscious. So, for the dead person, death isn't at all terrible. It's painless, physically and mentally. It's zero."

The explanation made Rachel feel uneasy. She looked at her watch.

"We have a minute," the doctor said. "I've done a lot of work in this area. I think you'll find it interesting." He indicated a gold-trimmed box on his desk. "Do you smoke?"

Rachel shook her head.

"The point is," he said, "the dysfunctional are, so to speak, like the dead. That is, they're not conscious of their condition, as we, the functional, see it. For instance, you see a mental patient—so called—wallowing around in her own filth, moaning, and your assumption is that she's in terrible agony. Not so, however. And why not?"

"How can she be anything else?"

"Because she's not *aware* of the filth—as filth," he told her. "If she were aware of it, conscious of the foulness, she would be functional, and—do you see?—she would not be there in the institution. She certainly would not be wallowing around in the filth."

"I understand," Rachel said.

"But you don't accept it. Neither, I'm sure, will you find it easy to accept the fact that our patient is really quite happy."

"She's mad and she's happy?"

"Yes. She has that world of her own into which she's withdrawn. It's a happy place—for her. It's the place she wants to be. In our world she was in constant anguish. The pressures got to her. Now—in her world, in her private world—she's found peace. Why shouldn't she be happy?"

Rachel picked up her purse.

"What I'm saying is this," the doctor went on. "There is no rational reason for you to fear dysfunction. I don't recommend it. But if you should happen to choose it for yourself—as opposed to remaining in this world—you can go to it with the knowledge that you will be happy there."

Rachel fidgeted. He was beginning to sound as if he were selling retirement property in Arizona.

"You're right, we are out of time," he said, rising. "In fact, we went over. I sometimes get carried away when I get started on dysfunction," he said, escorting her to the exit. He opened the door. "Next week."

Riding down in the elevator a few moments later and then waiting in the parking garage for the Eldorado to be brought around, Rachel puzzled over the session with the doctor. She had been prepared to do battle with him. But he had declined to fight. The first time, he had challenged everything she told him. This time, her every claim had been met with "very possible." His agreeableness hadn't been convincing, though. She had sensed all through the session that he was luring her into a trap.

He had certainly had a number of opportunities to spring a trap. Pressed, she would have had a hard time defending her assertions: that the masks that the children had been wearing and the masks in the painting were the same; that Sam wanted to marry her; that it was Jewel who had called her and screamed murder at her and that Jewel had turned on the heat under the pot; that it had been the power of suggestion that had caused her to fear the scissors. She had realized how vulnerable her claims were even while she was making them. Why hadn't he?

Ahh . . . the agreeableness, that *was* the trap. She had been in it all the time and hadn't known it. By not challenging her, he had kept her from becoming defensive. As a result, she had done the questioning herself—taking over his role—and had found her claims to be weak. She'd been had.

And had good. By his tactic, the tricky son of a bitch had almost had her believing that he was right about her, that she was a mental case. And that business about insanity being a kind of paradise. That was a lure, too. He wanted her to go quietly, willingly. He wasn't interested in determining whether she was sane or insane—he had already decided that—he was only interested in running her through the procedure with the least amount of bother to himself. Well, screw the bastard. She wasn't having any.

Seventeen

A COLD rain that looked as if it might become sleet was falling when Rachel left the parking garage. Even though it was still afternoon, the sky was dark. The turn in the weather added to her anger, and she drove belligerently in the city traffic, threatening jaywalkers with the Eldorado, as if she had been given a commission by the mayor to clear the streets. Because she had the windows tightly closed, she did not hear the curses that erupted in the car's wake, but she saw the cursers in the rearview mirror, mouthing and shaking their fists.

Because of the rain, movement was slow on the expressway. When the progress of the cars was occasionally halted temporarily and Rachel did not have to keep her attention on the road, she fumed anew about the way the doctor had tricked her. She reexperienced the helplessness and shame that she had felt when she had been trying to ask him if she was crazy and couldn't get the words out. She would never go back to him. She didn't need him to humiliate her; she could get that from Paul.

Instead of freezing, the rain had slackened and become a mist by the time Rachel left the expressway. With the sky darker, because late afternoon was evolving into early evening, the visibility was poor. Rachel was reminded of the night of the accident. As she approached the turnoff to Cedar Point Road, she felt herself tensing. When she finally entered the narrow, twisting road, she was gripping the steering wheel so fiercely that her arms were aching and the pain was beginning at the back of her neck and across her shoulders.

She tried not to think about the accident. Perhaps Sam had called her while she was in the city. Maybe there would be a message from him when she reached the house. Or would Mrs. Woolsay take a message for her from him? She might consider that collaboration in an infidelity. If he hadn't called, would that be significant? If he had called but hadn't left a message, should she call him back? He might be annoyed if she telephoned him at headquarters; he was so busy. But she didn't know his home phone number. She should have asked him for it. Why hadn't he given it to her? Maybe he didn't want her to have it.

The car's headlights picked up the sign at the entrance to

the first estate on the road, The Ridge, and Rachel's thoughts instantly returned to the night of the accident. She slowed the car. The road was slick, the way it had been that night. She steered the Eldorado carefully through a turn. Ahead, the sign at the entrance to the second estate, Vallum, appeared, its enamel lettering wet and glistening in the mist. Anticipating the next turn, Rachel nervously tested the brakes.

The turn was managed without any trouble. The sign at the entrance to Cooper's appeared from the darkness and was left behind. The Eldorado approached the rise and the sharp bend beyond which the accident occurred. What if, coming out of the turn, she saw the masks again? There was no excuse now; it was not Halloween. She would be imagining them, and it would be proof that she had hallucinated them the first time, too.

The rise came out of the darkness, looking higher than it actually was. Rachel wanted to stop the car and turn it around and flee. But she was afraid to stop; the children were waiting for her around the bend, watching, and they would come after her. The car reached the rise, and the nose lifted. Rachel was immobilized; she was going to miss the turn and crash into the trees. But somehow the Eldorado stayed on the road. The turn was made—and no children were waiting.

Rachel sighed thankfully, feeling limp. The Eldorado's lights were now illuminating the opening to the private road to Catawba. She looked into the rearview mirror. The mist had folded in behind the car, hiding the place where the accident happened. She allowed herself a small smile. Maybe the fact that she hadn't hallucinated the children this time didn't prove beyond a doubt that they had really been there the first time, but it was something.

Turning into the private road, Rachel began looking for the house lights. There would be glimpses of them through the trees at first. But the lights did not appear; there was only the grayish darkness ahead. Perhaps they were hidden by the mist. In the headlights she saw the entrance to the drive, then the shape of the house, broad and high, a black outline with cone-topped turrets. Still, she could see no lights. The house appeared completely dark.

Puzzling, wondering why there were no lights on, Rachel drove on to the rear. The children would be home from school. Even if they weren't, Mrs. Woolsey would be there. Perhaps there had been a power failure. That was the most logical answer. Certainly, Mrs. Woolsey wouldn't be bumping around in the house in the dark on purpose. Surely that was the explanation—there had been a storm in Cedar Point and a power line had gone down.

B.J.'s car was not in the parking area, nor was it in the garage. Walking back toward the front of the house after putting the Eldorado away, Rachel continued to look for a sign of light from inside. Not even a glint or a reflection did she see, however. She began to feel the tenseness again. She wondered why Mrs. Woolsey hadn't lighted candles. Maybe there weren't any. No, she recalled, there were candles in one of the cabinets in the kitchen. Maybe there were only a few, though, one or two, and she was saving them for later.

Rachel climbed the steps to the porch. Reaching the door, she hesitated. She now had a strong feeling that something was very wrong. Not just a power failure, a mechanical breakdown, but something human and evil. She listened at the door. But the only sounds she could hear came from the outside: water dripping from the eaves, arthritic old tree limbs creaking, younger branches rubbing elbows, the heavy breathing of the winter breeze.

She was being foolish, dramatizing, Rachel told herself. The feeling of apprehension was a leftover from the scare she had given herself on the road. Cautiously, she opened the door and stepped into the darkness, then reached for the light switch. Finding it, she pressed it—and the entryway light came on. No power failure. Rachel closed the door. She listened again. The house was silent.

"Mrs. Woolsey," she called.

No answer.

Rachel slipped out of her coat and hung it in the closet. Still standing in the entryway, peering toward the darkness in the foyer, she listened once more. The feeling of something being wrong had grown stronger.

"Mrs. Woolsey?" Her voice was shaky.

There was no response.

Carrying her satchellike purse by the long strap—a weapon—Rachel advanced warily. She turned on the light in the foyer. Nothing seemed changed. She moved on to the hall that led to the back of the house and switched on the light there, then proceeded to the kitchen. There was an empty nursing bottle on the kitchen counter, Rachel found when she switched on the light, but no other evidence of Mrs. Woolsey's presence in the house. Where in the devil had the woman gone?

Walking back toward the foyer, she at last heard a sound. It stopped her cold. It was the same sort of soft, shuffling sound that she had heard the night that the intruder had been in the house. He was back! He had done something to Mrs. Woolsey! Oh, God, he had murdered her! Rachel began backing away, retreating from the sound, which had come from the direction of the foyer. Then she heard the movement again, this time from behind. In terror, she whipped around—and found Kirk Franklin standing in the kitchen doorway.

He was smiling that same faint I-know-about-you smile that she had seen the day before. His eyes, as always, were icy and penetrating. Instinctively, Rachel began a slow retreat, keeping a steady watch on him. He wasn't following her yet. If she could get out of the house— But he would not let her reach the car. And she would not be able to outrun him.

"We didn't know it was you," he said. He looked past her.

Rachel swung around. Jewel Brill was at the other end of the hallway, blocking the opening. Rachel was between them, with no outlet for escape.

"We heard someone, but we didn't know who it was," Jewel said. She, too, was smiling the secretive smile.

"What have you done to Mrs. Woolsey?" Rachel said, her voice thin and pinched.

Jewel looked toward Kirk.

Rachel turned to him. "What have you done to her!"

He seemed amused. "She's gone," he told her.

"Where is B.J.? Where is Holly?"

From behind her, Jewel spoke. "Gone," she said. "They're all gone."

"But we're here . . . we're taking care of things," Kirk told Rachel.

"You killed them!"

He didn't deny it. His smile became a teasing grin. "Why would we do that?"

"I know you!" Rachel shrieked at him. "You're the ones! You were on the road! You chased me!"

Jewel spoke again. "Mrs. Woolsey has gone to see her sister," she said.

"No!" Rachel screamed at her. "She only goes to see her sister on Sunday!"

"Her sister is in the hospital," Kirk said.

The statement surprised Rachel. Why had he told her that? To confuse her?

"She fell," Jewel said.

Rachel faced her, staring at her befuddledly.

"She broke her hip, Mrs. Woolsey said." This from Kirk.

Rachel turned back to him.

"B.J. drove Mrs. Woolsey to the hospital," Jewel said. "He asked us to stay here."

"To take care of things," Kirk said.

"Things . . ." Rachel murmured.

"The baby," Jewel said. "We've been taking care of the baby."

Rachel nodded dumbly. "The baby. . . ."

"I fed her," Jewel said. "Then we took her upstairs. We were sitting up there, watching her, talking."

"We heard a noise down here," Kirk told Rachel. "We weren't sure who it was."

"You didn't have any lights on," Rachel said feebly.

"It was still sort of light when we went up," Jewel told her. "We were talking. I guess we didn't notice how dark it was getting."

It sounded right. But Rachel was still afraid. Testing, she moved tentatively in Jewel's direction. Jewel stepped back, opening the way to her. The story was true. Mrs. Woolsey *was* at the hospital, not murdered, and B.J. had taken her there.

"Holly . . ." Rachel said.

"She's at school," Kirk told her. "Late rehearsal."

Yes, that seemed right, too. Why, though, had Kirk and Jewel let her panic? Why hadn't they told her right at the beginning that B.J. and Mrs. Woolsey had gone to the hospital? Those sly smiles, that was the explanation. They thought she was crazy, and they were tormenting her, amusing themselves. The damn little sadists. She owed them no apology for the accusations she had made.

"You can go now," Rachel said curtly, moving on along the hallway.

She did not look at Jewel as she passed her; she did not want to see her smirking. Reaching the foyer, she made a sharp right turn, then went briskly up the stairs. Above, the second level was still in darkness. Behind her, the silence had settled in again. She hurried; the terror that she had felt when she thought that Kirk and Jewel intended to murder her was still with her, clinging to her skin like a dry saltiness after a cold sweat.

From the landing, Rachel went straight to the nursery. The room was dark except for the soft glow from the night-light. At the crib she leaned over the side and saw that the baby's eyes were nearly closed. She was breathing evenly, about to slip off into sleep. Rachel found, though, that she was in need of a change. Handling her gently, so as not to disturb the narcosis of sleep, she lifted her from the crib and took her to the Bathinette, then began removing the wet diaper.

Rachel became aware of a presence behind her. Looking back, she saw Jewel standing inside the doorway, leaning casually against the frame, watching. She sensed that Kirk was also nearby—in the darkness in the hall—even though she could not see him. She glared at Jewel through the dimness. But the show of belligerency had no effect. Jewel remained at the opening, silent, observing.

"I'm here now . . . I told you, you and Kirk can leave," Rachel said, resuming the diaper changing.

"We promised B.J. we'd stay and watch."

"But *I'm* here."

No answer.

Rachel realized after a moment what the silence meant. B.J. had asked them to stay and keep an eye on his crazy mother if she returned before he got back from the hospital. He didn't trust her to be alone with the baby.

"My sister had a baby," Jewel said. "She killed it."

Rachel looked back at her again. "What do you mean?"

"She killed it."

"How? What happened?"

"Nothing happened," Jewel replied.

"That's ridiculous. You can't kill a baby and have nothing happen."

"Yes, you can. It's all right. The law says it's all right." She smiled the mocking smile. "Actually, she didn't do it herself," she said. "The doctor did it. But she told him to."

"Are you talking about an abortion?"

Jewel nodded.

"That's not a baby," Rachel said, getting a fresh diaper.

"What is it?"

"A fetus."

"What would it have been if it hadn't been killed?"

"A baby, of course."

"Then it was a baby," Jewel said.

"I'm not going to argue with you. But aborting a fetus and killing a baby are just not the same."

"It was alive."

"Yes, I suppose it was . . . if you think of it in that way," Rachel said.

[204]

"It wasn't dead."

"I understand that."

"If it wasn't dead," Jewel said, "then it was alive. There isn't anything else. Either you're alive or you're dead."

"I didn't *say* it was dead."

"It didn't die of old age."

Rachel pinned the fresh diaper.

"If it was alive, but now it's dead, and it didn't die by itself, then it was killed," Jewel said.

Rachel lifted the baby from the Bathinette and took her back to the crib.

"So she killed her baby," Jewel said. "So it's all right to kill people, isn't it?"

Returning to the Bathinette, Rachel looked at her cautiously. She felt afraid again. "A fetus isn't people," she said.

"The father was a people. And my sister is a people. How could the fetus have been anything else?"

"You know what I mean," Rachel said, dropping the wet diaper into the waste container. "A fetus hasn't matured."

"But it's a people, isn't it? It isn't a tree. It isn't a rock."

"All right, *yes,* it's a people," Rachel replied sharply.

"Then it's all right to kill people, isn't it?" Jewel said. "The law says it's all right."

Rachel faced her again. Now she could see Kirk, a tall, narrow shape standing in the darkness in the hall. As before, she felt trapped. Maybe she had been right about them. Maybe the story about Mrs. Woolsey's sister had been a lie. Maybe they *had* done something to Mrs. Woolsey and B.J. and Holly. If not, why this talk about killing?

"If you kill somebody older . . . I mean, like you . . . isn't that an abortion . . . sort of delayed?" Jewel said.

Shocked, unable to speak, Rachel shook her head.

"Why not? What if my sister had decided that she wanted to think about the abortion for a while? It was her choice, if the baby lived or died. Why rush into it? What if it had taken her a couple of years to decide? Or ten? Or twenty? Or thirty? It would still be all right to kill the baby, wouldn't it? It was *her*, choice, not the baby's."

Kirk stepped out of the darkness. He stopped in the doorway, his icy eyes fixed on Rachel.

"So it's really all right to kill anybody at any age . . . if it's an abortion," Jewel said. The sly smile. "How old are *you*, Mrs. Barthelme?"

"I—I'm—" Rachel pressed against the Bathinette, trying to retreat. The meaning of Jewel's question was clear to her. Jewel was telling Rachel that she and Kirk intended to abort her, kill her.

A car was approaching the house.

"That's B.J.," Kirk said. He moved off into the darkness.

"The reason I asked about your age . . . you look so much younger than my mother," Jewel said, still smiling slyly. Then she, too, was gone.

Rachel stood rooted, staring at the space that Jewel had occupied. It was over, she was safe. But she wasn't entirely certain what had happened. Had Kirk and Jewel intended to kill her then, or had they been putting her on notice, sadistically, that they planned to kill her sometime in the future? Or—good God!—had she panicked again, imagining that she was being threatened?

She heard the sound of voices from downstairs and recognized the rhythm of Mrs. Woolsey's way of speaking. She was still too shaken to move, though. What should she do about the threat that—maybe—Jewel had made? She had to call Sam and tell him about it. She had no way of proving to him that it was a threat, though. If she kept crying wolf, he would stop believing in her.

The downstairs talking had stopped; at least, Rachel could no longer hear it. She left the nursery and switched on the hallway lights. When she looked down the stairs, she saw Mrs. Woolsey starting up. The woman was not yet aware of Rachel. She ascended the steps laboriously, as if she were pulling herself up hand over hand. Nearing the top, she raised her eyes. The lines in her face were deeper; her eyes had a wounded look.

"I'm sorry," Rachel said. "How is she?"

"As good as can be expected, at her age," Mrs. Woolsey replied. She reached the landing and halted. "The doctor give her some dope to make her rest, poor thing."

"Was it her hip?"

"Yes. She was putting in a new bulb in the porch light, and she fell off the stool. At our age, that's what always starts it, we break a hip. Mrs. Donnelly, Mary Meara, Mary Conlon, all hips. Mrs. Donnelly and Mary Conlon in their graves now, may they rest in peace. And Mary Meara in the old ladies' home, which is worse. I'd rather be dead."

"I'm sure your sister will be all right," Rachel said.

"Oh, she'll be all right, the doctor says. But it's the beginning of the end. It always starts with a hip."

"Why don't you get some rest?" Rachel said. "I'll take care of things."

Mrs. Woolsey nodded. "Yes, I got to lay down. Though, at my age, it's a risk. Once we lay down, we never know if we'll get up."

"Mrs. Woolsey, you're just feeling blue."

"The handwriting's on the wall," the woman said sorrowfully.

"Nonsense. You have a lot of—" Rachel heard her son's car leaving. "Where is B.J. going?"

"After his sister."

"Oh, yes." Rachel glanced down the steps. "Are Kirk and Jewel still here?" she asked.

"They was when I come up." Mrs. Woolsey lumbered on toward her room.

"Take a good nap," Rachel said. "Sleep as long as you can. We won't bother you."

"No, I just need a couple minutes to gather my thoughts. Then I'll fix supper."

When Mrs. Woolsey had entered her room, Rachel looked

[207]

down the stairs again. Kirk and Jewel were down there somewhere. In the sitting room, probably. She ought to go down and face them and have it out. But if they had threatened her, they would deny it—and smirk at her. And she had no proof. She wasn't even absolutely positive about it now in her own mind.

Wearily, Rachel walked to the bedroom. As she entered, she saw a reflection of car lights on the windows. In the darkness, she moved on to the windows and looked out. A car was approaching on the private road. It was too soon for B.J. to be getting back. As the car neared the drive, she saw that it was Sam's. He drove on toward the rear of the house. Elated, Rachel hurried from the bedroom to go to the door to meet him.

She was almost all the way down the stairs when the first scream came.

"You killed my brother! Murder!"

Stunned, Rachel halted. The scream had come from the sitting room.

Again. "You killed my brother! Murder!" It was Jewel's voice.

Terrified, Rachel backed up the steps.

Once more, the shriek. "You killed my brother! Murder! Murder! Mur-derrrrr!"

Rachel shouted. "Mrs. Woolsey!"

The scream. "Murder! Murder! You killed my brother!"

Rachel raced up the stairs. "Mrs. Woolsey!"

"Murder! Murder! Mur-derrrrr!"

Rachel reached the top of the stairs and fell, sprawling. As she scrambled frantically to rise, Mrs. Woolsey came bustling toward her along the hallway.

"Stop her!" Rachel cried.

"Stop who?" Mrs. Woolsey was helping her to her feet.

"That screaming! Didn't you hear it?"

"Hear it?" Mrs. Woolsey replied crossly. "They could hear it in Timbuktu!"

The doorbell chimed.

"Sam!" Rachel said, starting down the stairs. After a few steps, she stopped, then, proceeding slowly, descended until she could see into the sitting room. "I can't see her!" she called back to Mrs. Woolsey.

"Who're you looking for?"

The doorbell chimed again.

"I'm coming!"

Rachel ran down the steps and across the foyer and into the entryway. She yanked open the door. Sam was there.

"I've got her!" Rachel told him, grabbing his arm and pulling him into the house. "She's in the sitting room! She's *got* to be there! She can't get out!"

"Hey, what?"

"Jewel!" Rachel told him, tugging at him. "She was screaming at me again! The way she did on the phone! She's still in there!"

Sam allowed her to pull him along. When they reached the foyer, Mrs. Woolsey was there.

"She heard her!" Rachel told Sam. "I didn't imagine it. She heard her, too!" She pushed him toward the sitting room. "She's in there!"

As Sam moved through the opening, Rachel retreated. She stood beside Mrs. Woolsey, waiting. Mrs. Woolsey sighed martyredly.

Sam reappeared. "There's nobody in here," he said.

"She is!" Rachel insisted. "She *couldn't* get out! We were right here, how could she get out? She's in there!"

Sam stepped back, gesturing. "Look for yourself."

Rachel went to the doorway and peeked in. She could not see Jewel. Entering the sitting room, she looked around bafffledly. Jewel was nowhere in sight. "She's hiding," she said. She went to a couch and looked behind it. No Jewel. She looked behind the other couch and behind the chairs. Jewel was not in the room.

"The windows!" Rachel said. "She went out a window!"

"When did this happen?" Sam asked.

"Just after you drove in," Rachel replied. "I saw your car—I was up in my bedroom—and I started down the stairs to meet you and I heard her scream at me."

"Are you sure she was in here?"

"I'm positive. She went out a window."

"Why didn't I see her?"

Mrs. Woolsey spoke. "Because she's a magician," she said.

Sam and Rachel turned to her. She was standing just inside the wide doorway, her plump arms folded across her bosom, looking righteous.

"What does that mean?" Sam asked dryly.

"If she went out one of *those* windows, she's a magician," Mrs. Woolsey replied. "They're stuck."

Sam glanced at Rachel, then went to a window and tried to open it, pulling, then pushing, and failed. One by one, he attempted to raise the other windows. Not one would budge.

"She was in here!" Rachel insisted fiercely.

"Were you watching the doorway?" Sam asked. "Could she have slipped out?"

"No, I— Yes! I ran up the stairs," Rachel said. "That's it. That's how she did it. She got out while I was running up the stairs. But it was her; it was Jewel. I knew it immediately, when I heard that first scream." She faced Mrs. Woolsey again. "You heard her. Tell him."

"I heard the yelling," Mrs. Woolsey said to Sam. "I'm not going to say it was that little girl."

Rachel raged at her. "Then who the hell was it!"

"Take it easy," Sam said to Rachel. He addressed Mrs. Woolsey. "Did you recognize the voice?" he asked.

She shook her head. "To me, it was just a lot of yelling."

"You have no idea?"

"I know who was in the house," Mrs. Woolsey replied. "There was me"—she indicated Rachel—"and there was her."

"And Jewel!" Rachel said. "She was down here. So was Kirk. You told me that."

"I told you they was down here when I went up," Mrs. Woolsey said. "I don't know where anybody was after that. All I know is I heard yelling, bloody murder."

"I did it, you mean?" Rachel said indignantly. "Is that what you're saying?"

"All I'm saying is what I know. I don't say what I don't know."

"But you saw me," Rachel argued. "You saw me running up the stairs. Was I screaming?"

"You was yelling."

"Yes, I was yelling for you. I wanted help."

"Yelling is yelling," Mrs. Woolsey said.

Rachel threw up her hands and turned away, going to the windows.

"Do you want me anymore?" Mrs. Woolsey asked Sam. "If you don't, I might as well start supper. I'm not going to get any peace in *this* house, that's the God's truth."

"Go ahead," Sam said.

Mrs. Woolsey departed.

"I swear," Rachel said to Sam, pleading with him to believe her.

"Tell me everything that happened, step by step," he said.

Rachel sat down in the chair beside the telephone table. "I was upstairs," she said. "I saw your car coming. I knew it wasn't B.J.—he'd left just a few minutes before to pick up Holly at school. She's in a play. But before that, Mrs. Woolsey had come up. I talked to her. Her sister is in the hospital—she broke her hip. Well, when I saw that it was your car, I started down to meet you. Mrs. Woolsey was in her room. I was about halfway down the stairs—maybe a little farther—and the screaming started. The same thing. 'You killed my brother. Murder.' Over and over. I knew it was Jewel. But I was scared. I ran back up the stairs, yelling for Mrs. Woolsey. She came out of her room. Then the doorbell rang, and you were here." She looked at him hopefully. "That's it."

"I don't see how she could have got out the front without me seeing her," Sam said. "Possible, but not likely." He went to the doorway and looked toward the stairs. "If you were running up the steps, your back would be to the foyer. She could have gone through, maybe without you seeing her, and gone on out through the back." He walked back into the room. "That way I wouldn't have seen her. I was on my way to the front."

"That's how she did it," Rachel said.

He stood looking around the room.

"This proves everything," Rachel said. "I wasn't going to say anything about it—I wasn't sure. But earlier tonight, before B.J. and Mrs. Woolsey got back from the hospital, Kirk and Jewel threatened me. Threatened to *kill* me!"

Sam looked at her sideways.

"They made it sound like they were talking about abortion, killing babies, but they meant me," Rachel told him.

"What about killing babies?"

"A lot of nonsense. They said—actually, Jewel said it, but Kirk was there. They said it was all right to kill people because it would be the same as a delayed abortion."

He squinted at her. "I don't quite—"

"It wasn't *supposed* to make sense," Rachel said. "They just used that. They were telling me that they intend to kill me. To make me squirm. They're sadists. I've been telling everybody all along that they're after me. But nobody will listen. That damn psychiatrist! He thinks I'm loony. Wait till he finds out how much his textbooks *really* know. And Paul and the children and Mrs. Woolsey, they all think I'm nuts. You're the only one who's believed me."

Sam walked toward the bar. "What psychiatrist is that?" he asked.

"There's gin there," she said. "Paul made me go to him."

"What did he say—the psychiatrist?" He bent down, looking on the shelves behind the bar. "Unless you'd rather not tell me."

"No, I don't mind. It's funny, really, now that everything is cleared up," Rachel said. "He thought I was hallucinating it all. Those children in the masks, the dead little boy, the white shoes, everything. His textbooks told him so."

"Why did he think that?" Sam asked, leaving the bar and walking idly toward the other side of the room.

"Don't you want a drink?"

"In a minute, maybe. Did he give you a reason?"

"Oh, sure. It was supposed to be because I have a bad marriage and feel trapped in it. The dead little boy, for instance, was supposed to be the baby—*my* baby. See how it works? The baby is trapping me in the marriage, so I want the baby dead, so I hallucinate the dead little boy. It's crazy." She laughed exultantly. "Wait until he finds out what the *real* truth is."

Sam had picked up B.J.'s tape player, which B.J. had left on a table, and was examining it cursorily. Rachel had the feeling that he was more interested in avoiding eye contact with her than in inspecting the machine.

"Everything *is* cleared up, isn't it?" she said. "Kirk and Jewel are two of them. You can find out who the others are by asking Kirk and Jewel."

He put the tape player down. "Two of who?"

"The children in the masks."

Sam picked up a book that was resting at the other end of the table. "That doesn't necessarily follow," he said. "As I mentioned before, maybe Jewel Brill picked up that bit about 'You killed my brother' from your daughter." He riffled through the pages of the book. "I don't have anything that definitely puts her on that road that night, though. Kirk, either." He put the book down.

"Make them tell!" Rachel said fiercely.

Sam shrugged. "I intend to talk to them."

"Talk?"

"At the moment that's all I can do. Rachel, I can't even place Jewel Brill in this room, doing that screaming. Who saw her? You didn't. I didn't. Your woman didn't. All I have—"

"—is the word of a nut!" Rachel said, furious.

The phone rang.

Fuming, Rachel picked up the receiver. The call was for Sam. Glaring, she held out the receiver to him.

While Sam carried on the telephone conversation, Rachel stood at the windows staring out into the darkness. Her attention was divided between the depressing thoughts that were parading through her mind and what Sam was saying to the caller.

SAM: That pizza joint up the street? Christ! Why didn't we think of that?

What was he doing, ordering a snack for later? No, that wasn't fair. Maybe the pizza joint had something to do with drugs or something, a teenage hangout.

SAM: No, don't do that. Tail him. Put a twenty-four-hour watch on him.

How about a little fairness for her? It was obvious that Jewel had been here in the room, screaming. Who else could it have been? There wasn't anyone else. Sam had even figured out how she had managed to get away without being seen. Why couldn't he do something about it? Something besides talk to her. She would deny it. What was he going to do, wait until they killed her?

SAM: I'll be back in . . . a half hour. Get Morgan and Bellamy in. I've got something going, maybe. It's a wild one, but you know, who knows? Something else—pull all the area bulletins for me for . . . make it for the past two months. Three months, make it.

She shouldn't have told him about the psychiatrist. Why did she? It slipped out. Now he wasn't sure about her anymore. He was wondering: Maybe she *is* a psycho. Maybe her husband and the others, maybe they're right about her.

SAM: I can't say. (pause) Right.

He hung up.
"Rachel, I've got to go," he said. "Are you all right?"

"You, too."

"Me, too, what?"

"My children keep asking me if I'm all right. What they're saying is, of course, that they think there's something wrong with me. They keep expecting me to do something really mad, I guess. Like running naked through the woods with a rose in my teeth."

"That wasn't what I meant, and you know it."

She faced him. "Why did you come out here tonight?"

"When I talked to you on the phone, you sounded upset. I thought I might be able to calm you down a little."

"Don't you know *why* I'm upset?"

"This business—"

"*Not* this business," she said. "You and me. When I told Paul about us, he said that you found a pushover and you pushed. Was he right?"

He looked at her levelly. "No."

"Well, then?"

"Rachel, I'm not a kid. I don't call up my girl and talk to her a couple hours on the phone. I don't write love poems. I don't—"

She interrupted again. "Sam, that's not what I want. I want to know what we're going to do. Where do we go from here?"

"It's not that easy," he said. "I've got ten million things on my mind right now. And you've got a husband and kids. What do you want me to say, let's run off to some South Seas island? When we get a chance, we'll talk about it, we'll work it out, one way or another."

"*When?*"

"When I get some of these loose ends tied up," he told her. "I can't give you a day and an hour. My work isn't like that."

From outside came the sound of B.J.'s car.

"That's my son," Rachel said.

The car passed the house, going toward the rear.

Sam took Rachel into his arms. He held her tightly, and she clung to him. Sam kissed her hair.

"We'll work it out," he told her. "Hang on. That's the important thing."

"They'll be coming in," she said.

Sam released her. He kissed her lightly. "I'm doing my best."

"All right. I'll try to be patient."

He kissed her again, then moved toward the sitting-room doorway.

Rachel looked out a window. B.J. was climbing the steps to the porch. Holly was behind him. Then came Kirk and Jewel. She took in a sharp breath.

"What's the matter?" Sam asked.

"She— Jewel!"

"What about her?"

"She's with B.J. Kirk, too."

Sam looked at her searchingly. "Could you get your son in here?" he said.

"How did she—"

"I don't know. Let me talk to your son."

Rachel went to the foyer. B.J., Holly, Kirk and Jewel were in the entryway, getting out of their coats. She motioned to B.J., and when he came to her, she led him into the sitting room.

"This is Lieutenant Lomax," she told her son.

B.J. nodded but said nothing. He stood stiffly, like a wall, determined to resist.

"We think somebody might have been in the house tonight," Sam said to him. "Did you see anyone around?"

"Like who?"

"Anyone."

"No."

"What about your friends? Did any of them say anything about seeing anybody?"

B.J. shook his head.

"You didn't see anybody on the road either—the private road?"

"No."

"Who was with you?" Sam asked. "If I come across something, I might want to talk to them later."

"Going, Kirk and Jewel," B.J. said. "Coming back, Holly was with us."

"Kirk and Jewel, they were with you all the way? They left here with you?"

B.J. nodded again. "To get Holly."

Sam shrugged. "Well, if you didn't see anybody, you didn't see anybody." He smiled amiably. "Thanks."

B.J. turned to Rachel. "What was it, somebody like the last time?" he asked.

"Well. . . ."

Sam answered for her. "More or less," he told B.J. "Thanks again."

B.J. left, joining Holly, Kirk and Jewel, who had stopped in the foyer.

Rachel went to the heavy doors and closed them.

"Sam, she was here in this room, and she was screaming at me," she said defiantly.

"You think your son is covering for her?"

"No. He wouldn't do that."

"How could she be here in this room and with him in his car at the same time?"

"I don't know!"

Sam shook his head, as if he were trying to clear his thoughts. "She wasn't both places. She was here or she was with your son." He gestured defeatedly, then walked toward the doors. "I've got to go, Rachel."

"And just leave it like that?"

"I don't know the answer," he said. "I've got to think about it." He rolled back one of the doors. "Hang on," he said. But he didn't look at her. He moved on through the opening.

Rachel knew what he was thinking. His reluctance to look at her before he left had told her. He thought that she, not Jewel, had done the screaming, as Mrs. Woolsey had implied. He probably thought, too, that she didn't realize that she had done it. He was resisting, undoubtedly, but ever so surely he was coming around to the psychiatrist's and Paul's and the children's way of thinking, that her hold on reality was slipping . . . or had already slipped.

They were all wrong. She knew that the screams had not come from her. She could see herself hurrying down the stairs. She wasn't screaming. She was just as certain that the screams had come from the sitting room and from Jewel. At the same time she conceded that that couldn't be possible, that, as Sam had pointed out, Jewel couldn't have been in two places at once. Both were true. Jewel *had* been in the sitting room, screaming, and she hadn't. If both weren't true, then it followed that Rachel had been doing the screaming herself—and that she was insane. But she wasn't. She knew she wasn't.

Sam's car was leaving. Rachel went to the windows and watched the glow of the taillight as it faded into the darkness. She stood for another few minutes, thinking nothing, feeling nothing, then left the sitting room. In the foyer she heard the soft murmur of voices from the kitchen. They all were back there: Mrs. Woolsey, B.J., Holly, Kirk, Jewel. Talking about her.

Mrs. Woolsey was telling the others that Rachel had stood on the stairs screaming bloody murder and then had claimed that Jewel had been doing it. Kirk and Jewel were telling about their experiences with her in the hallway and the nursery, saying that she had accused them of intending to kill her, when all they had really been doing was keeping an eye on her, as B.J. had asked them to do.

Damn them. Damn them all. She *ought* to burn the house down. She ought to burn it down with them in it. They deserved it, damn them.

That night Rachel waited until Kirk and Jewel had left and B.J. and Holly and Mrs. Woolsey were in their rooms before she went down to the kitchen to eat. She had not wanted to see any of them or be forced by courtesy to speak to any of them. Her children and Mrs. Woolsey had made a pariah of her by what they were thinking about her. There was nothing that she could say that would change their minds. All the evidence was against her, and it was an article of the house faith now that she was incapable of differentiating between fact and fancy.

In the kitchen she behaved as an outcast. Getting food, she used the light from the refrigerator, then turned on the bottle warmer so that she could have the light from the dial while she ate. Eating, she listened for sounds. If she should hear someone approaching, she was prepared to flee. First, she would switch off the warmer; then she would escape by way of the back stairs if the sounds came from the hall or by the hall if the sounds came from the stairs. Most important, she had to remember to turn off the warmer.

She wondered what Sam was thinking now. There was only one thing he could be thinking: that she was dysfunctional. No, he didn't think in words like that. He was thinking, sympathetically, that she had had a nervous breakdown. Perhaps he was still in love with her a little bit. But he wouldn't want her now. Too many complications. She was married, necessitating a divorce. She had the baby. She was in need of psychiatric care. He would be crazy himself to take on that many burdens.

Finished eating, Rachel quietly put the dishes in the sink; opening the dishwasher would make too much noise, she didn't want to be heard. She switched off the bottle warmer, then carefully made her way through the darkness to the back stairs. There, she paused, looking back in the direction of the counter, expecting to find that the light on the warmer was glowing again. It wasn't. She didn't trust it, though. As soon as she started up the stairs, it would turn itself on. So, still being careful not to make any sounds, she returned to the counter and pulled the plug.

The solution, Rachel decided as she silently climbed the stairs, was to take treatment from Dr. Edwards. They all believed that she was crazy—even Sam—because that was what the evidence told them. Therefore, if she let the doctor treat her and in time he told them that he had cured her, they would, *ipso facto,* believe that she was sane again. The actual truth was no longer important; it was what they believed to be the truth that counted. She would hate it, pretending to be ill, knowing all the while that she was perfectly well. But she would do it. Survival and eventual escape depended on it.

Eighteen

IT was a little after ten when Rachel awakened the next morning, after a night of old movies on television, floor pacing, hand wringing and then finally falling asleep out of numbed exhaustion. Sitting on the edge of the bed in her pajamas, she telephoned Dr. Blalock Edwards' office. The nurse-receptionist answered. Rachel asked for an appointment for that day.

NURSE: I'm sorry, Mrs. Barthelme. We're full up today. In fact, Doctor even has two sessions scheduled for evening, after dinner. But you have an appointment on Friday—remember?

RACHEL: I remember. When my husband called, he got an emergency appointment for me, though. This is an emergency.

NURSE: Of what nature?

RACHEL: May I talk to the doctor?

NURSE: I'm sorry. He's in session.

RACHEL: When *can* I talk to him?

NURSE: If you'll tell me the nature of the problem—

RACHEL (sharply): I'm sick!

NURSE: I understand, Mrs. Barthelme. I'll talk to Doctor just as soon as this session ends. It will only be a few more minutes. He'll want to know, though—what is the emergency?

RACHEL (urgently): I confess!

NURSE: Pardon?

RACHEL: Not confess, I don't mean that. I mean I admit. I mean I realize. I realize now that he's right. About things . . . things we talked about. I want him to help me. It's very important. It has to start now. It can't wait.

NURSE: Can't it wait until Friday?

RACHEL: No. I might do something. I might change my mind. I don't know. It can't wait.

NURSE: All right. I'll talk to Doctor, Mrs. Barthelme; then I'll call you back.

RACHEL: Tell him it's important for me to start.

NURSE: Yes, I will. I'll call you.

Waiting for the call to be returned, Rachel remained seated on the edge of the bed. She was sure that the doctor would not see her. He was undoubtedly used to getting frantic calls from patients. She probably hadn't impressed the nurse with the dire need of seeing him immediately. She should have wept and begged and threatened to commit suicide. But perhaps between the two of them, the doctor and the nurse, they would work out a way to move her appointment up from Friday. That would help.

It *was* important. She was willing to admit now—even though she would be pretending—that she was dysfunctional. But that wasn't enough. Before the others would change their thinking about her, the treatment had to begin. That was what they wanted, for her to confess to her illness and accept treatment. After that the pressure would be off. And in time, if she played her part well enough, if she followed the text, the doctor would pronounce her cured.

Her children would stop being afraid of her.

Sam would want her again.

The phone rang. Rachel grabbed the receiver.

RACHEL: Yes. Hello. I'm here.

NURSE: Mrs. Barthelme?

RACHEL: Yes!

NURSE: Mrs. Barthelme, Doctor will make an exception.

He'll take you during his dinner hour. He'll have something sent in. Will you be available at that time? That's seven o'clock.

RACHEL: Yes, that's fine. That's wonderful.

NURSE: He's making an exception. He doesn't ever do this.

RACHEL: Thank you. Tell him I appreciate it—I really do. Seven? Seven o'clock? This evening?

NURSE: Yes. That's after his six o'clock session and before his eight o'clock session. It's his dinner hour, but he's making an exception in this case. Remember now—seven o'clock.

RACHEL: Yes. And thank you again. And thank the doctor.

Rachel hung up the phone, then fell back on the bed. She laughed explosively, hugging herself, venting her enormous feeling of relief. It was as if she had been given a release from a sentence of lifelong exile. Soon— Six months? A year? Then she would be acceptable to them again, certified sane.

The laughing made her weak. She had already been weary from being awake most of the night, and the tension of waiting for the nurse to return her call had drained her further. She felt that she ought to get out of bed—it was day. But she had nothing to do but wait for the time to leave for the city, and that would not be until late afternoon. So she gave in to the weariness and closed her eyes, and after only a few moments she was asleep again.

When Rachel awakened the second time, it was almost four o'clock. She wanted to be on her way by five. Rising quickly, she went straight into the bathroom to shower. Under the spray she decided that before she left she would tell Mrs. Woolsey—and the children if they were in the house—where she was going and why. That would start the rethinking. They would begin to look upon her not as a loony who was sinking deeper into lunacy but as a woman with a little problem who was doing something positive about solving it.

Leaving the bathroom, she saw that a light snow was falling. It wasn't sticking, though, so as yet it presented no particular difficulty. She chose a casual, flaring skirt, a soft, long-sleeved sweater and low-heeled slippers. They would give her a little-girl look. Dr. Edwards was, after all, a man. He would be more sympathetic to a little girl than to a woman. Girls were new, with clean whitewall tires and fresh-smelling upholstery, while women were used, with dents and scratches and the odor of oil leaks.

When Rachel left the bedroom, she heard baby sounds coming from the nursery and saw that the door was open. Assuming that Mrs. Woolsey was with the baby, she went to the nursery doorway. The baby was in her crib, but Mrs. Woolsey was nowhere in sight. As Rachel started to turn away, a reflection caught her attention. The long-bladed, dagger-like scissors were sitting out on the Bathinette again. The sight of them froze her. Then she heard Mrs. Woolsey's plodding footfalls approaching along the hallway.

"You left them out again!" Rachel cried angrily at the woman. "I told you to hide them!"

Mrs. Woolsey, carrying an armload of fresh diapers, glared at her belligerently. "What're you raving about now?"

"Those scissors!"

"Oh, them. My sister in the hospital, hung up in a harness, and you expect me to worry about a pair of damn scissors. I never lived in a house like this. It's a bughouse."

"I told you! Keep those scissors out of there!"

"Keep out yourself, if you're that buggy," Mrs. Woolsey said. "You ought to be in the crazy house, anyway. You're driving everybody nuts."

"Shut up!" Rachel shrieked.

"Shut up, yourself, you crazy whore!" Mrs. Woolsey shouted back.

Rachel snatched at the diapers and yanked them from the woman's arms, sending them scattering. "You witch! You witch!" she screamed.

"I ain't no crazy whore!"

Rachel ran to the stairs, then raced down the steps.

From the landing, Mrs. Woolsey shouted after her. "They ought to kick you out! A good husband and those nice kids and that little baby and you whoring around!"

Rachel stopped at the bottom of the steps. "Fat bitch!" she yelled up at the woman.

"Crazy whore!"

Rachel ran to the entryway and grabbed her raincoat from the closet, then slammed out of the house. In her fury she slipped in the film of slush that was collecting on the porch steps and almost fell. That enraged her even more. She kicked the bottom step. Striding on, she cursed Mrs. Woolsey, aloud and viciously. The old bitch had to go. Rachel would not have her in the house one more day. When she got back, she would tell her to pack her bags and get out. Out! Out! Out!

Rachel was nearly halfway to the city before her rage started to cool. Then she began to lament. The battle had been her fault, not Mrs. Woolsey's. The woman hadn't left the scissors on the Bathinette intentionally; it had been a slip of the mind, caused by her concern about her sister. Rachel shouldn't have erupted. When she returned to the house, she would apologize to Mrs. Woolsey. What would she do without her? Who would care for the baby?

Mrs. Woolsey shouldn't have said that Rachel belonged in a crazy house, though.

She shouldn't have said that Rachel was driving everybody nuts.

She shouldn't have called Rachel a crazy whore—even though, first, Rachel had called her a witch. A witch wasn't so bad. But a crazy whore, that was terrible.

Things wouldn't ever be the same between Rachel and Mrs. Woolsey again even if Rachel did apologize to her. The woman would always think of her as a whore. And Rachel still had six months to a year to live in the same house with her before she got her certification of sanity from the doctor and escaped and married Sam. Every time there was any contact between them Rachel would be conscious of what the woman was thinking about her. Whore. *Crazy* whore. Mrs. Woolsey wouldn't even believe that she was being cured. The woman was an ignorant, sanctimonious, fat old bitch. Once a nut, always a nut, she would think.

[224]

Paul would be dubious, too. She had been so adamant before about rejecting treatment, he would think, why now, all of a sudden, was she so amenable to the idea? He would have the children watching her. What if she slipped? What if the girl called her again and screamed at her that she had murdered her little brother? And what if the girl still sounded like Jewel? Rachel would not be able to tell anyone about the call—not even Sam. What if something else happened, something worse? What if Kirk and Jewel tried to abort her? She wouldn't even be able to scream for help—because B.J. and Holly would be watching and listening and they would know when they heard the scream that she was still crazy.

No, God, that didn't make sense.

Somehow, though, she had to keep Kirk and Jewel out of the house from now on. She couldn't ask B.J. and Holly to drop them. They would insist on knowing why. If she told them the truth—that Kirk and Jewel intended to abort her— they would be absolutely certain that she was out of her mind. Abort? A thirty-six-year-old woman? But damn it, that was exactly what they were planning to do. They didn't fool Rachel with their looks of innocence and their plausible explanations. The damn little fiends were going to abort her!

The steering wheel was slick from the perspiration on Rachel's hands. She had the pain at the back of her neck and across her shoulders. How could she ever go back to the house with what was waiting for her there? That woman thinking whore. Paul doubting her. B.J. and Holly watching her. Kirk and Jewel standing in the shadows, smirking, waiting for their chance. Waiting for a Sunday when Paul and the children were at a football game and Mrs. Woolsey was with her sister and Rachel and the baby were alone. Abortion Sunday.

The snow was thick and sticking. Rachel switched on the wipers to clear the windshield so that she could read the signs at the exits.

Six months to a year of sessions with Dr. Blalock Edwards, that was another dismal prospect. She wasn't even sure that he would free her in a year. Once they had their hooks into you, people said, they never let go. She would just quit. Would he certify her, though, if she refused to go to him anymore?

EDWARDS: A year isn't anywhere near enough time, Mrs. Barthelme.
RACHEL: But I'm well. I'm completely well.
EDWARDS: Oh, no. You're only pretending to be well. You've been pretending for a whole year, Mrs. Barthelme. I know. You still believe that you saw those youngsters in the masks and the dead child and the boy in the white shoes, don't you?
RACHEL: No! No! No! I'm well!
EDWARDS: I'm afraid not. We have a long way to go together, Mrs. Barthelme. We're only beginning.

The Eldorado was approaching the exit to the Loop. Rachel tightened her hold on the steering wheel. A hand slipped, and the car swerved, tail wagging on the snow-wet pavement. Rachel grappled with the weight. After a second she had the Eldorado straight in the lane again. But the feeling of alarm was still with her. She couldn't make herself turn the steering wheel, afraid of going into another swerve. The Eldorado drew even with the exit, then left it behind.

Rachel realized that it had not been a fear of losing control of the car that had caused her to drive by the turnoff. Another exit to the Loop was coming up, but she would not take it. She had made a decision. She would not keep the appointment with the doctor and she would not ever go back to the house in Cedar Point. She had freed herself. She would drive straight on to wherever the Eldorado took her.

She eased the car over into the center lane. In her mind the inner lane became a line that she was not allowed to cross, a bar between her and the exits. Her hold on the steering wheel relaxed, and the pain at the back of her neck and across her shoulders began to subside. The wipers, sweeping snow from the windshield, gave her a clear view of the road ahead. The heater provided warmth. The closed windows and the Eldorado's strong construction kept her dry and safe. She was free and secure.

She would have an apartment. She would furnish it in the same way that she had furnished the apartment in Manhattan. That would be fun. She would make new friends. They would be kind, gentle people who had no ambition. She would have a small summer place by the sea, and she would take long, idle walks along the beach. In winter—weather like this—she would go to the galleries. She would have a very special friend, and they would have long talks together, laughing a lot.

At first, she would have to hide. Paul would be looking for her. Not because he wanted her back but for the sake of appearances. She would check into a hotel and dye her hair and cut it short and get a whole new wardrobe and change her name. Something plain. Mary Jones. She would have to give up the Eldorado; the police, trying to find her, would be looking for it. She would park it and leave it. No, she would sell it; she needed the money. She couldn't sell it, though. It was registered in Paul's name. Damn it! It was her car, but he owned it.

The Eldorado passed the last of the turnoffs to the Loop.

All Rachel had was the clothes she was wearing and the money in her purse, fifty dollars or so. That wouldn't keep her in a hotel and fed very long. She would get a job. But doing what? Waiting tables, maybe. She had no experience, though. She had no experience at anything except being a wife. That didn't pay very well. Eighteen years at it and what did she have? The clothes she was wearing and fifty dollars more or less in cash.

The names on the signs at the exits were no longer familiar to her. She was entering the wilderness.

No job that she would be qualified for would pay much. She might not be able to afford an apartment. She could get a room, though, and furnish it the way she wanted it— eventually. Furnishings cost money. There would be no summer place by the sea. But she could go to seaside resorts on vacations—if it didn't cost too much. Maybe she could go back to school and train herself for something higher-paying. But going to school cost money, too. Night school, that was the answer. Working during the day and going to school at night. When would she go to the galleries? When would she have time to make new friends and have long talks? Where was the fun of it?

The exits were farther apart now.

Rachel had the pain at the back of her neck again. She wished she knew where she was. She wasn't accustomed to being free; she wasn't comfortable with it; it was too loose on her—she was used to something closer-fitting. The problem was that she hadn't ever been prepared for freedom. She had been brought up to be linked to a man, to be a wife. When she was a girl, any statement that referred to her future always began with "When you're married, Rachel—" That implied—or, evidently, she had assumed that it implied—that she would always be a dependent, cared for and protected.

With the dusk settling in and the snow drifting on the road and so many things on her mind, distracting her, she was having trouble keeping the Eldorado in the lane. It was a hell of a night to be running away from home. She wished that she wasn't leaving so many obligations behind. The appointment with the doctor; she should have stopped and telephoned him. The baby. She owed the baby her presence, her support while she was growing up. And B.J. and Holly. She was leaving them with the idea in their minds that their mother was a mental case. Psychologically, they might be scarred for life.

Rachel eased the Eldorado toward the right-hand lane. She had to go back. Freedom was not for her. The obligations owned her. She would do as she had originally planned: submit to treatment, get her certification of sanity, then divorce Paul and marry Sam, taking the baby with her. It would take time. And she would be afraid, especially on those Sundays when Paul and the children and Mrs. Woolsey were gone from the house and she was expecting Kirk and Jewel,

[228]

knowing what they had in mind for her. But in the end, if she survived, she would have peace of mind.

Before long, she saw the sign for the next exit, Dorset Avenue. The name gave her no clue to her whereabouts. But the information on the sign told her that the exit was a cloverleaf. Thus, there would be an entrance to the opposite side of the highway, enabling her to head the car toward Cedar Point. Somewhere along the way, at the first opportunity, she would stop and telephone Dr. Edwards and apologize to him for not appearing for the session. Then, if he would still have her, she would go to him on Friday, as previously scheduled.

The Eldorado sloshed fresh tracks in the wet snow in the turnoff lane beneath an overpass, then began circling, climbing. Rachel leaned forward at the wheel, nervous about being in unfamiliar territory. As the car neared the top of the ramp the engine suddenly coughed. The car lost momentum. Instinctively, Rachel pumped the gas pedal. The engine caught, and the Eldorado bucked forward, reaching the crest of the ramp. Relieved, but not sure that the engine had fully recovered, Rachel drove onto the shoulder. As she shifted into neutral, the engine coughed again, then wheezed, then died, as if its throat had been cut.

Rachel looked at the fuel indicator. It was pointing to empty. She groaned, sagging. She had been so upset when she left the house that she hadn't thought to make sure that she had plenty of gas. Now here she was, stuck. Snowing. She would have to tramp through the slush in shoes, no galoshes, to find a gas station. She didn't even know which way to go, ahead or back, to find a station. It was a hell of a goddamn sorry ending for a great escape.

She tied a kerchief around her head, then got out of the car. Because of the falling snow and the dusk, she could see only a short distance. Ahead and behind there was nothing but the misty, snow-flaked dimness, no lights. The choice seemed to be between setting out blindly or waiting for someone to come along and give her directions—and possibly a ride—to the nearest service station. She chose the latter of the alternatives and leaned back against the side of the Eldorado to wait.

All the traffic was on the highway that she had just left. A steady string of fuzzy yellow lights came toward her out of the dimness, then disappeared under the overpass. Dorset Avenue, though, appeared to be deserted. She began to suspect that she had found the only road in the world that was a dead end at both ends. She would wait five more minutes, she decided, then set out on foot, in one direction or the other.

Seconds later she saw lights approaching, coming from ahead. Leaving the car, Rachel went to the edge of the pavement. As the lights drew nearer she raised her arms and began waving. A car, an old yellow convertible, came out of the darkness, rattling and spraying slush. Waving vigorously, Rachel called out. But the car kept chugging on, passing her by. Rachel yelled after it. It became a rapidly fading spot of red light; then it was gone.

Returning to the Eldorado, she cursed the yellow convertible's driver. She got no time to sulk, though. Almost immediately another blur of yellow light appeared, approaching from the other way, on her side of the road. Quickly, she returned to the edge of the pavement and raised her arms once more. The blur became a pair of headlights. Rachel began waving. She saw the car, a dark sedan, and heard the motor, a muffled hum. The car was slowing. It passed her at a crawl, then turned off onto the shoulder a few yards beyond the Eldorado and stopped.

Hurrying to the car, Rachel saw the window opening. When she reached it, a man's face, long and lean, smiled out at her. It was an amiable, disarming smile, giving her hope.

"I'm out of gas, and I don't know where I am," she told the man. "Do you know where there's a service station?"

"Out of gas?" He had a soft, pleasant voice.

"Yes."

"How do you know?"

"The car stopped. And that thing says empty."

"Maybe it's your gauge," he said. He was opening the door. "It could have a short." He was out of the car, a tall man and thin, fortyish, wearing a heavy wool plaid jacket and faded jeans. He had a screwdriver in his hand. "I'll look at the wires," he told Rachel.

She had only a vague idea of what he was talking about, shorts and wires. "I'm sure it's gas," she said.

"If it's a short, it wouldn't do any good to put gas in it."

"Oh."

The man motioned toward the Eldorado with the screwdriver. "Go on," he said.

Walking back to the car, Rachel became apprehensive. "I don't want to bother you," she said to the man. "If you'll just tell me where there's a gas station. . . . They could probably fix it."

He didn't answer.

"It must be gas," Rachel said. "The motor stopped."

They had reached the Eldorado. "Get in back," the man told her, pointing the screwdriver at her.

Rachel stared at him. His expression had changed. His flesh appeared to have been drawn tight across his face, highlighting the bone structure. He looked as frightened as she felt.

"What are you going to do?" she asked. She had hardly any voice.

"Get in!" he said fiercely.

Rachel opened the rear door. "I have some money," she said. "Not much. But you can have it."

He jabbed at her with the screwdriver.

"All right—don't!"

Rachel got into the rear seat and retreated to the far corner, hugging herself protectively. Keeping his eyes on her and the screwdriver pointed at her, the man joined her, then pulled the door closed, slamming it.

"Don't hurt me," Rachel begged.

He was breathing hard, as if he had just completed a long run, and he still looked frightened. He was sweating in spite of the cold. Perspiration glistened on his thin cheeks and dripped from his narrow chin.

"Let me see you," he said.

"What?"

"Strip."

Rachel shook her head.

He leaned forward and put the point of the screwdriver at her throat. "I'm going to punch a hole right through your neck," he told her.

"No . . . please. . . ."

"Let me see you."

"I will."

He drew back, keeping the weapon pointed at her.

Struggling in the corner of the seat, Rachel began removing her raincoat. "Please don't hurt me," she begged again. "Promise you won't hurt me."

No answer.

"I won't tell anybody," she said. "You don't have to hurt me."

He wiped sweat from his chin.

With her raincoat off, Rachel began untying her kerchief. Her fingers fumbled at the knot. Then the man suddenly reached out and yanked the kerchief from her head and threw it to the floor.

"I'm sorry. . . ." She wept.

He made jabbing motions with the screwdriver.

Trembling, Rachel pulled her sweater up over her head and dropped it to the seat, then reached back and began unfastening her bra. She kept her eyes lowered so that she would not have to look at the man. As she removed the bra, the back seat suddenly started to fill with light. A car was approaching from the rear.

The man leaned toward her again. He put the point of the screwdriver at a breast, pressing. "Don't move!" he told her. The hand that held the weapon was shaking. "Don't say nothing. I'll punch you full of holes."

The car passed, and the back seat darkened.

[232]

The man withdrew the weapon. He was breathing hard again and making loud swallowing sounds. He closed his free hand over his crotch, holding himself.

"Go on," he told Rachel.

She unfastened her skirt. "Will you please not hurt me?" she said, pushing it down over her hips.

"Don't say that!" he said savagely, spraying her with his saliva.

"I'm sorry."

He threatened her with the screwdriver again. "Don't say nothing!"

She shook her head, telling him that she would not speak again.

With the skirt at her ankles, she began removing her pantyhose. The sounds coming from the man had changed; they were now grunts and wet sucks of air. Bending forward, Rachel pushed the pantyhose down to her ankles, then freed her legs. She had stopped crying, and even though, without clothes, she was cold, she was no longer trembling. She had resigned herself to the inevitable. The only thought on her mind was a hope that he would get it over with quickly.

"Let me see you," he said.

She sat back, turning her head so that she was looking out the side window, away from him.

"She's naked," he said, speaking to himself. "Jesus! Jesus!"

Rachel stared out the window, seeing nothing.

"Jesus! Oh, God!" He was grunting strenuously.

Maybe that was all he wanted, just to look at her, she thought.

But then that faint hope was quashed. "Get down on your knees," he told her.

This was not what she had prepared herself for. "How?" she asked.

"On the floor. Get down on your knees. Face me."

Still not looking at him, she edged forward on the seat. She heard a clinking sound and recognized it; he was unbuckling his belt. On the floor on her knees, between the back of the front seat and the front of the back seat, she kept her eyes lowered.

"Bastards!" the man said. He was frightened again.

Faintly, Rachel heard a siren.

The man was scrambling.

The sound of the siren rapidly became louder.

Rachel heard the door open. When she looked up, the man had already left the car. Straightening, she tried to look out the front window, but it was caked with snow. The sound of the siren was louder and closer. The man had left the door wide open and in the near distance Rachel saw a flashing red light. The police car or ambulance or whatever was on the highway, not on Dorset Avenue. The man would discover that, and he would be back.

She grabbed at her clothes. As she started to rise, a shoe escaped from her grasp and flew out through the open doorway. It seemed essential to her at that moment to have the shoe back, and she partly crawled and partly lunged after it. At the same time she was still conscious of the flashing red light and the shriek of the siren. As Rachel reached the open doorway on her knees the flashing red light disappeared beneath the overpass. For an instant the siren was muted. Then it became a strident wail again.

Rachel saw her shoe in the slush. The sound of the siren was fading. She stretched, leaning out through the opening, and felt the cold wetness of snow on her bare back. Retrieving the shoe, she looked quickly in the direction that the man had gone. His car was pulling away. It was already on the pavement, a dark, indistinct shape marked by two glowing red spots. But the sound of the siren could hardly be heard now. At any moment the man would realize that he was in no danger of being caught and would return.

Rachel put on her skirt. Carrying the rest of her clothes, she got out of the car and ran, going away from the direction that the man had gone. The cold snow stung her bare feet. Trying to pull her sweater on while she ran, she dropped a shoe. Bending to retrieve it, she lost the other shoe. Finally, with both of them in hand again, she fled once more, deciding to make no further attempt to dress until she had put considerably more distance between her and the Eldorado.

At last, she could run no more. Her chest ached; she could no longer breathe. Stopping, she stood still, gasping. She had no feeling in her feet; her legs were stumps. Looking ahead, she could see only falling snow and darkness. Panting, slowly recovering, she dropped her raincoat and shoes and pantyhose at her feet in the slush, then pulled her sweater on over her wet hair. That accomplished, she picked up the coat and put it on. The pantyhose she stuffed into a pocket of the coat. Hopping about, first on one foot then on the other, splashing in the slush, she put on the shoes. They were as wet as her feet.

Trudging on, Rachel felt somewhat less threatened; if the man were chasing her, surely he would have caught up to her by now. She was still conscious, though, of the feeling of absolute powerlessness that she had experienced when he had made her kneel, naked. No humiliation that she had ever known had been worse. It had been total. She had been a worm, completely hairless, completely vulnerable, about to be chopped in two. That was how it would have been if she had gone through with her plan to be free. There was no freedom for a woman, a natural prey; there was only a variety of ways to submit.

Rachel began to think that she would never find help. The snow and darkness were ever thicker and deeper. Then, dimly, she saw a crude wooden sign that was set back from the shoulder. Going to it, she sank halfway up to her knees in the slush that had collected in the drainage ditch along the road. The detour proved worthwhile, however, for the sign, ineptly hand-painted, told her that she had reached at least the fringe of a populated area.

A.A.A.A. JUNKYARD
Chas. Yates, prop.

Nearby she found a narrow dirt road, now mud, and peering along it, she saw a faint spot of light. The trek through the mud began, with the light becoming more distinct with each measure of distance covered. A dog started barking. Rachel hesitated. The barks were vicious, aggressive. The sound got no closer, though. So, assuming that the dog was either tied or penned, she proceeded.

A house, with a light at the door, a naked bulb, came into view. It was small, low and ramshackle. To one side, connected to the house, was a fenced-in area. It was a clutter of snow-covered junk. The dog, a savage-looking boxer, was behind the fence, making short, ferocious mock charges at Rachel. He was terrifying even though he was held back by the barrier. Making her way through an obstacle course of junk at the front of the house, Rachel glanced fearfully in the dog's direction every few steps, expecting an attack.

She pounded on the door.

Instantly there was a reply. "Who's there?" The voice was male and coarse.

"You don't know me!" Rachel replied, shouting. "I want to use your phone! I ran out of gas! I had trouble!"

"I'm closed."

"Please! A man tried to attack me! I'm wet and cold! Please!"

"Who you got with you?"

"Nobody! Honest! Its just me! I want to get help!"

Silence.

"Please! Please!"

The door opened a crack.

"Please. I just want to use your phone." A light suddenly flashed in her eyes, causing her to raise her arms to her face. "Don't!"

The light was lowered. There was an old man in the opening, thin and stooped and grizzle-faced, wearing a faded wool shirt and dirty bib overalls. He had a flashlight.

"You can come in," he told her. "I didn't know it wasn't a trick. You could be out here to rob me." He put his head out through the open doorway and shouted at the barking dog. "Shut up, you dumb-ass!"

[236]

The barking became a resentful growl.

"Where's your car?" the man asked Rachel, stepping back.

"At the exit."

When she was inside, the man closed the door, then, using the flashlight, plodded to a table and turned on a lamp. As the glow spread, Rachel got an impression of a jumble of mean furnishings; then she saw a mountain of an old woman seated in a wheelchair near a large, pedestal type of dining table. At the same time she became aware of a pervading odor of urine.

"That's my old lady," the man said. "She's feebleminded." He pointed toward a corner. "The phone's over there."

The telephone was on a rolltop desk, in a nest of scraps of paper. Rachel dialed the number of the Cedar Point police station and asked for Sam. Waiting, she saw that the old man was watching her, listening.

SAM: Yes? Rachel?

RACHEL: Sam, you've got to come and get me. Something terrible has happened. I was driving, and I ran out of gas. I got out of the car and I was standing there in the snow—

SAM: Where are you?

RACHEL: I don't know. I'm at a junkyard, but I don't know where. The man is letting me use his phone.

SAM: Can't you get gas?

RACHEL: I don't know. Yes. That's not the point. Will you listen?

SAM: I'm sorry.

RACHEL: I was standing out there in the snow and a man stopped. He made me get into the car—my car. He made me undress. He was going to rape me. Please come and get me.

SAM: Yes, of course I will. I didn't realize. I thought you were just out of gas. What do you mean he was going to?

RACHEL: There was a siren. He got scared and ran. I didn't have any clothes on, and I was out in the snow.

SAM: You didn't get any gas?

RACHEL: What? No.

SAM: Okay. Take it easy. Find out where you are.

Rachel turned to the old man. "He wants to know where I am," she said. "Would you tell him, please?"

He took the phone from her and began giving instructions to Sam.

Rachel looked at the old woman. Her eyes, nearly buried in fat, were vacant. Her gray hair was stringy, greasy. She was dressed in a faded flowered cotton print that was blotchy with oily stains. Her legs were thick, nearly as big around as the table pedestal, and gray-skinned. She was a mound of rotting garbage.

Rachel recalled what Dr. Blalock Edwards had said to her, speaking of the dysfunctional:

They do have an awareness. What they're aware of is that world of their own they've withdrawn into. It's a happy place.

She wondered if the woman was really happy in her world. It seemed impossible. But perhaps the doctor was right. The way he had explained it, it had a kind of logic to it. The woman certainly did not look *un*happy. She looked as if her mind and body had been anesthetized, making her insensible to all hurt. Perhaps that was happiness, an imperviousness to *un*happiness. For the moment, Rachel envied her.

The man handed the phone to Rachel.

RACHEL: Sam? Do you know where I am?
SAM: Yes. I'm on my way. It will take awhile.
RACHEL: Hurry. Please.

She hung up and faced the old man again. "Could I sit down?"

He pointed to a high backless stool near the doorway. "That your old man or your sweetie?" he asked as Rachel went to the stool.

"A friend." Perched on the stool, she hung her head and closed her eyes.

"I heard you say 'Lieutenant' when you asked for him. What is he, a soldier boy?"

"He's a policeman."

The old man grunted. "Where is he?"

"Cedar Point."

"That's up north. That's a toll call."

"I'll pay you," Rachel said. She realized that she had left her purse in the Eldorado. "Sam will pay you when he gets here."

"That'll be a time."

"I'm sorry. I don't have my purse with me."

"I'll give you five dollars," the old man said.

Rachel looked up. "What?"

"Five dollars." He indicated the old woman. "Don't pay no attention to her. She don't know nothing. We can go in the kitchen. I got an old mattress back there. It's the dog's."

"No," Rachel said. She was too exhausted, too miserable, to work up any indignation.

"You ain't no virgin," the man argued. "You done it once tonight. What's twice?"

"I didn't done it. The man ran away."

"Bull-malarkey."

"I don't want to talk about it. Just no."

The man got up and went to a dark corner. When he returned, he was carrying a short, flat length of iron.

"You owe me on that toll call," he said. He motioned with the piece of iron. "Go in the kitchen."

Rachel looked at him evenly. He was bluffing. "If you touch me," she told him, "when Sam gets here, he'll kill you."

The man thought about that. "Five fifty," he said, "and we'll call the toll call square."

"No."

Rachel lowered her head and closed her eyes again.

The dog began barking.

"That'll be your fella," the old man said. He was sitting at the round table playing solitaire.

Rachel got down from the stool and went to the door and opened it. The snow was no longer falling; the night had become clear. Headlights were approaching along the muddy road. She left the house and went to meet the car. When it stopped, Sam got out. He took her into his arms and held her tightly. Rachel tried to talk, to tell him what had happened, but sobs choked off the words. He caressed her gently, telling her that she was all right now, that she was safe, that she no longer had reason to cry. The comforting quieted her, and the tears stopped.

"I want to talk to Yates," Sam said. He reached into the car and pushed the front seat forward and motioned for Rachel to get into the back. "Did you leave anything in the house?"

"No," she answered, getting in. She saw her purse on the back seat. Then she saw that Joey, the flat-faced young policeman who had been to the house and whom she had met again at Saputo's, was seated in front on the passenger's side. "Hello," she said feebly.

"Hi. Tough," Joey said sympathetically.

Rachel nodded and sat back. Sam was walking toward the house. The dog had stopped barking.

"How did you find this place?" Joey asked.

"I walked."

Sam entered the house.

"You're all gassed up," Joey said.

"Did you find a station? Where was it?"

"We didn't look," Joey replied. "We brought the gas with us. We put it in and started the car up. It's okay."

"Fine."

"Sometimes if it goes completely dry, it's hard to start after that," Joey said.

"Oh."

"We didn't have any trouble, though. It started right up."

Sam had emerged from the house and was walking back to the car.

"Here he comes," Joey said.

Rachel nodded.

Sam got in behind the wheel. "I thanked him for you," he said to Rachel. He smiled. "I also paid him for the phone call. I didn't know what it would be. I gave him five bucks. Okay?"

"Yes," she said thinly.

[240]

Sam turned the car around and drove back through the mud. Nothing was said during the brief time it took to drive to where Rachel's car was waiting. When they reached there, Sam and Rachel got into the Eldorado, Sam at the wheel, and Joey drove off in Sam's car.

Sam held Rachel close again. "Now tell me what happened," he said.

She began crying again. Between sobs, she told him as much as she could remember.

"What did he look like?" Sam asked.

"Thin."

"What else?"

"I don't know. Ordinary. Thin. I didn't want to look at him."

"What was he wearing?"

"A jacket. Plaid. And— I don't remember. A plaid jacket."

"Nothing out of the ordinary?"

"No. I'm sorry."

"What about his car?"

"It was dark-colored, I remember that," Rachel said. "Black. Dark blue."

"A new car, an old car?"

"No, it wasn't new. It wasn't old, either. Sort of middle."

"You didn't get the license number."

"No."

"That makes it hard."

"What difference does it make?"

"You're supposed to report it," Sam told her.

Rachel pulled away from him. "No! I don't want to talk about it anymore. I want to forget it."

"Do you want him running around loose?"

"I couldn't tell them anything anyway," Rachel said. "He was thin, and he had on a plaid jacket. That could be a hundred men. I couldn't identify him."

"It's supposed to be reported."

"I don't want to *talk* about it!" She covered her face with her hands. "They wouldn't believe me." She wept. "That old man didn't believe me. He wanted me to go in the kitchen with him and do it on his dog's mattress. He was going to pay me five dollars."

"All right," Sam said. He started the engine.

"Are we going home?"

"Yes."

Rachel kept the space between them until they were on the highway; then she rested against Sam and he put his arm around her, holding her loosely.

"What were you doing way out here?" he asked.

"Running away. I had a fight with Mrs. Woolsey. She thinks I'm crazy. Everybody thinks I'm crazy. Even my children."

"Where were you going?"

"I don't know. Away. But I changed my mind. I was turning back when I ran out of gas." She pressed closer to him. "Do you think I'm crazy, Sam?"

He sighed deeply. "I don't know crazy," he said. "I know guilty and not guilty. That's my limit."

The answer hurt Rachel. She drew away from him again.

"I believe what I can see, whole," he said. "I have bits and pieces, I don't have anything whole."

"What you can see? I'm in love with you. You're in love with me. Doesn't that count for anything?"

He didn't answer.

"Are you in love with me?"

"Yes," he said.

"Then what the hell are you talking about, you can't see anything whole? If we're in love, that's whole, isn't it?"

"That's something else. I was talking about— If you have a problem or not."

"Why don't you say it? You think you're in love with a crazy lady!"

"I don't know. That's what I'm telling you: I don't know. Maybe those kids *were* out there on that road that night—with masks. Maybe there was a boy. Maybe he was dead. Maybe a couple of the kids were Kirk Franklin and Jewel Brill. All of it, maybe. But maybe not. I have little bits and pieces—"

"And maybe what happened tonight didn't happen either!" she said, furious.

"Maybe it didn't." He spoke calmly. "If the other things didn't happen, maybe this didn't happen tonight. You can't describe the man. You can't tell me anything about his car. But that doesn't prove anything." He looked at her. "Do you understand? Maybe you imagined it all, maybe some of it, maybe none. But *I don't know.*"

"You know you love me, though."

"Yes. I've got that whole, I know that."

"Even if I'm crazy?"

"That doesn't enter into it. If I loved you and you lost an arm or a leg, I'd still love you."

"Would you still marry me?"

"You're already married."

"I'm going to leave Paul."

"Evidently you think love means marriage," Sam said. "I don't think that way."

"No, not if marriage means having a crazy lady around."

"That's not the point. If you want to move in with me—or if you want us to get a place of our own—okay."

"Shack up, you mean." She moved farther away from him, into the corner of the seat. "I'm not a girl, Sam. I'm a woman with a baby. I need to be *Mrs.* Somebody."

"I can't offer you that. And as far as the baby is concerned—" He shook his head. "The way you're not a girl, I'm not a boy. I'm forty-two. I could be married. I could have children. I don't want either. To be in love, to have you with me, to be with you, that's fine. That I want. But not a contract and not a baby."

Rachel considered the proposal, living with him, leaving the baby behind. "I can't," she said. She looked out the side window. They were passing an exit to the Loop. "I guess things have changed. People live together, married or not. Nobody cares, nobody minds. I think I'm in favor of that—in theory. In practice, though, I couldn't do it. The contract is important to me. That's silly, I know. I have a contract with

Paul, and I'm miserable. But even so, I'm the way I am. I have the feeling that without the contract it isn't real, it's playlike."

"The only thing big I own is my car," he said.

She looked at him puzzledly. "What's that got to do with it?"

"You told me how you are. Now I'm telling you how I am. I don't own anything big. We rent the house. The boat is a partnership deal, and it's not in my name. Every commitment I have I could wind up in a day. I could take off tomorrow, anywhere, and never come back, and I'd be square. No debts, no obligations of any kind."

"Without a contract, you could do that to me."

"I wouldn't. I don't take off for nowhere. I stay on my job, I give it a hundred percent. I like staying put. I don't want to take off and never come back. It's important to me, though, to know that if I did want to, I could."

"I see. We're different."

He nodded.

That was that.

Rachel made herself as comfortable as possible in the corner of the seat. She closed her eyes and listened to the mixed sounds of the engine and the tires splattering through the wetness on the pavement. Drained, mentally and physically, she went quickly to sleep.

Nineteen

WHEN Sam woke Rachel, the Eldorado was parked in front of the Cedar Point police headquarters with the motor running.

"Can you make it from here?" he asked.

"Yes."

"If you don't think you can, say so. I'll get Joey to follow us in my car and I'll drive you home."

"No, I'm all right."

"Rachel, about the things that have happened to you—or haven't happened, whichever. Don't give up on yourself. Not yet. I'm still working on it."

"On the bits and pieces?" she said drearily.

"Yes. But a lot of cases are like that. Bits and pieces, then a few more bits and pieces, then there it is—whole."

"For instance?" she said. "What's one of the bits? What's one of the pieces?"

"I can't tell you that. It's police business. The bits and pieces might turn out to be nothing. Don't get the wrong idea, I'm not saying that I'm on the brink of breaking the case. That could happen. Sometimes it does. But most times. . . ."

"Well, thanks . . . for nothing." She looked at her watch in the light from the instrument panel. "It's almost midnight. Don't you want me to drop you at your house?"

"I still have work to do." He opened the door. "And my car is here," he said, getting out.

She scooted across the seat, getting behind the wheel.

"Hang on," he said.

"Good night, Sam."

He closed the door, and Rachel shifted into gear and drove away.

She was well on her way to the house, unfogging her mind after the nap, when the import of the evening's happenings suddenly became clear to her. She had lost Sam; rather, she had discovered that she had never had him. And she had suffered another hallucination; the intended attack on her by the man in the back seat of the Eldorado had not actually occurred, except in her mind.

DR. EDWARDS: You'd just had a severe shock. You were on your way to freedom and you found that you weren't up to it—in fact, that you would never be free.

RACHEL: Then I ran out of gas.

EDWARDS: Yes, you ran out of gas. It was dark, snowing. You needed help, but you couldn't get anyone to stop. Who could you get to help you? Who was strong? Who could cope? Who was sympathetic? Who had always been willing to help you before?

RACHEL: Sam.

EDWARDS: Of course. But Sam was far away. He wouldn't drive all that distance just to help you find a gas station. To get him to come to you, you needed a much more compelling reason.

RACHEL: I made up the story about the man.

EDWARDS: Oh, no. You'd never do that; you wouldn't make up a story. You created a happening in your mind. You made it real.

RACHEL: I'm insane.

EDWARDS: Dysfunctional.

Headlights, blinding, were coming straight at Rachel. A horn was blaring. She realized that she was driving in the middle of the road, with another car approaching from the opposite direction. Frantic, she whipped the Eldorado to the right. It left the road, plowing through the ditch. Tree branches lashed the windshield. The other car sped past, leaving the way ahead clear once more. Rachel swung the Eldorado to the left. It climbed from the ditch, swerved, swerved again, then found its proper lane on the road and straightened, going steadily on.

In the aftermath, Rachel shook violently. There was a club-like pounding inside her chest. She could see the headlights and hear the horn again, although the lights were no longer there and the only sounds that she could actually hear were the drone of the Eldorado's engine and her own convulsive breathing. Perspiration got into her eyes, causing her to blink spastically. The Eldorado was drifting toward the center of the road again. She jerked at the wheel, setting the car back on course. A few minutes later the entrance to the private road to the house came into view. For the first time ever she was happy to see it.

There were lights on all three floors, Rachel saw, as she

neared the house. She remembered that she had not told Mrs. Woolsey where she was going when she left. And the doctor had probably called to find out why she had not kept the appointment with him. They were probably concerned about her, waiting up for her. She would have to explain her absence to them. But what could she tell them? She wasn't sure what the truth was. She would say that she ran out of gas and leave it at that.

Paul's car was in the garage. That complicated the matter. He wouldn't accept the excuse that she had run out of gas as an explanation for the long absence. He would demand to know every detail. Well, she would tell him. That was the only thing she could do. The doctor was right about her; it wasn't her way to make up a story. If he didn't believe her, the hell with him. She didn't care anymore. She had no pride or dignity left to defend.

Paul, Holly, and B.J. were waiting for her in the entryway when she entered the house. For a moment nothing was said. She stood limply before them, presenting herself for inspection, feeling bedraggled. B.J. and Holly examined her concernedly and somewhat self-consciously. Paul's manner was controlled, noncommittal.

"Where have you been?" Paul asked evenly.

"I ran out of gas."

"Are you all right?"

"Yes."

"The doctor called," Holly said. "He said you had an appointment. We didn't know what happened to you."

"I ran out of gas."

"Okay, kids," Paul said to B.J. and Holly, "why don't you go on up to bed? It's all over."

They began backing away. Rachel followed. Paul closed the front door, which she had left open, then trailed after her. When they reached the foyer, B.J. and Holly said good-night and moved on toward the stairs. Rachel turned toward the sitting room. The children, she knew, would not go to their rooms. They would sit on the steps, listening, witnesses to the interrogation that was to come. In the sitting room she went to the chair that had the telephone beside it and dropped into it listlessly and closed her eyes.

Paul, of course, had followed her into the room. "The doctor said you told his nurse it was an emergency." His tone was still level. "He gave up his dinner hour for you. Then you didn't show up."

"I'm sorry."

"Where did you go?"

"I was running away," she told him. "I was driving, just driving, and I ran out of gas."

"Rachel, kids run away. Adults don't run away."

"I didn't know that. I was running away anyway."

"Running away from what?"

"Everything."

"Instead of going to the doctor and getting some help, is that what you were running away from?"

"Yes."

"How do you explain the way you look? You look like you've been through a wringer."

"A man stopped," Rachel said. "He made me get in the car—"

"Wait a minute. Where are we?"

"I ran out of gas. I was on a road. It was snowing and dark, and I didn't know where I was. I was trying to get some help. A man stopped. He made me get in the car. He made me take my clothes off. He was going to make me— He was going to rape me, I guess."

"He didn't?"

"He got scared and ran away," she said.

"Uh-huh."

"I found a house," Rachel said. "I called Sam, and he came and got me."

"Oh, I see—you've been with that cop. That's what I figured. That explains why you're carrying your pants around in your pocket."

Rachel opened her eyes and looked down. A leg of her pantyhose was hanging out of the pocket of her raincoat.

"Did he beat you up? Is that why you look like that?"

Rachel looked at him. It was clear that he didn't believe what she had told him.

"I'm no psychiatrist," Paul said, "but I can sure as hell see now what your problem is. You want somebody to treat you rough. What is it? Is there something you feel guilty about and you want to be punished?"

She closed her eyes again. "I don't know."

"That must be it. I've tried to be patient, I've tried to help you, getting you a doctor, but that hasn't worked. I've done everything I could. I've put up with all this crap. That cop. You and that cop. That I couldn't understand. A cop! But I can see it now. It makes sense. If you have a need to get beat up, where do you go? You go to a cop. Jesus Christ!"

Rachel wriggled her feet out of her shoes.

"Mrs. Woolsey is gone," Paul told her. "She finally got fed up."

Rachel looked at him again. "Gone for good?"

"Bag and baggage," he told her. "B.J. took her to her sister's. She said she wanted to be there when her sister gets out of the hospital. But that wasn't the reason. She told me what happened. Who am I going to get—"

The phone was ringing.

Paul picked up the receiver and identified himself. "No, that's all right, Art," he said. "I was waiting for you to call. Was it what you thought?"

Rachel listened to Paul's part of the conversation. The caller was Arthur Jahnke, the president of United Machinery. She soon deduced what they were talking about. Jahnke had just come from a meeting of a group of directors of the company. The chairman of United Machinery, William Hoag, was to be involuntarily retired. Jahnke would replace him.

"Art, you know how I feel," Paul said. "You're what we need. The whole team feels that way. With a few exceptions, naturally. But in a situation like this there are always one or two."

Pause.

"I shouldn't have said that. I don't want to name names. Look, it will blow over. When the change is made, they'll fall in line."

Pause.

"You're right, that is important. Either we're a team or we're not; there's no halfway about it. I agree with you. But they'll shape up. If they don't, I'm *your* man, you know that."

Pause.

"Well, when I said one or two, that was just a figure of speech. Art, I don't know. I haven't made a list. But let's let the dust settle."

Pause.

"Right. You're right. Just let the dust settle first."

Pause.

"I know that. I respect Bill, too. As I told you, though, Art, there comes a time. Nobody thinks more of Bill than I do, but at the same time, I realize that the time has come for him to step down. Hell, I love the guy. You know what I mean. But the company is in a new phase now. It's over his head."

A statement that B.J. had made flashed through Rachel's mind. People kill people. William Hoag was being killed.

"Don't think that," Paul said into the phone. "You didn't do it. I didn't do it. Nobody did it. Bill did it to himself. He can't swing it; that's what it boils down to. That's not your fault, Art. Your hands are clean."

Pause.

"I appreciate that. Even if nothing comes of it, I still appreciate it. Who's my competition?"

Pause.

"That's good company—I'm flattered by that. Frankly— I'm going to be completely frank about this, no holds barred. Frankly, I think it would be a mistake to bring in somebody from the outside. You and I think alike—you know that. We'd be a great team. The problem about bringing in somebody from the outside is you don't know what you're getting. A track record is fine. But this is a new track."

Pause.

"I know you will."

Pause.

"I'll keep my fingers crossed. In the meantime, Art, it's really great news. Not just for you, for the company, too. You're what we need."

Pause.

"All right. I can make a list. But let the dust settle first, the way you suggested. You know how to handle them."

Pause.

"You know what's best. I'll have it on your desk in the morning."

Pause.

"Well, I mean it. You're the man for the job."

Pause.

"Right. In the morning."

Paul hung up. "Tomorrow," he said to Rachel, "Holly can stay home and take care of the baby. But that's just one day. I'm not going to make a sitter out of her. She's in something at school. I'll turn Jenny loose on it. If anybody can get somebody quick to take over, she can."

"Who's Jenny?"

"My secretary. Don't you remember anything?" He sat down on a couch. "I had a long talk with Edwards," he said. "Do you remember who he is?"

"Yes. The doctor."

"Right. I told him about your latest trick, down here screaming your head off, then saying it was Holly's girlfriend. I put the cards on the table, Rachel. I told him what you're doing to us. You've got me climbing the walls. The kids don't know which end is up anymore. Mrs. Woolsey finally got enough of it. We're all at the end of our rope."

"I'll go back to the doctor," she said.

"Yes. But there's a little more to it than that. I want you to have a rest. The doctor agrees with me. He has an interest in a place that's not far from here—"

"An asylum!" Rachel said.

"No, not an asylum. Let me tell you about it. It's a place to rest; it's not an asylum. You're not locked in. It's like a hotel. And it's close. Once a week they'll drive you in, and you can have your session with the doctor. Then, when you get well, you can come back."

Rachel thought: People kill people. He's killing me.

"The doctor thinks this can all be traced back to the baby," Paul said. "Your age, having a baby. And at the same time, we moved out here from Manhattan. It was too much for you. Too much of a strain. It's as simple as that. You just need a good rest."

Rachel remembered the junkman's wife, her vacant eyes, smelling of urine. "Please," she said to Paul. "Don't put me away."

"Don't start that. I'm not putting you away. I'm giving you a rest."

"Don't," she begged. "I'll be good."

"Rachel, Jesus!" He got up and walked toward the bar. "I'm doing it for you. You make me sound like a monster."

"I'm better," she told him. "I'm almost well. I know now that none of those things happened. I imagined them all. The doctor is right. I didn't want a baby; that's what caused it. Now that I know that, I'll be all right."

He poured scotch into a tumbler. "I wish the hell I could believe that."

"Honest, Paul. I know what's real now. I was lying about tonight. I wasn't running away. I didn't run out of gas. I was with Sam. I went to see him to tell him I couldn't meet him any more. He got mad. He tried to force me. I wouldn't let him . . . that's how I got all messed up like this."

"I knew it was something like that," Paul said, dropping an ice cube into his drink. "Why did you lie to me?"

"I didn't want to hurt you anymore," she said. "I know what

I've done, how bad it's been for you. I'm sorry, Paul. I was sick. Not bad sick, but sick. Like a bad cold. I'm over it now, though. There's no reason to send me away."

He looked at her doubtfully.

"We don't need another Mrs. Woolsey," Rachel said. "I can take care of the baby . . . and the house and the meals and everything. I'm fine now. Healthy. Paul . . . eighteen years . . . don't I deserve a chance?"

He looked down at his drink.

"Give me a week. You'll see. I'll be perfect."

"You make me feel like a son of a bitch."

"Please, Paul."

"Okay." He sipped from the drink. "You'd better get yourself cleaned up and get some sleep."

Rachel rose. "Are you coming up?"

He shook his head. "I've got some work to do. A list for Arthur and a couple other things."

"Good night."

" 'Night."

She walked toward the doorway.

"Rachel . . ." he said.

She stopped.

"Last chance," he told her.

"I know. Last chance. I'll be good."

She left the sitting room and crossed the foyer and began the climb up the stairs. She felt bad about herself, ashamed. It did no good to tell herself that as a natural prey she had a right to use any means necessary to survive. She was not cleansed. She felt dirty all the way through.

Twenty

WHEN she awoke, Rachel was instantly alert. The bright daylight filling the bedroom told her that she was in trouble. A look at the clock confirmed it. It was after nine. She should have been up hours earlier, getting breakfast for B.J. and Holly, taking care of the baby. Scrambling from the bed, she heard her mother's scolding voice. *Get up! Get up! You'll be late for school!* She had set the alarm before she went to bed. Why hadn't it gone off? Checking the clock, she found that the alarm button had been disengaged. Paul had done it! He wanted her to fail!

In her pajamas she raced from the bedroom and ran to the nursery. From the doorway she saw that the baby was not in the crib. She hurried on to the stairs and scurried down the steps. Reaching the foyer, she heard Holly's voice coming from the sitting room. As Rachel started toward the sound, Holly came from the room, holding the baby in her arms and talking to her.

"Somebody turned off my alarm!" Rachel charged.

"Hi, Mom. Dad did," Holly said. "He said to let you sleep."

Rachel felt a wave of relief. Turning off the alarm had been an act of benevolence, not treachery. She had not lost her last chance.

"The baby's been playing," Holly said. She laughed. "Waving her arms and legs, anyway. But she's tired. I'm taking her up."

Rachel and Holly ascended the stairs together.

"You can go to school now," Rachel said. "There was no reason for you to stay home in the first place. I don't need you. I mean, it's nice to have you, but there isn't that much to do."

"Dad wanted to let you sleep."

"I know. But now, I mean," Rachel said, as they reached the landing.

"I don't have a ride."

"There's a taxi service in the village. Call a cab."

"Well, I'm home, I might as well stay," Holly said, going toward the nursery.

"Suit yourself."

Rachel went on to the bedroom. Obviously, Holly had orders from Paul to keep watch over her. He was skeptical about her recovery. Today would be a test. Holly would report to him on how she had performed. She had to be very careful not to make any mistakes. One slip and Paul would have her put away.

People kill people.

Nobody thinks more of Bill than I do, but at the same time I realize that the time has come for him to step down.

When she had dressed she went back downstairs. Music—if it could be called that—was coming from the sitting room, indicating that Holly was in there with her tape player. Rachel walked on to the kitchen and began preparing breakfast for herself, coffee and toast. As she waited for the water to boil for the coffee and the toast to pop up, she started on a list of things to do, things that Mrs. Woolsey would be doing if she hadn't left. Plan an evening meal. Run the sweeper in the sitting room.

The water was boiling.

A few minutes later, when Rachel was seated at the table with the coffee and toast, adding to the list, Holly came into the kitchen.

"Hi," she said.

"Hi."

Holly went to the sink and turned on the cold water and let it run, then opened a cabinet and got out a glass. Watching her, Rachel saw her look toward the stove. She was checking, making sure that Rachel had not left a burner on. Holly filled the glass with water, then stood leaning back against the counter, sipping. She was in no need of a drink, of course; she was keeping Rachel under observation.

"What about your play?" Rachel said. "Isn't there a rehearsal today?"

"Yes."

"It'd be a shame if you missed it."

"Maybe B.J. can take me when he gets home."

"How will that look? Out of school all day, missing classes, then showing up when all the fun starts."

Holly shrugged unconcernedly. "What are you doing?"

"This is a list of things to do. What would you like to have for dinner tonight? Anything special?"

"I don't care."

"I wonder what we have," Rachel said, rising and going to the freezer. She opened the door. "Steak?"

"Okay."

Rachel closed the door.

"You didn't take it out," Holly said. "It has to thaw."

Rachel felt caught. "I haven't decided," she said, bluffing, going back to the table. "I might make something else. Something fancy. Steak is so plain." She sat down. "Do you like chicken fricassee?"

"I don't think I've ever had it."

"Then maybe we'll have that."

"Don't you have to take a chicken out?"

"I'm still thinking about it," Rachel said. "We might have something else."

"Pizza is easy."

"I don't want it to be easy," Rachel said. "I want it to be special. Mrs. Woolsey didn't know how to cook. Everything was meat and potatoes."

Holly emptied the glass and departed.

Rachel was shaken, but she felt pleased nevertheless. She had made the first mistake and had managed to muddle through. It would be easier from now on. The first was always the worst.

Finished with breakfast, she left the kitchen and got the vacuum cleaner from the entryway closet and took it into the sitting room. Holly was lying on a couch, reading, with her tape player now silent.

"I hope this won't bother you," Rachel said, plugging in the vacuum cleaner.

"Unh-unh."

Rachel began cleaning in the vicinity of the telephone table. Holly was watching her. She realized all at once that she was doing it wrong, starting in the middle of the room. That wasn't efficient. She picked up the machine and took it to the corner where the bar was located and began again, working from the corner outward. After a few moments, she sneaked a look and saw that the correction had apparently satisfied Holly, for she had returned her attention to the book.

The drone of the machine was soothing, relaxing. It kept out all other sounds. Working with her back to her daughter, she had the feeling at last of having escaped from observation. Too, she was sure that she was doing well with the cleaning, covering every inch of space, proving to Holly, if she was watching again, that she was functional. Not only did she have privacy, but, she was certain, she also had approval. It was a nice, secure kind of isolation.

The euphoria abruptly disintegrated. Rachel realized that she had not taken anything out of the freezer, neither steak nor chicken. When it came time to prepare dinner, the meat or the fowl, whichever, would be frozen solid. It wouldn't be quite as bad as leaving a burner on under a pan. Still, it would be an error, a mistake, a sign of lingering dysfunction. She switched off the vacuum cleaner.

Holly had looked up from her book.

"Now, *I'm* thirsty," Rachel said, going toward the doorway. "I'll be back in a minute."

Holly smiled.

Rachel strolled casually across the foyer and then down the hallway—like someone who was going for a drink of water, she hoped—since there was the possibility that Holly was watching her from the doorway of the sitting room. When she reached the kitchen, though, she hurried, going straight to the freezer. There, she got out a chicken and put it aside to thaw. After making sure that the freezer door was closed—another possibility for error, leaving the freezer door open a crack—she headed back toward the sitting room. She was pleased with her choice of the chicken over the steak. Fricasseeing was much more complicated than broiling. It would show them how competent and confident she was.

As Rachel neared the sitting room, she heard her daughter speak.

"I feel so dumb," Holly said. "All she's doing is cleaning the house."

No one answered. Rachel realized that Holly was talking on the phone. She halted, listening.

"I know, but I'll miss rehearsal," Holly said. "I can't go in if I've been out all day."

She was reporting to Paul.

"Nothing. Just talking about what to have for dinner. She couldn't be any more normal. Can't I go in?"

Pause.

"I told you," Holly said, "running the sweeper. She doesn't need me. I'm just sitting around. Please can't I go in?"

Pause.

"Okay. Thanks. 'Bye."

When Rachel entered the room, Holly had the telephone book open.

"I'm looking up that taxi," Holly said. "I guess I'll go in to school. You don't need me, do you?"

"No. I'm fine."

When the cab had been ordered, Holly left the room, saying that she had to get her copy of the play from her room. Rachel resumed the cleaning, withdrawing once more into the isolation provided by the drone of the sweeper. She was pleased with the way she had handled Holly, getting her to go to school. She had used finesse. That wasn't the way a crazy woman would have done it.

A short while later Holly came back into the room with her coat on and carrying the play script and shouted over the sound of the vacuum cleaner that she was leaving. Rachel waved, then, when Holly left the room, went to the windows. The taxi was standing in the drive. She watched her daughter get in. When the taxi pulled away, she resumed the cleaning once more, happy. Holly no longer feared what she might do; she had not been at all reluctant to leave her alone. As Holly had told Paul on the phone, Rachel couldn't be any more normal.

By the time Rachel had finished cleaning in the sitting room and moved on to the foyer with the sweeper her joy had diminished a good bit. The work was becoming drudgery. She wondered if she would ever see Sam again. Probably not. He had offered to take her in as his lover, and she had turned him down, so that was the end of that. As far as the case was concerned, it was undoubtedly closed now. He hadn't believed what she told him about the man who made her undress in the back seat of the car, so it was unlikely that he still thought it possible that the other things had happened.

She was right back where she had started, only worse. She was still trapped in a dead marriage, and now she had lost Mrs. Woolsey. This was how she would spend the rest of her life, cleaning, cooking, pretending to be happy, proving to Paul that she was normal, sane. What was so damn sane about being happy being a drudge? Knowing that her future was so dismal and accepting it ought to be proof of just the opposite, that she was mad as a hatter. Dr. Edwards might be interested in that theory; perhaps she had isolated a new strain of insanity: the happy housewife, or Mrs. Barthelme's madness.

She should have moved in with Sam on his terms. A legal contract wasn't so important; it was no guarantee that the relationship would be compatible. Her relationship with Paul was legal, and it was a horror. Sam loved her and she loved Sam; that was all that actually mattered. She should have compromised—or, rather, acceded, since no compromise had been offered. If she had, she would be really happy now, instead of pretending to be.

Not entirely happy. There was the problem of the baby. Sam didn't want a baby. She couldn't blame him for that; she didn't want a baby either. But there the baby was, alive and kicking—or howling. That was the real obstacle. She could have done without a legal marriage, but she couldn't leave the baby behind. She owed the baby her presence. It was that debt, that responsibility, that had kept her from going to live with Sam.

If only she hadn't had the child. She should have had an abortion when she discovered that she was pregnant. That hadn't even occurred to her at the time. She had been brought up to believe that when you got pregnant, you had a baby. Times had changed. A lot of women had abortions these days. Jewel's sister, for one. In fact, the way Jewel thought, it was never too late for an abortion. Rachel could go upstairs right now and—

The idea shocked her. She tried to put it out of her mind, but it stayed, shaming her. She needed a distraction; perhaps if she gave up the cleaning for a while and did something else, the thought would go away. She turned off the machine. As the drone faded, she heard the baby crying. In a way she was thankful. After she fed the baby, she would play with her and, in that way, make up to her for the terrible thing she had been thinking.

Rachel went to the kitchen and put a bottle on to warm, then climbed to the second floor by way of the back stairs. The baby was howling angrily, demanding to be nourished. Rachel began talking to her soothingly as she entered the nursery. But she did not reach the crib. She saw the shiny, long-bladed scissors. They were still resting on the Bathinette. She stopped, horrified by the sight.

The terrible thought came to Rachel's mind again. She saw herself standing over the baby, with the scissors raised like a dagger. In panic, she fled, leaving the nursery and going to the bedroom. She slammed the bedroom door to shut out the sounds of the baby's cries. But the howls could still be heard, growing increasingly shrill as the baby exercised her only means of drawing attention to her hunger.

Rachel clapped her hands to her ears, gaining some relief, but not enough. She could not go back into the nursery. She was not sure that she could resist the temptation of the scissors. People killed people. The baby was the obstacle. If it weren't for the baby, she would be with Sam now. It wouldn't be murder; it would be a delayed abortion. She had the right to take the baby's life when she first became pregnant. Why didn't she have the right now?

The baby's cries were harsher, more demanding. Rachel ran from the bedroom and, with her hands at her ears, raced on to the landing and scurried down the stairs. The sounds of the baby's howls followed her, frenzied. Reaching the foyer, she came upon the means of her salvation, the vacuum cleaner. Quickly, she switched on the motor. Instantly the initial hum rose to a steady drone that was louder than the baby's cries, and she was enclosed once more in that splendid isolation.

Mechanically, she resumed the cleaning. Soon the baby would exhaust herself and, hungry or not, go back to sleep. One missed feeding would do her no harm. How, though, would Rachel ever get the scissors out of the nursery? She couldn't ask B.J. or Holly or Paul to take them out; they would know that she was afraid to handle them herself, afraid of what she might do. They wouldn't trust her with the baby anymore. They would say that she was still sick, and they would send her away to Dr. Blalock Edwards' rest home.

Angry and frustrated, Rachel punished the floor, scrubbing it savagely with the sweeper brush. In her mind she could see the baby, red-faced, shrieking wildly. Hating herself for not going to her, she began to cry. But she had to be strong; for the baby's sake she had to stay out of the nursery until the scissors were removed. She had to keep the sweeper going, insulating herself from the baby's cries, scrubbing, scrubbing.

From the foyer she moved into the entryway. Her arms were weary and aching from the tension and the fierceness with which she was working. She no longer had the strength to scrub; she could only push the brush forward feebly and pull it back powerlessly. Her anguish began to lessen. Isolated inside the sound of the sweeper, unable to hear the baby's cries, she was no longer driven by guilt and sympathy to go to her.

Finished with the entryway, Rachel took the cleaner into the hallway, then into the kitchen. After that she started on the empty rooms on the main floor. Now she had to unplug the machine each time she moved on to another room, and she was forced to suffer the sounds of the baby's howls. To her relief, the crying seemed to be abating. Soon, soon, Rachel hoped, the baby would wear herself out and go back to sleep. Then, before the next feeding, Rachel would figure out a way to get the scissors out of the nursery. No one would ever know what had happened.

Rachel was cleaning in the next to last empty room when B.J. arrived home from school. He was suddenly standing in front of her, speaking to her in competition with the sound of the sweeper. Surprised, she could only stare at him blankly for a moment. Then, becoming oriented, she took another moment to establish her attitude. She was calm. That done, she bent down and switched off the vacuum cleaner. The silence was deafening.

"The baby's crying," B.J. said.

Rachel listened and heard nothing.

"Not loud," B.J. said. "I was going up to my room, and I heard her. I guess she just woke up."

"Yes, I know," Rachel said. "She's hungry. I have a bottle on. Will you bring her down for me, please?"

"Okay."

They left the room together.

"Holly went to school after all," Rachel said.

"I saw her. She wants me to pick her up after rehearsal."

Now Rachel could hear the baby. She was whimpering.

[262]

"Where are Kirk and Jewel?" Rachel asked. "You usually have them with you."

"They're coming." He started up the stairs, then hesitated. "What if she needs changing?" he asked.

"I'll do it down here," Rachel replied, going on toward the kitchen. "Bring down a diaper."

She was delighted with the way she was managing. B.J. thought that the baby had been crying for only a short while and that Rachel had the situation well in hand. With quick thinking she had avoided going to the nursery to change the baby's diaper. Somehow, she was now sure, she would get the scissors out of the nursery without the assistance of B.J. or Holly or Paul. She couldn't even mention the scissors to them. They knew about her earlier fear of them and would become suspicious.

The baby was howling again when B.J. arrived in the kitchen with her. The moment she got hold of the nipple, though, she settled down, sucking ravenously, making only occasional gurgling sounds. Rachel talked to her comfortingly. B.J., meanwhile, began a search through the refrigerator for something to eat. Usually he would ask Mrs. Woolsey what was available. She always knew exactly what the refrigerator contained.

"I'm sorry I can't help you," Rachel said. "I haven't had time to take inventory. I've been cleaning all day."

"That's okay." He withdrew from the refrigerator with a leftover pork chop, a slab of Swiss cheese and an apple. "Anything I can do?" he asked.

"Not that I can think of. I have everything under control."

"Can we go to the Steelers game?" he asked.

"What's that?"

"The Pittsburgh Steelers. We were going to fly up in Mr. Jahnke's plane. But Dad said maybe me and Holly couldn't go."

"Holly and I," Rachel said, correcting him. "Are you talking about a football game? What have I got to do with it?"

"Dad said we might have to stay here. He said he'd see."

"You don't have to stay here on my account," Rachel told him.

"Great!" He took an enormous bite out of the apple, then, chewing, spoke to her again.

"I can't understand you," she said. "Don't talk with your mouth full."

He swallowed. "I said I'm going up to my room if you want me."

"I won't need you. Everything is completely under control."

B.J. departed.

When the feeding was finished and Rachel had fitted the baby into a clean diaper, she took her into the sitting room and put her down on her blanket on the floor, then sat down cross-legged beside her. The baby, bulging with milk, lay almost motionless, making contented bubbling sounds. Rachel talked to her again, softly, not apologizing but trying by her manner to make amends. The baby, sated, was not in the least interested; at least, she showed no sign of paying attention.

Rachel's thoughts refocused on the problem, the scissors. She devised a solution. When B.J. came down to go after Holly, she would ask him to sit with the baby for a few moments; then she would go to the nursery and get the scissors and break the blades. There would be no danger involved because the baby would be with B.J., safe, protected from the demon inside Rachel's head. The plan was perfect. Oops! She shouldn't think that. Bad luck.

Waiting, Rachel tried to remember how to make chicken fricassee. The chicken had to be browned first. Was that right? Yes. What were the herbs? Thyme, for one. Cloves? No, that was stupid. Chopped onion. Something else. Lemon juice. Rosemary, that was the other herb. Well, surely there was a cookbook in the kitchen with a recipe for chicken fricassee in it. Although Mrs. Woolsey had cooked, as she used to say, by thumb. Maybe she ought to make dumplings. Oh, God, no! She would ruin them; they would be like marbles. Save the grandstanding, dumplings and sauces, for later when she had a little more real confidence in herself.

Why didn't B.J. come down? Wasn't it time yet to go after Holly? What would she do if Kirk and Jewel arrived while B.J. was gone? Let them in, of course. But what would her attitude toward them be? Cool and proper. She had to make it clear to them, although not in words, that she knew that they were after her. She couldn't accuse them, naturally. They would tell B.J. and Holly. And B.J. and Holly would tell Paul. And Paul would decide that she hadn't recovered from the illness after all.

The baby began complaining. Rachel wrapped her in the blanket and picked her up and walked with her, to the windows, to the doorway, back to the windows. The fretting continued. Rachel rocked her as she walked and talked to her soothingly. The complaining persisted, however. Surely she wasn't asking to be put back to bed already; she hadn't been up that long. She couldn't possibly be hungry; she had finished off the whole bottle. Maybe, though, a bottle wasn't enough for her these days. B.J. had been that way right from the start, requiring a little extra.

Still rocking the baby gently and talking to her, Rachel took her back to the kitchen and put another bottle on to warm. Now, the baby began to kick and howl. Rachel placed her on the table and checked her diaper, on the possibility that a pin had become unfastened and was sticking her. Both pins, though, were closed. Feeling increasingly tense, Rachel picked her up and resumed the so far fruitless walking and talking. The baby shrieked.

"Stop it!" Rachel said.

She was immediately repentant.

"I'm sorry," she told the baby, holding her close.

The hugging caused the baby to squirm even more vigorously.

Rachel grabbed the bottle from the warmer, ready or not, and put the nipple to the baby's lips. She fought, wagging her

[265]

head from side to side to keep the nipple out of her mouth.

"Damn you! What do you want?" Rachel shouted. The loudness and sharpness of her voice frightened her. If B.J. heard her shouting at the baby, he would think that she couldn't handle her. Mrs. Woolsey *never* shouted. "Please," she whispered urgently to the baby. "Please stop! You'll get me in trouble!"

The baby howled all the more frantically.

Rachel heard a car. B.J.'s car. He was leaving, going after Holly. Holding the screaming baby tightly again, she ran toward the front of the house. She had to stop B.J. She needed him to sit with the baby while she went up to the nursery and broke the blades of the scissors. Reaching the sitting room, she ran to the windows. In the dusk she saw the dim outline and taillights of her son's car as it drew away.

"You spoil everything. You spoil everything," she told the wailing baby, crying.

Sobbing, Rachel resumed the walking, though not the talking. There seemed to be nothing else to do. Perhaps the baby's distress was a delayed reaction to the earlier hunger and crying when Rachel did not go to her, and all she needed now was to be put back in her crib. But Rachel could not take her up to the nursery with the scissors still there. She would simply have to walk and walk and walk and keep walking until B.J. returned with Holly. And what then? She couldn't ask them to sit with a screaming baby while she went upstairs without giving them a reason. She was under observation—possibly a crazy woman—she had to explain her actions. Somehow she had to quiet the baby before they arrived.

The carriage. The cold. That was how she had solved the problem that Sunday when the baby's screaming had become too much for her to bear. Hurrying, she took the baby to the empty room where the carriage was kept and put her into it, then wheeled the carriage to the foyer. She needed extra blankets, but they were all upstairs. Moving on to the entryway closet, she got out a winter coat for herself and one of B.J.'s coats and one of Holly's as substitutes for blankets. As she was tucking the coats in around the baby, she heard a car approaching.

It was too soon for B.J. to be returning. Paul, perhaps. She was too upset at the moment to face him. More than likely, though, it was Kirk and Jewel. That was worse. She couldn't be cool and proper with a baby's screams in her ears. They would intimidate her, threaten her with their manner—or maybe even worse. This might be the opportunity that they had been preparing her for. She had to get out of the house without their seeing her.

Running, Rachel wheeled the carriage toward the kitchen.

"Please don't," she begged the howling baby. "They'll hear you."

The baby, of course, ignored the plea.

In the kitchen Rachel left the carriage and went to the back door and looked out. There was a car in the parking area, but she could see no movement. She opened the door and got the carriage and wheeled it out into the early-evening cold and dimness. The abrupt change of temperature silenced the baby for a second. Her complaining, when it resumed, was quieter, less frantic. Rachel closed the door, then pushed the carriage toward the woods. Passing the car, she saw that it was Kirk's.

By the time Rachel reached the path with the carriage the baby's cries had become whimpers. She slowed her pace to a hurried walk, then, deeper into the woods, to a stroll. She was safe now. The risks and dangers were behind her. The baby was quiet. She would stay out until B.J. and Holly got home. A half hour or so. When she returned to the house, she would ask Holly to take the baby up to the nursery, saying that she wanted to get started on the chicken fricassee.

That would still leave the problem of the scissors. Perhaps she could arrange to be busy at something when it was time for the baby's night feeding. She could ask Holly to take care of her—as a favor, nothing suspicious about that—and then while Holly had the baby downstairs, she could go into the nursery—

Rachel thought she saw a flicker of light ahead. She stopped and peered through the trees, squinting. There was no light now. There seemed to be a shape, though, a figure moving. It was probably a shadow. But a shadow of what, and why would it be moving? She saw the light again. A flash; then it was gone. Alarmed, she turned the carriage around and started back along the path. Again, she saw a flicker of light. They were all around her! The light appeared again. For a second it held steady, a fiery glare. Then it was gone.

Kirk and Jewel! And the others! They knew she was in the woods. They had heard the baby crying and had followed the sounds. Now they were searching for her, tracking her. The light again! A flash and gone. A figure, a shape, moving. Fear-stricken, Rachel turned the carriage again. She fled, running, going deeper into the woods. She saw a spot of white. Litter or the white shoes? Slowing, she looked back. One light! Two lights! She raced on. The spot of white was gone. She ran faster, frantic, driving the carriage deeper into the forest.

Another light, ahead. Reaching a fork, Rachel steered the carriage onto the path that took her away from the light. Then, suddenly, she was trapped. She had reached the rocks. Beyond was the freezing water of the lake. She wheeled the carriage around. The lights were everywhere. One. Two. Three. Four. They were closing in on her. Screaming, she retreated. More lights! She was on the rocks, stumbling, dragging the carriage, falling, screaming all the while. The lights were coming at her, faster, crossing the rocks to get at her.

She saw the masks behind the lights. The frightened face of the man who had made her take off her clothes. The face of the junkman, sour and mean. The face of the junkman's wife, swollen, with sunken, empty eyes. Kirk's face, cruel. Jewel's face, mocking. Dr. Edwards' face, pink and piggish. The lights blinded her. Voices talked at her. Hands took hold of her. She fought, shrieking hysterically. But they were too many. They held her, restraining her.

Then they laid open her head and fell on her mind, tearing and shredding, and at the same time, feeding, slobbering over the sweet, spitting out the bitter.

[268]

Twenty-one

RACHEL was awakened by the baby's fussing. Sleepily, she raised her head from the pillow and looked at the luminous dial of the bedside clock. Six ten. Time for the first feeding. Rising, she recalled one of her mother's sayings: Men work from sun to sun, but women's work is never done. True. But there were compensations. Men couldn't ever know the satisfaction of giving birth and, even more fulfilling, bringing up the babies.

As Rachel put on her robe, she saw that Paul's place in the bed was empty. Evidently he was away again. Poor Paul. He worked too hard. But she couldn't complain. After all, she had known when she married him how ambitious he was. Anyway, he seemed to thrive on overwork. So, there was no sense in worrying, either.

"Oh, my, my, my, my, my, listen to you," she said melodiously to the fretting baby as she entered the nursery. "You want your breakfast, don't you? Yes, you do," she said, lifting the baby from the crib. Cuddling her, she carried her to the Bathinette. "You're so hungry, poor little baby, baby, baby."

The complaining stopped.

Rachel removed the baby's wet diaper and began powdering her. "Right after breakfast, you get a nice bath," she told her. "Yes, you do. A nice bath. Yes." She took a clean diaper from the pile. Noticing that it was frayed at an edge, she picked up the scissors that were resting on the Bathinette and clipped off the fringe of raveling threads. "There we are!" she said brightly to the baby. "Neat as a pin!"

When the baby had been diapered, Rachel left the nursery

with her and descended the stairs. As they reached the foyer, a sound of movement came from the sitting room. Rachel walked to the doorway and looked in. Paul was asleep on a couch, turning restlessly. There were papers on the cocktail table and wadded-up papers on the floor, indicating that he had fallen asleep while working.

"There's Daddy," Rachel whispered to the baby. "See Daddy? Yes, there he is. He's asleep, isn't he?" She tiptoed away, heading for the kitchen. "Daddy is a-sleeping . . . Daddy is a-sleeping," she sang softly. "Dee-dee-dee-dee-*dee*-dee. . . ."

In the kitchen, Rachel put a bottle on to warm, then, carrying the baby in one arm, cradled, began collecting the ingredients for pancake batter. Using the free hand, she put the ingredients together in a mixing bowl, crooning airily to the baby as she worked. By the time the batter was made, churned smooth in the electric mixer, the bottle was warm. Seated at the table, with the baby nestled in the curve of her arm, she began the feeding.

Holly came in a short while later.

"Good morning!" Rachel said cheerily. "Is your brother up?"

Holly nodded, looking at Rachel appraisingly.

"Honey, will you put some syrup on to warm?" Rachel said. "We're having pancakes."

Holly got the bottle of syrup from the cupboard. "I thought you'd be resting," she said.

"Good heavens, why?" The baby had finished the bottle. "I'll be right back," Rachel told Holly, rising. She put the bottle on the counter, then left the kitchen, rocking the baby gently. "Oh, my, she's so full, isn't she? Yes, she is, she's so full. Ohhhhh, look at those sleepy eyes. She wants her beddy-bye. Yes, she does. She wants her beddy-bye."

On the stairs she met B.J.

He seemed surprised to see her. "Hi—" he began.

"Shhhhh!" Rachel said. "Sleepy, sleepy," she said, indicating the baby.

In the nursery Rachel put the baby down in the crib and tucked a blanket around her. She hummed softly to her until her eyes closed. Then she returned to the kitchen.

Paul was there. "Are you okay?" he said.

"Why wouldn't I be?"

"That was a hell of a scare," Paul said. "Those cops said you were yelling your head off. Not that you didn't have good reason. The dumb bastards. They shouldn't have been out there without telling us."

Rachel got out the griddle and put it on a burner and turned on the heat under it.

"I never did find out what they were looking for," Paul said. "They'll never tell you anything."

"It must have been a who, not a what," Holly said. "They said they thought Mom was a suspect. That's a who."

Rachel stirred the batter.

"I don't care what they thought; there was no excuse for that," Paul said indignantly. "Running around out there, shining those damn flashlights. How in hell was your mother supposed to know who they were? And she had the baby with her. Christ, they'd have scared me, too." He addressed Rachel again. "Do you feel the shot?"

"The what?"

"Oh, yeah, you don't remember, you were out cold. I got Art Jahnke's doctor for you," he said. "He lives up the road. He gave you a shot, a sedative."

"I don't feel a thing," Rachel said, spooning batter onto the griddle.

"Well, as long as you're okay . . ." Paul said. "That's great."

Rachel put water on to heat for coffee. "I'm going in to do some shopping today," she said. "Is there anything anyone needs?"

"Shop for what?" Paul asked.

"Oh, my! I've got to get this house furnished!"

"Hey! Now you're talking!" Paul said elatedly. "Just like old times." He looked at the kitchen clock. "Got to get a move on," he said.

"Don't you want breakfast?" Rachel asked, turning the pancakes.

"No time. Got to shower, got to shave. Got an early meeting. Things are popping." He started to leave, then paused. "Oh, say," he said to Rachel, "we were going to fly up to Pittsburgh with Art for the Steelers game on Sunday. I told the kids I wasn't sure. What do you think? Can you get along here alone?"

"Why, of course."

"I told you," B.J. said to his father.

"All right, then it's set," Paul said, departing.

Rachel shook her head in dismay. "He should have at least had a cup of coffee," she said.

When breakfast was over and the children left for school, Rachel cleaned up in the kitchen, then planned the evening meal. Having noticed that there was a thawed chicken in the refrigerator she decided on fricassee, with dumplings and a green salad. That chore out of the way, she went up to the bedroom. After showering, she put her robe back on and gave her hair a good brushing. As she was selecting clothing for the day, she heard the baby stirring. Smiling lovingly, she went into the nursery.

"A bath for you, young lady," she told the baby, taking her from the crib. "Then you and I are going out. We have a busy day ahead of us. Oh, yes, yes, yes, yes, yes, yes, a busy, busy, busy day!"

By noon Rachel was on her way to the village in the Eldorado, with the baby beside her on the front seat. She hummed contentedly as she drove, a tune from the past. In the village she parked in front of McMillan's and, carrying the baby, entered and walked back to the gallery. The tall, slender young man who was in charge met her with a smile.

"I looked at a painting—" she began.

"I know—that voodoo picture. Lieutenant Lomax was in here yesterday about it."

"No, this was an ancestor portrait."

"You mean that stiff-looking guy in the business suit?"

"Yes, that one. I want to order some of those. You told me it could be done."

"That same painting? That same guy?"

Rachel laughed. "No, no. I want him to look like my husband. These are ancestor portraits." She handed the baby to the young man. "Please. . . ."

"Sure."

Rachel got the snapshot of Paul from the wallet she carried in her purse. "Like this," she said, passing the picture to the young man and retrieving the baby.

He still had trouble understanding. "You want that same painting . . . but you want the guy to look like this . . ."

Rachel was patient with him. "They'll all be *his* ancestors," she explained.

"All? How many do you want?"

Rachel pondered; what would be a good number? "Fifty," she decided. "We have a large house."

The young man accepted the order without any further debate, even though Rachel had the feeling that he still did not really understand.

When she left the art store, she drove on to Tuck's Barn to buy the furnishings for the house.

"Victorian," she told the man who wore the denim apron. "It's a Victorian house."

"That's upstairs," he said.

"I know. I don't need to see it. It's all the same. I'll need a dozen rooms' worth."

"Wait a minute," the man said. "Big rooms? Little rooms? What kind of rooms? Bedrooms? Parlors? What?"

"It doesn't matter," Rachel said. "We don't use them. They're just there. Make some of them parlors and some of them bedrooms, half and half."

Oddly, he seemed reluctant.

"I know," Rachel said, handing the baby to him, "you'll want a deposit."

With a check in hand, the man became wholly cooperative. He even complimented Rachel, telling her how smart she was to buy in bulk and get the discount rate.

Driving home, she was immensely pleased with what she had accomplished. And it was still early afternoon. There was plenty of time left for the other things she had to do. After she fed the baby and put her down for her nap, she would give the sitting room a good cleaning—Paul had left a mess in there, wads of crumpled paper all over—then start on the fricassee.

Heavens, it was nice to be busy!

Twenty-two

PAUL woke Rachel on Sunday morning by shaking her. He was standing beside the bed, dressed, holding the phone.

"The baby's awake," he told her.

As she rose, he walked toward the windows, speaking into the telephone. He was talking to someone about weather and an airplane and Pittsburgh. In her robe she went to the nursery. The baby was making happy sounds. Rachel took her from the crib. On the way to the Bathinette she looked out the windows and saw that several inches of snow had fallen during the night. Evidently that was the weather that Paul was concerned about.

When she had changed the baby's diaper, she took her down to the kitchen and put a bottle on to warm. As she was getting eggs from the refrigerator, planning on making French toast, Paul came into the kitchen. He had a wool scarf around his neck and was getting into his overcoat.

"No breakfast," he said to Rachel. "We don't have time to eat."

She put the eggs back.

"I thought the planes might be grounded," he said, going

into the pantry. "But Art checked with his pilot, and it's okay." He emerged from the pantry with a paper bag. "We're meeting Art at the airport," he said, taking fruit from the bowl on the table and putting it into the bag. "This will hold us. I want to leave now because I don't know how the roads will be."

"Have a nice trip," Rachel said.

"Yeah, the weather is supposed to clear up."

B.J. called from the hallway.

"I'm coming," Paul answered. "Warm up the car." He tucked in his scarf, then began buttoning his coat. "We'll be back sometime tonight late," he told Rachel. "Don't worry. Don't wait up." He picked up the bag of fruit. "See you," he said, leaving.

"Have a nice trip," Rachel said.

She fed the baby, then made coffee for herself and took the baby and the coffee into the sitting room. While the baby played on her blanket on the floor, Rachel sipped her coffee and thought about all the things around the house that had to be done. Before long the baby began to fret. So Rachel took her up to the nursery and put her down.

Still in her pajamas and robe, Rachel returned to the kitchen. She took inventory of the groceries and meats in the pantry and refrigerator and freezer, making a list of the supplies that she would order on Monday. That led to emptying the refrigerator and freezer and washing them out on the inside. With those tasks completed she went back upstairs and collected the laundry and dry cleaning for the man who would pick them up on Tuesday. Finally, she ran the sweeper in the bedroom and the second-floor and third-floor hallways.

In the early afternoon the baby woke. Rachel fed her and bathed her and played with her until she became cranky, then rocked her for a while. She was asleep again when Rachel put her back down in the crib. From the nursery Rachel went into the bedroom. She took off her robe and pajamas, then showered. When she left the bathroom and began dressing, she saw that the sky had darkened and the snowfall had become heavy. Combing her hair, she stood at a window looking out at the whiteness that was thickening on the ground and the trees.

A pair of lights appeared on the private road. A car was approaching the house. When it reached the drive, she saw that it was Sam's car. He was home from work. As always, he drove on to the rear. Happy that he was home, Rachel left the bedroom and went down to meet him. She was at the front door, holding it open, when he came up the porch steps. He was carrying a tape player.

"Are we going to be snowed in?" Rachel asked cheerfully.

"Hi," he said, smiling, entering the house. He began getting out of his floppy raincoat. "It looks like it, doesn't it? We've got everybody on overtime. The accident calls started coming in early this morning. It's a good thing it's Sunday or it would be worse."

Taking his coat, Rachel kissed him lightly. "It's so nice, though, all white and clean," she said, hanging the coat in the closet.

"I could live without it."

"What is that for?" Rachel asked, pointing to the tape player.

"I've got something for you to listen to."

"Oh."

They went into the sitting room.

"Is it all right if I close these doors?" Sam said.

"That will be nice—cozy," Rachel replied, going on toward the bar to make his drink for him.

"I don't want anybody to hear," Sam said, rolling the doors closed. "This is about the case, Rachel. It's still confidential."

She was pleased. He was going to tell her about his work while he unwound with his drink.

As she reached the bar, Rachel's attention was drawn to the outside. Through a window she saw several figures emerging from the woods. They appeared to be children, youngsters, and they were wearing masks. Curious, she watched them approach the house. At first, she thought that one of them had no feet, but then she saw that he was wearing white shoes, which were hard to see against the whiteness of the snow. Their masks were interesting: brightly colored, grotesque, with contorted features. Then, as the children neared the porch, Sam spoke to her.

"Rachel, can we talk?"

Obediently, she left the bar and went to him. He was seated on a couch. The tape player was on the cocktail table. It was running, but no sound other than the soft whir of its motor was coming from it. Rachel sat down in the chair that had the telephone table beside it.

"When does it begin?" she asked Sam, indicating the tape player.

"Forget that for a minute," he said. "First, I want to say this: The case is not yet tied up. There are still a couple loose ends. But I have enough now that I know where it's going. I know the end. I want you to know, too. Because I know how bugged you've been. But, remember, as of right now, what I'm going to tell you can't get out of this room. Okay?"

Rachel nodded solemnly. It was exciting.

A sound of movement came from outside the sitting-room doors.

"Who's that?" Sam asked.

"The children."

"All right." He edged forward on the couch. "The first break came when Joey spotted the kid in the white shoes again," he said. "As it turns out, he works in a pizza joint up the street from headquarters. No doctor, no connection with a hospital, a pizza hustler. He's a dropout. And he hangs around with Kirk Franklin."

Rachel nodded again.

"That wasn't a lot, of course," Sam said. "But it was one piece—maybe. Next—"

Suddenly, a female voice was screaming from the tape player. "You killed my brother! Murder! You murdered my brother!"

"That's how she did it," Sam said.

The screaming from the tape player continued. "Murder!

You murdered my brother!" Then, abruptly, silence. Not even the machine's motor could be heard.

"She put the player here in this room," Sam said. "Then, just before she left the house with your son, she turned it on. You didn't hear anything then, not right away, because she had the screaming at the very end of the reel. Otherwise, the tape is blank. That's what she did. Then—as you see—when the tape runs out, the machine turns itself off."

"That's fascinating," Rachel said.

"That's not Jewel, of course," he said, nodding in the direction of the tape player. "I had a woman at headquarters do the screaming for me."

"That was nice of her."

Sam smiled thinly. "Anyway, next," he said. "All along, the one thing that kept running through my mind, bothering me, was that the little boy had a baby face. If he was out on that road in the dark in that weather, he couldn't have been much of a baby—even if he was with his sister. I kicked that around and kicked it around, but nothing came of it."

"Mmmm," Rachel said sympathetically.

"Then it hit me," Sam said. "How did we really know that he was a boy or how old he was or anything? The girl was screaming about her brother. So we *assumed* that the kid was a boy. But you didn't see him. All you saw was his face. A *baby* face."

"Don't you want your drink?" Rachel asked.

He looked surprised. "In a minute—let me tell you this. So maybe the kid *wasn't* a boy," he said. "Maybe it was a baby. And maybe, for some reason, the girl didn't want you to know that. So, thinking quick, she yelled 'brother.' To make you think that the baby was a little boy—do you see?"

"Yes, I see."

Sam sat back. "Well, I went into the files," he said, "and got out all the bulletins for the whole region for that time. And there it was. On the same day that that business happened to you out there on the road, a baby was kidnapped. In Indiana, just across the line. It was a baby girl. She was taken out of her carriage from in front of a store in a shopping center."

"Oh, my!" Rachel said.

"That gave me the reason for the girl wanting you to think that the baby was a boy, a kid. If you'd told us that it was a baby, we might have made the connection, the baby that the girl had in her arms and the baby that had been kidnapped." He looked at Rachel closely. "Are you following me?"

"Yes, yes."

"My next guess was that the baby was dead," Sam said "I put my men out there in the woods and told them to cover it inch by inch by inch. I'm sorry they scared you the other night. They didn't know who you were; they thought you might be the girl. But anyway, the upshot was they found the grave. We sent the body to Indiana, and I got the confirmation just a short while ago, just before I came out here. It was the kidnapped baby."

"That's terrible!"

"They used a plastic bag or something like that," Sam said. "The cause of death was smothering." He leaned forward. "You know that painting, the masks? You were right about that, too. They copied the masks they were wearing from the masks in the painting. That word on the painting—Otu. That was a tribe of Indians in South America a long time ago. They lived on a little island off the coast of Peru, and they had a big population problem."

"How terrible."

"Yeah." He looked at her oddly again. "Anyway, the Otu came up with a solution," he said. "They sacrificed baby girls. Girls, of course, because girls produce children. That painting, that was a painting of a sacrificial ceremony. According to my research, the guys who did the sacrificing wore those masks. The masks made it okay. With the masks on, they weren't themselves, they were whoever or whatever the masks represented—gods of some kind. See?"

Rachel nodded.

"I went back to McMillan's and had that guy in the gallery check his records," Sam went on. "He told us that painting hadn't ever been out of storage. But he was wrong. They rent out paintings in batches, as many as you want for as long as you want, and that particular painting had gone out once in one of the batches. It was in the Franklin house."

"Now do you want your drink?" Rachel asked.

He looked annoyed.

"I'm sorry," she said. "I thought your story was over."

His expression softened. "I guess it is," he said. "Okay, I'll have a drink."

Rachel rose and walked toward the bar.

"Evidently Kirk got interested in the painting and did some research on it himself and liked the idea," Sam said. "And found some others who liked it, too—Jewel Brill and the kid in the pizza shop and a couple more. Of course, I'm sure there's a lot more to it than that. Their thinking is screwed up . . . but the whys and wherefores, that's not my department." He sighed sorrowfully. "Maybe they were somebody else when they put the masks on. Maybe that made it okay, the way they saw it."

Reaching the bar and glancing out the window, Rachel noticed the many footprints in the snow on the porch, leading to and from the door. There was a plastic bag on the steps that had not been there before. Raising her eyes, she saw the children again, the youngsters in the masks. They were going back into the woods. She smiled after them, then turned her attention to the business at hand, making the drink for Sam.

"Rachel, you understand, don't you?" he said. "It wasn't you they were after. They were trying to break you, yes—I guess. But that was only so that, afterward, we would all jump to the conclusion that you did it."

She poured a tall glass three-quarters full of gin.

"They were after your baby," Sam said.

Rachel smiled at him lovingly. "Olive or onion?" she asked.

She waited for him to do his little trick, pull either an onion or an olive from his ear.

[280]

But he sat completely still, staring at her. He seemed to be thinking very hard. At last, he spoke, one word. The word was soundless, but Rachel read it off his lips. "Mad. . . ." It baffled her and she tried to think what he might mean by it, but no answer came. She found at that point that the thinking had distracted her so that she could no longer remember where they had been in their little talk. There was no alternative, of course, but to begin again at the beginning.

"Tell me about your day," she said brightly, taking his drink to him.